Eden Prairie

Books by Frederick Manfred

NOVELS
The Golden Bowl (1944)
This Is the Year (1947)
The Chokecherry Tree (1948)
Morning Red (1956)
The Secret Place* (1965)
Eden Prairie (1968)

POEMS
Winter Count (1966)

RUMES
Boy Almighty (1945)
Wanderlust** (1962)

STORIES
Arrow of Love (1961)
Apples of Paradise (1968)

TALES
Lord Grizzly (1954)
Riders of Judgment (1957)
Conquering Horse (1959)
Scarlet Plume (1964)
King of Spades (1966)

* Originally published in hardback as *The Man Who Looked Like the Prince of Wales*; reprinted in paperback as *The Secret Place*.

** A new revised version of a trilogy that was originally published in three separate volumes, *The Primitive*, 1949, *The Brother*, 1950, *The Giant*, 1951. Mr. Manfred wrote under the name of Feike Feikema from 1944 through 1951.

Eden Prairie

FREDERICK *Feikema* MANFRED

Trident Press / New York

TO

John R. Milton
friend

ACKNOWLEDGMENT

To the directors of the Avon Foundation go my sincere thanks for a fellowship to help me write this book.

FREDERICK MANFRED

Contents

PART ONE   *Karen*   9

PART TWO   *Kon*   99

PART THREE   *Karen*   183

PART FOUR   *Brant*   205

PART FIVE   *Karen*   233

PART SIX   *Brant*   263

PART SEVEN   *Mildred*   303

PART EIGHT   *Karen*   319

Eden Prairie

PART ONE

❧◈❧◈❧◈❧◈❧◈❧◈❧◈❧◈❧◈❧◈❧

Karen

1

A pair of sulphur butterflies emerged from the leaves of a single cottonwood. They fluttered down like tumbling snowflakes. Erratic, yet strangely unerring, they headed straight for a patch of wild roses. They touched down with dusty legs on pliant blossoms. Slowly their pale yellow-blue wings closed to a single blade. They resembled two fallen autumn leaves, delicately veined, for the moment lovely, each a separate silence. Presently they uncoiled their tube mouths and sucked awhile. The nectar was sweeter than sunny air. The male butterfly had the longer antennae and he quivered ecstatically. The female sucked quietly.

Nectar gone, they rewound their tube mouths, opened their double wings, fluttered off.

They moved down the slough. They doubled the meanderings of a little trickling stream. They wafted slowly along.

They sipped the nectar of swamp buttercups. They tasted the bitter milk sap of a rosy dogbane. They suckled the purple florets of a tall bull thistle. They became flying yellow petals.

Suddenly two redwing birds, male and female, dove down out of the western sky. The shoulders of the male flashed a brilliant scarlet. The female was a solid brown shadow to the male. They speared straight for the two butterflies. Missed them.

Instantly the two butterflies separated. They darted frantically aside. They fluttered sharply erratic. They rose. They fell. They shot ahead. They stopped.

The two redwings made a second pass at the butterflies, this time hauling up short just as they reached them, hovering like heavy hummingbirds—then pecked them out of the air. Each, one. Gobbling, the two redwings flew on and up.

Karen was eleven years old when her mother died.

Her father, Alfred Alfredson V, was a restless man, a wanderer, and on the death of his wife abruptly decided he'd had enough of the town of Bonnie. He made up his mind to try homesteading in western South Dakota instead. His oldest child, Alfred VI, fourteen, he put out for hire with a rich farmer. Big Alfred was doing well in school, but that couldn't be helped, he had to go out and work anyway. The smaller children though, five of them, could go along to the Dakotas.

A neighbor lady, Mrs. Hamilton, stepped in. Mrs. Hamilton had often shaken her head at the way strongheaded Mr. Alfredson did things. Take all those poor little children out into the wilderness? Especially little Karen, the second child, with her wavy red-brown hair and her gentle ways? With all her talent? No. That was wrong. Mrs. Hamilton decided she would ask for Karen, be her foster mother.

Mr. Alfredson was known to be quite strict with his children and Mrs. Hamilton expected him to be possessive. She approached the subject of Karen warily one day when she ran into him on main street.

"You want Karen?" Mr. Alfredson was quite a short fellow, but standing with chunky legs wide apart on the boardwalk, he still had an imposing manner. "All right, take Karen. There probably ain't any schools out in South Dakota anyway. Not to speak of."

Mrs. Hamilton swallowed involuntarily. She hadn't expected him to agree so readily. But she recovered quickly. "Do you want my husband to draw up the papers?"

"No papers, Missus. I don't hold with papers."

"But suppose you want her back after a time? And suppose we don't want to give her up?"

He made an angry sideways gesture. "Woman, my word is better than my signature." He fixed her with high light-blue eyes. "Do you want her or don't you?"

"I do."

"You've got her." Then he held up a blunt hand. "But one thing though, Mrs. Hamilton. Don't raise her to be one of them overparticular old maids now. She's already got too much of that. Shake her loose some way."

"Thank you, Mr. Alfredson." Mrs. Hamilton had her own notion about how she should raise Karen.

Turning on his heel, Mr. Alfredson stumped across the street to the bank.

Mrs. Hamilton looked Karen up on the school playground and drew her to one side. "Karen, child. I've just had word with your father."

"Oh, Mrs. Hamilton, may I come and work for you?" Worry that Mrs. Hamilton might have made up her mind against her quirked the corners of Karen's gentle green eyes.

Mrs. Hamilton blinked. Gracious stars alive. So that stubby Mr. Alfredson had already prepared the child for the move. "Child—"

"I'll work hard for my board and room, Mrs. Hamilton." Karen touched a slim hand over her red-brown hair to make sure that all was in place.

"I know you will, Karen. But that isn't what I came over here for." Mrs. Hamilton smiled. "My three children must work a little too, you know. I can't be having you rob them of the privilege of doing their necessary chores." Mrs. Hamilton's smile deepened. "No, Karen, it's that we like you, Karen, and that we would like you to come live with us. Do you understand that? Live with us."

"Live with you, Mrs. Hamilton?" Karen's gentle green eyes gradually filled with wildest child joy.

"Yes. Would you like that?"

"Oh, Mrs. Hamilton . . . Oh, Mrs. Hamilton . . . If that's really true, I'm going to work hard for you anyway. Just you watch."

"We'll hold the thought, child. Meanwhile, what do you need for clothes?"

"Oh, I don't need any new clothes. I have plenty."

"Are you sure?"

"Well-l . . . I would very much like to have a sunbonnet someday. But that can wait until I earn some money."

"My dear child. A sunbonnet you shall have."

Karen moved in with the Hamiltons that same weekend. The next week her father and her brothers and sisters left for the far Dakotas.

Karen missed her strong-willed father. She'd been afraid of him but she loved him. She also missed her younger sisters, Janet and Gerda, as well as her little brothers, Richard and Abbott. Her pale tall mother, Kathryn Andringham Alfredson, she missed most of all, and she was haunted by the last sight she had of her just before the coffin lid closed, of taut white skin and sudden high cheekbones.

Big brother Alfred she saw Sunday mornings at the Congregational Church. Alf worked for Charlie Pullman north of town and seemed to be doing all right. But she didn't think about Alf much—for which she had her reasons.

It took Karen a while to get used to her foster family. The Hamiltons were from England by way of Vermont. Gordon Hamilton was the son of a fourth son of a titled English family. He had the airs but none of the inheritance. Yet Gordon Hamilton made the best of it. He married a grave-eyed Vermont girl named Grace Reynolds. He learned the printer's trade in Ohio. He migrated to Bonnie in Siouxland, where he bought out *The Bonnie Review*. When the grasshopper plagues hit Siouxland, followed by the panic of 1893, Gordon quietly bought up various tax-delinquent farms abandoned by busted homesteaders. By 1900 he was the richest man in Bonnie, if not in Leonhard County. He built himself a two-story house with a bay window trimmed with squares of colored glass and a big porch facing the south. The house set

high on a hill under the white town tower. It commanded main
street to the west all the way down to the Cannonball railroad
depot. He also built himself a new printshop near the post office,
just a few steps away from the Bonnie Hotel.

Gordon Hamilton was a gaunt man of few words. He saved his
talk for his *Review* editorials, where his remarks were full of solid
good sense. He advised pioneers to hold onto their Iowa farms,
instead of, say, running off to chase rumors of new gold strikes in
the Black Hills. In time, he wrote, the farm would prove to have
more gold in it than both of the Dakotas put together. He advised farmers to plant hackberries instead of box elders. The
hackberry was a clean tree; the box elder dirty. He recommended
that farmers rotate their crops—the soil needed regular rests from
the hungry corn plant.

Because Gordon Hamilton became independently wealthy he
could afford to reject advertisements that promised the moon
with a ring around it. When he did run such advertisements he
invariably spoofed them in his editorials. Of a catarrh specialist,
a certain itinerant Dr. J. Johnson Krider, who claimed he'd found
a specific while in South America, Gordon Hamilton once wrote:

For the loafers down at the pool hall, who are looking for easy money,
we suggest you pay this Dr. Krider a visit when he comes to town. Dr.
Krider claims he will seat you in a chair, place a towel around your neck
and a bowl in your lap, and in ten minutes will extract from one-half
to a pint of catarrh mucus from your head and throat—and will give
you $100 if he fails. *The Review* suggests you go right along and try it.
It's money in your pocket.

Gordon Hamilton reported on everything coming under his
purview. It was his stubborn notion that a newsman worth his
salt had to report on a representative sampling of what he came
upon in life. Thus on occasion he printed a sorry tale.

The officer from Hello arrived here Monday morning and placed one
of our esteemed citizens under arrest for bastardy, taking the prisoner
with him. The wife feels the double shame of her husband's perfidy and
her sister's weakness. The arrest was the first intimation here of the

nasty affair, and for a while the town pretty near went wild over it. It must be said in the prisoner's behalf that he strongly maintains his innocence and asserts that the prosecution is instigated not by the wronged girl, his sister-in-law, but by others who are using the girl to shield the real author of the crime. May he be able to establish his innocence, in which many of our people firmly believe. The family formerly lived in Hello, where he was regarded by some as lazy and good-for-nothing, but he seems to have some good traits notwithstanding. *The Review* hopes this case will come to a satisfactory conclusion for all concerned. The previous shameful scandal, in which a married man from Bonnie left the county with another man's wife and deserted two sets of poor helpless children, is still strong in our memory. Our town and our county has had enough of it.

Grace Hamilton often cringed when she read her husband's columns. She admired his forthrightness, but worried that her children's minds, including Karen's, might be corrupted. Yet she refused to hide *The Review* from the children. Father's work had to be honorable.

Grace Hamilton was both slender and durable. She'd accepted motherhood as a worthy task just as she'd accepted the embrace of a man as a necessary duty. She kept a neat house, and found time to read and to play the piano besides. She adored Thackeray and always felt sorry for his last lonely days; had her doubts about Dickens, volumes of whose work she'd won as a premium in a subscription drive; and thought Hawthorne a beast for having penned *The Scarlet Letter*. She favored blue for her clothes, a light blue for around the house and a dark blue for church, so that during the week her blue eyes took on a quietly friendly cast and on Sunday a quietly grave cast. She had her ship on course and was heading it straight for that final harbor—death in heaven.

Horace was the firstborn Hamilton, and very early had the gravity that went with the role. It was his dream to become a lawyer. He often went along with his father when his father covered the district court in Rock Falls. Horace aped his father's airs to perfection.

Joyce, the middle child, should have been spoiled. She was a lovely thing, and knew it, and occasionally played the brothers off against each other to get her way. But her basic nature was a good one. At ten she began to take on the bloom of a woman.

In Sylvester the mother had hopes for her own kind of child. When Sylvester was six she spotted that he had a talent at music. She had their piano tuned and sent him to Mrs. Poindexter for lessons. Sylvester learned rapidly at first. But he was facile rather than deep, and at eight his progress fell off. He was a daydreamer and full of what Mrs. Poindexter called daffy notions. He had a flappy way of walking, and always seemed to be dropping things, especially when helping with the dishes.

Mrs. Hamilton might have given up on Sylvester's talent if it hadn't been that Karen liked music too. Mrs. Hamilton thought Karen's slim fingers were just perfect for the violin so she bought her a lovely cherry-tone model, and sent her off to Mrs. Poindexter for lessons too. Soon Sylvester and Karen were giving recitals in the parlor for the family. Mrs. Hamilton was a little piqued that Karen proved to be the better musician, that Sylvester didn't mind playing second fiddle as accompanist.

Karen had a lot of fun with Sylvester. Together the two of them dreamed of a future in which they would tour the country giving concerts. Karen called him Syl. It fit the way he had of embroidering her playing with his chording. And he could be such a cutup sometimes. Karen in her mind was going to be the artist, oh, yes.

It also developed after a while that Karen could draw. Mrs. Hamilton happened to catch her doodling one day on the back page of a discarded *Bonnie Review*.

"Why, child, those look like real horses."

Karen turned grave green eyes on Mrs. Hamilton. "Thank you, Nanna."

"Where did you get the copy?"

"That's our Mr. Hamilton's horse Colonel."

Mrs. Hamilton looked out of the kitchen window onto the back lot where their bay Colonel was grazing. "Why, so it is."

"I had trouble getting his tail right though, Nanna. Colonel won't let me get near him. He doesn't like me."

"That's why you should use copies, not real horses, child. Whoever heard of anyone copying from real life? Except perhaps real artists like Rembrandt or Leonardo da Vinci? Today when I go downtown I'll get you some tracing paper. And a picture book about horses from the public library."

"You're too good to me, Nanna."

"Now, now."

"But it's true, Nanna."

"Karen, you're our sweet sunbonnet girl and we can't help but be nice to you."

When Karen tired of copying horses, Mrs. Hamilton bought her some paint and brushes, and got her to copying paintings she liked, especially the two pastoral scenes in the parson's study. Karen copied them so well that Mrs. Hamilton, ever thoughtful, bought some china bowls and plates, and had Karen paint designs on them—a spray of violets, a single rose, a cupid with a bow and arrow, all copies. Karen's painted china soon was the talk of the ladies' teas around town. Karen never did try anything original again with either pencil or brushes.

Mrs. Hamilton and Karen were shelling peas in the kitchen one day, when Mrs. Hamilton abruptly asked, "Child, where did your father live before he came to Bonnie?"

"In Missouri."

"And before that?"

"Near Chokecherry Corner."

"And before that?"

"Zion, Michigan."

"And before that?"

"Jerusalem, Iowa."

"And before that?"

"Friesland. On the North Sea."

"And why did he leave this Freese-land?"

"Because he didn't want to be just a common laborer. He thought he was meant for better things."

"And your mother was content to go along with him wherever he went?"

"She had to go along with him."

"Why was that?"

"Her family had cut her off without a penny because she married Father. You see, she eloped with him when they didn't want her to marry him. Because they were rich and he was poor."

"Then perhaps your father was a bit of an upstart for thinking he was meant for better things?"

"Oh, no, Mrs. Hamilton. The Alfredsons were once of a better class of people too. They lost everything through a pestilence."

"Oh."

"Yes." Karen slowly shook her head in memory. "My, how Father hates to talk about that time. Father is so proud. That's why he can be so wild and so strict at the same time. Wandering all over the world looking for a sure way to get rich quick. Get back his fortune and his station in life both."

"Did your mother ever talk about her family?"

"Many times. Oh, yes."

"Did she ever mention anybody being special in her family?"

"How do you mean, Nanna?"

"Well, like playing the violin? Or painting?"

"No-o. I think all she said in that line was that they could sing good in church. They were too high-toned to make spectacles of themselves."

"Spectacles? Is one making a spectacle of oneself if one plays a violin?"

"That's what they always thought. Such things were for clowns and public entertainers."

"Oh." Mrs. Hamilton thought to herself for a while.

Karen said, "I hope I haven't said anything wrong, Nanna."

"Oh, no, child." Mrs. Hamilton smiled. "And now, how about in your father's family? Was there ever anything special about them?"

"They were wonderfully handy with their hands. And they loved to tell stories." Karen accidentally spilled some peas over the side of the bowl onto the white table. She gathered them up one by one. "But I probably shouldn't even say that."

"Why is that, child?"

"Well, Father says an Alfredson is never supposed to brag about himself. Or about his relations."

"That's good." Mrs. Hamilton moved her white stool closer to

the table. "Your father sounds like a good man despite his being
so strict with you children."

"Yes, he was a good man, Nanna. Oh, we surely got the
dickens from him sometimes. And we never dared to lolly
around much. But . . ."

"But you loved him."

"Oh, yes." Karen laughed a short laugh in memory. "I even
did when he made me give back that ten cents."

"What was that, child?"

"Oh, it was nothing, really. It was my brother Alf's job to milk
the cow. Alf offered me ten cents if I would milk the cow so he
could go skating. Well, as I was milking the cow she kicked the
pail over. And we had to tell Father what happened, of course.
Well, Father said Alf shouldn't have given me the ten cents, not
until after the job was done. And done right. So I gave Alf back
his ten cents."

"That was a hard lesson."

"Yes." Karen's chest rose and fell in a deep sigh. "But then,
that's always happening to me and the animals. They just don't
like me. Ever. Like with your dog Trixie that time."

"Yes."

Both fell silent, remembering.

The very first day Karen moved in with the Hamiltons, the
Hamilton dog, Trixie, a rat terrier, came out of her blanket-lined
box in a corner of the kitchen and began barking at Karen. Karen
liked the looks of the little dog, brown with white spots over the
head. But the little dog barked and barked at her. Karen thought
perhaps she could quiet it by petting it. But when she reached
down a hand, she almost had it snapped off. Trixie was outraged
at the proffer of friendship and went into a paroxysm of barking.
She pranced in rage around Karen, filling the tight white kitchen
with a gathering crescendo of roaring, until Karen had to cover
her ears.

Mrs. Hamilton and the three Hamilton children were astounded. "Trixie! Why, what's the matter with you? Karen's a
nice girl. She's come to live with us. She's going to be part of the
family now. So you be nice to her and let her pet you."

But Trixie would have none of it. She almost snapped off Mrs. Hamilton's hand too. And when Trixie wasn't barking she was growling.

"I declare," Mrs. Hamilton cried, "but I do believe that dog has gone insane."

Karen, crestfallen, had to go to another part of the house for a while.

It wasn't until Mr. Hamilton came home that Trixie quit growling.

Karen stayed out of the kitchen until after supper. But when she went in to help do the supper dishes, Trixie started in again. This time Trixie got so worked up she frothed at the mouth.

"Well," Mr. Hamilton said from his armchair at the head of the table.

"I don't understand it," Mrs. Hamilton said.

The three Hamilton children stared at Karen.

Karen said, "I might have known. Animals just don't like me. I guess I better pack up and leave."

Mr. Hamilton was shocked. "But, dear child, you've only just arrived."

"That dog will never get to like me."

"Oh, yes, she will," Mr. Hamilton said. He got up from his armchair and went into the kitchen and reached down a hand to soothe Trixie's neck.

Trixie bit him, snarling.

Mr. Hamilton jerked erect. He gave Trixie a kick in the belly. "You bitch."

Trixie grunted, and for the moment shut up.

"Why, Mr. Hamilton!" Mrs. Hamilton exclaimed.

The upshot of it all was that the Hamiltons got rid of Trixie. They gave Trixie to Dud Mann, the rendering-plant man, who lived northwest of town. There were rumors that Dud Mann made corn whiskey on the side and that he needed a fierce dog to guard his still.

Karen cried over this.

"It's all right, child. You're still going to be our sunbonnet girl. Trixie was getting old anyway."

Karen felt awful. Trixie hadn't looked too old to her. "And here I really like animals so."

By the time Karen entered high school her long red-brown hair had become even more wavy and glossy and her green eyes more gentle and appealing. Her features had thinned some, become fine and feminine. And she moved with the gracile motion of a swan in water.

Teachers liked having her in class. They gave her by far the best marks.

A few of the teachers remarked on her personal reserve and wondered if she weren't a little too serious. She was almost too busy improving her mind.

The first two years in high school everything went as smooth as pie.

But then in her junior year she took to sleepwalking.

She had a room of her own upstairs on the southeast corner. Joyce had the northeast room across from her. The boys, Horace and Sylvester, had the coldest room in the house, on the northwest corner. The folks slept in the big bedroom, on the southwest corner.

Karen's first sleepwalking jaunt took her into Joyce's room. Joyce didn't scare. Joyce knew right away who it was.

"Karen?"

A moan escaped Karen.

"Karen?"

Karen shuddered in her long white nightgown. "Wh—a—t?"

"Do you know where you are?"

Karen's eyes fluttered open. "Joyce!"

Joyce giggled.

"Oh, Joyce, what am I doing in here?"

"That's what I was wondering."

"Oh, Joyce."

"Good thing you didn't sleepwalk into the boys' room."

"Oh, dear God, how awful! Oh, Joyce, Joyce, please don't tell Nanna."

"I won't." Joyce giggled some more in the dark. "But just you stay in your own bed after this."

A month later, with Mr. Hamilton and Horace gone up to Rock Falls to attend an important lawsuit, Karen sleepwalked again. This time she dreamed herself into Mrs. Hamilton's room.

Mrs. Hamilton had a question for Karen the next morning when they were alone together in the kitchen. "Is there something the matter with you, girl?"

"No, Nanna. Not that I know of anyway."

"You aren't unhappy about something?"

"No, Nanna. Why do you ask?"

"Oh . . . nothing."

"Nanna, what have I done now?"

Mrs. Hamilton folded her gaunt hands under her blue apron. "You don't remember coming into my room last night?"

"Why, no, Nanna. Did I?"

"You most certainly did."

"Ohh."

"It's all right, girl. Nothing happened."

"Why, what did I do?"

"Nothing. You just walked in. Like you were in a daze." Mrs. Hamilton sighed with a sharp intake of breath. "Luckily the moon was shining so I could see who it was right away."

"Ohh."

"After a minute you came straight for my bed and stroked my hair."

Karen stared wild green eyes at Mrs. Hamilton. "Dear God, how awful. I did? Why!"

"It's a good thing your eyes weren't open or I would have screamed."

"Oh, dear, dear! How terrible. Oh, I'm so sorry, Nanna. I'll try never to do it again. I'll pray God and ask his help when I go to bed at night so I won't do it again."

"You meant no harm, child."

Mrs. Poindexter, the music teacher, moved to Sioux Falls. It was decided there wasn't much point in having Sylvester go on with his music lessons if it meant he had to go all the way to Sioux Falls for them. But Karen it was decided should go on, and if possible with a teacher who was first of all a violin teacher.

Mr. Hamilton ran a small ad in his paper inquiring for a violin teacher, one preferably living nearby. Presently a letter came in the mail from a Peter Walling living in Hello. Peter Walling was a high school music teacher as well as a violinist in a local quintet. He sounded good to the Hamiltons, so every Saturday, when the weather was good, Horace hitched up Colonel and drove Karen eleven miles to Hello.

Karen's playing improved markedly for a couple of months and Mrs. Hamilton privately was pleased.

But the fourth month Karen's interest in the violin abruptly fell off.

"What seems to be the matter, child?"

"Nothing, Nanna."

Another month went by. Karen had to be prodded to practice her lessons. And she almost had to be pushed out to the buggy where Horace waited to take her to Hello.

"Now, child, there has to be something the matter. What is it?"

Karen decided to come out with it. "Peter Walling is a flirt."

"Mind what you say now, child. He is a teacher."

"Well, I don't care. I just know he is."

Mrs. Hamilton's lips pursed up as if she were sucking a plum pit. "Karen, by now you must have learned most men like to flirt a little. That's how they show their interest in you."

"I don't like it."

"How old a man is he?"

"In his middle twenties. At least."

Mrs. Hamilton smiled then. "Is he married?"

"No."

"Oh. You did make sure of that though."

"That's why I was suspicious of him in the first place."

"Well, Karen, it is true that as a teacher he should be on his good behavior with his pupils. But you shouldn't shy away from every young man's attention, you know. Not altogether. After all, someday you will be having a husband."

"I'm never going to get married."

"Oh, pshaw, child, that's just young-girl talk."

"But I'm not, Nanna."

"Do you want us to look for another violin teacher?"

"I wish you would. I can't stand it when he looks at me that way. Like he's a fox and I'm a pullet."

"Karen, you needn't take lessons from him, if that's your mind."

"I want to be the artist, Nanna. But not if it means taking lessons from him. He's too stuck on himself."

"All right, child."

Another violin teacher couldn't be found, and Karen's lessons were abandoned.

The summer between her junior and senior year, Karen, dressed in long flowing white, took to wandering out to the meadows south of town along the Little Rock River. Here the land was still unplowed and wild. She loved the prairie flowers, especially the wild sweet Williams with their five light-violet petals notched and shaped like fairy trumpets, and used to gather them up by the armful and bring them home for dinner-table decoration. She sometimes dreamed for hours on an ancient Hopewell mound overlooking the river, sitting a foot deep in wild grass and the year's first daisies.

Once a pink butterfly landed on the ring finger of her left hand. It sat quietly awhile, it's only motion the occasional folding of its wings and the alternate lifting of its chalky legs. Its wings appeared to be made of flakes of pink snow just barely held together.

"Oh, if I could only draw you. I'd just paint the best picture ever of you."

Song sparrows, shooting straight up out of the buffalo grass, shed widening rings of song.

Karen took off her blue sunbonnet and lay back in the grass. She let the blue skies fill her green eyes. This was the way life in heaven would be someday.

The Little Rock River below her flowed quietly between curving brown banks. Little wavelets sparkled over stony shallows. Occasional pickerel leaped free of the water and snapped at

hovering gnats. A mottled brown mud turtle soaked up the sun
on a flat pink rock.

After a while the bawl of a calf for its mother and in turn the
bellow of the mother cow for its calf awakened Karen from her
green reveries. She tied on her blue sunbonnet again, gathered
up her usual armful of wild sweet Williams, and stood up. As so
often happened when she stood up too quick, she felt faint for a
moment. Then, head cleared, green eyes steady again, she headed
for home.

She had just rolled herself, slim and angular, underthrough a
barbwire fence, when she heard a commotion coming down the
road from town. She first saw dust rising, just past the Henry
Cooper house. To get a better look at whatever it was, she
climbed up the steep side of the ditch onto the road. Then it
appeared, coming around the corner past the Cooper lilacs, two
black horses galloping out of control and a black carriage careen-
ing wildly from side to side. The driver seemed to be sitting as
if paralyzed in the front seat. One of the reins rode the wind in
a long serpentine flutter.

"That's the boy Alfred Engleking," Karen murmured. "By
ginger."

She would have been all right if the boy Alfred hadn't suddenly shrieked, "Look out! Here comes a runaway!" and then
jumped out of the carriage, hurtling himself headfirst into the
ditch, legs wild like a frog. The flying body and the shout, "Runaway!" scared Karen half out of her wits. She dropped her flowers
and swooped back down into the ditch. And in her hurry to get
on the other side of the fence, instead of going underthrough it,
she tried going over it. She got halfway across, when her petticoat
caught in the barbs. And there she sat, pinned down clothespin
fashion, blue sunbonnet bobbing.

It took her an hour to get herself unhooked. The barbs seemed
to go after her white clothes like an army of black ants after
bread.

The boy Alfred offered to help her, but this she rejected,
coldly, and ordered him down the road after his runaway horses.

That evening, between spells of self-laughter, Karen told about it at the supper table. "And there I was, all spread out over that prickly fence like a quilt spread out to dry. Lordy Lord." She laughed so heartily that even grave Mr. Hamilton had to laugh too.

"Now don't you go putting that in your paper," Mrs. Hamilton said with a look at Mr. Hamilton.

\ "I had no such intention," Mr. Hamilton said. "Though it was well described. Seems a pity such invention should go to waste."

"Well, don't."

"As you wish."

In her senior year Karen was elected to write the class poem. Karen responded by doing it in the manner of a Longfellow:

> By the rivers of the crimson rock,
> By the redman's fasting trail,
> In a council lodge on green hills,
> In our lonely prairie heaven,
> There lived a band of hardy pupils,
> Class of Nineteen Seven.

Her English teacher was surprised by the excellence of the poem.

Karen was surprised herself. The long poem proved that by studying and by doing she was continually improving her mind. And as long as that was true she could say to heck with the boys who thought her too thin and withdrawn.

2

Sunday in early June.

After a fine dinner of broiled beef and buttered fresh buns, the Hamiltons one by one wandered out onto the front porch to take in the beautiful day. Mr. and Mrs. Hamilton took their usual places in their white rockers, Horace and Joyce sat on the top step, and Sylvester and Karen settled on the bottom step. All were dressed in their Sunday best.

Soon the neighbors down the street also came out on their porches to enjoy the day.

Below, an occasional horse and buggy crossed main street. Farther on, the green maples along the Big Rock River flashed gleams of underleaf silver. And still farther west, soft cumulus clouds began to appear on the horizon and drift toward town.

Mr. Hamilton puffed quietly on a long black cigar. Every now and then his rocker slowed as some thought struck him. Mrs. Hamilton rocked to herself gently rhythmic, hands folded in her lap. From the way the toes of her shoes showed beneath her long blue Sunday dress it could be seen her feet were crossed at the ankles.

Horace and Joyce on the top step read a little, Horace in a brown book, *Cross Examinations*, and Joyce in a green book, *The Rise of Silas Lapham*.

Sylvester and Karen on the bottom step were like two colts occasionally grazing away from each other and then toward each other. Karen daydreamed; while Sylvester larked about. Karen dreamed of the day when her poetry would rival that of Elizabeth Barrett Browning. Sylvester made a whistle out of a blade of grass and blew shrilly on it for a while; then picked up a handful of pebbles and threw them one by one at sparrows feeding on a mound of horse dung near the hitching post out front; then gave a series of sly jerks on a stray red-brown hair floating on air above Karen's head.

When Sylvester finally managed to unhook the top button of Karen's right shoe, Karen slapped him lightly on the hand.

"Syl, quit being such a cutup always."

"So you got yourself some new shoes."

"You know perfectly well Nanna gave them to me for my graduation." Karen refastened the top button.

"They're pointy enough to prick a boil."

"Thanks."

"Though on you they look pretty nice."

"Thanks again."

"This time I meant it as a compliment."

"I bet."

"Cross my heart."

"I can't believe you any more. The way you're always fooling around."

"You were the prettiest girl at graduation."

Karen gave him a sour look. "Now I know you're lying."

"Really, Karen. Cross my heart."

"You're not fooling me, Mister Sylvester Hamilton, all of a sudden switching with the wind like that."

"Please, Karen."

"After what you first said, trying to butter me up isn't going to do you a whit of good."

Sylvester fell silent. A sad look came over his blond boyish face.

The little clouds approached rapidly; began to drift across the sky overhead.

A carriage rolled out of a narrow lane where it joined the high east end of main street. The lane came out of a farm which the Hamiltons owned, and the folk in the carriage were their renters coming to town, the Peter Foresters. The Foresters had a flock of boys, perfect for the big farm. Everybody in the carriage, including the little toddler sitting on the mother's lap, waved at the Hamiltons; and the Hamiltons waved back.

Presently Mrs. Hamilton brought out a basket of bananas and passed them around. Even Mr. Hamilton put aside his cigar and took one.

Karen loved bananas. She split hers open at one end and pulled the strips of yellow peeling back a little at a time. She more sucked hers away than ate it. What a wonderful sweet world it really was. Karen said, "Sunday afternoon is always the bestest time."

Mr. Hamilton bent a kindly eye upon her. "And why is that, Karen?"

"Because then I can put on my brand-new shoes and sit out on the front porch and eat a big yellow banana."

Mrs. Hamilton stirred in her rocker. "Well, now, isn't that nice."

Shadows from the boulevard maples lengthened across the lawn. Vaporing perfumes drifted over the white lilacs bordering the drive.

Karen gazed up at the sky. Some of the milk-foam clouds began to build up into golden domes. All had fat blue bottoms. While far to the south, over Sioux Center, the largest domes, colliding, soon became a tumbled line of mountain peaks. Karen measured their movement against the roofline of the Mathews house across the street and finally decided that the fat clusters of clouds were moving into the wind, going straight east. Behind them, northwest of Bonnie, more clouds were coming.

Sylvester was irrepressible. He soon got over feeling hurt. He gave Karen a light push on the knee. "Have you heard the latest downtown?"

"I suppose this is going to be another one of your—"

"You didn't hear what the oldest Forester boy did the other night? Our renter's boy Jim?"

"No. And besides, I already feel sorry for him."

"Then you don't want to hear it, I take it."

"Well, go ahead, if you must."

"If you're going to act that way I'm not going to tell it."

"Go ahead. You won't be happy until you do."

"You want to hear it?"

"Go ahead." Karen finished the last of her banana and laid the peeling to one side.

"Well, our Jim took in the latest play down at the Bonnie Opera House. *The Highway Man*. About halfway through the second act, when the sheriff starts to run around on the stage, and wrings his hands, and cries out, 'A horse! a horse! will somebody please furnish me with a horse so I can go after that dastardly robber?' our boy Jim jumps up from his seat and sings out, 'Will a jackass do?' "

"Jim didn't."

"He did. And quick as a whip, the fellow playing the sheriff says, 'Yes, a jackass will do. Step right up, kind sir.' "

"You made that up."

"I did not."

"Were you there?"

"No, but—"

"You made that up."

"No, I did not."

When Karen looked around for support, she found Horace and Joyce and Mr. Hamilton smiling.

Mrs. Hamilton wasn't smiling. She was quietly rocking to herself, lost in some inner reverie. She hadn't heard a thing of Sylvester's story.

After a bit, relaxing, Karen said, "Poor Jim Forester."

At that, Sylvester cackled with delight.

Mr. Hamilton, having taken up his cigar again, pointed it at the dark gathering of clouds over far Sioux Center. "That's beginning to look like a bad one."

Everybody looked.

An explosion seemed to have occurred within the distant creamy domes. The domes mushroomed into an enormous thunderhead, mounting and mounting until all of it hit a barrier, very high, then gradually flattened out into the shape of a monster graduation cap. The whole underside of the thunderhead turned swiftly black and became as ominously slick as a racing river. The sun in the west caught the thundercloud at a slant, giving the upper reaches on the front side a luminant white cast and the backside a molten gold glow. The blue in the sky immediately east of the massy cloud deepened into the purple of dark wet violets.

"That isn't coming this way?" Mrs. Hamilton wondered.

Horace spoke up for the first time. "It better not. It's beginning to look dangerous."

Mr. Hamilton hooked his thumbs in his vest pockets. He chewed on his cigar. "It won't. It's heading out toward Mill Creek way."

"Look," Joyce cried. "It's doubling up on itself."

Out of the top of the first thunderhead a second and an unbelievably higher cloud vaulted up, mounting up like a mighty Jacob's ladder. It swelled very rapidly, and like the parent thunderhead below, it too took on, where the sun caught it, the ineffable sweet texture of creamy white foam.

Presently beneath the mounted thunderheads, out of the absolutely black underside, out of its slickest flat portion, a small tit appeared. The tit varied in size for a few moments, then suddenly lengthened and thickened into a slick gray hose, then began to lower toward the earth.

Mr. Hamilton stood up. He whispered, "Now that's a tornado."

Mrs. Hamilton stood up too. She crossed her arms over her slim bosom, as if cold. "Is that really a cyclone, Gordon?"

"I'm afraid so."

"Those poor people."

The slick gray hose slowly, inevitably, devilishly lowered toward the earth, wide at the top, snakelike at the bottom.

Karen said, "The whole thing looks like a great big double-dip ice cream cone."

Then the gray hose touched earth and immediately turned black. Even from where the Hamiltons sat, trees, buildings, windmills could be made out exploding skyward.

"Those poor people," Mrs. Hamilton whispered again, raising a hand to her lips.

Mr. Hamilton went for his hat and cane. "I better hustle down to the depot and get the story on the telegraph."

"A real tornado," everybody said.

They watched the lashing black vortex until it vanished into the east.

It was an hour later. The sun had begun to settle toward the horizon beyond the river. Light streamed across the rolling countryside. All the earth was once more an innocent green garden. The water towers of the little towns around—Sioux Center, Hello, Chokecherry Corner—rose into sight over the groves like puffballs.

Joyce and Horace got to their feet, stretched, and went inside. Presently Sylvester joined them.

Karen and Mrs. Hamilton were left alone on the porch.

It became very still out. The gentle tinkle of forks and knives as Joyce set the supper table came through the open front door.

Mrs. Hamilton rocked awhile in silence, then said, "Karen?"

"Yes?"

"What are you doing sitting there so silent by yourself?"

Karen thrust her button shoes straight out before her. "Oh, nothing really, Nanna. Just thinking my thoughts."

"And what thoughts are those, Karen?"

"Oh, about what my future shall be."

"About some boy maybe?"

"Oh, no, Nanna. Not a boy. I should say not."

"You're sure not?"

"Of course, Mrs. Hamilton."

"Hmm."

"Whatever made you ask such a question, Nanna?"

Mrs. Hamilton got up from her rocker. She brushed her blue dress down at the back. She took a couple of steps toward Karen. "Child, I want to have a talk with you."

Startled, Karen got to her feet too. Her green eyes opened wide. "Of course, Mrs. Hamilton."

"Come with me then."

Mrs. Hamilton went directly to Karen's room upstairs, with Karen following apprehensively. Mrs. Hamilton closed the door behind them, then settled in the white chair by the south window, while Karen sat down on the white quilted spread of her bed.

Mrs. Hamilton sat very stiff for several moments, looking out on the street below. Her lips moved as though her tongue were searching for something caught in her teeth. A deeply grave, even ominous, expression quirked the corners of her eyes, almost into catlike triangles.

Karen's heart began to beat loudly. It pulsed in her throat like a series of swallows going the wrong way. She held a hand to her biscuit breasts.

A soft wind breathed through the open window. The iron rims of buggy wheels crunching on gravel streets downtown could be heard all the way up the hill.

"Karen," Mrs. Hamilton said at last.

"Yes?"

"I must ask you something personal."

"Yes, Mrs. Hamilton."

"Please bear with me."

"Of course, Mrs. Hamilton."

"Why is it that I never see . . . Oh, this is so hard to ask, child."

"Why, Nanna, I have no secrets from you."

"You're sure of that?"

"Of course. I've never kept a secret from you ever."

"Karen, have you ever noticed anything different about Joyce from time to time?"

"I don't know what you mean."

Mrs. Hamilton's eyes were round and blue for several moments. Then gradually Mrs. Hamilton hardened into what she must do. "Karen, child, you're not in a family way, are you?"

Karen's eyes turned a light yellow-blue. Her mind raced, trying to make out what Mrs. Hamilton meant. "You mean, I'm in the family's way?"

"No, no, I mean—"

"When I've always worked so hard to please you?"

"I don't mean that, child. I mean . . ." Again Mrs. Hamilton had to hunch forward to do what she must do. "I mean, Karen, child, why is it that I've never seen any sign of the flowers on you?"

Karen blinked.

"I mean, the wild roses. You know."

Karen still blinked.

"Don't you understand me, child?"

"No."

"Well, then let me ask it this way: Don't you ever have friends to stay?"

Again Karen blinked.

"How do you manage to hide your periods from me?"

Karen's heart began to beat irregularly.

"To put it in plain words, don't you ever menstruate, Karen? Have the monthlies?"

Karen stared at her.

"Don't you know what I mean?"

"No."

"Don't your girl chums ever talk to you about their periods?"

"I don't have any girl chums, Mrs. Hamilton. You know that."

"Well, hasn't even Joyce talked to you about them?"

"No."

"No? You really haven't noticed them on Joyce then?"

"Well, Joyce does act secretive once in a while."

"That's what I mean."

Karen still sat with big ignorant green eyes.

Mrs. Hamilton hitched her chair closer and placed a hand on Karen's knee. "Child, haven't you ever noticed spots in your bloomers?" Mrs. Hamilton flushed. "Or in your nightie in the morning?"

Green silence.

"No spots of blood?"

"No."

"And you've never noticed them in Joyce's nightie?"

"Well, yes, that I have. But I thought they was just from scratching a mosquito bite or so." Of a sudden Karen turned red. "Oh! Now I remember some girls talking dirty once. In the girls' toilet at school. About getting gramma's roses once a month. In that place."

"That's what I mean, child."

"No, I don't."

"You don't?"

"No."

"Oh." Mrs. Hamilton sat in quandary for a few moments. Then once again, biting in, she caught Karen's eyes firmly with her own. "Karen, child, then I must yet ask you another painful question."

"Of course, Mrs. Hamilton. I have no secrets from you."

"Have you ever fooled with a boy? With, say, maybe Sylvester?"

"Mrs. Hamilton, I'm ashamed of you."

Mrs. Hamilton's eyes opened a very whitish blue. Mrs. Hamilton stared at Karen a long time. Then gradually her eyes lost their catlike preying look and became round and tender with deepest concern. "Dear, if you haven't. . . . Oh, my."

"Mrs. Hamilton, have I done something wrong?"

"My dear. One would almost wish you had." Slender Mrs. Hamilton heaved a long sigh. "Well, I guess there is only one thing to do then, and that is to take you to a doctor."

"A doctor, Mrs. Hamilton?"

"Karen, I don't mean to frighten you, but you should long ago have had your periods. Since when you were about thirteen."

Karen began to puff. She was seventeen. For four years something had not happened to her that should have. "Does that mean I'm sick, Mrs. Hamilton? That what I am is not natural in some way?"

Mrs. Hamilton inclined her head to one side. Her hands clinched and unclinched in her lap like active clams. Blue veins stood out on the backs of her slender fingers. She heaved a long, long sigh. "We shall see what the doctor says."

"Must I really go to the doctor?" Karen said.

"Yes."

"To Doctor Drury?"

"Yes."

"But I don't like him."

"Child. Why not?"

"He's a nasty man."

"Oh, come now. Doctor Tom is all right."

"Doctor Tomcat, that's what he is."

"Why, child, wherever did you get that notion?"

"The girls in school talk awful about him."

"Oh, then you did know something, a little, about these things?"

"Only because I couldn't run away from them talking fast enough."

"Well." Mrs. Hamilton bit on her lips. "Nevertheless, to the doctor you shall go."

"But I don't wish to, Mrs. Hamilton." Karen turned a different red. "And I won't go."

"Karen, I've been made your guardian. And I say you must go. After you're twenty-one, then you can do as you please."

Karen looked down at her hands in her lap. Her slender shoulders came up a little, stubborn.

Mrs. Hamilton got up to go. "We'll talk about it some more in the morning."

Promptly at nine the next day, Mrs. Hamilton took Karen firmly in hand and marched her down the street to Dr. Thomas Drury's office.

Karen felt horribly self-conscious. She was sure that everybody along main street was looking at her, and that they knew where she was going, and why. The worst was that she and Mrs. Hamilton had to walk the whole length of main street to get to Dr. Drury's office next to the Bonnie Hotel.

Mrs. Hamilton and Karen entered the waiting room with a rustle of well-ironed dresses and closed silk parasols. A bell rang as the door closed. Together they settled on a wicker settee. Everything in the waiting room was done in white: chairs, walls, ceiling, even the floor.

There was a click in the next room as if a scissors were being snapped shut. A moment later booted feet hit the floor, and then Dr. Drury loomed through the inner door.

Dr. Drury was a large man, a good six feet tall, heavy-shouldered, slim-waisted. His arms appeared to be almost as thick as his legs. He had knowing black eyes, heavy black brows, a high balding forehead.

"Yes?"

Karen blushed, looked down at her hands.

"Well?"

Mrs. Hamilton said, "We're here about Karen, Doctor Tom. A personal matter."

"Ah."

Dr. Drury ushered them into his inner office. Here the furnishings were darker: brown rolltop desk and swivel chair, plain tan wallpaper, oak flooring, several black-framed diplomas and testimonials. A strange contraption stood in a far corner. On it was a brass plate with the words: 24-PLATE X-RAY MACHINE. An examining table and a medical cabinet were the only things white. Dr. Drury offered them each a chair, then he settled in his swivel chair facing them.

"Well, now, what seems to be the matter?" He addressed Mrs. Hamilton but flicked Karen a piercing look.

Karen threw Mrs. Hamilton an agonized green look.

"Go ahead, Karen," Mrs. Hamilton said.

Karen shook her head.

Mrs. Hamilton placed a hand on Karen's knee. "Come, child. Tell him. He is a doctor."

"I can't."

"You can always tell a doctor what's wrong."

Karen turned very red; wouldn't say a word.

Mrs. Hamilton sighed. "She's so shy about some things."

Dr. Drury nodded. "That's understandable."

Karen just knew that behind those deep-set black eyes Doctor Tom was thinking bad of her. She burned.

Mrs. Hamilton heaved a long sigh. "The plain truth is, Doctor Tom, that Karen is seventeen and hasn't menstruated yet."

From the way Dr. Drury reacted Karen was sure she'd been right about what he was thinking. First his eyes narrowed; then opened in astonishment.

"Never?"

"So she says, Doctor Tom."

"Is this true, Karen?"

Karen didn't like it that he called her by her first name, and showed it.

"Miss Alfredson, this is really true?"

"Yes."

"Have you ever had the measles?"

"No."

"The mumps?"

"No."

"Hmm." He settled his chin in his hand. It gave his face a squared look. "Tell me, Miss Alfredson, do you know if your mother was also late with her periods?"

Karen bridled. "We never talked about such things. Besides, she died when I was eleven."

"Have you ever been seriously ill?"

"No."

Dr. Drury studied her. Then he apparently made up his mind about something. "Well, for a start, we'll prescribe some exercises for you."

Karen brightened a little.

Dr. Drury talked as he wrote on a prescription pad. "Walk as much as you can. Long walks. Vigorous walks. And go to dances. And now I mean that about dances, young lady. I know you're probably quite religious, but do it anyway, you hear? And sing. Sing loud and lustily. Let it fly like a bird." He threw Mrs. Hamilton a look. "Now, Grace, what I'm going to say next I know you won't approve of, remembering your feelings about that dirty Charles Dickens. But I urge you to get Karen here . . . errh . . . Miss Alfredson here . . . some romantic novels. Even sexy novels."

"Dear God," Mrs. Hamilton whispered.

"Now I mean that," Dr. Drury said.

"But why such books?"

"Grace, what else but to stir her up? Get her vital juices flowing."

"Oh," Mrs. Hamilton said.

"Oh," Karen said.

Dr. Drury went on. "Also, I want you to get her a pony." He shot Karen a look. "You ride horseback, don't you?"

"I never have," Karen said. "Animals and I don't get along very well."

Dr. Drury gave Mrs. Hamilton a firm look. "In all seriousness now, Grace, I advise you to get her a good lively pony. And I specifically recommend that she does not ride sidesaddle, but rides like men do. Clothespin fashion. That way maybe we can jiggle it loose."

"For heaven's sakes," Mrs. Hamilton said.

"And generally, Miss Alfredson, I want you to keep the head cool, the bowels open, and the feet warm. Mind that you do this now. Or there might be results that we shall all regret. Come back in two months."

Karen took the long walks. That she liked.

She also sang, with Sylvester accompanying her on the piano. She had a tolerable soprano voice and was at her best singing Stephen Foster's songs:

> Beautiful dreamer, wake unto me,
> Starlight and dewdrops are waiting for thee,
> Sounds of the rude world heard in the day,
> Lulled by the moonlight have all passed away.

She read novels. Mrs. Hamilton refused to buy Karen the sexy novels, but she did let her read Charles Dickens' *Little Dorrit*.

Dances Karen refused to go to. She had heard that some of the boys liked to dance close.

From Lakewood Farm, where a Jim McAllister raised prize horses, Mr. Hamilton bought a bay pony mare guaranteed to be tame. "A baby can ride it," Jim McAllister promised. "We raised it as a pet."

Karen named the pony Bets after a heroine she'd read about in a book called *Betsy's Vow*. In the story the heroine, Betsy, had vowed to dedicate her whole life to proving that her father had not committed suicide, as alleged, but had instead been the victim of dastardly assassins.

Mr. Hamilton taught Karen how to halter Bets, feed her, curry her. "The more you yourself handle the pony, the more it'll get used to you."

Karen was a little trembly about it but Bets didn't seem to mind.

Mr. Hamilton bought her a boy's saddle. He showed her how to put it on Bets and pull up the cinch straps, snug but not too tight.

Karen thought she noticed something the first time she pulled up the cinch. "Is that the way her ears are supposed to be?"

Mr. Hamilton studied Bets's lowered ears. "Perhaps it's a little too tight at that." Mr. Hamilton loosened the cinch strap some, and the pony's ears came up.

Two weeks later, on a Sunday after church, Mr. Hamilton decided that Karen was ready for her first ride alone. Karen bridled and saddled Bets, and led her out of the barn and up the drive beside the house. With all the Hamiltons watching, Karen stuck her pointed shoe into the stirrup and, gathering up her long green dress, mounted and settled into the saddle.

Bets had been rudely interrupted in the middle of an alfalfa dinner and had ideas about going back to the barn.

"Here, you! Not that way." Karen gave the lines a hard jerk. "This way, Bets. We're going for a ride downtown."

Bets hesitated; thought it over; finally decided to give in for the moment. She headed for the street and then turned downtown.

The Hamiltons cheered lightly from the front porch.

A block down, Bets stopped and craned her head around and had a good look at Karen. She stared at Karen for almost a full minute. Then, mind made up, she whinnied shrilly, snapped down her ears, threw up her tail, and went into action. Bets broke into a hard gallop straight down the hill. She ran so wild her rear hoofs on each gallop landed well between her front hoofs.

Some citizens saw the two coming, and ran out onto the street waving their arms. "Runaway! Runaway!"

Bets brushed through them as if they were cobwebs.

When Bets got in front of the long veranda of the Bonnie Hotel, right next door to Dr. Drury's office, she abruptly slid to a full stop. Her stiffened hoofs threw up a sleet of gravel and dust across the street. Then, to the delight of a half-dozen loafers, Bets humped her back and bucked Karen off.

Karen sailed through the air in a long flowing fall and hit the graveled street with a heavy thud.

But before anybody could come over and help her, Karen jumped to her feet on her own. With some dignity she brushed off her green dress.

The Hamiltons came running up. "Are you all right?" Mr. Hamilton gasped, out of breath, red-faced.

"Of course, Mister Hamilton."

"Thank God."

Karen threw a withering look at the lettering on Dr. Thomas Drury's office door. "I knew something like this was going to happen. And I told him so too. Karen Alfredson and animals just don't mix."

Sylvester went over to secure Bets.

Bets kicked her heels at him.

Karen got a mite of satisfaction out of that. "I see Beast doesn't like you either. Well, it's all right, Syl. We're both too fine for her."

"Bets, you mean," Joyce said.

"No, Beast," Karen said. "That's what she is to me now."

Mr. Hamilton sold Bets at a loss to one of the Engleking families who'd rented one of his farms.

Four months passed by before Mrs. Hamilton dared to ask Karen about her female trouble again. When Karen told her that the sign of the flowers still hadn't shown up, Mrs. Hamilton put on her firmest manner and took Karen to see Dr. Drury in his office once more.

Dr. Drury appeared to be surprised. "When you didn't come back after a couple of months, I thought, well, good, everything's working out all right."

Karen's lower lip thinned.

"But I see it hasn't."

"No," Mrs. Hamilton said.

"Not even that wild ride downtown helped then." Dr. Drury allowed himself a glimmering smile.

"No."

"Well." Dr. Drury's black brows sharpened at the corners. "Let's take the young lady's temperature." He dug out a heavy thermometer and slipped it under Karen's tongue. "And now your left hand, please."

Karen gave her hand reluctantly. She flinched when his hairy fingers felt for her pulse above the wrist.

In the following silence, Dr. Drury looked down at the floor. He appeared to be thinking to himself as well as counting.

Mrs. Hamilton waited in blue-veined silence.

Dr. Drury let go of Karen's wrist. "Your pulse is somewhat slow. Sixty-six." He waited a bit longer and then withdrew the thermometer. "Hmm. Ninety-eight degrees. And that even after you walked downtown." He pondered some more to himself. "Lethargic." He shot Karen a drilling look as he addressed Mrs.

Hamilton. "Except for giving up horseback riding, she's been doing everything else I prescribed?"

"Mostly. Though she won't go dancing."

"Why not?"

"She doesn't like the way the boys dance so close, she says."

Dr. Drury's face darkened in irritation. "But that's precisely why she must dance. Get her blood heated a little." Again he drilled Karen with a look as he addressed Mrs. Hamilton. "All right, if she won't dance, and can't ride horseback, then I want you to make her take a daily hot bath. Sitz bath, we call it. Where the seat of the patient is immersed in hot water. For the therapeutic effect of the moist heat in the perineal and anal regions. In as hot a water as she can stand on her bottom."

Both Karen and Mrs. Hamilton stiffened on their chairs.

"And," Dr. Drury continued, a sardonic edge in his heavy voice, "while she's taking these sitz baths, she might as well be massaging her bosoms with rubbing alcohol. Harshly, if possible. If only to stimulate them into growing."

Again both women tightened on their chairs.

"Meanwhile, feed her all the meat you can. Bloody meat even."

"I don't care for meat," Karen said evenly.

"Then for godsakes, woman . . ." Dr. Drury paused. "Child, I should perhaps say." He shook his big head. "Anyway, for godsakes eat some eggs then."

"That we can manage," Mrs. Hamilton said.

Karen said, "Doctor, it almost sounds to me like you want me to grow up to be one of them highbinder bloomer girls."

Dr. Drury held her look. "You need roughing up, girl."

Karen turned white with fury.

"And this time, don't wait four months. If these things don't work."

"All right," Mrs. Hamilton said.

When Mrs. Hamilton learned that Karen's mother's mother, Gramma Andringham, was still alive in Zion, Michigan, she suggested that Karen write her, and among other things mention

what her trouble was and ask if any of the other womenfolk in
that branch of the family had that trouble.

Karen, with some reluctance, did write.

In two weeks Karen got her answer. It was written by her un-
married aunt, Aunt Gertrude, who was living with Gramma Andringham, and it came in the form of a postscript to a curt formal
letter. "Gramma says not to worry about being late with your
flowers. It's in the Andringham family to have them late. She also
says that the Andringham women usually have trouble breast-
feeding their children because they do not have enough milk."

Mrs. Hamilton smiled when she saw the postscript. "Maybe
everything will be all right after all, Karen."

"Well, I always felt all right," Karen said.

"Up until now," Mrs. Hamilton added. "Because it had still
better come soon."

Karen sitz-bathed every night. She sang. She took long walks.
She ate eggs.

Nothing happened. Her hips remained gracile. Her bosom did
not swell. Her mouth, though soft and pink, remained small.

On occasion she had bad stomachaches; or, as she sometimes
said with a light laugh to Joyce, "The skitters."

What with all her sitz-bathing, and her having the skitters, the
word "sitter" began to show up in her talk.

Six months later, on her eighteenth birthday, Karen still hadn't
had her wild roses.

Once again Mrs. Hamilton took things in hand. Mrs. Hamilton
was helping Karen with the breakfast dishes, she drying and Karen
washing. "Karen, it's down to the doctor you must go. And this
time you go alone."

"Why alone?"

"My goodness, girl, because you're of age now."

"I'm not going. I hate him."

"But why?"

"I've told you before I think he's one of them flirts."

"Silly girls' talk."

"Where there's smoke there's fire."

"Why, Karen, he's a doctor."

"He's a flirt. I can see through him like cheesecloth."

"He has a lovely wife. He's devoted to Lydia."

"He's as crooked as a dog's hind leg when it comes to being faithful to her. Everybody says so."

"Who says so?"

"Everybody."

"Karen, you must go." Mrs. Hamilton, finished wiping the butcher knife, for emphasis tapped its bone handle on the enamel top of the auxiliary kitchen table. "And I repeat: This—time—you—go—alone."

"He's stuck on himself. I can tell."

"Gracious stars alive, child, if you don't start having your periods pretty soon . . . why, you'll have to have an operation."

Operation?

An hour later, giving in, Karen put on her high-button pointy shoes and her blue cloak and gray shawl, took up her green parasol, and, alone, went down to Dr. Drury's office.

All too soon Dr. Drury was fixing her with those wise black eyes of his. "Still nothing?"

"Nothing."

Dr. Drury looked down at his hairy hands. He sat in thought awhile. Finally he said, "What I wish I could do would be to send you to live in a hot climate somewhere. In a close atmosphere. And make you sleep under heavy bedclothing."

"Then there really is something the matter with me?"

Dr. Drury spoke more to himself than to her. "True sexual hypesthesia perhaps." He paused. He looked at her heavily. "Tell me something . . . when you dream at night . . . have you ever dreamt of a lover kissing you?"

"No!"

"Not even when lying flat on your back?"

"None but the pure shall enter here."

"What was that?"

Karen sat with tight lips.

Dr. Drury's large mobile lips drew back in a sneer. "Don't tell

me you're one of those pure young ladies who believes she can
live in the world without shedding a little blood?"

"Were this truly God's world, yes, I believe I could live without having to shed a little blood."

"Bull. Bull. Man is a beast. And the most we can expect, even
from the very best of men, is an occasional soaring swine."

"Doctor Drury!" Karen jumped up from her chair, insulted. "I
am a human being. And I hope a child of God. And not a beast.
So I think I shall leave now."

"Sit down."

"No. I'm going."

Dr. Drury seized her by the arm and more bent than pushed
her down. "Listen, young lady, this is serious. And I've made up
my mind to help you. Because the Gordon Hamiltons are friends
of mine." He fixed fierce eyes on her. "I tell you that you need
opening up."

"No!"

"And I say yes."

"Haven't you smart doctors been able to make some kind of pill
for this?"

"Pills are mostly nonsense."

"I thought maybe there might be one by now."

"Sure I can give you a pill. But not one that would be effica-
cious." He continued to fix her with merciless eyes. "The trouble
with you is, young lady, you lack strong passions." Then he
snorted as he added, "Except when it comes to saying no."

Karen's eyes kept straying toward the door. She wished she had
the nerve to just get up again and go.

Dr. Drury stood up. "Well, I guess there's nothing for it but
to go in and see what's what."

"What does that mean?"

Dr. Drury gestured toward the white examination table. "Why
don't you just lie down on this a moment and then we'll find
out."

Karen sat heavy. Memory of her mother's sad life passed
through her mind.

"Come. It's only a routine examination. One that all women

finally have to undergo at one time or another. Before they die."
He took her by the hand and pulled her to her feet.

Karen hung back.

With male firmness he drew her toward the table and then helped her onto it.

Karen lay stiff on her back. Her eyes rolled back under her eyelids. Oh, God, now what.

"Relax, young lady."

Karen tightened even more.

"Please. It won't hurt you."

A spasm moved through the muscles on the insides of her thighs.

"Here, take this peppermint." Dr. Drury placed a white mint on her lips. When she didn't open up right away, he pushed the peppermint down between her lips. It clicked against her teeth. Almost automatically her mouth opened and her tongue accepted the peppermint and placed it in her cheek.

"That's better." Dr. Drury's voice for the first time became gentle. "Now please relax. Please. I promise you that the more you relax the easier it will be for you." He spread a white sheet over her, covering her face.

Karen lay as stiff as an icicle inside her darkened gray world under the sheet. She heard him moving about. She heard the click of metal instruments. She kept wondering how in the world she'd let herself get into this fix. Then, unbelievably, both the sheet and her dress were folded back and cold air touched the length of her legs. She swallowed her peppermint whole. She cried out, "Here you! You leave my skirts alone."

"This is not going to hurt you."

She felt her legs being lifted at the knee and her feet being placed into a sort of stirrup, first one, then the other. She felt his hand slide under her. "Don't!"

"Quiet now."

Eyes tight shut, she cried muffled through the sheet, "But you're tearing the buttons off my drawers!"

Dr. Drury sighed with a patient male sound. "Unbutton your own drawers then. Why the fashion-makers ever decided to put buttons at the back instead of at the side will always remain a mystery to me. Probably because they used manikins for models. No holes in their bottoms."

"No."

"What's the matter now?"

"I want to get out of here."

"Dear God, you are a case."

"You have no business inside my drawers. I shall never unbutton them."

"My God, young lady, just where do you imagine the flow is supposed to come from?"

"I don't care. You just let me alone."

Dr. Drury looked up at the ceiling. "Jesus Hippocrates Christ! What we medicine men don't have to endure to keep that damned Oath." Then Dr. Drury's teeth came together. "Well, I guess at last after all I'll have to take matters in my own hands at that. To do what medicine considers the best and right thing." Once more his hand slid under her, and quickly, deftly, he undid her buttons and pulled down her drawers.

"Ohh."

"I know you suffer from a very bad case of maiden shame. But what comes next will be good for it." He bent down to examine her.

"Mother!" Karen squeaked through the sheet covering her face.

"Not so loud. Or you'll have everybody on main street in here, thinking I'm raping you."

"Mrs. Hamilton!"

"Please, Karen. Still, now. I know it's sad that women these days never speak to anyone on the subject of sex. How they live out their tragedy all alone with a brave smile on their face."

"That hurt." She flipped back the sheet and tried to sit up to see what it was he was doing to her.

Instantly he flipped the sheet back over her face and pushed her down. "Lie still."

"Oh, God."

Pause. "No maidenhead. Well." Pause. "Are you sure you've never felt a tickling sensation here? Ever?"

"No!"

"No sense of dilation even?"

"What's that? No."

"It's hard to believe."

"Oh, Doctor Tom, I was feeling perfectly fine until everybody started making this fuss over me."

"Hard to believe."

"It seems to me a person has a perfect right to be exactly what she is."

Dr. Drury hovered bulky over her. Then he reached for something, an instrument, took hold of it firmly and, shoulders hunching up, moved upon her. With the flat of one of his hands he held her down, also firmly.

There was a cruel and cold invasion.

"Ow!" she shrieked.

"Ahh. There. Now let's have a real look." Pause. "Well-l. Everything appears to be normal."

She dared not move against the cold piercing thing that had her pinned down.

"No obstruction that I can see."

"It's outrageous," Karen cried aloud. "That's what it is. Everybody has a right to be let alone and I want to be let alone."

"Yes, everything seems to be shipshape."

"If God wanted me this way, then that's the way I'm supposed to be."

"Good."

"Everybody keeps getting after me that something's the matter with me. When all along I like being exactly what I am."

"Very good."

For one fleeting second, where his warm hairy fingers touched her, she felt pleasure. "Oh, why must I be tormented so by everybody? Why can't they just let me alone? I don't bother them."

"All right, young lady. It's all over."

The moment the prying pain let go of her, she flipped the sheet off her face, drew up her drawers and rebuttoned them, swung off the examination table, then, grabbing her cloak, shawl, parasol, sailed outside.

White-faced, hardly seeing a thing, aware only of an opening avenue of space between trees, she headed uphill for home.

May breezes touched her face. Spiders of spring trailed faint ropes of gossamer across her brow. Slowly leafing trees dropped their debris of broken buds on her wavy red-brown hair. Shimmers of heat rose from the sidewalk and touched her on her slender calves. She hardly noticed any of it.

It seemed but a moment and then she was entering the back door into the Hamilton kitchen, parasol and cloak and shawl still clutched in her hand.

"Why, Karen, you look a wreck." Mrs. Hamilton was sitting at the white work-table peeling potatoes.

"I have a perfect right to keep on being just what God made me."

"Of course you have, child. Why, what happened?"

"That Doctor Tomcat!"

"What did he say to you?"

Karen stood directly in front of Mrs. Hamilton, facing her across the work-table. Karen's eyes were blazing green. "Mrs. Hamilton, I've been attacked."

Mrs. Hamilton stared back her. "Now, Karen—"

"I have, though."

"Sit down, Karen. I'll go get you a glass of cool cistern water."

"I don't want a glass of cool cistern water. I've been attacked."

"Oh, shh."

"But I have been."

"That's strong talk."

"It seems to me I should know what I've been, Mrs. Hamilton."

"By Doctor Drury?"

"By Doctor Drury."

"Not really."

"But I have been, Mrs. Hamilton. And it still hurts awful."

Mrs. Hamilton then turned a scared white. "Hurts? Awful? You mean, you've really been raped?"

"No. Not raped. Attacked."

"By our Doctor Drury?"

"By our Doctor Drury." Karen closed her eyes. "I'll never forget it to my dying day."

Mrs. Hamilton wiped trembling fingertips in her apron, then came around the table and placed a hand on Karen's shoulder. "Come, let's go sit in the living room and I'll quick make us a cup of tea."

"A cup of tea will hardly help me now."

"Go on in there anyway." Mrs. Hamilton gave her a push. "Go, now."

Karen went, stiff-kneed. She settled on a hardback chair near the bay window. It hurt to sit. It felt like the eye of a potato had been pared out of her. She held herself painfully erect.

Mrs. Hamilton set the teakettle at the head of the kitchen range. She brought in the tea tray with its set of two thin, almost transparent cups and saucers and a sugar bowl. It was the set which Karen had decorated with wild roses. The texture of the striped pink petals was hauntingly real.

The clocks in the house beat in time for several moments.

Soon white vapor gushed out of the spout of the teakettle and the lid began to bobble on rising air. Mrs. Hamilton poured boiling water onto the tea leaves in the teapot, then brought the tea into the living room and set it to steep on the tea tray.

"Now, Karen. Tell me about it again."

Karen looked out of the bay window. The lilacs out front threshed gently in soft purple raptures

"Tell me."

"I went down there like you wanted me to."

"Yes. Go on."

"Then he asked me some questions. Like, did I ever dream of a lover kissing me. Like, did I lie flat on my back."

"Well, that's to be expected, isn't it?"

"Then he said we were all mostly nothing but soaring swine."

"He didn't."

"He did. I got up to leave. He made me stay. He used force. He said pills were mostly nonsense." Karen quivered. She began to speak in a rush. "Then he said for me to get up on his examination table, and I didn't want to, but he made me anyway, and he drugged me with a special peppermint, and then he put a sheet over me, and threw my dress back and tore loose the buttons of my drawers, and attacked me with something long and cold."

Mrs. Hamilton stared at Karen. Her face gradually blued over.

"He did, Mrs. Hamilton."

"But it seems impossible that a member in good standing in our church could conceive of such a thing."

"But he did, Mrs. Hamilton."

"Poor Lydia. If true."

"It hurt something awful, and I told him a person had a perfect right to be exactly what God made her, but he went ahead and did this awful thing anyway."

Mrs. Hamilton poured them each some tea. Her veined hand trembled and she spilled a little over the side of each cup. She set the teapot down and then emptied what she'd spilled in each saucer back into the cup. "Child, we must be very careful of what we say here now. The reputation of a professional man is at stake and what he means to our community."

"And what I am doesn't count?"

"Of course it does, child. Come, take a sip of your tea."

"In a minute. I don't like it when it's so hot."

Mrs. Hamilton tested her tea. "It's really not too hot. Come, take a sip."

Karen picked up her cup and her lips came out in a reluctant kiss to test the tea.

"There. That's better. Now. Let's look at this again. Are you sure that it wasn't just a plain and simple examination? As you know, when we women are finally really sick we must submit to such examinations."

"It's not decent. They can give us a pill instead."

"Then it was only an examination after all?"

Karen's voice became shrill. "Mrs. Hamilton, don't you believe me when I say he attacked me?"

Mrs. Hamilton took several sips of tea. "I hardly know what to say."

"And aren't you going to do something about it? Get after that awful man?"

"What do you want me to do, child?"

"He needs to be arrested, doing these things to innocent young girls."

"Karen."

"But he did it to me, Mrs. Hamilton."

"What did he do to you?"

"He attacked me."

"It's difficult for me to believe that he—"

"You don't believe me?" A sudden chill passed through Karen. "Oh." Shivers moved in waves up her backbone. "Mrs. Hamilton." Her green eyes crossed at the corners. "Oh. Oh. Oh."

"Karen!"

Karen let go with a high short shriek. Then she slid out of her chair onto the floor, hitting the leg of the table and making the tea spill over into the saucers again. She beat the floor with her hands and toes until pale dust began to rise out of the blue pattern rug.

"Stars alive," Mrs. Hamilton whispered.

Karen kicked and shrilled and undulated until the big room began to reverberate with it.

Mrs. Hamilton gaped.

"And now what shall I say to my Lord on Judgment Day?" Karen moaned.

Mrs. Hamilton swallowed with a click, then had to work to make the swallow stay down in her stomach.

"Picked when still green."

Mrs. Hamilton's head came down in a sudden nod. She put a hand to each knee and got up. She stood over Karen. "Karen, stop it. That's enough of that now."

"Ruined."

Mrs. Hamilton stamped her foot. "Karen, that's enough of that now!"

"My God. My God."

Mrs. Hamilton took hold of one of Karen's arms and gave it a tug.

Karen jerked free of Mrs. Hamilton's grasp.

"Karen, that's enough of that nonsense now."

Bubbles of froth appeared in the corners of Karen's mouth.

"Karen, if you will quit making a spectacle of yourself, I promise that I shall take the matter up with Mister Hamilton tonight. And then we can decide what to do."

Karen's eyes slowly turned up under her eyelids.

"Karen!"

Karen's hands crossed stiffly at her thighs. All color leached out of her face.

Mrs. Hamilton stared down at Karen in disbelief. "Why, gracious me! The child's fainted dead away." Pause. "Now what shall I do? I can't call Doctor Drury."

Karen hardly breathed.

Mrs. Hamilton took a deep breath; thought a moment; then rushed out and fetched a basin of cool cistern water. She dashed it into Karen's face. "Karen! That's enough of that now."

No response. Light from the bay window glinted in the splashes of water on the blue rug.

"Mercy me." Mrs. Hamilton clutched her side. "What a spirited child she is."

There were firm steps on the sidewalk outside and up the front steps.

"Oh, thank God, there's Gordon."

Gordon Hamilton entered quietly and clapped his black hat on the hall tree. Then he spotted Karen lying stiff in a pool of water. His gaunt face lengthened in surprise. "My Lord, woman, what is this?"

"Karen has fainted dead away." Mrs. Hamilton wrung her hands. "The poor dear."

"What happened?"

Mrs. Hamilton told him Karen's story.

"Not our Tom."

"Gordon, I'm afraid it's true."

"My Lord."

"I'm convinced of it. Though I wasn't sure at first."

"My Lord." Mr. Hamilton set his feet apart and stared. Then he said, "Well, let's bring her around." He got a flask of brandy from a little locked cupboard under the sideboard. "This should do it." He knelt beside Karen, careful not to settle in the splashes of water, and poured a tiny flip of brandy into Karen's open mouth.

Karen coughed; then sat up exploding little spumes of brandy.

"Ah," Mrs. Hamilton breathed. "Good."

Mr. Hamilton tried to pour some more into Karen's mouth.

Karen's hand instantly came up and pushed the bottle away.

"Ah," Mr. Hamilton said. Setting the bottle to one side, he helped Karen up off the floor and to a chair.

Karen was outraged. She scraped out her mouth with a harsh clearing sound like she might be cleaning it out with an abrasive soap. "Filthy liquor."

"It was only to bring you around," Mr. Hamilton said.

"First I'm attacked. Then I'm being made a drunk of."

Mr. Hamilton gave her a sideways look.

"And all along I felt fine until that man invaded my privities."

"Karen," Mr. Hamilton said, "Karen, truly now . . . are you sure Doctor Tom did this?"

"Oh, Mr. Hamilton, are you going to doubt me too?"

Mrs. Hamilton's hands began to flutter. "Now, now, child, let's not . . . Of course we believe you. Only we must make quite certain of so grave a charge."

Mr. Hamilton's thumbs found their favorite roost in his vest pockets. The cool air of the professional newspaperman came over his face. "Karen, I trust you understand the gravity of your charge. Because if Mrs. Hamilton and I finally believe that this thing is true, then this is what we shall have to do—we shall have to hire a lawyer and place a charge against Doctor Tom."

Karen hid her face in her hands. "I wish I'd never been born. Then I wouldn't have brought this disgrace to your home."

Mr. and Mrs. Hamilton exchanged a look.

"I was feeling perfectly fine until everybody started making this fuss over me. And here I always thought a person had a perfect right to be just what God made her."

Mr. Hamilton's lips cracked open a little. "Grace, there she has a point."

Mrs. Hamilton began to cry.

Karen heard Mrs. Hamilton cry. She turned to look at her. And when she saw there were actual tears in Mrs. Hamilton's eyes, she promptly passed out again.

Later, after Karen had once again been revived, this time with a swallow of vinegar, and after Mr. Hamilton had finished his dinner, it was decided that Mr. Hamilton should speak to Titus Fowler, the local lawyer.

The next day Mr. Titus Fowler interviewed Karen in the Hamilton living room. Mrs. Hamilton sat beside Karen on the black horsehair sofa. Mr. Fowler sat at a small table across from them, pencil and pad ready.

Mr. Fowler was dressed in black shoes, black suit, white shirt with wing collar, black bowtie. He had a strong chin, a high square forehead, relentless black eyes. He had more the air of a judge than a lawyer.

It was a lovely sunny day out and the living room rug took on the color of bluebirds.

As Karen told her tale by fits and starts, helped along by Mrs. Hamilton, her green eyes resembled frost-pinched violets.

After she'd finished, Mr. Fowler sat awhile in thought, looking at his notes, looking out of the window. It was apparent he had heard worse stories.

A horse and buggy clattered by on the graveled street outside.

Finally Mr. Fowler cleared his throat. "Hum."

"You don't believe me?" Karen challenged.

"I should like to ask you a few questions."

"I suppose you're a friend of his too. You men."

"Miss Alfredson, listen to me." Mr. Fowler leaned a hard look into her. "You have made a very serious charge here. And before I can make it a matter of law I have to make certain of my ground."

Karen stared right back at him. "Well, if that's your mind, mister, you can go to thunder for all of me. Because I can see already you're afraid to go after him."

"Karen," Mrs. Hamilton said.

Mr. Fowler continued to look her right in the eye. "When it comes to that, young lady, I fear no man. If Doctor Tom is guilty,

guilty he is, and I shall personally see to it that he be prosecuted to the full limit of the law."

Karen also continued to stare back at him.

"Now, a few questions. All right?"

Karen slowly nodded.

"You are absolutely sure now that Doctor Drury had intercourse with you?"

"What's that?"

"That he got on top of you. Did he?"

"He most certainly did."

Mr. Fowler's heavy black brows slowly came up. "Right there in his office?"

"Yes."

"He did do it to you then?"

"Well, he did something to me."

"What did he do to you?"

"Something he had in his hand came into me." Karen crossed her legs. "It did. It most certainly did."

Mr. Fowler's lips became thin and precise. "What was this something that came into you?"

"Something he took up in his hand."

"Are you speaking of his . . . ah"—Mr. Fowler threw a sidelong look at Mrs. Hamilton—"his member?"

"Whatever it was, it was hard on me." Karen snapped off her words. "It hurt like the dickens."

"Or was it a surgeon's instrument of some sort?"

"He violated my person with something."

"Something else besides his hand?"

"He entered my person. He attacked me."

"Are you sure?"

"He attacked me."

"Do you know what is meant by a physical examination?"

"Yes."

"What does it mean?"

"A doctor looks you over."

"So that if you have something wrong with your nose, for example, he looks up your nose?"

"Yes."

"And if, say, there's something the matter with your throat, he looks into the back of your mouth?"

"Yes."

"Now, couldn't this also be true if there was something the matter with your womb? That he would look into it?"

Karen uncrossed her legs and stretched her toes straight out before her. "I think it's disgusting."

"What was that?"

"A doctor doesn't have to look into one's privities. A womb belongs to God and mortal man has not business in it."

"How else can a doctor tell?"

"He can take your temperature. And feel your pulse."

"He can tell by feeling your pulse if there is something wrong with your womb?"

"I think so. Because God will take care of the rest."

Mr. Fowler stared square-headed at her. Here at last was something he had never run into before. "Young lady, let me ask you a blunt question."

"Go ahead."

"Have you ever heard of people having the piles?"

"Yes."

"And you know where such piles are usually located?"

"Yes."

"Now, isn't it true that if you were to go to a doctor with a complaint of having the piles, the doctor would look into your behind?"

"It's disgusting, that's what it is. Besides, a person has a right to be let alone."

"Answer the question."

"Besides, having something the matter with your sitter is different from having something the matter with that other place."

"How so?"

"Well, it's where a girl is supposed to stay pure. And where if you're a good girl you are pure. And I've been a good girl."

Mr. Fowler exchanged a crinkled look with Mrs. Hamilton.

Karen recrossed her legs. "He was even afraid that everybody on main street would hear me cry out in there. In his office."

Mr. Fowler stared some more at Karen.

"He made me take a piece of doctored peppermint candy and drugged me with it. Then he pulled down my drawers and said I needed opening up."

Mr. Fowler's eyes widened and began to shine at the corners.

"Then he said the most horrible things, about tickling and such, and then he did it."

"He raped you?"

"He attacked me."

"Miss Alfredson. Are you prepared to charge, under oath, that Doctor Thomas Drury is guilty of rape?"

"He needs to be arrested, doing such awful things to young girls."

Mr. Fowler put away his pencil in his vest and picked up his pad. He got to his feet.

"You aren't going to do anything to him then?" Karen cried.

Mr. Fowler turned to Mrs. Hamilton. "Let me give this whole matter some thought in the next couple of days."

Mrs. Hamilton also got to her feet. "Certainly, Titus."

Mr. Fowler gave Karen a polite nod. "Thank you, young lady. I'll be back later."

Mr. Fowler left.

Karen's eyes became very wide and green. "He didn't believe me either." It still hurt a little when she sat.

"Now, Karen, please."

"Well, I don't care. I have a right to be let alone."

"Karen."

"Mrs. Hamilton, God shall not hold you guiltless if He finds something wrong with me on Judgment Day."

Early the next Saturday morning there was a knock on the front door. Karen, home alone, answered it.

There stood her brother Alfred VI. Alf had driven up in a spanking new black buggy. A stylish roan mare, bespangled with brightly colored celluloid rings, stamped at flies where she stood tied to the Hamilton hitching post. There was a quietly sly expression about the mare's mouth.

Alfred was dressed up like an ambassador: black hat, black tie, black suit, black shoes. Karen had never seen him in such splendor. She was used to seeing him at church in hand-me-downs. It took her a moment to adjust. Also, he seemed taller than his usual six-foot-five.

"Alf!" she cried. "What are you doing here all dressed up like that?" She was both happy and sorry to see him; happy because he was all she had of her own darling family around, sorry because she all too well remembered a certain dark thought about him. "Did you get fired?"

Alf removed his black hat. His black wavy hair slid out of place a little. "Naw, I didn't get fired."

"Well, don't you work Saturdays?" She stood back, holding the door open for him.

Alf stepped inside. Besides his hat, he carried a small hatbox. "Charlie Pullman gave me the day off so I could see my new gal in Jerusalem."

Karen stared amazed. "You've got a new girl where? That far away? Who?"

"Ada Engleking."

"What are you doing going with one of those trembling Englekings?" Karen scolded. "They're always in trouble, with their shotgun weddings."

"Wait'll you meet Ada. She's different. You'll like her."

"Ha."

"Oh, she ain't one of your Bonnie Englekings."

"I'll bet."

"Her dad's that Alfred Engleking what lives in Jerusalem. And he's awful strict."

"Wherever did you meet her all the way from there?"

"She was visiting her cousins here on the section. Down below Pullman's there."

Karen couldn't keep her eyes off Alf's brand-new clothes, nor off the dashing horse and buggy outdoors. "Where'd you get all those fancy clothes? And that fancy rig?"

"Earned it."

"Oh, Alf, didn't Pa say we had to send our earnings to him?"

"I did send him everything . . . until I hit twenty-one. Then according to the law I didn't have to anymore."

"Hoh!" she gasped. "You dare to do that?"

" 'Course. It's my turn to get married now." A smile touched his handsome face; then vanished. He handed her the small hatbox. "Here, I brought you a present from the Pullmans."

"For me?" Karen took the box and held it preciously. "What is it?"

"Open it up."

She sat down. Holding the box in her lap, she removed the lid. "A kitty."

"Yep."

"Oh, and I always wanted one." She lifted out a spotted kitten, a lovely gold-and-black-and-white thing. "Oh, isn't she a beauty. I hope Mrs. Hamilton will let me keep her." Karen began to stroke it. "Aii, kitty. Aii, kitty." The kitten slinked down a little to slide under her touch each time. "Let's hope this'll be the one animal that likes me. For once."

"It'll be your own fault if it don't." Alf spoke shortly, looking down at her from his great height.

"Don't say that."

"You're too fine for the animals. And they know it. They always do."

"Please, Alf." She continued to stroke the multicolored kitten. "Aii, pussy. Aii, pussycat." She laughed for joy at its soft wondrous fur. "I'm going to call her Josephine. After Joseph's coat. It is a she, isn't it?"

"Take a look for yourself."

"Oh, Alf, I couldn't tell the difference."

"It's a she all right."

"Little Josephine."

"Wal," Alf said, setting one leg forward stylishly the way the clothier advertisements had it in *The Bonnie Review*, "wal, I also come here to find out what the heck's this business about you and our Doctor Tom."

Karen paled. And accidentally she pinched the kitten over the belly. "Who told you about that?"

"Mister Fowler came out to see me."

"He did! The nerve of that man. Whatever for?"

"Just wanted to ask some questions about you, is all."

"Like what?"

"Oh, like, was you honest. And, did you make up stories sometimes."

"What did you tell him?"

"Wal, the truth, of course. That you was always a little finicky to play with as a kid. And what Pa once said about you, that you already was too much like an overparticular old maid."

"Alf, did you really tell him that?"

"I sure did."

"Why, you awful thing, you, blacking my name like that."

"Wal, it was the truth."

"When I'm blacked enough as it is already."

"Says who?"

"Everybody."

"You talk about blacking. . . . Listen, Sis, what do you think you're doing to our Doctor Tom? If that ain't blacking somebody's name I'll eat it."

Karen was white furious. "I can tell a few things about you too that will make everybody sit up."

"Pah."

"You once got on top of me. And if I hadn't've bit you, you wouldn't've got off."

"Aw, shucks, Karen, that was when we was kids."

"And then as if that wasn't bad enough, you had to start trying to get on top of Gerda."

A quietly sly expression appeared about Alfred's mouth. "You always did favor Abbott over me."

Karen immediately turned righteous. "Say, listen here, you. Abbott is a sweet clean boy." She looked at the dark hair over the backs of Alf's hands. "He's a silver boy with a soul as pure as snow."

"Wal, I gotta go now. But I came to tell you that you better be careful what you say about our Doctor Tom. He can sue you for damaging his reputation."

"An old fool is the worst fool of all."

"Mind, now." For a moment Alfred's deep-set eyes burned into her. They had the light-blue intensity of a buggy's carbide lamps. "I'm the oldest in the family and as long as Pa ain't here it's my duty to tell you."

Karen wanted to say: "You tell me off? When you didn't even finish the eighth grade, let alone high school?" But she knew it was a mean thing to say, and certainly not something a good Congregationalist would say, so she said instead, "You can leave now."

"That's what I mean to do. It's a long ways to Jerusalem. I'm going to have to go like Billy Blixen to make it in one day. Thirty miles. But Daise can do her." Alf caught up his wavy black hair in one hand and pushed it back in place, clapped on his black hat, and, turning hugely and easily, was out of the door and down the steps.

The buggy squeaked as he mounted the footplate. He settled on the black leather seat and spread a yellow silk duster over his knees. Then his strong male voice rang out clearly. "All right, Daise, old girl, let's get high behind and eat up them miles."

There was a swift patter of hoofs, a crinching of steel rims on sand, and Alf and horse were gone.

"You men always stick together against us poor women, no matter what."

The kitten Josephine suddenly squirted out of Karen's hands. It landed tail-over-head on the floor, then darted out of sight under the horsehair sofa.

A forlorn look edged into the corners of Karen's green eyes.

The next Monday, in the morning, Mr. Titus Fowler appeared at the Hamilton door again, this time carrying a thick brown folder of papers. And once more Karen and Mrs. Hamilton sat down with him in the living room to have a talk, the two women on the black horsehair sofa and he at the small table.

Mr. Fowler had the air about him that what he was about to

say wasn't going to be good. It was in the way he wielded his high square forehead.

"Well, now," Mr. Fowler said, catching up both Karen and Mrs. Hamilton in his relentless glance, "here we are again."

Karen waited, a hand to her lips, a guarded look in her eyes.

Mrs. Hamilton picked up the kitten Josephine from where it was purring at her feet. She held it in her lap, stroking it over its white tab ears.

Mr. Fowler opened his brown folder. "Karen, I've investigated the matter of Alfredson versus Drury as thoroughly as it is humanly possible to see if any legal action could be taken against Doctor Drury. I even investigated around town to see if any other young girl, or if any other woman of any age whatsoever"—a vinegar smile touched his lips for a moment—"had a complaint about Doctor Drury as to his professional behavior as a doctor. But I didn't come across a single instance of it." Again a puckered grimace tugged at the corners of Mr. Fowler's lips. "Doctor Drury does have, in his private life as apart from his professional life, what might be termed a roving eye. I myself have noticed this with regard to my own wife. So it is rather obvious that he does like the girls. But, in any event, I have not been able to find anything concrete that could be termed wrong or actionable. Certainly, at any rate, nothing more than dark remarks by jealous husbands and spicy talk by flirtatious wives. And you know that one cannot hang either a case or a man on such evidence."

Slowly Karen sat more and more erect.

"I've . . . uhh . . ." Mr. Fowler riffled through his flake-stiff legal papers. "I've also had occasion to discuss this matter with Hy Snapp, our local justice of the peace. Hy took the matter under advisement; and, after giving it all some thought, went over and had a long talk with Doctor Tom. Hy says Tom was shocked to hear of the possible charge. Hy says that Tom categorically and emphatically and absolutely denied that anything other occurred in his office than the usual normal examination of a woman for female trouble."

Karen blanched.

"So, Miss Alfredson, what it comes down to, finally, is this: your word against his word."

That liar. That devil.

"And I'm afraid that in a court of law a jury would be more apt to believe a doctor than a patient."

"Then there is no hope of getting after him?" Karen cried.

"Frankly, no."

"Then what are we going to do?"

"I recommend that we do nothing. That we drop the matter entirely."

"Ohh!" Karen cried. All along it had also been bothering her that her many-colored Josephine was enjoying herself preening under Mrs. Hamilton's soft stroking hand. The kitten had never let her pet it that way. Karen so wanted it to love her, so wanted to be able to touch it.

Mr. Fowler looked at Mrs. Hamilton. "So, Grace, I guess that winds up the case. I'm sorry."

Mrs. Hamilton spoke quietly. "Well, you know how it is. We had to make sure."

Mr. Fowler got to his feet. "I know."

"Mister Hamilton said to be sure and send him the bill."

Karen gave a low wounded cry and suddenly clutched her chest. Her green eyes rolled up fish-white. Then her hands fell slack and she slid angularly off the black horsehair sofa onto the blue rug.

"I declare," Mrs. Hamilton said. She set the kitten aside gently, and gently reached down to touch Karen. "The child has fainted dead away again."

Mr. Fowler nodded his head to himself, once, as if he had expected this.

Mrs. Hamilton knelt beside Karen. She straightened out Karen's awkwardly tumbled legs, then took hold of Karen's hands and began to chafe them over their backs and up over the wrists. "Karen! that's enough of this nonsense now. Wake up. Come."

Mr. Fowler watched calmly from his square-headed stance. "Shall I get some cold water?"

"Oh, dear. And we'll have that all over the rug again. Well, all right. Yes, go get some."

Mr. Fowler get the bucket of water from under the kitchen cistern pump. "Shall I splash her a little?"

"Yes. A small one at first."

Water slapped Karen in the face.

Karen, if anything, turned more white. Her cheekbones showed through her skin like pieces of blue ice.

Mrs. Hamilton pointed. "Titus, quickly. The brandy in the cupboard there. Under the sideboard."

Again Mr. Fowler obliged. With a finger he gently pried open Karen's mouth and gave her a shot.

Karen didn't even gag. The brown liquid went into her mouth and then spilled out of it again, running down under her chin.

"Oh, dear," Mrs. Hamilton whispered. "I fear this time it's a good one."

Mr. Fowler got down on his hands and knees beside Karen and placed an ear on her bosom. "Her heart's still beating. Erratically."

"Lord in heaven."

"Like a pony that can't make up its mind whether to gallop or to trot."

"Karen! You! Here now."

"We'd best get Doctor Tom."

"What! And have her suffer an even worse one after what's happened?"

"That's true."

"No." Mrs. Hamilton thought hard, so hard that sweat appeared over her temples. "No, this is what we'll do. You go downtown, Titus, and right away send a message on the telegraph to Dr. Case in Rock Falls. He knows us. Tell him to come down on the Bonnie Omaha this afternoon immediately."

"All right." Mr. Fowler got to his feet.

"Meanwhile, I'll try and keep her alive until he arrives."

Mr. Fowler hurried out of the door.

Mrs. Hamilton chafed Karen, and covered her with a warm quilt; and chafed her some more, and doused her with smelling salts; and kept it up until Dr. Case arrived late in the afternoon.

Dr. Case pronounced it a severe heart attack due to shock. He prescribed rest, asafœtida, rusk with beef broth, and as much goat's milk as the patient could tolerate.

3

Karen lay spiritless in bed for a long time.

Karen drifted; dreamed; slept. The only time she showed any life at all was when Alf came to visit her. Then for a moment she showed some fire as she bitterly sent him on his way.

Karen became well acquainted with the white ceiling above her bed. Her skin turned almost transparent, until little river systems of blue veins appeared under it. Her hair lost its red tint and turned a plain brown.

The Hamiltons were very good about it. Mrs. Hamilton became Karen's patient nursemaid. Joyce got married during this time to the local cashier, but helped her mother with such housework as she could. Horace got a job with a law firm in Sioux City, but thoughtfully sent Karen an occasional book he thought might interest her. Mr. Hamilton, upon hearing that Karen had always wanted a trunk of her very own in which to store her own precious things, ordered her a new black model with brass trimmings from Chicago. And Sylvester, having got a job as music teacher at the local high school, brought home the latest gossip about town.

Karen acknowledged it all with a languid smile. And slept.

One day, while on her knees helping Karen store something in the new trunk, Mrs. Hamilton came upon a sheaf of papers with neat lines of writing on them. Mrs. Hamilton recognized the handwriting immediately. Karen wrote much as she looked—angular, with long strokes across her *t*'s, and *n*'s as wide as *w*'s.

"Why, Karen, this looks like poetry of some sort."

Karen said shortly, "Just some things I copied." Karen had only that day dared to get out of bed to sit in a rocker.

"May I read them?"

"If it pleases you, Nanna." Karen didn't relish the idea very much.

Mrs. Hamilton read several of the poems. She looked up from

where she knelt on the floor. Her measured glance held Karen's eyes. "I don't ever remember having read them in our library. Where did you copy them from?"

Karen sucked on her lower lip and held it lightly between her white teeth. Now that she was out from under the quilt she smelled strangely of asafœtida even to herself.

"Karen?"

"They're not very good, are they?"

"Well-l . . . it's just that I never read anything like them before." Mrs. Hamilton glanced further through the poems. "Some of them are about our town of Bonnie. And they've never been printed in our local paper. That I know of anyway."

Karen looked to one side.

"And this one. It seems to fit how you feel about your father. How you are different." Mrs. Hamilton read the poem aloud:

> Sometimes
> I wonder if my father understood
> In leaving me he did me good.
> He never knew, couldn't, what it meant to me
> To love a tulip two or three.
>
> Most times
> He drove wild horses
> And built sod houses
> And sat out claims
> And beat out flames.
>
> Sometimes
> I moon a month of sweetest angel dreams
> My bed a slough beside some streams.
> I walk alone, alone, completely free
> To love a tulip two or three.

Karen quickly winked away a tear.

"Karen?"

"Guess I might as well tell you." Karen could feel her lips trembling. "I made them up."

"Aha. I thought so."

"I didn't mean to fib about it."

"Fib, nothing." Mrs. Hamilton got to her feet. "It's perfectly understandable." Mrs. Hamilton stared down at the sheaf in her hand. "Would you mind if I showed them to Mister Hamilton?"

"Oh, he wouldn't care to see them. He'd only laugh at them."

"May I?"

"Oh, all right." Karen drew up her shoulders. "But I want them back."

"Never fear."

After Karen had written the class poem, other ideas for poems had come to her. She'd put them all down, faithfully, just as they came to her. Never once did she have to scratch out a word. When a line came, it came complete. Occasionally a line would come slow to her, even tough. But if she waited patiently, the little kitty in her head would eventually untangle the snarl in the ball by itself, and then once again there the words and phrases would come. The poetry writing lasted a little over a year. Then, when the ball was all used up, the poems stopped.

Karen wondered a little why Mrs. Hamilton should want to show the poems to Mr. Hamilton.

A February snowstorm went by. Then a warm March came. The buds on the lilacs gradually thickened, resembling drops of dark rainwater about to let go.

On the fifteenth of April, early in the morning, Meard Borman, the drayman, drove up and unloaded a large package at the front door.

Karen heard Mrs. Hamilton downstairs talking pleasantly with Borman. Then Karen heard Borman moving the box inside the house. Next, incredibly, she heard Borman laboring up the steps with the heavy package and then into her room, with Mrs. Hamilton holding open the door.

Karen sat up in bed. She pulled a white woolen comforter over her shoulders.

"Karen, look what we have here."

Karen stared at the package. It had heavy brown strings. "Oh, Mrs. Hamilton, whatever is that?"

"You'll see in a moment." Mrs. Hamilton turned to Borman. "How much to carry it up here, Meard?"

"That comes with the price of delivery." Borman's tongue chased a chew of tobacco around in his left cheek. "How do you do, Miss Alfredson."

Karen hated men who chewed tobacco. Alf sometimes did it. She drew up the white bedspread as high as she could. "Hello."

"How you feelin'?"

"Fine."

"For somebody that's supposed to be sick you look mighty pert to me."

"Thanks."

Borman gave her a broad brown wink. "I suppose one of these days you'll be out gardening bright and early with the robins."

"I hope so." What would a man who chewed filthy tobacco know about robins in a garden? "If only to get myself off Mrs. Hamilton's hands. Poor soul."

"One of these days you're gonna surprise yourself. Just you watch."

"I hope so."

"You will." Borman gave her another brown wink. "Well, so long. Easy does it now."

After Borman left, Karen said, "Nanna, whatever it is, you shouldn't have done it. You've already been too kind to me."

Mrs. Hamilton gave Karen a special smile. She drew up Karen's rocker beside the package. "Come, climb out of bed and we'll both have a look."

"Oh, Nanna, you shouldn't't've."

"Come now, out of bed with you."

Karen began to puff. Trembling, she got out of bed. She slipped into her blue wrapper and settled in the rocker.

Mrs. Hamilton handed her the shears to cut the heavy brown strings.

"Is it really for me?"

"Open it."

Karen cut away the strings. Then she opened the top of the package, unfolding the brown paper and bending back the brown cardboard lids. She parted soft folds of aromatic excelsior.

Bundles. Of what seemed to be books. Or magazines.

Karen opened the top bundle. Books all right. Slim blue volumes. In packs of ten each.

Karen picked up one of the books and held it wonderingly in her pale blue-veined hands. There was gold lettering on the blue cover:

POEMS

* * *

Karen Alfredson

Karen stared. Slowly her eyes sought out Mrs. Hamilton's. "My poems? Published in a book?"

Mrs. Hamilton beamed. "Mister Hamilton and I both thought the poems were worth preserving."

Elation blazed in Karen's eyes. The green in them turned into a glittering blue.

Karen leafed through the little book. One of her poems caught her eye and she paused to read it. It looked so distinguished in print:

> What kind of life is this if you postpone
> Climbing some hill to dream alone,
>
> Postpone a walk to Hopewell mound
> To look at all the sights around,
>
> Give up the chance to pick puccoons
> To taste the dews of Indian moons—
>
> This is no life if you postpone
> Climbing some hill to dream alone.

Then, after a long moment, a shadow closed down her eyes. It was as though she'd deliberately put on a pair of blinders.

"What's the matter now?" Mrs. Hamilton said.

"Nothing."

"But why so all of a sudden downcast?"

"Oh, nothing, Nanna. It's just that I don't want to make a

spectacle of myself. Become one of those vain things too smart for her own good."

"Gracious, child, but you have a right to be proud of what you did. Happy. It's a wonderful thing to be able to write poetry."

"No, Nanna. The first thing you know I'll start bragging about myself. Besides, such things are for clowns and public entertainers."

"My dear child. My dear child."

Nevertheless the little blue book of poems did change things. Karen's health took an immediate turn for the better. And soon she had trouble keeping up with her own recovery.

Nights Karen slept soundly. She dreamt good dreams. And she invariably awakened refreshed.

Mr. Hamilton loved a hearty meal to begin the day with, and Karen, by imitation, found herself eating not only a dish of oatmeal porridge with him, but also, on occasion, a strip of bacon with an egg.

In a couple of weeks she was helping Mrs. Hamilton around the house, washing the breakfast dishes, tidying up the bedrooms, emptying out the chamberpots, dusting the furniture, redding up the front entryway, and sweeping off the stoop. The egg peel look of her skin changed to peony white. The tiny river systems of blue veins sank from sight. The tint of red returned to her hair.

Karen knew Mrs. Hamilton would never accept payment of any kind for all the care she'd been given during her long convalescence, neither money nor hard work. "Nanna mothered me without complaint even though I wasn't her own flesh and blood. And she may not have believed me altogether either in that Doctor Drury business, but she was tender with me anyway. She felt sorry for me. The dear."

Yet Karen felt she had to do something in token of her appreciation. Karen had always been good at sewing and knitting, and one day, coming upon a catchy ad in *The Bonnie Review*—"TATTING TAUGHT. IDA COGSWELL."—she knew what she had to do.

Karen took lessons from Ida Cogswell. She soon learned to loop and knot a single cotton thread so well that within a week she was making expert edgings for Mrs. Hamilton's tablecloths. After a time the small cream-colored tatting shuttle was like a sixth finger to Karen's hand.

Mrs. Hamilton was astounded, and most pleased, at all the lovely fragile wheels and complex snowflakes that evolved out of her foster daughter's slender supple fingers.

"That Karen is a most clever girl," she told Mr. Hamilton in the privacy of their bedroom at night. "I declare, when she sets her mind to it, there's hardly a thing she can't do. Those doilies she made for my flowerpots are the best I've ever seen. Really."

"A singular girl."

During the night a northwest wind cleaned off the sky and the next morning the sun shone dazzling in Karen's room. Even while still in dreamland Karen's eyes trembled as though they were egg yolks full of dark yellow life. She heard a happy voice cry, "Blessed day!" She opened her eyes and yellow became green. She was awake.

She took in the details of the room: sun-tinted white ceiling, gold-tinted blue walls, lemon-tinted bedspread, yellow-flashing mirror.

Her flesh felt full. Her groin felt warm and itchy.

"Change of weather. I can feel it in my bones."

She leaped out of bed. She brushed her teeth and washed herself in the white bowl. She let her white nightie fall on a blue throw rug, where it immediately took on the look of a bled-out pullet. Modestly she stretched her arms. She slipped into her drawers buttoned at the back, drew on her black stockings, using Mason jar rubbers for garters, shucked herself into a white petticoat, flourished a blue dress up over her head, and, one foot at a time, buttoned on her pointy black shoes.

She tiptoed downstairs and found she was the first one up. She started a fire in the kitchen range, put on the coffee and the oatmeal, sliced some bread and placed the bread in the oven to toast on a grill, sliced some bacon and filled the frying pan.

She was cracking eggs when Mrs. Hamilton appeared, sleepy but smiling. "Child."

"Good morning, Nanna."

"You're up bright and early."

"I woke up feeling so good I just had to hustle out of bed and get at things."

"I'm glad, child."

"It's going to be one of those wonderful June days."

"Let's hope so."

"Nanna, I'd like to go for a long walk. Do you think I'm strong enough?"

"You're strong enough to do anything now, Karen."

"Then I shall go to my favorite place."

"Just so we know where you are."

Later Karen tied on her blue sunbonnet, fixed herself a picnic basket of lunch—a dried-beef sandwich and a jar of lemonade—tucked in her tatting carefully, with some waxed paper between it and the food, and set off across town.

Lettuce and radish flourished in neat green rows in black gardens. Dandelions speckled the lawns, utterly yellow, toddling sturdily in a morning breeze. Lilacs lingered white and purple. Overhead the leaves of the ash trees showed two greens, the undersides a hint of silver and the sun side a touch of sky.

Karen stepped along, slim, stately.

The high school grounds opened ahead, a sweep of green fringed with new young hackberries. Six boys played a game of ball behind a fence. The apse of the Congregational Church resembled a vase of frozen nasturtiums, red and yellow and green. Martins moved in loving swoops around tiny houses high up on poles; and then, coming in for a landing, just as they were about to light, stood for a moment on fanning blue tails.

Karen dreamed along.

The last sidewalk at the edge of town dropped off into a cinder path, grayish red in green grass. The path wound through a patch of gray-tinged wolfberries. Gophers, erect beside their holes, whistled shrill warnings. Flashing blue swallows cleared the air of insects. A single heron took a heavy undulant route across the point, from the Little Rock River to the Big Rock River.

Karen crossed the south road out of town, rolled under through the barbwire fence, brushed herself off, walked stately to the

Hopewell mound on the brow of the last hill. She stopped to catch her breath.

Below flowed the rippling Little Rock, curving and recurving slenderly down the valley. Light-green buffalo grass showed through the darker bluegrass. Islands of joint-grass told where old springs were working. A herd of black cattle grazed on the far side of the little river, each animal moving in turn as if a cowrie in a whimsical game of Parcheesi.

Karen walked down to the bank of the river. She liked to sit near running water. She selected a spot on a little point that still lay pure and ungrazed. A single plum tree stood exactly in the middle of it. She turned on her toes twice before setting down her basket and settling herself in the grass. The grass was very thick and it smelled like the hair of a collie puppy.

Below her a fat maple hung sloping, almost toppling, over the water, its topmost branches touching the sandy shore on the other side of the river. The bottom branches had been neatly sheared off by the ice of a flooding spring breakup. A little forest of spindling willows grew on a far slope of sand. A sandpiper ran along the near sandy shore. Occasional quick little winds ruffled the water, until sharp wavelets raced upriver against the stream. A single pickerel rimpled the silver surface, jumping to full gleaming length, identical with errant thought. It was all one, the river, the grass, the plum tree, Karen Alfredson, the northwest breeze, the June sun.

She picked a puccoon, sucked at its drop of honey, then ate its orange petals one by one, savoring them as if they were crumbs of sweetbread.

"I shall be happy. I shall not. I shall have joy. I shall not."

She leaned to kiss a tall buttercup. She licked up some of its vivid yellow-red dust. The dust tasted musty-saltish.

She picked some wild daisies and some tall dandelions. Thoughtfully, artfully, she braided the white and yellow flowers into a crown, the petals on the outside and the turned-in ends on the inside. She took off her sunbonnet and tried on the crown for size. It was too big. So she undid her hair, got out her ivory comb and combed it, then separated it into gleaming red-brown strands, redid it all in a heavier braid, and formed it into a thick coil about her head. This time the crown fit. The circlet of white and yellow flowers appeared to be growing out of her red-brown hair.

A wind rose and occasional wisps of clouds began to drift across the sky. Soon shadows stroked dark blue through the wide valley and up over the far green hills. Once a shadow raced across where she sat. Instantly a chill rose out of the earth. In a few seconds the shadow was gone, and equally sudden, wonderfully warm, the sun shone on the backs of her hands again.

Swallows dippled by. "Weeb weeb."

Meadowlarks sang the June greens. "It's lovely blue, all, where I am! Yessiree."

Robins slept fatly.

Pink below the bank caught Karen's eye. "Wild roses. Down there?"

Taking her embroidery scissors, she carefully slid down the dirt bank, set herself at the water's black gummy edge, and reaching as far as she could at the same time that she sank in the mud a little, managed to snip off several stems of the wild roses. She took a long and deep smell of the petals, then climbed back to her seat on the little point.

She held the wild roses across her wrists, the petals in her open palms. The petals already had the touch of age upon them, sun-blanched along the delicate edges. She smelled them again.

"Why must there be Doctor Toms?"

The petals seemed to crimple a little more before her very eyes.

"It's the brother Abbotts that are the fine ones."

She felt hungry. Thoughtfully, between sips of lemonade, she nibbled at her sandwich. Swallowing was always a little noisy.

She opened her basket further and took up a half-done edging for a piano runner. Silk thread instead of the usual cotton was tricky to work with. She set up a net around the outspread fingers of her left hand, then with the pursed fingers of her right hand wove the shuttle in and out, deftly, expertly, swiftly. The ivory shuttle resembled a little flying fish. Her lips pinched up into a smiling frown.

She tatted a strip some seven inches long.

Swallows swept up the midges about her head.

She tired. She laid aside her embroidery work. She removed her crown of wild flowers and stretched out on the grass. Sunlight lay upon her belly like warm fatherly hands. She nuzzled her red-brown head down into the thick grass. She let her head turn naturally to one side. Grass tickled the lobe of her ear. Distant soft sounds stirred in the grass. Once she thought she heard a whimpering deep under the sod.

She napped. She dreamed of wild roses: blooming, withering, reblooming. The perfume of them fairly suffocated her. Songs pulsed in her nose.

Shadows touched her in swift succession and she awoke to clouding skies. Yet she felt warm in her limbs, over her slender belly. Life was good in the grass.

She lay musing at the skies. Shifting blue openings appeared in the centers of the soft cumulus clouds. Delicate skies seen through shrouds of vapor overpassing and underpassing each other evoked delicious tastes inside her eyelashes.

Through one of the larger blue openings she saw that the sun was halfway down.

"Time to go home. It's my night to help Nanna with the supper."

She gathered up her things, and her crown of flowers, and packed them neatly in the picnic basket. She tied on her sun-bonnet. Then, with a last look around, sighing, she said, "Good-bye, river."

She was about to climb the little hill above the river, when she felt warmth descend the inside of her left thigh.

"That's strange. Can't be wetting without my knowing at my age."

She stopped and set down her basket. Gathering up her dress and petticoat at the sides with both hands, she looked.

By ginger. It had come. The wild roses.

"Won't Nanna be glad about that. At last."

She studied her feelings. It wasn't bad, after all, to have them. No pain. No uproar like everybody seemed to think she was supposed to have. Just a plain ordinary all-right feeling.

"I always did say that I'd become whatever it was I was supposed to become in my own good time."

She let her dress fall into place and proceeded home.

Mrs. Hamilton helped her handle it. Mrs. Hamilton was like an older sister to her.

4

That summer she got word of a teaching job. It was in the country five miles north of Bonnie and the school was known as Rock Township No. 3. The idea of becoming a teacher and of paying her own way in life excited her. At last she truly was going to be like everybody else.

Sylvester drove her out to see the chairman of the township school board, a farmer named Alan Weatherly.

Mr. Weatherly turned out to be tall and blond. He had a slow outdoors smile and every now and then had a way of catching his big potato chin in a fond freckled hand. He wore freshly laundered overalls and shirt and an old straw hat. He invited her inside.

They sat down across from each other at a white kitchen table. He took off his straw hat and placed it between them, beside a blue sugar bowl.

"So you want to teach?"

"Yes. If you will accept me."

"You've had some normal-school training?"

"No. I'm just a high school graduate."

"You'll have to be approved special by the county superintendent then. By Ben Grinder in Rock Falls."

"Must I see him too?"

"You'll have to." Mr. Weatherly played with the rim of his straw hat. "Grinder will interview you and then, if he thinks you've got the goods to become a teacher, give you a written examination. If you pass, our local board votes on your application."

"Do you think there's a chance for me?"

Mr. Weatherly smiled a stiff weathered smile. "Teachers are pretty scarce these days." His mild blue eyes were quietly watchful. "You have a horse so you can drive out?"

Karen sucked her lower lip between her white teeth for a moment. "Mr. Weatherly, I fear that animals and I do not get along."

"Then you'll have to board out with a neighbor." He folded his heavy hands together. "We'll find you a place somewhere. It'll work out." He paused. A reflective, almost chilly, look crept into the corners of his blue eyes. "We don't pay much, you know."

"That's all right. Just so I get a start."

"The going rate in the county for new teachers is thirty-five a month. And you furnish your own room and board."

Karen thought the salary handsome. "Shall I let you know if Mister Grinder approves of me?"

"He'll let us know. And then we'll let you know."

"Fine." Karen's eyes crossed inward a little. "Oh, I surely hope I pass."

"You will." Mr. Weatherly stroked his big potato chin. He began to smile his slow outdoors smile again. "There'll be eight classes, you know. Plus the primary grade. Two or three pupils to a class. Some twenty two in all by the last count."

"I'll manage."

"So you think you can keep order with a bunch of wild country kids?" His eyes went over her slender frame in a kindly manner.

"I'll manage."

Mr. Weatherly cast a slightly vexed look over his shoulder at the kitchen range. "I'm sorry my wife ain't home today or I'd offer you some tea. She's gone quilting."

"That's perfectly all right, Mister Weatherly." Karen stood up. "Well, I should be on my way. Sylvester's in the town band and he has to hurry back and practice."

Mr. Weatherly saw her to the gate. "We'll have you over for supper sometime."

Karen took the Bonnie Omaha to Rock Falls; met with Mr. Benjamin Grinder; took the teacher's examination; passed it.

Mr. Grinder appeared to like her, and afterward, as a favor, suggested that she take normal-school training during her summer vacations, preferably at Morningside College in Sioux City. The time would come, he said, when teaching requirements would be stiffer.

A week later Karen received a penciled letter from Mr. Weatherly stating that she'd been hired. He suggested that she room and board at the Frank Murray home. The Murrays had no children and would welcome a boarder.

Sylvester hitched up old Colonel again, tied Karen's trunk to the back of the buggy, and brought her out the Saturday before school began.

They first had a look at the Rock No. 3 school itself. It stood white and alone in an acre of land in the southeast corner of the section. There were a dozen tall angular ash trees along the road out front. It had a lean-to for a woodshed, built onto the back of the schoolhouse.

For water Mr. Weatherly said they'd have to use a well in an abandoned farmstead kittycorner across the road. The abandoned place with its weather-grayed collapsing buildings and its half-dead grove and its jungle of ragweeds gave Karen the shivers. The place meant trouble.

Nor did Karen like the outhouse situation on the school grounds. Two privies had been built together as one unit out in back with only a thin partition between them. No doubt the school board had meant well in trying to save on lumber. But. Karen right then and there made up her mind that she'd never let a boy and a girl go out to the toilet at the same time. There'd be no moral declension in any school she ran.

The desks inside the schoolhouse were in good condition, from the smallest to the largest. There were several good maps, a globe, plenty of blackboard space up front, a new United States flag, a good teacher's desk with an armchair, an organ, a black wood-burning stove in the northwest corner, and a pail with a dipper out in the hall. There was even a new dictionary on a stand, and a bookshelf with a hymnal, a Bible, a book on Indian wars, a new almanac, and a set of junior classics.

Karen was happy to see that the school board had held a clean-up bee, the men giving the outside of the building a fresh coat of white paint and cutting down the weeds, the women painting the inside walls a light green and giving the floor a scrubbing with soap and hot water, and then an oiling.

"The children here at Rock Number Three could be a good bunch," Karen commented.

Sylvester's brows came up. "What makes you think that?"

"Neat parents can't help but have good kids."

"I wouldn't bet on it. There's always one bad onion in the bunch."

"My very own school to teach."

"Good luck."

"You know I don't believe in luck. Or chance."

"Happy times then."

Sylvester next brought her out to the Murrays'. He and Karen carried her trunk inside; then he left for home.

Karen's room was upstairs in the northwest corner. In addition to her trunk, the room was furnished with a white iron double bed, a blue-trimmed chamberpot, a white pitcher in a white bowl standing on a blue dresser, a rag rug, and a side chair.

Mrs. Murray proved to have furtive brown eyes. She said she wasn't well, that she often had to take to bed because of a bad case of the female complaint. Would Karen be interested in earning her room and board instead of paying for it?

Karen wondered a little what Mrs. Murray meant by the female complaint. Karen hoped it wasn't what she'd had. Poor woman.

"Then you'll help me with the housework to earn your room and board?"

"Yes, Mrs. Murray."

"It means getting up at four."

"Four o'clock?"

"Mister Murray doesn't want to waste a minute. He's out to get rich quick."

Karen bit back a comment. "I'll do it."

Mrs. Murray had hands that were always busy with something. If she wasn't brushing back her hair, or stroking her dress down over her thin thighs, she was busy washing her hands. The ends of her fingers, even her fingernails, were white from all the cleansing.

Mr. Murray, when he came in from the field, had little to say. He too had something that was continually in motion. His mouth. Eating, chewing tobacco, spitting, cursing. Brown stain always seemed to be dripping from the ends of his moustache.

The next day, Sunday, turned out to be a very lonesome one for Karen. Mr. Murray worked all day, plowing, while Mrs. Murray lay in bed, reading the Bible, praying, weeping, fasting. The Murrays were strange creatures.

"But God must have had a reason for creating them," Karen thought to herself. "He always has a purpose."

It was with relief that Karen sallied forth on Monday morning to teach her first day of school. She had to walk a mile and a half along a country road. She loved all the wild flowers she met. She'd already been up four hours, yet felt fresh and was full of eagerness for the day ahead.

The children arrived a good half hour early. Walking along the country roads, they came from all four directions. Most of them, after putting their dinner pails out in the front hall, went outside to play a game of tag, pump-pump-pullaway. Several of the older boys went off by themselves behind the woodshed.

Karen spent the half hour making sure she had all the class books ready to hand out, that there was fresh water in the water bucket, that the American flag was properly draped up front, that there was a window open on each side for cross ventilation. Then, at exactly nine o'clock, she picked up the school bell and went out on the front stoop and rang it.

On the first clang the pump-pump-pullawayers left off playing, and obediently, with big round wondering eyes for their new teacher, filed into the schoolhouse. All the boys wore blue overalls and frosty chambray shirts. The girls wore gingham dresses of varied colors and designs.

The boys who'd gone behind the woodshed came in last. They were big fellows, two of them at least sixteen, and already built like men. The tallest of them stopped for a sip of water; poured what he didn't drink back into the bucket.

Karen stopped him. "What's your name, young man?"

The fellow looked at her, up and down, slowly, calculatingly—at her red-brown hair coiled on top of her head, at her tight waist with its neat white apron, at her high black shoes just barely showing below her long blue skirt. He had close-set brows, hair cut as if with a hedge shears, and a wet nether lip. He had the swayback slouch of the tired lover.

"Your name, young man." Even Karen was surprised at the amount of gravel she suddenly had in her voice. She might be timid around animals, but of young brute men she apparently wasn't in the least afraid.

The fellow's brown eyes retreated under his brows. He too was somewhat surprised. "Adolph Horsberg."

"Adolph, is it? All right, Adolph, I want you to listen carefully to me." Karen turned her head slightly so that those already inside the schoolhouse could hear her too. "In this school we do not pour water back into the bucket after we've had our drink out of the dipper. It's not sanitary. And it's not decent. You're to throw what's left in the dipper outdoors. Do you understand?"

Adolph tried very hard to hold up to her.

The fire in Karen's green eyes increased. "Well, young man?"

Adolph's glance finally slid off. "Okay."

"That's better. Now, go in and take a seat." Karen waited for him to precede her, then closed the door after them.

Adolph dragged his feet over to a desk in back.

Karen, watching everything with heightened air, caught a look passing between Adolph and a slim easy-eyed blond girl in the back row as he sat down.

Karen stepped firmly to the front of the room. "We'll start with the seating first. All those in the primary grade raise their hand."

Two small hands came up directly in front of her.

"Good. You'll sit in the two smallest desks over there. And now who's in the first grade?"

One hand came up.

"You take the next biggest desk."

Karen went through all the classes. She found she had twenty-two pupils all right, as Mr. Weatherly had said there would be.

Karen asked for their names and carefully entered them in a red book that was specially ruled for recording marks, times tardy and absent, deportment, and comment.

The last name Karen entered in her red book turned out to be that of the girl who had exchanged a look with Adolph. Tessie Windmiller. Tessie was fourteen and in the seventh grade. She had two sisters in school, much younger, Dorothy in the second grade and Lucy in the primary grade. Karen noted that Adolph and Tessie continued to have occasional sliding eyes for each other. Karen didn't like it. But for the moment she decided to let them alone. There would be plenty of time to take care of them later. She also spotted the interesting fact that Adolph's two younger brothers, Darl and Karl, were sweet on Dorothy and Lucy.

Karen began the school day with the singing of the national anthem. She played the organ while the pupils stood beside their desks facing the flag. Most of the voices were rusty, even ragged. But there was one voice that was not. It was a girl's. Karen glanced over her shoulder as she played along to see who it might be.

Tessie Windmiller. Tessie?

Karen played a few more bars and looked again. Yes, it was Tessie all right. And what a glorious soprano it was. Tessie sang with her head thrown back a little so that her silvery spider-thread hair hung freely to her shoulders. Tessie sang herself so completely into the song that she seemed oblivious of her surroundings, even of that Horsberg fellow. Tessie's voice reminded Karen of brother Abbott's silvery voice. Tessie was the girl soprano to what must surely be by now Abbott's male tenor. When they finished singing Tessie for once didn't bother to slide eyes at Adolph. Karen made a special note of it. Maybe with the singing she could help save Tessie from Adolph. Karen was fond of Tessie already.

Karen organized the classes: spelling, reading, writing, arithmetic, language, geography, history, music. She passed out the study books and assigned the lessons.

Karen had a steady smile for them all, for the slow as well as the swift, for the mutt as well as the sweetface. They were all God's children.

The boys tended to erase their slates with their shirt sleeves, smudging themselves white over the elbows. Karen smiled wryly at this, and gently wondered out loud why they didn't do as the girls did, use dampened rags to clean their slates. When a boy or a girl asked to leave the room, go to the toilet outside, Karen granted easy permission, one at a time. It was God's will that such things be taken care of at their proper times. "But mind that you don't linger now. We've got a nice surprise coming pretty soon and none of us wants to miss out on that now, do we?" Karen promised them that if they would be good all week long, at their best behavior, she would reward them the last hour Friday afternoon with a story, probably reading from that wonderful book *Black Beauty*.

Recess times went well too. In the morning recess period, at ten-thirty, Karen took the whole school on a fifteen-minute tour of their little schoolground acre. She pointed out the various wild September flowers—black-eyed Susan, sunflower, rosin aster, wild clover. She told them that if one had to, one could live off the prairie for several days just eating ground cherries and rose hips and wild onions and wild plums. She discovered for them the varied insect world—the dragonfly, the katydid, the stinkbug, the bumblebee.

Everybody had their lunch during the first part of the noon hour recess, Karen included. The children scattered out under the trees to eat in groups of threes and fours. Each one had his or her little lunch bucket, what had once been a syrup pail or a tobacco pail and still smelling a little of its former contents. Adolph and Tessie sat in the northwest corner, as far away from everybody as they could get. Lunch finished, the children played different games: drop the handkerchief, king's X, wink, London bridge.

During the afternoon recess period, at two-thirty, one of the boys found an old weathered baseball lost in the grass. Adolph promptly made a bat out of a fallen ash bough and soon they were playing work-up baseball. This separated the girls from the boys. Except for Tessie. Adolph made a special ruling in the case of Tessie. She proved to be as fleet-footed as any of the boys and could catch a ball like a man. She almost hit as well as most of the boys. But of them all Adolph was the best player. For all his tired lover's slouch he could run with the supple ease of a swift hunting dog.

At three-twenty-five Karen ordered all study books closed. "All right, children. Neaten up your desks now. Clean your slates and put them away. Be sure to pick up any loose crayons underfoot. And set your books neatly inside your desk. That's it, Peter. You show the rest how it's done."

At precisely three-thirty all were ready. "Good. Attention now, please. All faces this way. Sit erect. You too, Adolph. Now, now, you don't need sympathy from your neighbor. All right." Karen clapped her hands twice, sharply. "Turn in your seats. That's it. Rise from your seats. That's it. Pass outdoors, the little ones first. In order now. School is dismissed."

After the last child's happy voice had faded away down the country road, and all had become silent again in the little white schoolhouse, Karen settled into her armchair with a wonderful tired sigh. Her first day of teaching had been a good one. She'd been able to keep good discipline. She'd been right to think that neat parents couldn't help but have good kids. And she was also pleased to discover that she had one exceptional child in school. Tessie Windmiller. Though it was too bad Tessie was sweet on that brute Horsberg boy.

Karen looked around to see how she might improve her schoolhouse. She probably should put up some white curtains. And paste some clever cutouts on the bottom panes of the windows. And she should also bring along a vase sometime in which to put wild flowers.

She sighed another tired sigh, had another long look around, then, gathering herself up, set to work chalking the alphabet on the blackboard in a clear legible hand for the next day, sweeping up the place, and closing all the windows.

It was four-thirty when she set out for home a mile and a half away. She had yet to make dinner for the Murrays as part of her room and board.

The next morning when she arrived at the schoolhouse she found a drowned mouse in the water bucket. It was floating on its belly, head and feet hanging down.

"That'll teach me never to leave water in the bucket overnight. Ugh."

She poured the mess out in the ditch along the road. She scrubbed out the bucket with a bar of soap and then got fresh water from the well in the deserted farmstead across the road.

"I'll set some traps, just you watch."

That day everything went along smoothly until shortly after lunch, during noon recess. Then a short burst of shrill girl cries coming through the open window caught Karen's ears. She went to the window to look. The children were all gathered around Adolph Horsberg in the northwest corner of the school lot, almost exactly where Tessie and Adolph had their lunch. Adolph was holding the water bucket in one hand and something else in the other hand. Karen's eyes opened very green. She'd already been wondering a little why Adolph had volunteered to get a bucket of fresh water for her that noon.

Karen sailed outside and across the schoolyard. The sun was brilliant and it caught the silverheads in the group with especial sharpness. All eyes turned as she approached.

Then Karen saw. She shuddered. In the other hand Adolph was holding a live striped gopher by the tail.

The gopher was sopping dark-brown wet. Water dripped from its open mouth. It was gasping for breath. Every few seconds it curled up on itself as if to climb its own tail to get at Adolph's fingers. Each time Adolph gave it a little snap and made it give up. Adolph was smiling a hero's smile.

"Adolph Horsberg! Whatever are you doing?"

Adoph, startled to be accosted so peremptorily, turned sober. "Why, nothing, Teach. Except catching me a gopher." He pointed at a small hole in the ground with his toe. "I drowned him out." Grass had been carefully parted back from the hole and its edges were sloshing wet.

Karen was revolted. "Drop that poor creature. This instant!"

Adolph gaped at her. "But why, Teach?"

"Because I say so. Let him go."

"But, Teach—"

"Drop it." Karen stamped her foot in the grass. "Drop it, I say."

Adolph, dumbfounded, dropped the gopher.

The miserable soaked gopher lit on its nose, tumbled tail over, lay prone. It gasped and gasped for breath.

Everybody stared at it.

Gradually the gopher's popped bead eyes cleared. And gradually too it began to understand that it was free. It took a couple more moments for the idea to take hold, then, suddenly, scrambling, the wet gopher slithered through the assembled legs of the schoolchildren, and in a whip, its tail flinging off a last clear drop of water in a little arch, was gone, down yet another hole.

"There, that's better," Karen said.

Adolph still stood dumbfounded.

Tessie moved close to Adolph. She too was struck dumb by Karen's order.

"Isn't that better now," Karen said.

Adolph gave his blond Tessie a look and a shake of the head. "Well, Tess, old girl, there went a sure ten cents."

"Ten cents?" Karen said.

Adolph gave Karen a withering look. "Yeh. The county pays a ten-cent bounty for every pair of gopher front feet you turn in."

"They do?"

"Yeh."

"But why?"

"Because gophers eat seed corn, that's why. Seed corn that my paw plants so hard to get into the ground." Adolph continued to give Karen a scornful look. "Why, Paw says he's seen it already where a gopher come after him down the row digging out the kernels as fast as he could stick 'em in."

"That I believe."

Tessie spoke up. "It's true though, Teacher. That's what my dad says too." Tessie looked at the hole down which the gopher had disappeared. "It's not an easy thing to catch a gopher. But Adolph, he done it." Tessie touched Adolph's forearm in pride, her eyes gleaming a high blue.

Adolph kicked at the grass, so hard that a piece of turf flew up and hit his younger brother Karl in the belly. "Somebody's gonna have to pay for this and pay right smart, if it turns out we're ten cents short come our wedding day. Not, Tess?"

Karen was astounded. "Wedding day?"

Adolph threw Karen a bold look. "Sure, Tess and me are planning on getting married as soon as she's through the eighth grade."

Why! the young snips, thinking of getting married already. What kind of parents. . . .

Karen recalled the hour of the day. "All right. You, Peter Stickney, you go run and ring the bell. Landsakes, we've wasted half the day over a poor miserable gopher."

A week later, again during the noon recess, Karen noticed that something was amiss in the schoolyard. The children had gone to sit in the far southwest corner of the grounds and were talking together as if they knew an awful secret of some kind. Occasionally they would look at the woodshed at the back of the school building.

"I wonder what now."

Karen counted the children. Counted twice. There were exactly twenty. Two were missing. Who could they be?

She saw that the older boys, buddies of Adolph, were giving each other knowing jaws at the same time that they threw occasional catcalls in the direction of the woodshed.

The woodshed?

It came to her. Adolph and Tessie. They were missing.

Karen hated to think what that might mean.

That Adolph. That rascal. Did he think that she was running the school for his personal benefit alone?

Well, he was going to find out about that in short order. This was her first charge and she was responsible for the morals of the whole school and she was not going to let a brute of a farm boy spoil her record. She liked teaching and she was going to be a success at it. She took in a great breath, picked up the poker behind the wood stove, and set out.

Karen slipped around the north side of the school, out of sight of the twenty children on the southwest corner, so they couldn't warn the culprits. She stepped lightly around the west side of the woodshed and approached the door on the south side.

She smelled old cobs. There was also the faint aroma of heated rosin.

The children in the southwest corner at last spotted her. But she'd appeared so suddenly that they didn't have time to cry out a warning. The knowing jaws of Adolph's buddies fell.

The woodshed door was only partly closed. Sunlight a foot broad struck through the opening, lighting up the interior as though it was a powerful four-cell flashlight. Neat stacks of wood lined the east and west sides. Red cobs lay in a sloping pile below the scoop hole on the north side. On this pile, partly indented into it, lay two intertwined undulating figures. The red cobs under them were squeaking rhythmically.

Karen's green eyes blinked. Slowly they cleared of themselves, as if on their own they were making sure that they saw what they saw.

Tessie's dress was up over her hips. Her pink pants lay thrown to one side. Her eyes were half-closed in bliss, as if at last she'd found heaven itself. And Adolph, slightly humped up, was galloping between her legs.

Karen couldn't understand why Tessie was clutching Adolph so hard to her bosom, instead of fighting him off.

So this is what people did. Too bad the stork story wasn't true.

Karen's stomach hiccuped.

Animals.

Karen pushed the door all the way open. Light exploded around the two schoolyard lovers. Cobs turned a bright red. Gripping her iron poker, Karen gave Adolph an awful jab in the sitter.

"You stinkers!" Karen cried. "The both of you."

The two young lovers quivered. Adolph began to jerk as if he'd suddenly got the fits.

Adolph's involuntary jerking infuriated Karen. Dropping her poker, Karen grabbed Adolph by the ankles and gave him a tremendous pull backward.

Adolph came free of Tessie with a wounded cry. And Tessie let go a screech as though she'd been chopped in half.

"By ginger! There's going to be no baby-making at any school that I'm in charge of."

Adolph's feet curled up. He stirred like a crab that'd just lost its tail. Tessie reached wildly for her pants and failed to find them.

"You stinkers. Get up!"

Adolph made motions under himself as he tried to button up. With her pointed toe Karen gave Adolph an awful kick.

Adolph screamed in mortal agony.

Karen next grabbed Tessie by the arms and jerked her to her feet. "You come with me, you hussy!"

Tessie's dress fell into place but her sense of balance didn't. Tessie slumped against Karen, arms slack, knees buckling in opposite directions.

"Aren't you ashamed of yourself, you cheap thing?" With her free hand, Karen picked up Tessie's pink pants and thrust them into Tessie's pocket. "Doing something that even married people are ashamed of."

Only the whites of Tessie's eyes showed through partly closed lids.

Karen held Tessie close. Thoughts raced through Karen a mile a minute. She should send them home in punishment, if only for them to be made an example of, for the sake of the other children, especially Dorothy and Lucy, Tessie's younger sisters, and Darl and Karl, Adolph's younger brothers. If things weren't handled just right, the younger children would soon be doing the same awful thing.

Yet Karen knew she couldn't. First, because sending the two culprits home in the middle of the day might get the parents into an uproar, and eventually mad at her. Second, the two culprits lived along the same road and would walk home together.

What an awful rotten stinking way for the two families, the Horsbergs and the Windmillers, to be neighborly with each other. "And I'll just bet a cookie the parents know about it too, have guessed already, when their dear little darlings play together. Disgusting."

Still holding Tessie close, Karen gave Adolph another kick. "Get up, you awful pig."

"Oww!" Adolph yelled, throwing back his head.

Karen kicked him an awful one again. "You stinker, you get up and go right straight to your seat. You hear?"

"Oww!"

"Get!"

"Owww!"

"Get! Get!"

All of a sudden Adolph bounded to his feet and shot out of the cob shed.

Hanging onto Tessie, Karen followed after as fast as she could. She and Tessie came around the front of the school just in time to see Adolph leap over a fence and disappear into a deep corn-field.

Karen glared after him. "Just as I thought. He was thinking to himself all along."

Tessie tried to break free of Karen. She'd seen where Adolph had vanished.

"Oh, no you don't." Karen threw both her arms around Tessie. And forcibly, almost carrying her, Karen made her march into the schoolhouse and straight to her seat. "Now you just sit there, young lady, until I figure out what to do with you."

At two-thirty, just before last recess, Karen decided what she had to do. She would consult with the teacher at Rock No. 4, two miles to the north. She'd never met the Rock No. 4 teacher but since she was in the same profession she was bound to have some ideas on the problem.

Karen dismissed school early. The moment the children were out of sight, she put on her blue sunbonnet and took the dirt road north. The Frank Murrays might have to eat a late supper that night but it couldn't be helped.

The first place on the left was the Windmillers'. It was just as Karen had suspected. The Windmillers kept a slovenly yard: machinery left any old place, several wind-flattened cob piles rotting along the edges, paper caught in fences, weeds head high between the buildings.

There was no sign of any of the Windmiller children around, neither Tessie nor her little sisters Dorothy and Lucy.

Karen hurried on. A single row of young ash trees grew along the road on the left. In several places the fence was nailed to the young trees. The shadows of the young trees touched the edge of the dirt road.

Soon the road sloped down toward a culvert. Beyond the culvert, and also on the west side of the road, lived the Horsbergs. The Windmillers and the Horsbergs shared a line fence. It helped explain a little why the children of the two families were so intimate.

Karen also gave the Horsberg yard and its green house close scrutiny to see if Adolph and his brothers Darl and Karl had arrived home safely. All she saw moving were gray chickens scratching dirt near the corncrib and horses reaching for straw across a barbwire fence behind the cattleshed. The windmill south of the barn, near the draw, clanked regularly and at its foot water was spilling out of a stock tank.

At the mile corner gleamed four galvanized tin mailboxes, each up on a separate pole. One of the mailboxes had the name Horsberg splashed loosely in black on it. The other three mailboxes had the names Windmiller, Johnson, and Stoefen. A fringe of wild roses grew under them, where the county road maintenance men couldn't get at them with their mowers. The roses were spangled with orange hips.

A half mile farther north, on the east side of the road, lay a neat modest farmstead: red barn with windows trimmed in white, light-blue house with windows also trimmed in white, house yard clipped close by grazing sheep, barnyard cut with scythe. The pigs were fat, the cows had heavy bags, the horses were sleek.

Karen thought: "Now here would be a good place to room and board. Too bad they live in the wrong school district."

A herd of dark-red cattle, all without horns, grazed in the pasture on the west side of the road. They were fanned out in an irregular line. All cropped steadily. Several of the cows every now and then butted each other in frisky play. One of the older cows mounted a runt in the group exactly as if she were a bull, even to trying to give the runt the double thrust.

Karen looked the other way. "Ugh."

Then Karen looked again. Something had struck her as odd about the horny performance. "Why, that wasn't even a gentleman cow."

Karen walked on several steps. "Dear Lord. Just a plain old cow pretending."

The road sloped down. Below and across a creek, on the corner on the left, stood the Rock No. 4 schoolhouse. It was like her own, except that it faced north, not east, with its woodshed and outhouses on the south side. Even as Karen crossed the culvert, children began streaming out of its north door and then up the road. Three of the children came her way.

"Good," Karen thought, "just as I'd hoped. In time for me to catch the teacher alone." Karen gave the three children a good smile as they passed by her.

As she approached the front door, Karen was pleased to see how spick and span everything was kept. Even the shoe cleaner near the cement stoop was swept off. The teacher here was neat.

Karen stepped inside the vestibule. She knocked gently, standing to one side of the open door, out of politeness not looking inside before being invited in.

Silence.

She knocked again.

Then came footsteps. The footsteps were quick, strong.

The vigorous footsteps worried Karen. "Just so she isn't one of those big women teachers with a moustache."

"Yes?"

The voice was boyish. It was that of a young man, not a woman.

Karen stared. A young man teacher? No one had told her about this. And a neat young man teacher?

Karen tried a tentative smile. "I'm Karen Alfredson. Teacher at Rock Number Three. You know, two miles south of here?"

"Oh." The young man smiled. "Yes. I've heard of you. I'm Konstant Harmer."

They shook hands. His hand though slender was firm. Karen spotted immediately that the hair on the backs of his fingers was fine, blond, just like little brother Abbott's.

Konstant Harmer's eyes were exactly level with hers, of a light-blue cast, as if just barely tinctured with bluing, with the pupils a gleaming gray. His hair was the most perfect silver blond she'd ever seen, and he wore it combed mostly pompadour with a slight part on the right side. His face was light-complected, so clean it was apparent he didn't need to shave very often. He had the deft gestures of one who hadn't done much farm work. Most surprising, he wore a light-gray suit with a blue shirt, a yellow tie, two-tone shoes. Most men wore dark blues and blacks. There was a gladsome air about him. Though at the same time there was no hint that he might be either frivolous or flirtatious. He was one of those fine boys sometimes seen in the country.

Karen liked him. He was like her little brother Abbott all right. Probably about the same age too, a couple of years younger than she was. Here was someone she could trust.

As she stood there looking at Konstant Harmer, a scene from her childhood flashed through her mind.

. . . It happened when she was ten. She was standing by the sink in the kitchen and combing little Abbott's hair. She combed and combed, until Abbott's fine silver hair came up in crackling fluffs. She reached the comb into the basin to wet it. It was the only way to get rid of the electricity. She was aware of Pa sitting by the stove, smoking his corncob pipe, his eyes now and then on them. Pa's eyes were a light blue and his hair a red-brown and he sat stubby and strong.

Presently Abbott stirred under her combing.

"Stand still, Abbott."

Abbott continued to squirm, finally said, "But I gotta go do number one."

"Oh," she said.

Modestly Abbott ran outdoors.

In a couple of minutes he was back.

She smiled at him. "So you want your hair combed some more, do you?"

Abbott gave her a shy smile, and waited.

She began combing as before. Soon the electricity built up again so that his hair almost stood on end. Again she wetted the comb to settle his hair.

And once more Abbott began to squirm and once more he had to run and do number one.

At that point Pa cleared his throat at the stove. "You don't have to comb his hair all day, do you? Find something else to do."

Go help your poor mother with something. You know she hasn't been feeling well lately. Go. March. . . ."

"Won't you come in?"

Karen blinked. Konstant Harmer was talking to her. "Yes?"

"Won't you come in?"

"It'll be all right?"

"Certainly." Konstant smiled. "We have no secrets here." His smile widened, revealing healthy white teeth. "We'll leave the door open in case anybody comes."

"Good." Karen removed her sunbonnet. She brushed several loose strands of her hair back into place.

The schoolhouse was also pin-neat inside. The writing on the blackboard was the best penmanship she'd ever seen. Good crayon drawings done by pupils hung in a neat row across the west wall. Pictures of recent Presidents lined the east wall. All the windows had white-and-blue curtains. Every desk was in place, with all the books and papers carefully stacked away under the lid. The smell of fresh oil rose from the floor.

"Here, have my desk chair."

"Thanks. Whew, I'm tired."

"Did you walk over?"

"Yes. And I'll have to walk back too. Besides having to make supper for the dratted Murrays. Though she's been all right to me otherwise."

"I know them."

"Well, then you know."

"Yes."

Karen looked at the rows of desks. "Well. And how many pupils do you have?"

"Eighteen."

"I've got twenty-two." She heaved a deep sigh. "Though I surely wish it was only twenty."

"How so?"

"That's why I came here." She looked down at where her slender hands lay in her lap. Now that she had got this far she didn't know what to say. What an awful thing to have to talk about, what that Tessie and Adolph had done. She wished with all her heart that Tessie and Adolph could be enrolled in his school. A man would know better what to do. She felt a blush moving up out of the collar of her green blouse.

Konstant waited. He stood across the desk from her, neat, eyes alert and courteous, slim hands hanging free. The late sun coming through the west windows glinted in the silver hairs over the backs of his fingers.

"I've got a real poser in my school. It's about a boy and a girl."

Konstant's head came up ever so little, as though he wasn't sure he wanted to hear about a boy and a girl.

Karen liked that. Yes, here was one she could trust. She could tell him anything, even disgusting things, and he wouldn't take advantage of her. "Do you know that Horsberg family living a mile south of here?"

"Yes. They go to our church."

"What do you know about them?" Karen looked him in the eye.

"The folks seem to be nice enough."

"Are they religious?"

"They go to church regular."

"Do they take their kids with them?"

Konstant hesitated. "Well, not always."

"There. You see." Karen shook her head sadly. "I knew there had to be something."

Konstant waited.

Karen shook her head some more. "It's such an awful thing to talk about. Yet I can't permit it to happen in my school again. And I didn't want to run to the parents right away either. Or go to the school board. So I thought I'd come over and visit with you to see what you thought. Though I never expected to meet a man teacher."

Konstant smiled. "There's a good reason why I'm teaching here." His smile widened. "I live in this district and everybody on the school board thought what a nice thing it would be if one of their own people could teach their children. Even if I was a man and really should be out in the fields working."

"So your folks live here?"

"Yes. A mile and a half from here. That way. Northwest."

"Then you walk it like I do."

"Every day."

"Mr. Weatherly told me that they really prefer an older teacher with more education."

"If they can get one."

"Yes. If they can get one."

Konstant's fingers still hung free. "I don't intend to make a career of it here. My plan is to go to college summers until I get my degree. Then I'll teach in high school."

"Where will you go to college?"

"Morningside in Sioux City. I hope."

"Too bad you can't go four straight years and be done with it."

"I don't mind. I'm lucky even to have gone to high school. My father doesn't hold much with education. Unless it's for agriculture. My father told me that after I was through with high school I would have to make my own way. And my father's right too to be that hard. That's why I work for my room and board at home."

"But just summers—why, it'll take you a coon's age, dear man, to get through college that way. Why, you'll be too old to get married by the time you finish."

"I don't plan to get married. My older brothers are married and that's enough in the family."

Karen nodded, thoughtfully. "That's where I agree with you. Marriage, what I've seen of it, the way men are with women, that's not for me either." She played her fingers through each other. "I suspect if I'm to keep my job teaching I'd better take normal-school training summers at Morningside too." She brightened. "Maybe we'll see each other there."

Konstant's light-blue eyes turned watchful. "Maybe."

Karen recalled what she'd come for. "Oh, dear. I suppose I better get at it." Again a blush moved up out of the collar of her blouse. "No use in beating about the bush any longer. So." She took a deep breath. "I caught a boy doing it to one of my girls in the woodshed this noon. Adolph Horsberg with Tessie Windmiller."

"Oh."

Her blush deepened. "Yes, it was awful. And the little dickens of a Tessie, she didn't even fight back."

Silence.

"Of course the whole school knew what'd happened the minute I ferreted them out." Karen's face burned. "What I want to know is, what do I do now?"

Silence.

"What would you do?"

Konstant swallowed with an audible click. "I don't know."

"But suppose you were to find two of them doing it tomorrow here in your woodshed?"

Konstant stood straighter. "I won't."

"Why not?"

"Because I keep close watch on all my boys."

"Oh."

"I know my boys."

So that's the way he does it.

"I've got only one I've got to keep an eye on. And I do."

That means Tessie's got to be watched closer.

"I don't know about girls. They're mostly nice though."

"Not my little Tessie. That darn little fool. Why, she's gone and done this thing before she's lost all her milk teeth even."

"Isn't this Tessie one of the Windmiller children?"

"Yes."

"I know that family too." Konstant shook his head. "Poor stock. The missus had a poor reputation even before she got married. Though I have to say that I now hear she does most of the work on the farm. While he can be seen uptown almost any day drunk."

"Well! It sure helps to know that."

He sat down on the edge of the desk. "It won't do you much good to see the parents. Neither the Windmillers nor the Horsbergs."

"Would you tell the school board then?"

"Maybe you should give the children another chance. Keep a close watch on the girl after this. Make her your friend. Counsel her in God's ways. It's about the only thing you can do."

"I suppose so." Karen pressed a hand to her stomach. "Maybe I can keep them apart in school more." She paused in thought. "But oh, glory, what about out of school? On the way home? They live on the same road, you know. And their farms join. And I can just imagine them sneaking back and forth across the line fence."

"The best thing is for you to make yourself a close friend of Tessie's. Real close. Like I do with my boy Thomas Priester."

"Maybe you're right. Because the funny thing is, I like Tessie. She's one of my best students. And oh, has she got a glorious voice. Just glorious."

"That helps. I'd spend some extra time with her then, developing that talent. So she feels obligated to you."

"A good idea. I'll do just that." Gradually Karen began to feel better about the matter. "Then you wouldn't report it to the school board right away?"

"I wouldn't."

"Then I shan't either."

That night when Karen went to bed at twelve, exhausted, she thought again of the fine young man she'd met that day.

Some girl someday would have a good life with him. There weren't many like him around. In spirit he was an awful lot like little brother Abbott all right.

And the last thing she thought of as she fell asleep was the silver fuzz on the back of Konstant Harmer's long slender thumb.

PART TWO

⊛◇⊛◇⊛◇⊛◇⊛◇⊛◇⊛◇⊛◇⊛◇⊛◇⊛◇⊛◇⊛

Kon

1

On the way home that night, Konstant Harmer remembered that earlier in the day he'd promised himself to go take a look at a strange wildflower. The boy Tom Priester had talked about finding it growing in the middle of the section north of the schoolhouse. The thought that the flower might be a new find made Kon prickle inside. If it turned out to be true, wouldn't his old botany teacher be proud of him? Maybe his name, Konstant, would be associated with it for all time to come.

Halfway down the road west Kon slipped through a barbwire fence and then followed a line fence north. The Lorenson pasture lay on the west side of the line fence and a Priester field of corn grew on the east side.

Kon stopped every now and then to nibble on a wild rose hip, and to ruffle the rusty combs of the burdock, and to smell the droopy aromatic petals of the coneflowers. His father, Anse Harmer, considered anything not corn or grain a pure straight weed. Kon could understand his father's attitude, but he himself loved the wild free growing things. Kon smiled to himself as he recalled how suspicious his father was of even the tame flowers in the garden, that they might go wild and spread into the fields. It was hard work to keep the fields clean, even with the new riding cultivators.

The boy Tom Priester had said the strange flower was growing beside a big red granite boulder. The cows in the Lorenson pasture across the fence hadn't quite been able to get at them, he'd said.

Presently Kon spotted the big red boulder where it protruded from the rise ahead. It rode half-buried in the prairie loess like some lost red iceberg. The growth around the boulder was different, a band at least three feet wide, where neither plow nor cultivator had ever disturbed the virgin sod. The grass stood taller and the wild roses grew better. It was where the turf—old roots, decayed stems, matted humus—lay fatter.

Kon put a hand to the red boulder. It was cool to the touch. At hip height it was also wondrously smooth where passing buffalo by the millions had rubbed themselves. Kon stroked it lovingly. He saw that the boulder wasn't granite after all, but Sioux quartzite, similar to the rock in the great Blue Mounds outcropping north of Whitebone. Natives often called quartzite granite.

Kon spotted the strange flower growing at the north end of the red boulder. There were a dozen of them, all in a cluster, forming a tight mat like bunch grass. Each stem was topped off by a small bronze cylinder.

He approached the flowers almost shyly. His fingers trembled a little as he knelt beside them. He held a hand over them, not quite touching them.

They weren't in any botany or flower book that he knew of.

The stem was tannish, hairy. The leaves grew in clusters of three from each notch and they too were hairy, like velvet, their green texture barely showing through tan. Each flower had five silky pink petals about the size of mouse ears. The core of the flower stuck out like a tiny bronze cob.

He resisted the impulse to pick one of them. Instead he leaned to smell them. Their aroma was dusky, of some other ancient time, salad and spice of the buffalo. They would most certainly have disappeared under the plow had there been no boulder to protect them.

Already he loved them. What a fine contrast there was between the silver hairs over the back of his hand and the bronze velvet of the flower. Next spring he would separate a small corner from the clump with a spade and bring it home to the wildflower corner in their garden.

The sun struck the boulder from the side, lighting up its red tones, giving it a glassy pink texture. The dark side resembled a jellied wine.

His glance moved over the sloping, slowly rolling land. Two rises lay between him and Karen Alfredson's school, hiding it from him. He wondered again what she was going to do with that Horsberg-Windmiller mess. He was glad he didn't have it in his school. He wouldn't have known what to do with it, what with every parent around knowing him so well. It wasn't a very good idea for him to be teaching in his own neighborhood really. It was lucky for him that he'd sensed trouble in that Priester boy early in the game and had made it a point to make friends with him. Look at the results—a new flower instead of infant fornication.

Karen Alfredson. The shape of her face was like a gaunted oval. Yet her complexion was young and tender. Her eyes had the pure green of grass in May. No flirt there.

It surprised him to be thinking of Karen. He rarely gave the womenfolk much thought. The cats. He loved Mother all right, but then everyone loved Mother Reka. No, it was mostly of his brother Brant that he always had warm thoughts. He and Brant had been the best buddies in the world since when they were kids. They'd done things together they'd never forget. Especially that wild apple wonder day when there'd almost been a drowning. Karen could never come up to Brant.

The shadow on the east side of the sloping red rock widened. It was time to head for home and chores.

Kon climbed the fence and started across the Lorenson pasture. The Lorenson cattle hadn't been able to keep up with the grass and every now and then he had to walk through islands of

seeded bluegrass. Finally, not being able to resist it, he took off
his shoes and socks and stroked white-footed through the deep
grass. Bleached seed caught between his toes. He imagined himself walking across the fur of a giant puma. It gave a little where
it lay over hollows. A coneflower, catching between his big toe
and the little toes, tugged at his foot and almost tripped him.
He walked barefooted until he reached the fence along the road.

Better get the shoes back on. Pa don't like mudlarking much.

Kon settled on a white stone and slipped on his socks and
shoes. Then, climbing the fence, he got ready to face his father
and mother.

Ahead along the road loomed a familiar landmark, a huge
corpulent old cottonwood. No one knew how old it was. Pa said
it was already an old tree when he first saw it as a pioneer. It
stood alone in the run south of the Harmer farm. For years it
had been known as the Harmer Lone Tree.

White chickens met him near the Harmer line fence. There
were always a few such feathered adventurers. How could they
have known that the last fox in the township had been caught
the year before? Though they were always careful to stay within
sight of the farm buildings. Perhaps because the buildings were
painted white. In its blurred cockeyed vision, the chicken probably felt safe so long as it could see white.

Kon walked under the giant cottonwood. Its cool shadow
touched his neck. Kon always associated cool air with the cottonwood.

Kon was proud of the Harmer yard. It was one of the showplaces in Siouxland. Every two years Pa gave all the buildings
except the barn a fresh coat of white paint. The barn he always
painted a deep bull red. Given plenty of rain, the white buildings,
even the barn, always stood out glinting sharp against the green
grass and the green walnut trees in the windbreak. Only the white
chickens were given free run of the yard. Otherwise all the other
animals were kept in their proper pen or pasture. Pa couldn't
stand clutter on his yard and was always gathering up bits of
paper or recribbing collapsing cob piles or burning tumbling

weeds. Done with a cultivator or a plow or a rake, Pa promptly put it in the machine shed.

As he approached the yard, Kon spotted his father emerging from the white corncrib next to the road. Pa was carrying a bushel of corn on his shoulder, head crooked to one side and one arm up to hold the basket in place, and heading for the white hog barn. Pa threw the corn in a spraying motion over the fence, with the young pigs chasing after the throw of the corn like kids following the scattering of coins. And before Kon could gain the yard, Pa appeared yet again with a second basket of corn, this time to feed the horses in the red barn on the far side of the yard. Kon admired the erect slim vigor of his father. Anse Harmer at sixty was probably good for another twenty years on the farm.

Mother Reka appeared on the steps of the veranda, shaking out a dust mop. She too was thin, but in contrast to Anse was a tiny thing, like the difference between a red squirrel and a red fox. Even their natures were like those of the red squirrel and the red fox, the one fierce and voluble and everywhere at once and the other crafty and persistent and philosophic.

Mother waited for Kon on the steps. She held the dust mop across her body like a pikestaff. "You're late, Konstant." She always used his full first name.

Kon closed the house yard gate behind him. "I had a visitor after school."

" 'Twasn't them Priesters complaining again?"

Kon smiled. "No. Just the teacher from Rock Number Three."

"What'd he want?" There were times when Mother appeared to have more of an upper lip than a lower.

"Oh, she came over to compare notes. Talk shop."

"She?"

"Yes, Mother. You know I'm the only man teacher around."

"Hmpf. Probably one of them flighty scared things, I betcha."

"No, Mother, Karen Alfredson struck me as being quite sensible."

Mother gave her dust mop an involuntary shake, quick, hard. A tiny plume of pale dust wafted out of it. Mother's gray hair was caught up in a tight knot on the top of her head, giving it all the look of a gourd mounted on a pumpkin. There still were streaks of young brown hair running through the gray. Mother's eyes opened and narrowed by turns, a shimmering piercing light blue. "Pa's had to do most of the chores alone, you're home so late."

"He hasn't milked yet though, has he?"

"No."

"I'll catch up then."

"Well, the milking will help keep your hands soft at least."

Kon smiled quietly. "Like a good schoolteacher's hands are supposed to be."

Mother didn't smile. A breeze rose off the green lawn and lightly pushed against her, outlining her small bony frame inside her gray dress and gray apron. She was put together like a stick figure with all sorts of strange knots showing here and there. Her eyes caught movement near the barn. "Here comes your pa now."

"I'd better hurry then." Kon went inside and ran lightly up the stairs to his room.

Kon's room had a big window on both the east and the south sides. The room was airy and full of September evening light, making bright the multicolored coverlet on his bed and the oval rag rug lying between the bed and the white dresser. Even the old oak rolltop desk and chair as well as an old black trunk shone as if they'd just been revarnished.

Kon slipped into his yard clothes: faded blue shirt, overalls patched over the knees, brown socks. He hurried downstairs and picked up his straw hat from a peg behind the stair door and his shoes from behind the kitchen door. When he stepped outside he found Pa already seated in his rocker on the far end of the veranda.

"Sorry I'm late tonight, Pa. But I had an unexpected visitor."

"That'll happen."

Kon sat down on the top step. He pulled on his shoes and one by one laced them up.

Pa rocked to himself, light-gray eyes musing on his fields. Pa was a mouth breather and had a loose lower lip on which a drop of moisture was always forming.

"Did you have a good day, Pa?"

Pa's head swiveled around until he could look Kon straight in the eye. "What'd you find by the red rock?"

"You saw me?"

"I was up in the cupola. Closing a hole where the pigeons was getting in. From that wind we had last week."

"The Priester boy told me about a new flower there."

"A new weed, you mean." Pa wiped his lower lip with the back of his hand just as a drop of moisture began to form.

"I guess so."

"Well, you can make up for it by mowing the lawn after supper tonight."

"I promised Mother I'd mulch the strawberries for her."

"Do that too then."

A crow lit on the veranda railing. It was one that Pa had tamed the past year. It cocked its head at Pa, then, as if part of an act, prinked out a figure eight by circling first one post and then the other of the double-pillared support at the corner.

Pa smiled; and just in time caught another drop forming on his lower lip.

The crow next cocked a bright eye at Kon, said as clear as could be, "Weaklings are soon weeded out."

Kon didn't like the crow, and showed it.

"He doesn't mean you, son. As I told you before, I taught him that for the benefit of that grain shocker we had in July."

Kon said nothing. He hurried down to the rack by the gate where the milk cans and pails were set mouth up to catch the sun. He selected two pails and two ten-gallon cans, then pushed through the gate and headed for the barn.

"A little early for that, ain't it, son?" Pa called after him.

"A few minutes early won't hurt none."

"You know I want them cows milked every day right on the dot at six and six."

"I know. But I'd like to get started. Do something."

"Well, go ahead. We should probably begin drying up your cows anyway. I'll sit here a minute and catch my breath. Been going all day."

By the time Pa had settled behind his first cow, Kon had an inch of milk in his pail. The sound of milk striking into the foam at the bottom of the pail had just changed from a tinny noise to a troubled drumming.

Pa always began his milking routine the same old way, the squirts first coming slow and rhythmic, then gradually increasing in tempo, until at last, with deep bubbling sprays, he caught up and passed Kon.

Kon sat very erect beside his cow, careful to keep every part of himself except his hands from touching her. Cows sometimes had lice. Though this was something Pa always denied. His white-face Herefords have lice? They were too healthy for that. Pa kept a clean barn in the winter and the sun and rain kept the cows groomed in the summer. Pa claimed besides that cow lice couldn't stand the human smell and soon left one. But Kon'd once had a pupil who came to school loaded with them; even to having his hair speckled with nits.

Thank God the tits were clean and dry. Kon hated to find black rings along his fingers and over the back of his thumbs after milking. Dirty tits were awful. Kon always made it a point to wash them when they were caked with mud. Pa thought this a good idea. Milk was human drink and should be kept clean.

Sitting back from his cow, Kon spotted a mouse peering down at him from the top of the stanchion. The mouse's nose was up, sniffing, and its tail was down, twitching delicately. Kon couldn't help but smile to himself at the nervy thing. Where was their cat, Old Tom? He'd catch it quick enough if he was around.

Kon wiggled his ears.

Flip! and the mouse was gone.

Pa got up from his first cow, pail running over with a head of creamy foam. Pa emptied his milk into one of the ten-gallon cans and covered the can with a lid.

Kon envied the old man his chorsing skills.

As he settled under his second cow, Pa said, "Forgot to tell you, but the boys are coming over tonight."

"Brant and Charlie?"

"Charlie wants a family jawing."

"Wonder what about?"

"Dunno. He called while I was out plowing. Mother talked to him."

Kon's eyes fixed on the red hair of the cow immediately in front of him.

So Brant was coming over. Kon hoped Brant would take Mildred and the little nieces, Edna and Pauline, along. The little tykes were dead ringers for Brant. Too bad they weren't nephews.

But Charlie coming over? There was bound to be a fight. Good thing Charlie didn't have any kids. They might have turned out to be like him. Bullies. And if not like him, then like his wife Inez. Deadheads.

Pa went on, mostly to himself. "Thought I did all right by the two boys, giving them each an eighty when they got married."

"Think it's got something to do with Charlie wanting more land?"

" 'Spect so. Charlie'll even borrow money from a bank, he's such a plunger."

Kon finished his cow and got up. He'd filled his pail with foaming milk too. He emptied the milk into the ten-gallon can, then settled under his next cow.

Pa spat into the gutter. "Now me, I wouldn't want to pay interest. It's always working against you. If I had to pay interest I couldn't sleep nights thinking about it."

Kon milked along steadily. The aroma of cream fresh out of the cow rose from his pail.

"Well, we'll see when they get here. If it don't rain."

"It won't rain. The sky was clear when I came home, Pa."

"I kinda feel it in my bones though, son."

Kon sat as far away as he could from his second cow too, except that with this one he also had to keep a wary eye out for her lashing tail. A rich smell of hay wafted down from the loft overhead. His cow drooled spit into the wooden feed bunk in front of her. She could've almost been of Harmer blood the way she drooled. A fly settled on Kon's cheek. He twitched it off. A second later his cow felt the fly on her back; and of a sudden let fly with her tail. The tail caught Kon across the back of his neck, almost knocking off his straw hat. "Here! here!" Kon warned.

"Tie her tail down then, son. To her legs."

"But if you do that she starts to dancing around. And you have an awful time getting the milk out of her."

"Hrm," Pa grunted, and spat into the gutter.

"Here, you!"

Far in the distance, to the southwest, there was a low crack of thunder, suddenly.

Kon's ear prickled. Now from what corner of the heavens had that storm come up so quick?

"Told you," Pa said.

The cows stood placidly in their stanchions, drooling, waiting, their burdens of milk pendant.

A shrill voice cried from the house. "Anse? Anse? Yoo-hoo!"

"That'll be Mother calling," Pa said. "For us to help her get the chickens in."

"It's going to hit us then." Kon knew Pa hated to be interrupted with his milking. It broke into the cow's mood of giving. And sometimes a cow even ceased giving, and that led to complications, clots in the milk, infections. Kon could feel Pa struggling with himself—should he or shouldn't he let go of his cow?

Mother's voice was all of a sudden in the barn, in the doorway, crackling with impatience. "Anse! I've already got the windows closed. Now help me with the chickens."

"Shoot," Pa said. Then he got up, threw his one-legged stool to one side, set his pail against the wall. "C'mon, Kon, I guess chickens is more important than cows at that."

Kon got up with a groan and hurried outside after his father.

A quick look to the west and Kon saw that the sudden summer shower was already almost upon them. It was only a single thunderhead, narrow at the bottom, from which hung a veil of amber rain, but it was immensely tall, flattening off at the top against the stratosphere. It was coming on very fast, which was surprising, as there was no surface wind.

Mother took command. "Konstant, you quick go take the road

and chase 'em up from there. Anse, you go take the yard. And I'll take the grove."

Kon ran. The chickens he'd met when he came home from school had heard the thunder too and were already picking their way back through the grass. The last white straggler was down by the great old cottonwood in the run. Kon got behind the last straggler, then began to wave them all home. "Shoo! get home now. Shoo! you foolish biddies."

The veil of amber rain began to strike across the Harmer line fence beyond the cottonwood. It appeared to be deepening. Where it hit the standing corn it set up an awful racket.

"Shoo! hurry! you silly things."

Once a chicken got soaked through it could catch the croup. There were already enough enemies of the chickens around—lice, weasels, cholera—without letting a rainstorm wipe them out.

"Shoo, you. Shh-up now."

Kon got his white flock well into the yard at about the same time that Pa came around the side of the barn with his white flutterings. Both bunches were going to make it, heading nicely for the lath gate in the chicken coop.

But Mother still wasn't in sight. She was still in the grove somewhere.

Rain enveloped the windmill at the far end of the night yard.

"Pa?" Kon cried. "Can you drive them in alone now? I'll go help Mother."

Pa nodded, waved him on.

Kon found Mother near the beehives in the apple orchard just inside the walnut tree windbreak. She was shooing along a dozen reluctant chickens. Ordinarily the bees would have been after her. But bees were quick to sense when storms were on the way and long ago had already massed safely inside their hives.

Mother was outwardly calm for the chickens' sake, but inwardly Kon could see that she was a knot of fury. "Shoo! Konstant, stand there by the lilacs and keep them from going that way . . . shoo! . . . while I get these last wretches up . . . shoo!"

Flails of rain began to play on the tin roof of the machine shed.

"You're going to get soaked, Mother!"

"I don't care about me." Mother made a sudden run at the irregularly moving white line of chickens. "Shoo!" She gave the last one a pointed toe in its fanned-up tail. The chicken almost rolled over; squawked loudly; then turned to challenge Mother. It was an old brood hen, the kind that were almost as bossy as Mother herself.

A lasso of rain lapped around the house, then enveloped them —Kon, Mother, the white chickens. At the same instant a sucking surface wind caught at them too, tugging at Kon's pant legs, lifting Mother's skirts high up over her head and revealing a stark naked skinny bony body with an odd moustache in the middle, and almost upsetting all the chickens like sailboats caught out with the mainmast sail still up. Then lightning suddenly dazzled down in the center of the yard, illuminating everything garishly. It was only the cloud's second bolt. Then thunder opened up the air. That scared the devil out of everyone, most of all the chickens, and ducking down, heads out like pointed snakes, the chickens made a beeline for the chicken coop, all of them going so fast that neither Kon nor Mother could keep up with them. The chickens vanished, every one of them, sailing through the open lath gate.

Mother, her dress now under control, beat Kon to the coop gate, slid it shut.

"Got 'em!" Kon cried happily.

"But some wet," Mother said.

"We better run ourselves."

"Run!"

They scurried for the barn.

Pa was waiting for them, holding open the cow door.

"Whough!" Mother beat beads of rain from her clothes. "That was a close call."

Kon laughed, clear, boylike. "It's always such a hassle with them chickens."

Rain dropped heavy on the farmstead for a long minute, forming a splashing sheet of water over the dusty ground; then, as suddenly as it began, was over. The veils of rain moved beyond the walnut grove, going northeast toward brother Brant's place. The backside of the little rainstorm was a wreathing wall of gray.

"God be thanked there was no hail," Mother said.

Pa nodded. Then he turned to Kon. "Well, son, let's get back to pailing them cows. Before their milk turns to cottage cheese."

A half hour later, Pa finished his tenth and last cow just as Kon finished his seventh and last cow.

Kon was mulching the strawberries after supper with a mixture of leaves and old hay when Brant and family drove onto the yard. It was still light out. Brant always came early when visiting the folks. If he said eight he'd be there seven-fifty. But everywhere else, church, trips to Sioux Falls or Sioux City, creamery meetings, he'd be a half hour late. Pa was a trifle contemptuous of this two-way habit of Brant's. The trouble with Brant, Pa said, was that he was still hungry for the old home tit.

Brant had just bought a new car, a black-and-copper Ford, and he pulled up at his father's gate with a smile of quiet triumph. His lower lip was also usually moist in its center cleft, though not quite as pronounced as Pa's. Kon always felt that if Brant had only worked at it he could have had lips like Mother's or his own, with slightly more of an upper lip than a lower. But Brant was a mouth-breather like Pa and Charlie and so was probably doomed to having a moist lower lip.

Kon set his fork against the milk shed and headed for the gate. Mother and Pa came down the front steps off the veranda at the same time. Kon held the gate open for them.

It made Kon smile to see the little girls Edna and Pauline and their dog Bill sitting in a row in the back seat of the car, all three heads almost evenly high and all three with the same open-eyed expectant look. Bill was a collie and so his hair was golden-brown in contrast to the girls' black hair. "And then too," Kon thought, his smile deepening, "his nose is colder and some longer."

Mildred was the first to get out of the car. She was a big handsome woman, with a broad swarthy face, wise brown eyes, and very black hair. She was several inches taller than Brant, and more than twice as big as scrawny Mother. Mildred brushed down her dress front and back. The brushing down accentuated her full bosom, making it stand out so amply her dress hung a foot in front of her knees.

Kon held out his hand to Mildred. "Sister."

"Kon." Mildred's hand was both browner and broader than Kon's. Her handshake was firm. She squared her shoulders and stood in the grass like a walnut tree. "You're looking good, Kon." Mildred had a soothing alto voice.

"Thanks. So are you." Kon next leaned over the side of the car and reached for Brant's hand. "Everything all right, Brant?"

Brant returned Kon's warm squeeze. "Couldn't be better. And you?"

"The same."

They gave each other a lingering gaze. Where Kon was light-complected, Brant was dark, even to the hairs over the backs of their thumbs. They loved each other.

Kon then turned to smile at Edna and Pauline in the back seat. "So the little girlies came too. Good."

"Oh, you can't keep them home when you're going to Gramma's," Mildred said.

The spell for the three in the back seat broke, and the two little girls and the dog Bill came tumbling out.

Kon couldn't tell if he was being kissed more than he was being licked.

"Down, Bill," Mildred scolded.

That only made Bill all the wilder and he got up on two legs and began licking Mother and Pa too.

"Ptuey!" Mother spat. "Get away from me."

"Dummed dog," Pa grunted. Pa almost went down under Bill's impetuous wet rush and Pa's lip for once thinned tight and dry across his teeth.

Mildred surveyed it all with a warm female smile.

"Bill!" Brant finally called out.

Bill instantly sank to the ground, obedient, quiet.

"My, that dog!" Mother said, rubbing hair off her face. "And the worst is, he's bigger than me."

Pa let go with a short laugh. "Ha."

"It's because he loves everybody, Gramma," Edna said.

"When he licks you he's really only kissing you, Gramma," Pauline said.

Mother finally smiled. She threw her arms around the little children, kissing and loving them up. The little children responded by including Grampa in their embraces. To that Pa relaxed and his lip began to hang a little again. Everyone smiled, warm toward each other. Even Brant, who continued to sit behind his steering wheel, appeared to be in part pleased.

Presently Pa, disentangling himself from his grandchildren, had a question for Brant. "Get any of that rain a little while ago?"

"Naw. Just settled the dust, is all."

"You know it was more than that," Mildred said. "It's going to help that last crop of radishes."

Brant threw his wife a sidewise gleaming look. "I still say it was only a dust-settler."

Pa passed over the exchange. He grunted a short laugh. "Well, here it gave us a chance to get acquainted with our chickens again."

A klaxon blasted down the road beyond the fat old cottonwood.

"There comes Charlie in his old Luverne," Pa announced. Genuine pleasure opened Pa's face. "Right on time, like he said. Never a minute too early, never a minute too late."

Brant's lips curled in jealousy as he caught the look of love Pa had for Charlie.

Charlie and wife Inez appeared past the white corncrib, Charlie sitting erect at the wheel like a pompous fireman and Inez sitting crestfallen beside him like a caught firebug. With a whirl of arms and shoulders, Charlie wheeled his old brown Luverne onto the yard, and with a hard pull on the hand brake, rolled to a stop beside Brant's new Ford. Charlie gave the klaxon another blast, then followed it up by giving the bulb horn several

rhythmic pinches, making it bleat the tune "Shave and a Hair-
cut, Six Bits."

A look of concern came over Pa's face. "Why, Charlie, you
still got you your summer cold."

"Yeh," Charlie rasped low, hoarse, touching a thick rag around
his throat, "and I finally got so sick of it that I had Inez fix me
up a red flannel full of raw onions and swab it around my neck.
By God, I've never had me such a sore throat in my life."

"That's too bad, son," Pa said. "It looks awful."

Charlie was a big man, big-shouldered, big-armed. People had
trouble thinking of him as the son of so slender a father and so
tiny a mother. A tousle head, and quite blond, Charlie had yellow freckles over his bare arms and over the backs of his hands.
Charlie also had yellow eyes, and this too was surprising in a
family of mostly blue eyes. Pa always said that Charlie was a
throwback to another Charlie Harmer, a great-uncle of his, who
was a cattleman in Texas and who later took up gambling and
got shot up in a poker den in Oklahoma.

Yet in one thing Charlie was truly Pa's son. He had the
Harmer lip, hanging even looser than Pa's, especially when he
sulked, with a bigger drop of moisture.

An onion ring had begun to slip out of the folds of the red
flannel around Charlie's neck. Inez spotted it and with a blunt
finger poked it back in place.

Inez was a chunk of a woman, having a high fat middle, small
breasts, and heavy matronly arms. Her hair was the color of dried
hay and she wore it in a tight wispy knot in back. Her cheekbones
were high and sharp and her eyes so sunken it was hard to make
out their true color. Her lips were shaped in what had once been
a natural smile but which over the years had become utterly
meaningless.

Charlie's hard yellow glance fell on Kon's white hands. "Been
laying in the shade again, I see."

Kon pretended he hadn't heard.

Mother chewed once. "Ten minutes ago you'd've caught him in
the garden working."

"I still say Kon'll never learn the Siouxland step." Charlie opened the door on his side and with a grunt stepped down. He limped around to the front of his car. He had once stepped on a hay knife and got himself a toe that stuck up like the head of a startled turtle. The heel of the crippled foot scuffed at the ground, hard enough to kick up dust from underneath the top layer of wet. Charlie spotted the dust. "Didn't get much of that shower here, I see."

Pa said, "Did you?"

"There was a half inch in an empty tobacco can by the tool-shed."

Brant drew back his upper lip. "That's the pure truth, I suppose."

"Yessir, the pure plumb truth, if you must know. And the hell with you, Brant Harmer."

"The hell with you yourself," Brant flared back. "With you the first liar doesn't have a chance."

"Anybody what believes in witches hadn't oughter talk."

"Oh, yeah? Well, I wouldn't talk so loud either if I was you. Because one of these days we'll all regret that we didn't put up a hexafoos over our doors. To keep out the trouble that's coming."

"Fairy tales from when we was kids."

"Boys," Pa said.

Mother chewed over a dark thought to herself.

Charlie gave Brant's glistening new Ford a look of contempt, at the same time that he patted the radiator of his old brown Luverne. "Still throwing your money away like a drunken sailor, I see."

"It's my money."

"Some of it is."

"And that some of it is no less than yours is."

Charlie gave his car another pat on the head. "Hell, long after you've wore out your third Ford, I'll still be driving this sweet paloosey of an old Luverne."

Inez got out of the car too. She brushed her dress down in back, then shyly approached the children. Having no children of her own, she was always trying to make up to her nieces.

Edna and Pauline would have none of her though, just as Bill would have nothing to do with Charlie. The two girls and the dog retreated behind Mildred.

"Here, here, you two," Mildred said, pushing her girls forward. "That's no way to act to your aunt. Now you go over and give Aunt Inez a big tight hug and a kiss."

The girls hardly budged.

"Remember, she's the only aunt you've got."

Charlie smiled a big loose smile. "Your only aunt, that's right. Unless'n Kon here should happen to get married. Ha."

Mother chewed once again. "Konstant has more important things to do right now than think of getting married."

"Like what?"

"Never mind that now."

Charlie had a big loose leer for Kon. "I hear that new schoolteacher over at Rock Number Three has dropped her handkerchief for you."

Kon ignored Charlie; instead smiled at his nieces, encouraging them to go kiss their Aunt Inez.

Still the girls held back.

Charlie went on, slowly, hoarsely. "Kon, let me give you a piece of advice. And you can take it from a man who's been married at least once. Instead of tying yourself up with a skinny old dried-up schoolteacher, marry yourself a breed. Say a woman who's part Indian and part Scotch. Then you'll have yourself a wife that'll be a little wild and a little tight both."

Out of Inez' dead smile there abruptly came a strange wild cackling. It sounded a little like an alarm clock going off. After a moment it stuttered to a stop.

Charlie shuddered. He'd reached the point where he could hardly stand her laugh anymore. He whirled on his gimpy leg once, then pointed a finger at Kon. "Pa, you've got to do something about this son of yours here. Because if you don't he'll disgrace us Harmer men. Take him to Sioux City, for godsakes, and lock him up in a room with a Nellie Snow for a night. Or something."

Mother said, "Let the boy alone. He will get over it in time."

Brant slowly got out of his Ford. He was white. He walked up to Charlie and stuck a finger into Charlie's belly. He was a good foot shorter than Charlie, yet for the moment, in his rage, he appeared to be the more formidable. It never paid to get Brant too mad because then he became animal mad, worse even than a tormented badger in a barrel. Brant snarled, "Charlie, when I see you go on like this with your great big blab . . . by God, if I don't think I'm looking at the most wonderful ass in all of Siouxland. And in his highest glory."

Charlie reared up on his gimpy leg. "For that remark I'll have your guts for garters."

"Boys," Pa said.

Heat rose in Kon's belly at the way Brant came to his defense. Kon wanted to pitch in himself but didn't quite know how to go about it.

Again Brant speared Charlie in the belly with his finger. "Just because you personally don't mind risking your health playing around with open-legged women don't mean that Kon has to."

Again Inez let go with a wild mechanical cackle of a laugh.

"Let every tub stand on his own bottom," Mother cried.

Mildred smiled at the ground. She'd heard the Harmers before.

But the children were scared and showed it. Their eyes were glowing wide.

The dog Bill watched it all with his own kind of silent regard.

Charlie decided he had enough of it. He brushed Brant's finger aside. "I didn't come over here to fight with you." Charlie looked around. "Where's the dog Bill? Ah, there he is. Bill, come here." Charlie grabbed Bill by the collar before he could escape. Bill knew what was expected of him and he hung back as hard as he could. But Charlie dragged him up the walk toward the house anyway. "Come on, everybody, what are we doin' standing around here when we can sit comfortable up on the porch?"

There was a gradual turning of faces toward the veranda.

Charlie lifted the entire dog off the ground as he ascended the steps. He flopped Bill back and forth a couple of times as though the dog were a blanket, then folded him into a curve, and, stretching out on the plank flooring himself, made a pillow out of Bill.

The dog Bill squirmed and whimpered. And his nose screwed up at the awful onion stink coming out of the red flannel around Charlie's neck.

"Lay still, Bill," Charlie growled.

Pa settled in his rocker at the far end, Mother took the near rocker, Mildred commandeered the remaining two comb-back chairs for herself and Inez, and Kon and Brant took the top step, with the little girls sitting between them. All but Charlie looked out over the yard. Charlie, center stage, stared up at the white ceiling of the veranda.

Light lingered. Earth and sky hung floating as if riding in a deep sea of lemonade.

It was remarkable that none of the Harmer men smoked. Smoking might have cured them of the hanging wet lip. But Mother was death on tobacco. She said smoking was a filthy habit. Also, it stunk up her curtains so.

A meteor streaked across the southern skies.

After a while Mother began to rock a little. "Yes, we should all be thankful that we're still alive and healthy. It could easy have been different."

Pa began to rock then too. "That's right."

Mother said, "And not fight so. You boys always fight so."

Pa said, "That's right."

Mother said, "Because when I remember them old times, we're lucky to be here at all."

Brant said, "Mother, be careful or you'll get Pa started again on the old days."

Pa bristled. "What's wrong with that? I suppose you're too up-to-date to hear about them?"

"Brant," Mother said, "what's wrong with Pa sometimes talking about them days? You came out of them days."

Brant said, "I know. But the trouble is, once Pa gets started, you can't get him stopped."

Mother said, "He's your father. And you can listen to him once in a while. Even if it is old stuff."

Pa said, "Those first years here on the prairie . . . you either lived as mean as a coyote or you was as fat as a snake full of frogs."

Brant said, "You see, there he goes."

Mother said, "But it was hard, them days, Brant. With all that wild open prairie around, no neighbors . . . Why, it was hard even to get a town started."

Pa said, "That's right. Why, there's a town east of here that had a barrel of whiskey for its foundation. The fumes of that whiskey caught the nose of every loafer within a thousand miles. And the town still shows it. It still looks like the yard of a shiftless farmer."

"Lay still, Bill," Charlie growled, resettling his head into the dog's belly.

Brant said, "We can't help it you folks never had any fun then."

Pa cried, "Fun? Hch. We had a barrel of fun them days. Why, once, after an Indian scare, we sent for a fiddle in a buckboard ten miles away and had us a dance."

Brant sighed elaborately. "Well, folks, Mother's tapped the barrel and now we're in for it."

Pa rubbed his lean thigh. "Why, we young folks thought nothing of it to go visit a neighbor thirty miles away and have us a hoedown on a cold winter's night. And with a horse and buggy yet."

"Lay still, Bill."

Mildred said, "The dog can't stand the smell of them onions, Charlie."

"Damn you, Bill, lay still."

Inez sat near Charlie's head. She reached down and pushed back a protruding onion.

Mother rocked some more. "Though I have to say that I have one regret about them days."

Pa said, "And what might that be?"

"That we didn't go to church more often."

"We did too go to church a lot them days."

"No, we didn't either. We was pretty much out-and-out infidels."

"Why, we did too go to church. You was with me the Sunday when old Theophalia Atherton preached his own funeral sermon and then dropped dead right there on the pulpit."

"I wasn't either."

"Don't you remember that? Why, we all talked about him reaching ninety-nine and how it was too bad that since he'd got that far he didn't reach a hundred."

"No, I don't remember."

"Why, and you used to go with me to hear Pastor Caleb Allen, the Presbyterian preacher." Pa allowed himself a short laugh. "We used to call him Old Protoplasm. He always begun his sermon away back in ancient history. Before Creation even."

Mother's face softened. "But what I do remember about them days is that I could walk in any direction from our sodhouse and soon be swimming in perfume. Why, in the swales it was like the perfume lay there in little silver fogs."

"Now you're talking," Pa said.

"You almost fainted, it was all so sweet."

"Reka, remember that spring when we was out of meat and I happened to spot a great big crane in the run below our old cottonwood there? He had a broken leg and couldn't get up enough of a run to fly. So I took up my ax to get him. No use wasting gunpowder. We had to be saving on gunpowder then. Well, say! when the smoke cleared away, I looked like I'd been up against a corn sheller, my clothes was so tore up. But I got the crane."

Brant shook his head. "What's that crane got to do with perfume, I wonder."

"Reka, what was that joke again that was going the rounds about why we got that locust plague that time?"

"Governor Pillsbury of Minnesota appointed a day for fasting and prayer."

"Oh, yeh. And that was the signal for all them insects to up and fly down here to Iowa. They was afraid that if all them two-legged gophers up in Minnesota started fasting for one day they'd get eaten up the next day."

"Wasn't that about the time when that rich Englishman came stomping across the prairie here like he was God himself?"

"With his dogs and his glass eye, and a tin bathtub bigger than a claim shanty, yeh. And then he ups and buys everything he can see and plants a patch of larchwood trees right in the middle of it and calls it Larchwood."

Charlie coughed hoarsely, deep.

The dog Bill broke wind under the weight of Charlie's head.

"Lay still, Bill. You did that on purpose."

Mother said down to Charlie, "Son, taking a severe cold in the summer can quick turn into black pneumonia and then galloping consumption. You better watch out."

Brant sneered. "Let Charlie die if that's what he wants, Mother."

Kon reached across the children to touch Brant on the arm. "Don't rile him up. What do you gain by it?"

"Nothing like a little alum to settle muddy water, I say."

"Kon," Charlie growled, "you stay out of it. I can fight my own fights."

Kon stiffened. "And don't you take my milk for gall either."

Mother hunched herself up into a tight ball. "Boys! Now."

Inez said, "I says too, Charlie, I said, Kon says not to take his milk bag for a gall bladder. Besides, I said—"

"Oh, shut up, woman," Charlie snapped. "You never said that. You always talk mixed up."

"I did so now."

"Oh, shut up."

Dusk, then darkness, settled rapidly. The white buildings turned gray, the red barn purple.

Pa roughed his chin with the palm of his hand. "Summers, every identical day I hauled wood from the Big Sioux. Winters, every identical day I hauled rocks on my stone boat."

Brant pushed out his lower lip. "Suppose Charlie does die of black pneumonia tomorrow? Who's going to be your favorite then, Pa?"

"Hum!" Mother warned.

After a pause Pa moved up his rocker and put his feet up on the railing and said, "You're all my favorites."

Of a sudden Charlie sat up. "OK, Bill, you've done your job." Charlie gave the dog a light whack over the neck. "Thanks."

At first Bill couldn't believe it. When it did finally penetrate his brain that he was free, he sprang to his feet, shook himself until loose hair wafted up on the air, then romped over to where the two little girls sat and crowded joyfully in between them. His crowding in pushed Brant off his perch so that Brant had to move down a step. The little girls loved up Bill.

Charlie slid on his seat to one of the double-pillared supports and, leaning back, sat facing them all. He ran his tongue all around between his teeth and his lips. He coughed hoarsely several times. Then he finally let fly with why he wanted the family meeting. "Pa, I've been thinkin' it's time you retired."

All the grown-ups cried out. "What!"

"That's right. This farm is too much for the old man to run alone."

"Why!" Pa cried. "I got Kon to help me, if it comes to that."

"Him?" Charlie snorted a large snort. "Kon? Hell, Pa, he's too busy making whistles out of pigs' ears to help you much. Besides, he don't plan to stay long. First thing you know he'll be off to college somewhere."

Kon turned pale in the dark.

Charlie went on. "In another five years this place will be an eyesore the way you run it. Instead of a showplace."

"What!"

"You can't keep it up now."

Pa let both feet drop to the board floor of the veranda. Hard. "Charlie, you better get this straight. I'm stayin' put."

"Well, now, Anse," Mother put in, "maybe you ought to think it over a little, what Charlie said. You ain't gettin' any younger."

Pa glared across at Mother. "Why, hell, woman, there ain't but seventy wrinkles on my horn yet. Why, I'm still young yet. Why, if I had me a young wife I could still have me a second family of kids yet. Easy. One, two, three, four, five. If I was of a mind to."

Mother rocked once. "Anse, if you can lie, I can keep still."

"Lie about what?"

"That you could still be good with a young wife."

Charlie bulled in some more. "Pa, next summer sometime, when everybody's busier than a bee in a tar bucket getting in his own crops, supposin' you was to suddenly drop dead crossin' the yard here, then what, huh? Who'd finish the year for Mother here? Huh?"

Kon spoke up. "I would. Despite what you may think of me."

"You?"

Brant said, "Yes, Kon. And I could come over and help Kon and Mother."

Charlie sucked his lip at them in contempt. He turned back to Pa. "It could happen, you know, that you'd drop dead suddenly. Just as well as that I could get black pneumonia."

Pa abruptly turned his rocker about so that he could face Charlie head on. "Charlie, why don't you speak your whole mind? Lay everything out on the table. Your whole hand."

"All right, I will speak my whole mind. It's this. It's time for you and Ma to live on easy street. Go live in town. And I know just the place for you too. A dandy little house that's for sale in Bonnie right now."

"Right now, eh? And who'll take over this farm right now?"

"Me."

"I thought so."

"As the oldest son, I'll take over. And I'll get a renter for my place."

Mildred had a scoffing look for Charlie. "You and Inez live in this big house? With no kids? Why, you two'd rattle around in it like two peas in a chamberpot, it'd be so empty. It's too empty now, with just Mother and Pa and Kon in it. All that room going to waste."

Mother gave her daughter-in-law a look. "This is a matter of blood now, Millie."

"Two peas, did you say?" Charlie wondered with a hoarse laugh.

"Two peas, I said."

"Millie."

Mildred subsided.

"Hell," Pa said, "I'm tougher than you think. If I have to I can still lick any one of you boys. Arm wrestling. Walking behind the plow."

Charlie's voice slowly worsened. "Pa, you couldn't even lick Kon, if it came to that."

Pa leaned forward in his rocker. "Listen. Get this straight. No son of mine is going to butt me off my place."

Mother got to her feet. She'd heard enough and wanted the subject changed. "Kon?"

"Yes, Mother." Kon got to his feet too.

"I'll go get the mix from the icebox."

"I'm ready if you are."

Mother went into the kitchen. She lighted the gas lamp and then came out with a gleaming nickel container shaped like a cylinder. She gave it to Kon.

Kon smiled down at Edna and Pauline. "How would you two like to help me make some ice cream?"

The two little girls already knew but they pretended to be surprised. "Ice cream? Oh, goodie."

"Come then."

Kon got out the old wooden freezer from the milkhouse and placed the cylinder of mix in it. Then he got some ice from the icehouse and crushed it to fine bits inside a gunny sack. With cupped hands he shoveled the fine ice along with some salt in around the cylinder. And taking a seat on the bottom step, he set to work, slowly turning the crank of the old freezer. The two nieces sat on their heels in front of him, watching him grind the cylinder around and around in the crunching ice.

Edna, the oldest, liked her Uncle Kon very much. She showed it by touching him shyly on the leg.

Kon smiled down at her.

"Uncle Kon, pretty soon, after we've had some ice cream, can we go play hide and seek in the dark behind the house?"

"If you want to."

"Will you really play with us?"

"If you want me to."

"Pinching and such?"

Kon laughed.

"Why does Gramma keep your hexafoos up in the attic?"

Kon was startled. "Who told you about that?"

"Daddy."

"He did?"

"He says the hexafoos won't do you any good up there. In that old black trunk. Better that it should be tacked up over the front door."

"Your daddy can't be serious."

"Oh, yes, he is. He says if you don't have it tacked up over the front door, the hex witches will sneak into your house at night and come around and pinch you and such."

Kon threw a wondering look across at Brant.

Little Pauline's dark eyes fastened on Kon next. "Uncle Charlie is so big, Uncle Kon."

"He is?"

"He's even bigger than our own Daddy."

"Mmm."

"But that's not good, is it, Uncle Kon?"

"Why not?"

"Well," Pauline said, leaning over Kon's knee, "if he grows too big he'll die."

"Oh, Pauline, whatever are you talking about? Charlie will live forever."

"But that can't be, Uncle Kon, because he's supposed to die when he's all done growing."

"Oh, Pauline, people don't die when they're all done growing."

"But corn does."

"People are people, Pauline, and corn is corn. They're not the same thing."

"But then that isn't fair, Uncle Kon, if corn has to die when it's all done growing and people don't."

Mildred spoke from her chair. "Don't talk so much, Pauline. Can't you see Uncle Kon is busy making the ice cream?"

"Mother, may I please ask him one more question?"

Mildred sighed. "Oh, go ahead if you must."

"When I'm all done growing, Uncle Kon, then I won't have to die like corn does, will I, because I'm people?"

Brant broke in caustically from the top step. "Not unless a corn borer comes along and eats the heart right out of you."

The dark eyes of both Pauline and Edna swiveled around to their father above them.

"Corn borer? Mildred said. "Are you already worrying about them this year?"

Pauline still wanted her answer. "Uncle Kon, will I?"

"Uncle Kon?"

"Let's just think about the ice cream now. Because you see, if you don't help it by thinking about it, it won't get hard."

The sharp white light of the gas lamp in the kitchen shone through the open door upon them. For the moment it gave Kon the silver hair of an old man. It gave the hair of the little girls the black gloss of a pair of lively crows.

Mother could be heard relighting the fire in the range and putting on the kettle.

Kon turned the crank around and around. The whirling cylinder of mix made squeezing sounds against the salted ice. Sometimes the cylinder caught a piece of ice sideways and crunched it with a loud crack.

Soon salty water began to run out of the holes high in the wall of the freezer. It trickled blackly across the walk.

Brant couldn't resist getting in one last sticker. "Well, Charlie, I see where Pa didn't think much of your idea."

"No, he didn't, that's a fact. But you can bet your narrer ass that that's where he's making a big mistake. Because I mean to make him retire."

Pa shook his head, emphatic. "After what I done in my life, you still think you can make me retire?"

"I'm gonna keep after you until you do."

"Well, it won't do you a bit of good. Because I mean to die right here beside our old cottonwood. With the handles of my plow in my hands."

"That's what I'm afraid of, Pa."

"Not after all the things I done."

. . . It was when Anse was fifteen. His father and mother farmed the bottoms near the Great Serpent Mound in Ohio. They had just gotten a pretty good start, when all of a sudden they took sick with a bad case of the black blood. A country doctor prescribed some pukeweed extract, *Lobelia inflata*, to raise their body heat and so purify the blood. But he couldn't even get them to sweat, and they died.

Young Anse couldn't farm the place alone, so he held a public sale, auctioning off both the land and their movables. From the proceeds he paid off his father's debts and back taxes. Then, with only twenty-one dollars and seventy-six cents, and his father's rifle, Anse struck out for himself into the great wide world.

He headed for Chicago. He had a longing to go west and hoped to catch on with some cow outfit come to town with a shipment of cattle.

Anse hung around the Chicago stockyards for a month, watching, waiting. He paid his way taking on odd jobs: bus boy, waiter in a restaurant, night watchman in a boot shop, handyman in a livery stable.

No likely cow outfit came along to hire him.

Then a rancher from near Sioux Falls, South Dakota, purchased a hundred head of Kentucky riding horses, most of them bays, and turned over the job of driving them home to his horse wrangler. But the night before the horse wrangler was to set out with the cavvy, he decided to have himself one more hot time on the old town, and upon coming out of an upstairs whorehouse, gaunt with fatigue, fell down and broke his leg.

Anse heard of the wrangler's plight at the horse barns. Here was his chance. He promptly applied for the job. The wrangler's name was Tim Wray.

It was first things first with Anse. "Mr. Wray, how much do I get if I take on the job?"

"A dollar a head for those you deliver."

"I'll take it."

"You know horses?"

Anse sucked back a drop of moisture from his lip. "Well, I drove and rode my dad's horses, both."

"A hundred horses suddenly let loose out in the open country is going to take some doing."

"Could you have done it if you hadn't broken your leg?"

"Hell, yes."

"Then I can."

"How old are you again?"

"Going on twenty-one."

"Fellow down at the livery stable claims you ain't seen sixteen yet."

"Well, if you can get somebody else, go ahead."

"Oh, hell, you take the job, kid. I was just wondering, is all."

"When do I start?"

"I'll fix it up with the yard boys that they're to help you as far as Oak Park tomorrow. After that you'll have to drive them alone."

"When are the horses due in South Dakota?"

"Mr. Beresford wants them by June first. It's April first tomorrow. Two months should give you plenty of time."

"Mr. Beresford will have his horses on time."

"Now don't chase them too fast. Let them graze their way west."

"I won't."

"If you handle it right they should be fat by the time you get there."

"They will be."

"Good boy. And good luck."

"What about you and your leg?"

"Doc says I can take the stagecoach home in about a month."

"I'll see you there then."

"Right."

All went well at first. The horses were lonesome enough in the strange country to stay well bunched. There were no stragglers or loners. Quite soon one of the older bay mares took over the role of bell mare. Anse named her Molly. Anse rode a bay gelding whom he named General. Soon he and General took over the role of head stallion.

Across northern Illinois Anse had to keep to the roads. Most farmers already had their places fenced in. The new grass in the ditches was up early that spring and the horses did well on it. In a few weeks they were velvet sleek. The weather groomed them until they shone a bronze red in the sun.

Crossing the flooding Mississippi turned out to be quite a problem. The captain running the ferry at Dubuque refused to take the horses across unless Anse agreed to halter and tie them down. Anse had neither the lasso with which to catch them nor the halters.

Anse pondered awhile; finally hit on an idea. The bell mare, Molly, who had already been reading his thoughts like she might be a wife, could take his place at the tail of the herd while he himself rode the point on General.

Anse gave Molly a long stare and then urged General into the waters of the Mississippi. General hadn't any more than got his hocks wet when Molly caught on. She let out with a shrill whistle and immediately wheeled around and went back to the tail of the herd and began to chouse them in after Anse and General.

Some hundred feet in, when General stepped off into deep water, Anse swung off and grabbed General's tail. The spring floodwaters were burning cold.

The rest of the hundred horses followed, spreading out a little as they headed for the opposite shore, with only their tan heads and black manes showing. Far in back, pumping vigorously, and still chousing in the water, Molly brought up the rear.

General, stroking powerfully, easily made it across and Anse rode him up a high cutbank.

Shivering, sopping wet, but safe on high ground, Anse turned to watch them all come ashore. It was a sight he was never to forget.

When the last horse, Molly, emerged and shook herself, and whinnied sweetly up at him, Anse laughed a young boy's free laugh and, high with triumph, saluted the captain of the ferry across the river with a double thumb to the nose. Then he exchanged places with Molly, giving her the point again. Soon the sun warmed, then dried him.

On they went, west. They trotted; they grazed; then trotted some more.

Anse learned that prairie chickens liked to feed on dried wild strawberries caught in hay, so for meat he only had to ride up to a haystack and shoot what he needed from the back of his horse. Cottontails were everywhere and he also shot them as he needed them. Sometimes he traded a brace of prairie chickens for cornmeal with some farmer and then he had cornmeal and cottontail for breakfast. Every settler ran a hotel in his hut and many a time Anse was invited to stay the night. There was always room for one more man on the floor, the settler said. But Anse, smiling, always refused the invitation. Homes made of Iowa brick, prairie sod, were flea heavens. He stuck with Molly and the horses. He had come to love sleeping rolled up in a tarp on clean grass.

He ran into one cloudburst. It came down the Des Moines River in a wide flash flood. But after his experience crossing the Mississippi, crossing the swollen Des Moines was nothing.

The worst was the occasional horse traders he ran into. One look at Anse's streaming herd of bronzy peckernecks, and the traders were after him to sell off part of the herd, or at least make single trades with him. Sometimes horse traders followed him for miles in their top buggies, hoping they would change his mind. After all, he was only a boy and could hardly know his mind so early in life. Anse learned from observing them work with each other that they always watched each other's eyes. Where a man looked for defects in a stranger's horse was where the defects were in his own horse.

By the middle of May he was in Siouxland and crossing the Big Rock River below the Falls. He had only to cross the Big Sioux some twenty miles farther west and then he'd have clear sailing right onto Mr. Beresford's ranch.

To make sure that he'd keep heading straight west, he took a sighting on a treetop he could just make out over the horizon slightly to the southwest. He headed his horses toward it.

To his considerable surprise he didn't gain very fast on the tree. It remained in sight for most of an afternoon. When he finally arrived at its foot he was astounded to discover that he'd come upon a great giant of a cottonwood. Somehow, though standing alone, it had outlasted summer windstorm as well as prairie fire. It'd been a natural target for lightning and several of its topmost branches were dead, peeled white, with rippled scars down the length of its trunk, but it was still a great healthy monster of a tree.

Young Anse marveled at it; and fell in love with it.

Below and west of the fat cottonwood he came upon slough grass so deep that when he rode into it both he and his horse disappeared from sight. For the fun of it he reached up and tied some of the grass ends together into an arch and then rode under it.

"I ought to get down and cut me off a couple of handfuls," he said aloud. "Just to show people. Because nobody will believe me when I tell them."

He rode over to examine a slight rise in the land north of the cottonwood. Buffalo skulls and skeletons lay bleaching in the sun.

He liked what he saw.

"This is where I'm going to live. Build me a house on this little hump of land. Why, this prairie here is like the Garden of Eden itself." He gazed and gazed from the back of his horse, to all sides. "Yessir, after I've delivered the horses, and've got my pay, I'm heading right back here and homestead me a farm." He looked down at where a little stream in the slough ran through heavy black loam. "Look at how rich that is. It's been building up into rich soil for thousands of years and all I'll have to do is to tickle it a little and it'll come to life with a bang. First open it up with a prairie breaker, then plant a crop of sod corn, then later wheat. With a little work and some luck, I'll make this one of the showplaces in the country. Yessir, with a farm still in the state of nature, watch me make a killing. Pa dreamed of becoming a solid citizen in Ohio, rich. And didn't make it. But, by God, here in Siouxland, between two of the world's biggest rivers, I sure as hell will."

The hundred horses seemed to have taken a fancy to the single cottonwood too. When Anse decided to move on, he had some trouble chousing them away from it. They liked resting in its shade. It made a good center for them.

Late that day, at dusk, as the horses were streaming nicely down the face of a light-green bluff, heading for an evening drink in the dark-green Big Sioux River, suddenly there was a commotion at the head, where Molly the mare ran the point. A lurking party of Pawnee Indians, a dozen of them, hunters, also lovers of horseflesh, had flashed out of a brush-filled ravine. They came waving scaring blankets, hallooing like fiends from hell. This Molly had never seen before. Nor had any of the other Kentucky bays. In an instant the bronze-red horses broke, stampeding, and in another instant they were galloping wildly up over the light-green bluff, all of them, heading east and for home again.

Gone.

Anse pulled out his rifle and fired one shot at the Pawnees; and then General under him broke for it too.

Anse fought General up and down the light-green bluff, through sticky grapevine tangles and fearsome prickly ash, into and out of sloshy swales.

After a long struggle, after it had turned dark, Anse finally managed to get control of General again. Both were covered with slaver and blood.

"Well, if that don't swipe the rag off'n the bush."

The moon came up. In its milky light Anse led the horse into some river shallows and washed them both off.

General liked the washing and became friends with Anse again. He nuzzled Anse. He gave himself several hide-rippling shakes.

Mosquitoes rose out of the wet swale. They swarmed around Anse and his horse like a blizzard. Where the mosquitoes touched bare skin they burned. To be quit of them Anse finally had to ride General up the green bluff again, up to where the night breeze cleared the air. They slept standing together.

The next morning Anse took stock. Both he and General were pretty well cut up by the prickly ash. Anse's leather boots were all ripped up and his pants had been torn to shreds. There were deep gashes over General's chest and forelegs.

Anse sewed up General's deeper wounds with boiled string. As for his own deep cuts, he poured a sprinkling of gunpowder in them and touched them off with a match to cauterize them.

"Lost me everything but the one horse."

Anse boiled himself some jerky in a tin and ate hurriedly.

"But I ain't licked yet. I said I'd deliver them horses to Mr. Beresford, and, by God, I mean to deliver them horses."

He checked the saddle and the bridle, then swung aboard.

"Though I could be a mite late delivering them. June first stands just over the hill there."

All day he trailed the hoofmarks of the horses, going east. It was as easy as pie. The Pawnees had chased hard after them for a considerable distance, and then had fallen behind and lost them. The sign in the soft spring grass was clear-cut and easy to read.

When he reached the Des Moines River, he found it still in flood. From all signs it was obvious the horses had been hesitant to swim it. A good share of them had veered south, going down-river into lower Iowa, while another part had gone upriver, into Minnesota.

The remainder were grazing in a nearby meadow. They recognized Anse and General and, neighing joyously, came running up.

Anse was sitting there puzzling over how he could round up the other horses, when a granger on horseback came over a knoll. Anse brightened. Anse and the granger had a talk. It turned out that the granger had gone in for hay farming and stock grazing generally some ten miles to the northwest along a creek. The granger said he'd be glad to help the lad out by pasturing the bunch just found plus any other strays found, provided he could select a team from the whole herd for pay once Anse had them all rounded up. Anse agreed to the terms. He would settle with Mr. Beresford later about the cost.

Anse headed south, going after the biggest band first. He

chevied across flat Iowa all summer long, until far into the fall, and tracked every one of them down, even the singletons, and brought them back to the granger.

Then Anse headed north into Minnesota. Though the northern bunch was the smallest, it took the longest to round up. Winter set in early, and then it became slow, cruel going. He nearly froze to death a half dozen times. Occasionally he stayed overnight in flea-ridden sod houses. Often he crawled into a lonely haystack with General standing outside in its lee.

He asked everywhere after the horses. "Seen a loose bunch of bays lately?"

"Naw. Nary a one."

Or, "There ain't been any strays around here lately? Bays?"

"Strays, yes. Bays, no."

Or, "May I ask where you got that bay?"

"Found him one morning with my horses."

When May came around again, he'd finally rounded up every single one of his original hundred.

The granger couldn't get over it. "Kid, when you get through delivering them horses, you can come work for me. And name your own pay."

"Thanks. But I found me my Garden of Eden. And I mean to make my home there."

"Kid, you is grit, you is. And I tell you what. I'm not going to take a grazing fee for pasturing them horses. You know that team of bays I was to pick for myself? I ain't got the heart. So be on your way. This time you'll make it."

Anse and his hundred bays crossed the Big Rock River again on the twenty-ninth of May. They bedded down under the lone giant cottonwood on the thirtieth. They crossed the Big Sioux on the thirty-first. And they arrived on Mr. Beresford's ranch on June first, a year late exactly to the day.

Tim Wray, the wrangler who'd broken his leg in a whorehouse in Chicago, met Anse at the gate to the Beresford corral.

Tim Wray was dumbfounded. He kept blinking his eyes. "By the Lord, kid, I never expected to see you again."

"There they are. All hundred of them."

"Holy sufferin' swollen catfish, kid."

"Mr. Beresford still wants 'em, don't he?"

"Kid, I give you up for dead long ago. And the horses scattered to hell and gone."

"Does Mr. Beresford pay on delivery? Even if it's a year late?"

"He ain't home just now. But, kid, it's such a treat to see you, I'll pay you myself out of my own pocket."

The two of them ran the horses into the corral.

Tim Wray made the tally. "By God, kid, you're right. They are all here. The whole hundred of them."

"Could I trouble you for the hundred bucks now?"

"Today?"

"Yes, please."

"You damn tootin' you can, kid. And I tell you what else I'm gonna do. I'm gonna throw in the gelding. You've earned him."

"I'm much obliged."

"Say, kid, you wouldn't want to go get another hundred for Mr. Beresford, would you, now that you know the way so well?"

"No."

"Well, anyway, you'll at least stay for supper?"

"No."

"Why not?"

"I'm in a hurry to stake out my new home."

"Tell me, kid, before you run off . . . what really did happen in all that time?"

Anse told him.

"Pawnees? Just across the river from here? So close? I'll be goddamned. Man! Well, all I can say is, you'll do out here. You're broke in now, if you wasn't before."

That same night in the moonlight Anse crossed the Big Sioux and rode east until he came to his giant cottonwood. There he bedded down in deep grass.

Every now and then as he slept his hand touched the pocket where he'd stowed away the hundred dollars.

General stood over him, head down, patiently waiting for dawn.

The rest of that summer he got ready for next year. He built a log barn for his horse General and a small sod shanty for himself. He got ash wood for fencing from the groves along the Big Sioux. He planted a windbreak of walnut seedlings. He broke a small piece of sod to let air and rain sweeten the soil for the next spring. For food he shot deer, grouse, prairie chickens, and picked wild plums and bullberries, and grubbed up wild onions.

He was just in time. By September prairie schooners were sailing across the rolling land, heading for Sioux Falls and vicinity. Before the first snow fell, he had three neighbors only a half dozen miles away.

Anse prospered. Inside of four years he had his entire quarter section broke up as well as fenced in, and he had a good orchard and a garden going.

One spring day when he was twenty-two a covered wagon stopped under his big cottonwood. He wondered about the covered wagon a little and after a while went down to see who it might be.

And there she was, sitting on the wagon tongue, brown hair falling to her shoulders, light-blue eyes spearing right through him. She was the oldest of four children. Her mother had died suddenly back in western Pennsylvania and she'd become the woman of the house, caring for her father Donald Heath, as well as for her two younger sisters Amy and Mirabel and little brother Joseph. Anse instantly noted that though she was a little thing she was all there and then some.

Anse mostly visited with Mr. Heath. But all the while Anse noticed that the brown-haired girl listened closely to what he had to say and that her light burning blue eyes never once left his face. It was as if she meant to specially catch his eye, as though she had something to tell him but couldn't. A secret.

The next day, as the Heaths pulled out for the West, Anse couldn't help but remark, "Too bad you can't leave one of your daughters behind. I surely could use one of them."

Mr. Heath shook his head. "No. The littlest ones is too young and the oldest one I need for myself." Up until then Mr. Heath had had bold blue eyes, but now he couldn't hold up to Anse.

"What's the oldest one's name?"

"You don't need to know that."

"But supposin' I took a fancy to her?"

"She ain't staying, so it don't concern you. Giddap, you plugs."

The oldest girl spoke up for the first time. "My name is Reka."

Mr. Heath threw his Reka a soulful look, and his shoulders sagged, but he said nothing.

Two mornings later, as Anse was about to plow corn with his new walking cultivator, he spotted Reka coming down the row toward him. She was carrying something that looked like a wooden bird with a clamp for legs. He would have recognized her brown hair and her shimmering light-blue eyes anywhere.

Reka came directly up to him. "You meant that the other day? That you could use one of us?"

Anse's heart beat up fast for a moment. What a feisty little thing she was. Full of ginger. He looked at her clothes: plain spun gray dress, a pair of boy's heavy shoes, a faded light-blue ribbon in her hair. The ribbon was neatly tied in a bow. She'd put it on specially for him, he knew. Yes, he could use her all right. "Your pa know you're here?"

"I'm eighteen."

Anse smiled to make it easier between them. "Well, and here I thought you was only a sweet sixteen."

"I'm eighteen all right."

"What's that thing you got in your hand?"

"A sewing bird."

"What's it for?"

"To hold things down with while you sew. It's like having a maid hold down a dress for you while you sew on it."

"Never saw one before."

"It was my mother's. Pa give it to me when she died."

"Hmm. Well, let's tie the horses to a post here and I'll show you the house."

That noon when he came in from work he found dinner ready for him: boiled potatoes, fried rabbit, oiled lettuce, sugared crab apples.

After he'd had his fill, Anse leaned back to pick his teeth. "Well, and I suppose this is what they call keeping house together."

"Any complaints?"

"Not even one."

"There better not be."

That night Reka opened Anse's only bed on both sides.

Anse accepted the fact with an inward smile. He sat down on his side, and took off his shoes and shirt and overalls, and in his underwear got in on his side. The slats below cracked as he stretched out.

Reka checked the door, slipped a nightgown over her head and took off her dress underneath it, blew out the lamp, and got in on the other side. She moved in a kind of clamped-down frenzy.

Anse, tired, about to drift off into sleep, suddenly felt the point of an elbow in his ribs. He opened his eyes in the dark. "Huh? What? What's the matter?"

Reka gave him another jab in the ribs, this time almost playfully.

He lay very still for several moments; began to throb like everything.

Again Reka gave him a jab, this time with meaning.

Anse knew what the point was all right.

They became man and wife.

That fall they invited the neighbors over for a social hop. So many people came, they had to use cow pumpkins for chairs and halved gourds for drinking cups. Fiddles cried all night long.

Time went on. Anse, instead of selling his crops direct to the elevator, turned more and more to raising beef and to milking cows. He had winning ways with animals. He taught himself animal husbandry by way of university bulletins, soon became one of the most successful breeders and milk producers in the county. For his prize Hereford bulls and heifers he commanded fancy prices; for his milking he got fat cream checks. While Reka kept an immaculate house. She darned and patched and sewed like a professional seamstress. She took charge of the chickens and with them earned their grocery money. With a stove poker and an old beat-up tin dishpan she flagged down many a colony of bees flying by and successfully lured them into her homemade hives. Their land flowed with milk and honey.

As the children came, first big Charlie, then slender Brant, then fine-limbed Konstant, Anse bought more land, an eighty for each of them, for the day when they'd get married.

"You know, woman, by golly, you can't beat living in Siouxland, now can you?"

"No, I guess you can't."

"That's why I mean to live here to the end right beside our fat old cottonwood. With the handles of my plow in my hands." . . .

In the kitchen Mother felt sorry for Pa. What Charlie had just done to Pa shouldn't have happened to even an old horse. Pa deserved better from Charlie.

Mother was also sorry she'd said Pa wasn't getting any younger. She hadn't meant to be mean. But it was in her blood to be blunt.

Mother set the big white kitchen table, putting out tan bowls and silver spoons. She placed a pitcher of honey on the back of the stove to warm. She got a bench from the storage room and slipped it between the table and the wall. It was here Kon and the little girls and the dog Bill would sit. She got some extra chairs from the living room and ringed them around the rest of the table.

The truth was she herself was against retiring and moving to town. What would they do with all their extra time? Fight? They'd be on top of each other like a couple of old useless dogs trying to lay down in the same pile of straw. Snarling and yapping and complaining.

Charlie was wasting his breath if he thought he could talk Pa into it. Nobody changed Pa's mind. On some things Pa could be as stubborn as a badger.

That's a fact.

. . . Reka remembered the day she'd tried to get Anse to build her a new privy. What a time that'd been. He'd dig her a new hole, he said, and he'd move the old privy onto the new hole, and he'd repaint the old privy, but he'd be damned if he'd build her a new one. "The old one is plenty good enough for you. I notice that the hard wind last night still wasn't able to knock it over."

"It's good enough for you," she'd snapped, "because you can use your new barn. In the straw behind the horses there. Or you can go out into your new-tasseled cornfield. Behind the grove there. But me, the only place for me to do number two, let alone number one, is in that rickety old thing."

"Rickety? Why, if it was rickety it'd be all wet in there after a rain. But I notice that even that old catalog hanging in there is still always cork dry."

"If you can have a new barn, I can have a new privy over a new hole."

"And I say no."

"Well, I guess there's nothing for it but for me to use your new barn like you do. Or go out into your new-tasseled corn. First a red cob, then a white one."

Anse jerked; let out one short blat of laughter; fell silent.

"Because I'm not going to use that disgrace of a privy anymore."

Anse wriggled his nose; said nothing; did nothing.

Finally she made up her mind to do what she had to do. She'd saved some chicken money, which was hers to spend as she wished. She checked through the four mail order catalogs she had in the house—Montgomery Ward, Mast & Foos, Sears Roebuck, Savage.

After much soul searching, she decided on Mast & Foos and ordered a privy from them. Theirs was not only the fanciest one, a red affair trimmed in white, but it came with a warranty. "Satisfaction guaranteed for one year or your money back."

When drayman Meard Borman delivered it from Bonnie one day, Anse was outraged. And he spoke his mind about it. "You durn fool woman, so you've throwed your money away on a store-bought craphouse, have you? It won't last out the year."

"We'll see."

"It'll roll on the first good wind."

"We'll see."

Anse absolutely refused to help Meard lift it off the dray. So Reka had to help Meard. Anse also refused to dig her a new hole and put the new privy over it, let alone tear down the old privy and fill the old hole. Charlie and Brant had to come over and do the job.

"And the worst is," Anse said, "it's painted red like my barn is. The only other building."

"Just so it works."

Well, Anse had the last laugh about that. The new fancy privy was a two-and-a-half-holer: a big hole for the men, a more modest one for the women, and a little bitty one for the kids. Reka, and she didn't know why, always preferred the big one. Probably because Anse never used it.

After a while it became apparent that something was wrong with the big hole.

Reka was too proud to ask Anse to fix it.

Finally one day, aggravated, Reka wrote Mast & Foos about her troubles.

The company wrote back a polite letter, asking her to be more specific about her complaint.

Reka tried to oblige them. "It ain't that I want my money back. It's that I ain't satisfied with the way it works. And the way it works ain't for a woman to say."

The company again wrote politely to say that she still should be more specific if she expected them to help her.

Reka and the company exchanged letters back and forth for a month. She wouldn't be specific; and they couldn't help her if she wasn't.

Finally, Mast & Foos, intrigued, and knowing that a year's guarantee was at stake, decided to send down a company trouble-shooter to investigate the matter. Having gathered from the correspondence that they were dealing with an elderly lady, they chose an old-timer by the name of Otis Smylie to represent them. Otis Smylie was an office dandy with a goatee, who had impeccable manners, wore a top hat and a swallowtail coat on all occasions, wore gray spats even in the summertime, and sported a gold-headed cane.

One day Otis Smylie arrived on the Harmer yard.

Anse met him at the gate. When Anse discovered who it was, he called Reka, and then stepped back to watch developments.

The sudden appearance of the old dandy with his white goatee and his gray spats and gold-headed cane didn't faze Reka a particle. It seemed perfectly proper to her that Mast & Foos should send out a respectable gentleman to investigate a complaint about one of their products.

First she invited the old gentleman into the house. Would he like a glass of lemonade?

He would.

A piece of chocolate raisin cake, sir?

Delighted.

"Anse? How about you?"

"I never pass up a piece of chocolate raisin cake. Not when it's served along with a glass of lemonade."

The three exchanged small talk around the kitchen table, pleasantries about relations, gossip about government rascals, rumors of tornadoes in Ohio.

"More lemonade, Mr. Smylie?"

"No, thanks."

"More cake?"

"Thanks, no. It's very good though."

"Anse?"

"I've had sufficient."

Pause.

Otis Smylie took the cue. "Well, now, Mrs. Harmer, about your complaint . . . could you, uh, somehow, uh . . . where do you have our product located?"

Reka got up. "This way."

The two of them went out back.

Anse trailed along behind, lower lip smiling a drop of moisture.

"Hmm," the old gentleman said. "Fine location you have for it, Mrs. Harmer."

"Yes. My boys dug it there for me."

"Setting there up on cement blocks, it looks all right from the outside. What really seems to be the matter with it?"

"It ain't for a woman to say."

"Unless you tell me what it is I won't be able to help you."

"You'll have to look for yourself."

Otis Smylie slowly nodded. And he proceeded to make an in-spection. "Well, now, the door seems to be all right. Swings in without sticking or squeaking. And out."

Reka said nothing.

"The half moon in the door seems to be cut at the proper angle."

Silence.

Otis Smylie stepped inside. He stomped his foot. "The floor seems to feel level and solid. Are you sure there's anything the matter with it?"

"It ain't for a woman to say."

"Hmm." Otis Smylie investigated further. "The inside isn't painted or papered. But of course that wasn't part of the price."

Reka waited.

Otis Smylie ran an exploratory finger around the insides of the two smaller holes. "The baby hole seems to be all right. So does the aperture for the ladies." He looked around at Reka. "Your complaint can't be about the hole for the man, can it?"

"It ain't for a woman to say."

"Well." He ran an exploratory finger around the inner edge of the larger opening too. "Feels all right. No cracks. No, it can't be this one either."

Reka's nostrils opened slightly.

Something in the way she held her head told him that he'd hit on or near the seat of the trouble. Again he ran his finger around the inner edge of the larger opening. "Smooth as a stone crock, I'd say." He looked at her again.

Reka looked back at him, standing very erect.

"That's funny. Must be something I can't see." Otis Smylie re-moved his black top hat, set it circumspectly over the baby hole, tucked back his white goatee and, gray curls first, lowered his head down into the man's hole, into the privy vault itself. Head upside down, Otis Smylie carefully looked around to all sides, swiveling first one way and then the other, face slowly reddening. "Hmm. Everything seems to be shipshape in here too." His voice came partially muffled. "That I can see anyway."

Reka waited alertly.

"Not even a black widow spider around. No. Everything's fine here too." Otis Smylie slowly withdrew his head. As he did so, one of the hairs in his white goatee caught in a tiny invisible crack on the underside of the seat. "Ow," he exclaimed mildly. He paused; then with two fingers gently jerked the caught hair free. He stood up. Red-faced, he threw Reka a glance.

"Aggravatin', ain't it?" Reka said.

Anse almost busted a gut, he laughed so hard.

Reka got her privy fixed. Mast & Foos sent her a check to have it done by a local Bonnie woodworker.

Reka also had it painted a solid white to match the house. . . .

Long after the event Reka sometimes had to laugh about it. Though she was always careful never to laugh about it when Anse was around.

She loved Anse Harmer.

Too bad she had to keep one secret from him. A secret that would have shattered their good life together had he known of it.

. . . Reka's life with her own pa and ma started out innocently enough.

Pa and Ma, Donald and Carrie Heath, were loving parents. They owned a small rocky farm among some low hills in western Pennsylvania. They just barely managed to scratch out a living. But they were happy together. Pa and Ma were always hugging and kissing each other. Or else hugging and kissing the kids. The family grew up very close.

At the same time Ma was one of those who believed in hex witches. She was deathly afraid of their power for evil over cattle. She made Pa put up a hexafoos over the door to the cow barn.

She also wanted Pa to put up a three-toed mark over the door to their house. This Pa refused to do. He thought it a woman's silly notion. Human beings didn't need one.

Ma proved to be right. One awful night she got a terrible case of the cramps. And died.

Pa Heath grieved and grieved for his lost Carrie. He lamented that he hadn't listened to Carrie about putting a hexafoos over the door to their house.

The children felt sorry for Pa. To comfort him they loved him up every chance they got. They'd help him get over losing Ma. Sometimes people visiting them found them all practically sitting in each other's laps on the same sofa.

Pa Heath kept grieving so much, and so long, for his lost lovey Carrie that friends began to worry about him.

Finally the minister came over. It was he who wondered if a change might not be in order. Perhaps Pa should move to another town and get a fresh start. For one thing, the children needed a mother and no local widow would ever want to take up with him the way he had carried on about Carrie.

"We realize," the minister said, "that the death of your wife has been a great affliction to you. But, Donald, you must live for life, not death. The daily sight of your grief is not good for your children. Even if you have no concern for yourself, you must at least think of your children."

"I'll hold the thought, Reverend."

"Of course you still read your Bible, don't you?"

"Never miss a day, Reverend."

"Good."

"But I surely wisht I'd put up that hexafoos over the house door, like Carrie wanted me to. She would be here today, alive and well."

At this the minister became slightly enraged. "What? You still believe in that superstition? Lord God of hosts, when will you people hereabouts be rid of it? Oh. Oh."

"But—"

"Get rid of it. You hear? It is of the Devil. Hellfire beckons those who persist in this superstition."

"But—"

"Better that you were dead and in heaven, than alive because of a hexafoos and aimed for hell."

"All right, Reverend."

Reka was fifteen when Pa Heath finally decided the minister

was right. Like Lot, and like Abraham before him, he would go seek a new way of life in a new land. So he sold his farm, destroyed all sign of the hexafoos, traded his four old plugs in for two new young bay geldings, bought a brand-new covered wagon, put what money he had left into gold pieces, and bid his friends and relatives good-bye.

They headed west. Ohio. Indiana. Illinois.

Near Sheldon, in Siouxland, they rented a quarter section of land. The original owner had gone busted and the bank had taken over the farm. It had a good house, a good barn, a good pig house, and good soil. Pa Heath immediately began dreaming of buying it someday.

They still felt lonesome for Ma Heath. And they remained close as a family. Nights when they went to bed they still gave each other a good tight hug and a warm good-night kiss.

They slept upstairs, Pa and the boy Joseph in the bedroom at the head of the stairs, Reka and her two sisters Amy and Mirabel in the far bedroom.

One summer night, as Reka was about to drop off to sleep, very tired from cooking and cleaning and darning and patching and chicken raising, she heard Pa calling her. His voice was tender, though there was also in it a slight note of accusation. It startled her.

"Reka?"

"Yes?"

"Reka."

Reka sat up in bed. What had she forgotten now? "Yes, Pa?"

"I'm waiting."

Reka scratched through her memory. What was he talking about? Sisters Amy and Mirabel slept soundly beside her.

"Ain't you forgot something, girl?"

"Not that I know of, Pa."

"Something you do every night, lovey."

Her mind blinked. She was tired.

"You don't remember, girl?"

"I'm so tired, Pa."

"It's something you do every night before you go to bed."

He couldn't mean she hadn't gone to the privy, could he? That was none of his business.

"You don't love your pa anymore, I see."

Silence.

"And that even after I give you your mother's sewing bird."

Silence.

"Do you now?"

"Tell me what I forgot, Pa, so I can quick go do it and then go back to sleep."

"Why, lovey, don't you remember? You didn't give me a good-night kiss yet."

"Oh. That."

"Yes."

"Oh, Pa."

"I can see it coming already. My favorite daughter slowly drifting away from me."

Poor Pa. He did like it a lot that she always gave him a tight hug and a kiss at night before she went to bed. Like the other kids did. How could she have forgotten? Poor Pa.

Moonlight was in the room like the soft light of a just lighted kerosene lamp. Moonlight was a lot different from sunlight. Sunlight in a room was like the light of a gas lamp.

"Reka?"

What a pest Pa was about that silly old kiss. Here she was in bed already.

"Reka?"

Sighing, she got up and headed for his room. The hem of her cotton nightgown swished against her ankles.

She entered his bedroom and in bright moonlight stepped toward his bed. She could make out his form under the sheet, gaunt yet strong. His tanned face lay in dark contrast to his white pillow. Beside him lay little Joseph, sound asleep.

Reka smiled, and leaned down to give Pa his kiss, a quick one.

He rose up on one elbow to receive it.

Just as their lips were to touch, she stepped on one of his work shoes lying beside the bed. It startled her, and she misstepped, and they missed lips. She tried again, and this time her foot slipped, and she fell against him so that he sank under her unexpected weight.

He held her tight a second. "Hurt yourself?"

Her knee did hurt where it had hit the edge of the iron bed. "It's all right."

"You sure now?"

"It's all right."

"It'll never do to have the woman of the house hurt, you know."

"Just skun my knee a little is all. It don't hurt none."

"That's good." He held her tighter. "And now, let's have that kiss you forgot to give me." He pushed his rough chin under her chin so as to turn her lips toward him.

"Pa."

He gave her another tight hug and then kissed her soundly.

She liked lying on him. It was high time she got a man of her own. For the hundredth time she felt sorry for her father. It was also high time he got himself a bed partner.

Crickets whirred in the grass outdoors. Very far away some dog howled into the night. A breath of air rising off the alfalfa field behind the grove came in through the open window. The alfalfa air touched her face. It was swooning sweet.

Dear God, but she was tired.

A groan escaped him.

There were sudden tears in her eyes. She remembered how he'd groaned the day they lowered Ma into her grave. Poor Pa. In the moonlight through her tears the whole room became a silver hall. She turned and threw her arms around Pa and kissed him fulsomely on the lips.

Another groan escaped him.

"Poor Pa."

Suddenly he kissed her back. He hugged her. And also of a sudden his big broad hands were touching her everywheres through her flimsy cotton nightgown. "Little Carrie."

She whispered, "Pa, there's Joseph there."

His hand next slipped under her nightgown. "He's dead to the world. Sound asleep."

"Pa."

"I know. I shouldn't be doing this."

"No, you shouldn't."

"But, oh, it's so hard to live without a wife. For a man that's already knowed a wife."

"I know, Pa. Because pretty soon I'd better have a partner too."

"And you're so like her."

"Pa."

"So like her when we first got married."

"Pa!"

"God!" Pause. "All right."

"That's better."

They lay in loving suspense. Dangling. The one knowing, the other wondering. Yet neither the one nor the other.

Moonlight dreamed into the bedroom. The biceps of his right arm was like a corn ear against her breasts. His arm trembled at moments.

This was risky. Yes, it was time they both found themselves a sweetheart. Poor Pa.

She thought of Lot and of Lot's daughters, and of how they too were lonesome when they dwelt in the mountains. She remembered the saying of Lot's firstborn daughter, that their father was old, and that they had not a man to come into them after the manner of all the earth, that they should make their father drink wine and lie with them so that they might preserve his seed.

Of course Lot's story did not quite fit their case. Ma Heath had been a loving and an obedient wife. Nor had she turned to a pillar of salt. And Pa Heath also had a son Joseph through whom his seed might pass on.

She moved to withdraw from Pa's embrace. To raise herself she had to brace her hand. Her hand fell on his hard thigh. She could feel it jump to her touch inside his long-handled underwear.

He mistook her touching for something else.

It was begun in a moment. Moonlight became sudden sunlight. She received him before she realized what it meant.

Too late.

In a daze she dreamed back to her room.

She slipped into bed. She pressed the back of her head deep into her pillow. She lay staring at the ceiling.

It was darker. The moon was almost down.

The single white house in the lonesome green country cracked and rested and cracked and waited.

No sound came from her father's bedroom.

Pa shouldn't have got rid of Ma's hexafoos.

At last, with a groan of her own, she turned to her sleeping sisters, Amy and Mirabel, and embraced them and wept on their tender necks.

The next morning at sunup when she went down to make breakfast, she found Pa had already had his coffee and left for the fields.

That noon he didn't come in to dinner. She had to put his share of the steaming potatoes and fried beef away. The children looked a little lost that Pa didn't come in to eat.

But he came in for supper. He spent a lot of time at the washstand out by the gate, scrubbing his neck, parting and reparting his brown hair, thoroughly cleaning his shoes on the shoe scraper. When he entered the white kitchen, he avoided her eyes. He answered the children's queries with short grunts. He appeared to be so deep in the dumps that the children finally fell silent.

Reka's thighs burned. She wondered what would become of them. She wondered what sin the people of Sodom and Gomorrah had committed that they should deserve destruction by brimstone and fire. Was the sin she and her father had committed the unforgivable sin? Would it put them in jeopardy of eternal hellfire?

For two months they lived in a strange silence on the farm.

Gradually the children Amy and Mirabel and Joseph got used to it.

Reka got used to it too. She hadn't been got with child and so slowly the incident began to stand off to one side in her mind.

The next fall Pa talked about moving again. He'd heard of a farm for sale near Whitebone, in Minnesota.

The children liked it where they were. They told Pa they didn't want to move yet again.

Pa shook his head. Sorry. But he just had to move on. Had to. But why, Pa?

Because he didn't like it by Sheldon anymore. Besides, he missed the hills back in Pennsylvania, and at this new place near Whitebone there were some stone hills called the Blue Mounds, and he thought maybe he might feel more to home there.

"But we like it where it's flat, Pa."

"I know. But for old time's sake let's just get out our old prairie schooner again and drive over and have a look at this new place. A look won't hurt, will it? We'll make a kind of a picnic trip out of it. The good Lord knows we could all use a little fun once, we've all been so down in the mouth lately."

A picnic trip?

They packed a few clothes and several hampers of food, and off they rolled across the country, going northwest.

The farm proved to be too stony. It was worse even than the one they'd had in Pennsylvania. It lay some half dozen miles north of Whitebone up on the plateau behind the Blue Mounds escarpment. It had a few trees, some scrub oaks, but they were very old, gnarly, and only head high. Pa shook his head. Unless they got a lot of rain there'd be no crops.

They lingered in the area a few days. They stopped to camp at the springs near the Blue Mounds. It was a soft autumn and it was wonderful sleeping out on the grass under the open skies. Happy that they weren't going to be moving after all, and that the trip had truly turned out to be only a picnic trip, the three little ones played and played in the deep grass.

That night when they went to bed they each gave Pa a kiss and a hug like in the old days.

Because the children expected her to do likewise, Reka kissed Pa too. The kiss burned her.

Darkness came on.

She lay tossing in her blanket on the grass. She couldn't erase the touch of his rough lips on her mouth.

The stars slowly moved by overhead.

When later he came creeping over the grass, with the children sound asleep, she didn't deny him.

The fog of silence returned to their family life, deeper than ever.

Then the next spring he made up his mind to really pull up stakes and head farther west. He'd heard of some good land near Lost Lake, west of Sioux Falls. And rolling west, it was then that she met Anse under the giant cottonwood tree. . . .

Mother wept for Pa.

Soon the honey on the back of the stove began to seethe. She pushed it farther back, over the reservoir.

She went to the door and looked out on the darkened veranda.

Kon was sweating. The ice cream freezer began to turn heavier and heavier. Kon had to kneel on it to keep it from straying off the walk. Deep bass crunching noises came out of the freezer's innards. A dozen or so more turns and the ice cream would be done.

Charlie was talking in a softer tone of voice. "You see, Pa, it's this way. You can't always be up there swinging. Now it's our turn to bat."

Pa rocked in his rocker. "I see already where I made a mistake giving you two older boys your eighty. I should've kept you down more. Made you wait until my will was read. Kept you guessing."

"Wait," Brant said. "Don't you go putting me in with Charlie. I didn't know he had this in mind when he called this meeting tonight. It ain't my idea."

Charlie said, "Each generation has got a right to show what it can do at bat."

Pa said, "The trouble is, you boys take me for an old piece of potato. You think you can plant me in the ground and then suck me for my juice so you can get your start."

Kon grunted as the handle turned slower and slower.

Edna was already licking her lips thinking of the wonderful homemade ice cream to come.

Pauline put her arms around the dog Bill and gave him a kiss.

The dog Bill, delighted, licked her back, slurping her from chin to forehead, once, with a long red tongue.

Edna gave Pauline a disgusted look. "You let Bill kiss you!"

Pauline rubbed heads with Bill. "I love Bill."

"I suppose you're gonna let him lick your ice cream too."

"If he wants to."

"He's not going to lick my ice cream."

"That's cuz you're selfish."

"Uncle Kon, am I selfish if I don't let Bill lick my ice cream?"

"What?" Kon hadn't been listening. "Nobody's going to lick anybody."

Pa got to his feet. "Boys, my mind's made up. I found this place alone. I earned this place alone. I built it up alone. And, by the Lord, I intend to die on it alone." Pa pointed a finger at Charlie. In the reflected gas light from the kitchen door he resembled an aged angel disappointed by what he'd found on earth. "And, Charlie, I'll hear no more about this. You hear?"

"Rrm."

Kon turned the freezer handle one more turn. It took all his strength.

Edna and Pauline, who'd been watching for that last turn, beat Kon to the announcement. "Ice cream's ready!" they cried together.

Kon, puffing, had to laugh. "Yes, I guess it's ready."

Mother pushed out through the screen door and held it open. "All right then, everybody. Inside for the refreshments."

"I get to lick the dasher," Edna cried.

"But it's my turn," Pauline cried.

"Shh, now," Kon said. "Or I'll make it Bill's turn."

"Good," Charlie said. "Now I can throw away this durned choker." And with one swipe of his hand he jerked off the red flannel rag with its onion rings.

Soon they were all seated around the table, Pa at the head, the children and the dog Bill and Kon on the bench against the wall, Mother nearest the stove, the rest of the grown-ups opposite the children. Each had his tan bowl heaping full of dark gold ice cream, even Bill, and all, except Bill, had his ice cream topped with hot running honey. The gas lamp over the table shed a clear brilliant light upon them. All the tanned faces had the luminous orange luster of ripe pumpkins.

All waited until Mother picked up her spoon and took the first taste. After she savored it, and had nodded her head that it would pass, all pitched in, nine flashing silver spoons and one long red tongue.

"Mmmm," the little girls said.

"Mmm," Kon said.

"Llurrp," Bill said.

"Rrm," Charlie said.

While the ladies proved out the ice cream with delicate little licks.

Pa listened to all the mmming around him and couldn't help but smile a little. "It's like I always said . . . a land flowing with milk and honey."

Little more was said until the last bit was spooned and licked up from all the tan bowls.

"More, anyone?" Mother called out.

Mildred placed a hand over her middle. "Not for me. I'm too fat for Brant already."

"And I'm full to the gills," Brant said.

"And I says to Charlie too, I said, I better not either," Inez said.

Charlie glared at Inez. "You ain't said nothing to me yet about gettin' too fat."

"Well, I have too. Now."

Charlie shook his head. "That dumb woman of mine. You never know when she's telling you something if it's yet gonna happen or if it's happened already."

Mother smiled down at Edna and Pauline and the dog Bill. "Children?"

Both girls gave their father and mother a look, then shyly pushed their bowls forward. It was plain both had been told before coming over not to act like little pigs. The dog Bill sat with a slightly more expectant look than usual, his eyebrows quirked and his brow gravely wrinkled.

Both Mildred and Brant frowned warning smiles.

Kon felt tender toward his little nieces. Brant held them at arm's length too much. Kon gave the girls a wide flashing smile. "Oh, give them all some more, Gramma. Bill too. They've still got to catch up with us."

Mother gave the girls a warm grave smile. "It's good to see you little ones obeying your pa and ma. But around Gramma, you always obey her first, nah?" Mother reached for their bowls and filled them from the freezer and once again topped their ice creams with a liberal helping of hot honey. The dog Bill got a plain dish of ice cream.

"Thank you very much, Gramma." Both girls gave Mildred and Brant twisted little smiles.

"Anyone else?" Gramma called out.

Charlie pushed his bowl forward. "I'll take some. I work hard."

Inez wrinkled her lips at Charlie.

Pa had a warm smile for the children too as he in turn pushed his bowl forward. "I think maybe I ought to have a little more. Just to stay ahead of you two tykes, the way you're catching up so fast."

Mother filled both Charlie's and Pa's bowls.

Melted ice cream in the bottom of his bowl reminded Brant of something. "Anybody know how to keep a cow from sucking herself?"

Charlie ate his ice cream with quick tiny dips. It melted faster in his mouth that way. "You got one of them?"

"Yeh. At first I thought it was maybe milk snakes draining her. But then one day I caught her at it. She's a heavy giver, or I'd sell her."

"Rrm. A cow sucking herself comes pretty close to bein' perpetual motion."

Brant grunted a grudging laugh.

Charlie said, "So you want to know what to do about it?"

"Yeh."

"You'll take some advice from me then?"

"I'll try."

"All right. I tell you what you do." Charlie enjoyed playing the role of the master stallion. "And you can bet your sweet life it'll work too." Charlie licked up yet another quick dip of ice cream. "You take and get you a tough piece of ash board an inch thick. Cut off a piece about eight inches long and four inches wide. Shape it to look like the pincers of a crab. The opening of the pincers shouldn't be any more'n a quarter of an inch wide, just big enough for the divider in the cow's nose to pop into it. Round the whole thing off, rasp it down nice and smooth, so the edges won't cut the animal and cause sores."

"Rasp it down t'while the cow's got it on?"

"Oh, for godsakes, Brant, don't rag me. You know what I mean. With this hobble in her nose she can't get at her own tits. The hobble keeps pushing her tits away just as she reaches for 'em. At the same time it allows her to drink water from a tank and eat grass from the ground."

Brant held his head to one side, considering the idea, trying to find something wrong with it.

The children and the dog Bill finished their ice creams.

Mildred decided that that was enough for one day. She pushed back her chair and got to her feet. With a warm womanly smile she looked down at the children and the dog. "I think it's high time for little children to be in bed. Come, now. Into the car with you."

Edna didn't think much of the idea. She looked to Uncle Kon for support.

Kon smiled at them at the same time that he shook his head at them. "Now, now, you better mind your mother now."

Edna said, "You say that 'cause you're a teacher."

"Now!" Brant warned.

Kon laughed. "No flies on her."

"But I don't like it that she makes smart remarks like that," Brant said.

"Oh, it's all right. The child was only speaking the truth." Kon laughed some more. "They should obey, of course. But sometimes they should also be allowed to have their say."

Pa smiled upon Edna. "I can see already where that little girl's gonna be a dead ringer for her gramma. Blunt."

Mother threw Pa a darting look. "Ha. Another country heard from."

Then Charlie finished his second bowl of ice cream and they all went home.

2

A month later, curious to know what Karen Alfredson had done about the Horsberg-Windmiller mess, Kon decided to return her visit. He dismissed school early and walked the two miles across country and arrived at Karen's school just as her pupils were heading down the road for home.

Kon mounted the stoop, and there was Karen, emerging with the school bucket to throw the stale water away.

"Well," Kon said, "hello, neighbor."

Karen stared offish at him.

Kon smiled. "Are you busy?"

"What are you doing here?"

"Why . . . just that it was my turn to visit you."

She shook herself; and then a little smile broke through her blunt manner. "I'm sorry, but I guess I just had a bad day." Slowly a warm gold crept into the edges of her green eyes. She threw the stale water out onto the grass and then set the bucket to one side. "Won't you come in?"

"Thank you. Yes."

Kon noted instantly that her schoolhouse smelled different from his. And it wasn't just the smell of a different brand of floor compound either. It had something to do with overly scrubbed flesh, like he sometimes smelled on Mother.

Karen offered him the visitor's chair in back and drew up another for herself. She sat facing him. She had on a light-green dress with a black belt.

Kon crossed his legs, careful to pull up his light-gray trousers at the knees to save the crease.

Karen said, "I'm sorry if everything's still a little topsy-turvy. I haven't finished redding up the place yet."

"I know what you mean."

Karen sighed. "The way things've been going lately I'm not going to last out the year."

Kon thought: "Now if I'll just have a little patience she'll bring up the subject of Adolph and Tessie herself. Which is better than if I did it."

"Work work. Rush rush. And I'm not getting nearly enough sleep."

Kon sat back and folded his arms.

Karen sighed again. "Yes. And then there's that Tessie and Adolph poser I told you about."

"I've been wondering what'd happened to them."

"Oh, it's not that they haven't behaved while in school. Because they have. No, it's what they've been doing after they leave the school grounds that grinds me."

Kon waited.

"Oh, if only the parents could catch them little stinkers at it once. Then they'd know. But of course they never will. Because now those little stinkers are careful to do it in a secret place."

"Where?"

Karen didn't answer right away. The green in her eyes turned milky. The slim fingertips of her right hand played absentmindedly over the back of her left hand.

"You don't have to tell me."

Her eyes were quickly clear and green again. "Oh, but I want to. Come. Follow me. It's in the deserted farmstead."

"Well . . ."

"Come."

"All right."

Outside, the late-afternoon sun struck at them from behind the schoolhouse, strewing some of the whiteness of the building over the lemon leaves of the ash trees ahead of them and giving the air above them the clarity of fresh well water.

As they stepped through the ditch, a song sparrow fell out from underfoot. They'd almost stepped on its nest in the grass. The song sparrow spurted straight up.

"Whoa'p!" Kon said, quickly holding up a hand.

Karen stopped beside him, one foot up on toetip.

Kon knelt. "Ah. Look. See how cunningly our little mother hid her little home under this bull thistle? Down under it right on the ground? No wonder the schoolchildren never found it. Or any other marauders."

Karen's eyes opened very green at the lovely discovery.

"Well, now," he said, "that was fun, wasn't it? To spot that little home?"

"Yes. Too bad I don't dare to show the children."

Kon nodded. "Isn't it the truth. There's always one rascal who'll go poking in and break the eggs just for the fun of it."

They crossed the road.

The deserted farmstead lay catercorner across from the schoolyard. A windbreak of dying box elders ran along the north and west sides. Just inside the windbreak a row of lilacs still stood a strong and vivid green. The garden had grown over with pigweed. The yard was deep with waving plumes of foxtail and gay white daisies.

A barely discernible path led down the middle of the lane and then veered toward the house. Karen and Kon followed it, going single file. They dodged past a patch of light-green bull thistles, vicious and spiny, and standing higher than their heads.

The barn and the sheds were completely weathered gray. All their windows and doors were out. The house, never the best building in the old days, was in even worse shape. Wind had peeled off most of the curled brown shingles as well as a good share of the clapboards on all sides. The house resembled the skeletal remains of an almost devoured prairie mammoth. Great ragweeds under the gaping bay window appeared to be growing inside as well as outside the house.

Karen took a careful step onto the porch and then on light toes entered the open door. Kon followed, equally careful.

Karen led the way across what had once been the kitchen, then across the living room, and last into a side room. Chunks of fallen plaster lay everywhere. The place was already full of evening shadows. "There. Right there they do it now." Karen pointed at an old rusty spring on the floor. It was covered with a spotted khaki army blanket. There were black mouse droppings everywhere, on the yellowish-brown blanket as well as on the floor.

"No."

Karen nodded. "They come here Sundays. I know because I happened to catch them once. Sometimes on Sundays after church, I come to the schoolhouse to put the next day's lessons on the blackboard. Last week I hadn't more'n started chalking away, when I happened to look out of the front door, and there was Adolph Horsberg sneaking by. Along the edge of the cornfield there. 'Oho,' I says to myself, 'I bet I know what you're up to.' I watched, and sure enough, there comes Tessie Windmiller sneaking down the other side of the cornfield. Then they both disappeared into the grove of this deserted farm."

"You followed them?"

"Yes, on tiptoe. And caught them."

Kon stared down at the khaki blanket, then at the falling walls and the collapsing ceiling. Those children were playing house with a vengeance.

"I can't understand what they see in it. I just simply can't. It's just like they're a couple of dope fiends. I guess when it's once in them they can't help themselves. They've just simply got to have more of it."

"Maybe they should get married."

"Crazy with it . . . What? Get married? So young? They shouldn't have babies yet, Mr. Harmer, when they're still babies themselves."

Kon allowed himself a chuckle. "And I'm not saying that because I'm the marrying kind either."

"Well, at least that's good to hear."

"Though some animals do mate early. Pa's often mentioned it."

"But surely not human beings, Mr. Harmer."

"Well, maybe not."

"I'm a Christian, Mr. Harmer, and I believe that the good Lord created the human being apart."

"You're sure about that?" Kon was thinking of his brother Charlie.

"I've seen flies go after raisin pies but this has them beat."

The shadows deepened inside the house. Mice squealed in a far upstairs bedroom.

Kon asked, "How old is this Horsberg boy?"

"Sixteen."

"Hum. Old enough to be a father then."

"Is that the age?"

"I've heard of some becoming fathers at fifteen."

"Disgraceful!"

"How old is this Windmiller girl?"

"Tessie is fourteen."

"Hmm. She's old enough too."

"Disgraceful!"

"It wouldn't be the first time. Out on the frontier people often got married that young."

"And their lives wrecked forever."

"No, not necessarily." Kon threw her a sidewise look, then quickly added, "Of course, you understand I'm for late marriages myself. If at all."

"I was going to say."

"But some people do grow up early."

"Those stinkers. I'm having a worse time breaking them of it than Pa did breaking our old dog Sport of sucking eggs."

Kon had to smile.

"I just wish lightning could strike this awful place and burn it down to the ground, trees and all. It's of no use to anyone, really."

"Well, now, perhaps we shouldn't wish anybody any back luck. When they've probably had enough already."

Karen couldn't keep her eyes off the spotted khaki blanket. Suddenly she bent down and snapped it off the rusty spring. Mouse droppings sprayed around them like spent shot. Her face wrinkled up in savage disgust as she gingerly rolled it up into a ball. "I'm going to at least burn this. In the school stove."

"It's going to take more than that to break our dog of sucking eggs."

"I suppose it is."

"I've seen some strange lovers' lanes in my time but this one has them all beat."

"You can say that again."

They stood a moment longer in the brown gathering dusk and then Karen, done with it, led the way outside.

The setting sun struck sideways through the windbreak. Tall gaunt shadows lay like specters on the gaping barn. The waving plumes of foxtail glowed like just poured molten copper. The gay white daisies nodded, sometimes by twos and threes, sometimes in crowds.

Kon spotted something that was a different white in the weeds. He stepped over for a look. Bones. "Look here."

Karen stepped over too, long green dress rustling in the weeds. "They aren't human, are they?"

Kon knelt for a closer look. "I don't know. Too big for a sheep. Too small for a cow."

"You know, seeing this place from my school window, I've often wondered what might have happened to the owners that they should have deserted it."

"It does make a person wonder, doesn't it? From the way the weeds grow, it's got to be good land. So they couldn't have left because it was a bad farm."

"I asked the Murrays about it once. But they wouldn't talk about it. There seems to be some kind of mystery here that makes people clam up. A murder. Or something else awful."

"Maybe another case of some suck-egg dog. But this time he got shot up for it."

"You think so?"

"Could be. Stranger things than that have happened out here in the country, you know."

Karen stood looking at it all—at the bones, at the old buildings, at the masses of waving weeds, at the hip-deep grass growing wild in the fields—and then said, with a deep sigh, "Poor people, to be so in the grip of it."

"Yes."

Karen fell into a reverie. Her green eyes half closed. She stood very still.

Kon watched her, intrigued.

After a moment her lips parted, and she whispered, more to herself than to him,

> "Bones white,
> Boards gray,
> Fields in blight
> Even the daisy hay."

Kon's eyes opened in admiration. Why, she was making poetry out of it. This strange slim girl who was almost taller than he, why, she was full of surprises. "You made that up, didn't you?"

"Made what up—that about Tessie and Adolph?"

"No, no. I mean, that lovely little poem you just now made up."

"Oh, that."

"It sounded impromptu."

"Well . . . I guess it was at that."

"You write poetry?"

"Not any more." Slowly, even a little sadly, she shook her head. "And anyway, there was something wrong with that third line."

"Sounded fine to me."

"No, there was something wrong with it. 'Fields in blight' . . . no, that doesn't go with the rest very well."

"Well, then, think about it some more. Maybe it'll come right later."

"No, I've given that all up. What you just now heard just happened to slip out of me before I knew it."

"You're too hard on yourself."

"Oh, but, Mr. Harmer, I'm not a genius. So it's silly of me to be even thinking about writing poetry."

The sun burned a red hole for itself into the horizon; then fell into it. In another moment a deep maroon suffused the dying yellow box elders and the dark-green lilacs and the old gray collapsing buildings.

They left the grove.

Karen said, "Oh, dear. Well, I guess now I'd better get on home and start earning my room and board."

"Here too. Next thing you know, Pa and Mother'll be sending out a posse, wondering what happened to me."

A look of mild envy quirked the outer corners of her green eyes. "You're fortunate you have a family to worry about you."

"Heh. Sometimes they can be an awful handicap. Worse even than having your legs paralyzed from the hips down."

"I'd give anything if I could just have my little brother Abbott here for an hour." Karen glanced at Kon's hands. "Oh, how I'd just love to hug him up again. And kiss him."

"Well, good day to you."

"Thank you. And thank you for coming."

Each went their own way.

Two weeks after Christmas, Kon was surprised to have Karen pay him her second visit. It was a mild winter day and lovely for walking. There was only a light film of snow on the ground.

First thing she said was, "Well, you were right about Adolph and Tessie."

"What happened?"

"The two were missing when school started after vacation."

Kon waited.

"Of course, I knew right away something was up. Especially by the way my pupils were staring at me when they arrived at school. So I took Adolph's young brother Darl to one side and asked him where his brother was."

"What did he say?"

"That he'd eloped with Tessie to Nebraska."

"He did!"

"Disgraceful."

"Maybe it was high time."

"Mr. Harmer!"

"Well, Miss Alfredson, that's the way things are out here in the country."

"You may be glad you didn't have that mess in your school."

"Well, they keep seeing the pigs and the cows at it day after day."

"Maybe so. But if that's true then there is no hope."

"Oh, I wouldn't say that."

"Well, anyway, with those stinkers gone maybe now I can have a smoother time of it the rest of the year."

Kon looked down at the nails of his fingers. "Come to think of it, though, I almost did have a mess on my hands once. With that Tom Priester boy."

"A mess like mine?"

"No, not like yours. Different."

"How different?"

Kon couldn't hold up to her suddenly piercing green eyes. "Let's just say that there was a lot of trouble ready to break loose in my Tom and that I just barely managed to steer him straight."

3

The boy Thomas Priester was a fine-looking youngster. He was a slight fellow with slim arms and legs and a lithe blade of a body. He had well-shaped hands. He had an especially noble head, which he carried like a Greek runner. His light hair flashed white in the summer and flowed like foxtail silver in the winter. His skin had one color summer or winter—a light healthy-looking gold. His eyes were a very light blue, almost without any hue at all, and so keen not many could hold up to him. He was especially quick to sense other people's moods. He was as much at home with whimsy as he was with serious talk. His mother, Sarah Priester, was quite aware that her baby Tom was an exceptional child, and she went to some trouble to keep him in good clothes at school. Since he was her last child, she lavished love on him that she had not been able to give her older children. It hurt one to see how pleased she was when Kon took a special interest in Tom, and she hoped out loud that of all her boys at least Tom might make something of himself in the great wide world. He was their fine boy; perhaps even God's chosen.

Of Tom's older brothers, four were baseball players. Two of them were good enough to make the Bonnie town team. Thus when the Priesters began to limber up the old soup bone in late April, it was quite natural for Tom to carry the Priester baseball fever with him to school. From somewhere he rounded up an old baseball, and a cracked bat, and two old tattered fielder's gloves, one for the catcher and the other for the first baseman. The baseball had been resewn a dozen times, the bat was heavily taped up with black friction tape all the way from the knob to the trademark, and the gloves had about as much padding in them as a buttermilk pancake.

The very first warm spring day Tom got a work-up game going during noon recess, with everybody playing, the swift as well as the clumsy, even the girls. Tom explained the rules as they went along and within a half hour he had them knowing enough about the game for them to quarrel with authority.

Kon, grading papers at his desk, became vaguely aware that there'd been a change in the school ground play. New and different cries were coming in through the open windows. But it wasn't until a foul ball just missed hitting a near window that he learned what it was. The thud of the ball on the window frame made him jump up and run over to go see what the dickens was going on.

Baseball.

Baseball? Now there was something he didn't like at all. Certainly not at any school he taught. He wanted the children to have good clean fun during recess hour, their own fun if possible and not started by him. But baseball? Baseball was despised by the Harmers even more perhaps than smoking or drinking. Baseball was the Devil's own play and made for lazy good-for-nothing loafers.

Kon stared out at the playground. Yes, and worse yet, there was his dear boy Tom Priester running the show.

Kon had never seen Tom so alive. Tom was all over the place like a two-legged silver hound, running, leaping, frolicking. A couple of elastic strides and a rising jump, and he'd catch the ball over his shoulder. When Tom threw to first, or to home, the ball seemed to shoot out of his hand as if propelled by a slingshot. When some little toddler came clumsily up to bat, or made a poor play in the field, Tom stopped play and patiently showed him how to do it. He also had time to help the girls, giggle as they might, which was quite surprising as he never had time for them otherwise.

The more Kon watched Tom play, the more he realized he was seeing a side of Tom he hadn't known was there. What he'd had in mind for Tom to become was a botany teacher. Like he himself should have been. But a tobacco-chewing baseball player? God forbid.

The boy must have got it from the father, old Jake Priester. Old Jake had been a renowned ball player. While Sarah Priester, remembering their second son, Clarence, must have decided to let Tom play because she didn't want another Clarence on their hands.

Kon recalled the uproar Clarence had caused a few years back. Clarence had never dated a girl, had never cared about Saturday-night fun uptown, hadn't even cared a snap for baseball. Clarence'd had only one real interest in life—his baby brother Tom.

Tom for his part had loved Clarence to idolatry. Tom imitated Clarence in everything he did. He followed him everywhere he went on the farm. He slept with his brother Clarence. He even refused to listen to old Jake unless Clarence said it was all right.

Kon remembered the day Sarah Priester came to him, face strained, and pale and red by turns. She asked him if there wasn't something wrong with brothers liking each other that much. "It's like Clarence is poisoning him."

Kon didn't know what to say. He almost loved Tom that much himself.

"I've talked to the minister about it. But he says it's just an unusual case of brother love. That it's perfectly all right. That I should just let nature take its course. But I don't know."

Kon wondered out loud, "Why doesn't your husband kick Clarence out of the nest and make him go it on his own?"

"That's just what Jake has got to do," Sarah said. "Somehow."

Later on, Kon was to wonder more than once if his casual remark hadn't brought about what happened next. Clarence drowned in the Big Sioux River.

The drowning was a strange one. It happened that swimming was the only sport Clarence enjoyed a little, because Tom loved water, and he'd made himself into a strong swimmer. When they found Clarence's pale body with its dark tanned face and arms floating in the river, there was no sign of cramps to account for his going down. . . .

Looking out of the school window, Kon saw that it was Tom's turn to bat.

The fielders all backed up when they saw Tom pick up the old taped-up bat, some all the way to the fence. Even the pitcher stood farther back than usual. Tom stood slightly crouched, bat poised behind his right ear. The pitcher threw. Whack! and the ball took off like a pheasant flushed out of grass, slowly rising in a straight line, soaring over the fence, then slowly settling into the cornfield beyond. That ended the game for the moment. Tom first ran around the bases, with everybody shouting, "Home run! Home run!" and then he and the rest sallied out into the cornfield to look for the ball.

Kon's chin came down. Leaving the school grounds was against the rules. Now he had them where he wanted them. This was as good a time as any to crush the boy's craze for baseball.

By the time Kon got outside, the children had found the ball and were piling out of the cornfield again, some under the fence, some over, and were running back to their positions to play some more.

"Just a moment!"

All turned to stare at their teacher.

"Have you children forgotten the rule about leaving the schoolyard? That you must first have permission?"

Some of the flushed faces blanched a little.

"And you, Tom, you of all people."

Tom pretended surprise.

"Yes, you, Tom."

At that Tom flashed Kon a burning blue look.

"What do you have to say for yourself, Tom?"

"Nothing."

"You didn't know about the rule?"

Tom scuffed at the grass, disgusted. "Sure I knew about the rule."

"Well, then?"

"Oh, Teach, we can't always be running in to you to get permission for every little thing we do. It was just an old ball that went over the fence a little ways. And we didn't go running across the road either. It was for running across the road that you made the rule in the first place."

Kon couldn't help but admire the boy. Tom had grit. "Just the same, I'm not sure I like the idea of you playing a game that takes you off the school ground every so often."

"Oh, Teach."

"Well, suppose you'd have hit the ball over the road?"

Tom had only contempt for that idea.

"Strange things do happen in a baseball game, you know."

"That's why it's so much fun."

The boy really did have spunk, didn't he? Kon forced a pleasant smile to his lips. "Tom, I tell you, I'm not sure I'm in favor of you playing baseball at all."

"Why not?" Again Tom flashed Kon a burning blue look.

"It tends to make loafers out of people."

"My brothers ain't loafers."

"Tom."

"Well, they ain't."

"They aren't, Tom."

"Don't you dare to say anything bad about my brothers."

"Why, Tom!"

"Baseball is a wonderful game. They wouldn't have a World Series every year if they didn't think it was all right. And look at the great Ty Cobb. That's what I'm going to be."

"That's enough of that now! There'll be no more baseball this noon." Kon grabbed hold of his fob and pulled out his watch. "Besides, noon recess is about over. Nancy Beers, will you go ring the bell?"

Tom was furious. He took a step toward Kon. "But why, Teach? We need them couple of minutes to finish our work-up game. So that everybody's had a chance to bat. Them's our minutes. Just because I hit a home run."

"Nancy, go ring that bell."

The next day, just before noon recess, Kon announced that right after they'd all had lunch the whole school would go for a hike. They were going to look at a rare new flower.

Fifteen young faces stared up at him dismayed.

"It's a rare flower that our own Thomas Priester found last fall. It grows beside a big red boulder just inside the Priester line fence." Kon let his glance slide over to where Tom sat in back to see how he was taking it.

Tom was staring at him from his desk with hate in his eyes.

"We know what this flower looks like in the fall," Kon went on to say, "but not in the spring. And I thought it would be great fun if we could all go have a look at it when it's just beginning to shoot up out of the grass." Again Kon couldn't resist a look at Tom.

Tom's nostrils were slowly turning white along the edges.

"Don't you think that'll be great fun, children?"

There wasn't a wiggle in the room.

"What about you, Tom? You discovered it. It may even be named after you someday. If it proves to be truly a new flower."

"No!" Tom shouted.

"What?"

"No!"

Kon began to tremble. Why, the ungrateful little brat. After all he'd done for him. Opening up to him the wonderful world of botany. He ought to go over and grab the boy by the neck and give him a good choking.

Heads slowly craned around in the schoolroom to have a look

at this strange creature who'd dared to defy the teacher. Was this their own goodhearted Tom Priester?

Kon swallowed. He bit back angry words. He made up his mind that no little upstart of a Jake Priester boy was going to get his goat. He swallowed some more. And, after a moment, Kon could feel a smile of a kind slowly edging along his lips. "Well, in any case, the rest of us are going to enjoy our flower hunt, aren't we, even if Tom isn't?" Kon's smile gathered strength. "Tell you what let's do. We'll take our lunch with us and go sit on the big red rock and eat it there. What do you say?"

Nancy Beers was the only one to nod her head in agreement. Nancy had naturally curly brown hair and was quite vain about it. She had long wanted to be teacher's pet and had been jealous of Tom.

"But if Master Thomas doesn't care to go with us, to make further study concerning his own find, well, I guess that is his American privilege. He can man the fort here while we're gone."

Nancy turned her head slightly and gave Tom a pair of glittering eyes; and then very deliberately, with a side eye for Kon, stuck out her tongue at Tom. For a second the tip of her tongue actually seemed to flitter a little like a garter snake's.

But the skies decreed otherwise. About a minute later there was a rattle of thunder above the schoolhouse. Even as Kon strolled to the near window to have a look, a high shadow struck the schoolhouse. Well. A blackish-blue cloud bank stood off to the west. Already its ends were rushing off to either side of them, to the north and to the south, as if to encircle them.

Kon watched it come on for a moment. He saw rain striking the old Walker place. South of them it had already hit Karen Alfredson's school.

Kon turned to face the room. "Well," he said, a touch of the sheepish edging into his smile, "well, it seems the good Lord has other plans for us. We're going to have to postpone our jaunt."

A smile slowly crept over Tom's face just as he hid it behind a geography book.

Kon took some comfort in the fact that Tom had tried to hide the smile.

The next day Kon didn't bring up the matter of a possible hike to the Priester pasture. By that time he just didn't have the heart to. He couldn't deny Tom his fun. So the children went back to playing work-up baseball.

4

Ever since the night Charlie had tried to talk Pa into retiring, Pa had gone out of his way to show them how tough and self-sufficient he still was. Pa rejected Brant's offer to help him with the threshing and the corn picking. Pa even cut down on what he expected of Kon. Charlie's cruel words had the effect of rousing Pa to his full powers again.

One night late in May, Pa told Kon he could at last start college that summer if he still wanted to go. He wasn't needed on the farm. Of course he'd be expected to pay his own way.

Kon jumped at the chance, and early in June took the Cannonball for Morningside College in Sioux City. Thus began for him the long treadmill of going to summer sessions during vacation and teaching the rest of the year.

Kon scrimped and saved. He never went out, neither in Sioux City nor at home. The only person he ever saw much of outside of his family was Karen Alfredson at Rock No. 3, and that only at county meetings.

Kon's heavy schedule was interrupted only once. In 1918, during World War I, he was drafted into the Army for six months. But he wasn't sent abroad. He spent most of his time as a male nurse in an Army hospital near Sioux City. He helped in a venereal disease ward, and while there learned just enough about the amorous side of life to be even more offish with the women.

Eight years after he'd begun going to summer school at Morningside, he still had only managed to complete three years of college. Disgusted at how long it was taking him, Kon decided to ask Pa to help him his senior year.

It was May again, Sunday after supper, and he and Pa were sitting each in a rocker on the veranda. Mother could be heard washing dishes in the kitchen. The yard was darkening. A last shaft of sunlight pinkened the topmost leaves of the fat old cottonwood in the draw.

Kon started up a slow rocking. "Pa, I got a proposition to make to you."

"Shoot, son."

"You know that quarter you're supposed to have bought for me when I was born?"

"Yes?"

"But that you said wasn't to be mine if I went on to high school and didn't become a farmer?"

"Yes?"

"Could I take a loan against it at the bank if I agreed to pay the interest and later on paid the loan back?"

"What for?"

"I'd like to go full time at Morningside next fall."

"And quit teaching?"

"For one year, yes."

"Let someone else take your place here at Rock Number Four?"

"Yes."

"Suppose the school board decides to keep the new teacher after the year is up?"

"I won't worry about that. I've been wanting to teach in high school anyway."

"Think you're good enough?"

"Yes."

"No."

"Pa, a man should spend at least one full year on a campus to get the full benefit out of college. Contacts with good profs are especially helpful. As it is now I only get to see the poor profs during the summer. Or the hot tired ones."

Mother came out on the porch, hands still damp from doing the dishes.

Kon offered her his rocker.

"No, no, you stay right where you are, son. I like to sit on the steps better."

"Please, Mother."

"No. I'll sit here on the top step."

Compared to Pa, dear Mother had really begun to age the last few years. She'd become so wrinkled that the various cords and knots of her stuck out like she might be encased in a net. Her hair had turned completely white, and had become so thin she had trouble making up the usual coil at the back of her head. Only her eyes remained young, a piercing shimmering blue.

Pa rocked. A runner beneath him squeaked.

Mother turned on her top step, said suddenly, "How much do you need, son?"

Kon stopped his slow rocking. "Four hundred."

Mother next gave Pa the full blue force of her eyes. "Give it to him."

"No."

"Give it to him."

"But why?"

"Give it to him, I say. Four hundred dollars is a whole lot cheaper than giving him that whole quarter. Which you once promised him."

"Well, and I say no."

"He's been a good boy. He deserves it. So give it to him."

"Goddam it, and I still say no."

Reka set her head against Pa. "So that's your mind, is it? All right then, son, we'll go borrow it without his blessing at the First National Bank in Bonnie. I'll cosign the note with you."

Kon sat up very straight in his rocker. "Mother, now. . . ."

Pa rocked once, abruptly said, "Hell, woman, the interest will eat him up."

Mother said, "Just because you can't sleep nights worrying about interest doesn't mean he won't sleep."

Pa said, "Woman, I've told you a thousand times if I've told you once—interest is always working against you once you get it started."

"That'll be our business."

Kon said, "Oh, let's just forget it. It's not worth all this bickering. I'll manage somehow." Kon got up from his rocker and went upstairs to his room.

The next Saturday morning, Mother spotted Karen Alfredson coming up the front steps. Mother had taken a liking to tall Karen and she ran out to greet her, warmly taking her long slim hand in both of hers.

Karen laughed a slow green-eyed laugh. Karen was dressed in white: shoes, dress, blouse, wide hat. She stood out like a prairie schooner against the green grass of May. "Good morning, Mrs. Harmer. And how are you today?"

"You're staying for dinner?" Mother demanded peremptorily.

"Well, yes, I'd like to, if I may. But I didn't come for that though, Mrs. Harmer."

"Kon!" Mother called into the house. "You better come down. Your girl friend Karen has come to see you."

"Coming."

Karen laughed some more. "And I didn't really come to see Kon either, Mrs. Harmer. I came to see you."

Mother held the screen door open for her. "Never mind now. The boy ain't done nothing but mope around here all morning long anyway. Kon?"

Kon called down, "I'm tying my shoes first a minute, Mother."

Karen said, "But really, Mrs. Harmer, I mostly came to see you. Mrs. Weatherly told me about an antique sewing bird you have."

"Oh." Mother stood very still; spoke shortly. "Well, that ain't for sale."

Karen smiled. "I just came to see it. My mother had one, but in all of Father's moving around it got lost."

"Oh." Mother brooded to herself a moment. "I see. Well, all right, you can look at it. But remember now, it ain't for sale. All right?"

"Of course, Mrs. Harmer."

"Come."

Mother led the way into the sitting room. She pointed to a brown leather sofa. "Have a seat, child."

All the furnishings had been done in light golden oak: the round center table, the sideboard for glassware, the big paneled cupboards for dishes, the straight chairs, the door and window frames. The quarter-oak floor gleamed like fossil resin. Sunlight pouring in through the white lace curtains gave the big room a cheerful country brightness.

"Kon?" Mother called again.

Kon came downstairs and stepped through a pair of tan drapes separating the sitting room from the parlor. "Hello." Kon gave Karen a fair smile, then shook hands. "And how have you been, neighbor?"

"Just fine." A small light came on in Karen's green eyes. "And you?"

"I'll manage, I guess." Kon sat down on the sofa beside Karen.

Neither Kon nor Karen looked their age. Both had just turned thirty but still looked as though they might be in their early twenties. Neither had a gray hair nor a wrinkle around the eye or under the ear.

Mother studied them with a hooded look. "Now, Kon, you know you're not telling the truth."

"Mother."

"Tell her the truth. Tell her that you're down in the mouth. Sitting there smiling like that."

"Now, Mother."

Mother settled in her favorite chair, a platform rocker. "Well, if you won't tell her, by jickery, I will. Karen, that boy of mine—"

"Mother!" Kon warned.

At that moment Karen spotted the sewing bird in the sewing corner. "Ah, there it is. Just like my mother's."

Mother immediately fell silent.

Karen's green eyes slowly softened. "Sitting here I can just see Mother's slender fingers weaving back and forth under its beak."

Kon watched Mother. Mother had always been touchy about that sewing bird. As a little boy Kon had often asked if he could play with it but she had never given him permission.

Karen slowly got to her feet. "May I just touch it, Mrs. Harmer?"

Mother stared down at the backs of her hands, darkly.

"Mrs. Harmer?"

"Well . . . if you think you have to," Mother said, brusque. A look came over her as if steam were about to shoot out of her nostrils.

The sewing bird resembled a blue jay as to both color and size. It was fastened to the open lid of the sewing machine by means of a big nickel clamp taking the place of claws. Its birdlike beak was designed to hold work to be sewed by hand. A small velvet pincushion the size of a crab apple was fastened to its back.

Karen pressed down the sewing bird's tail to open its beak. "Yours still has a strong spring, Mrs. Harmer. It'll hold most anything in place."

Mother leaned forward in her rocker as if she were having an attack of some kind.

Karen stroked the back of the sewing bird. "In the old days this was one of the best helpmates a lonely farm wife ever had. What I wouldn't give to know where Mother's went."

Mother leaned forward still farther. The platform rocker came up in back so high it looked like it was going to tip.

Kon spoke sharply. "Mother?"

Then Mother's small head with its little white bun of hair at the back came up with a jerk. She fixed seething eyes on Karen. "Child, I give it to you."

Kon and Karen were both astounded. "What!"

"You're still young and you can put it to good use for years to come. While me, I'm old and about to die and won't need it much anymore."

Karen gasped. "But . . . Mrs. Harmer . . . I don't want you to do that. I didn't come here for that."

Kon got up and went over and put a hand on his mother's shoulder. "Mother . . . ?"

Mother brushed his hand aside. "Don't touch me."

"But, Mother, for a minute there . . ."

"Get away." Mother smiled sourish. "I'm fine."

Kon stared down at his mother, eyes wide.

Karen retreated from the sewing bird. "Oh, but Mrs. Harmer, I can't accept this from you. It's a precious family heirloom."

"I've given you the bird. Now take it."

Karen shook her head. She settled back on the sofa. "I can't do that. It means so much to you. I can see that."

Mother got up with a bound, went over and unscrewed the nickel clamp from the sewing machine lid, and almost threw the sewing bird into Karen's lap. "Take it, I say."

"But. . . ."

"I'll get mad if you don't."

"Oh, Mrs. Harmer. . . ."

Mother's eyes almost closed over. "The finger of God pointed the way to me. That I give it to you."

The blue sewing bird lay in Karen's lap. She touched it as if it were something precious and very fragile. She couldn't believe her good luck.

Mother said, "And I can't think of a better person to give it to."

Kon laughed nervously. "Well, Karen, one thing about Mother, when she gives you something she gives it."

"It's so strange."

Kon said, "Take it. Mother means it. I know that none of us boys will ever want it."

A grateful smile melted Karen's face. "Why, this is the nicest thing to happen to me in a long time. Since the Hamiltons had my poems printed."

Karen stayed for dinner. They had canned beef, boiled potatoes, flour gravy, creamed asparagus, fresh-baked bread, butter and honey. And chilled tea from the cooler.

Kon noted that Karen was a light eater. No wonder she was so thin.

Mother noticed the same thing. When she served dessert, she quite deliberately gave Karen as large a dish of pale slim pears as she did the menfolks, Kon and Pa.

Up to that time Karen had served herself. But with the full dish in front of her she raised both her hands. "Oh, Mrs. Harmer, but this is far too much for me." Her green glance stole across to Kon. "Maybe Kon'll help me. Take half."

"Don't you feel good?" Mother said.

"I feel fine."

"Maybe I'm failing as a cook then. I know I'm getting on."

"You're a wonder at the stove, Mrs. Harmer."

"Well, then, what is it, child?"

"It's just that I never eat much."

"A cricket couldn't live on what you eat."

Karen smiled. She thought Mother a card with her strange remarks.

Kon had a wrinkled look for his father at the head of the table. "Maybe if I was to cut down on my eating like Karen here, maybe I could make it on three hundred my final year in college. Instead of four."

Pa, drowsing, seemed not to have heard.

Mother chewed once, old streaked teeth showing for a second. "I still say I'll be glad to sign a note for you at the bank, son."

Karen's eyes opened. "You need to borrow some money to go to school this summer?"

Kon cut up a pear with the side of his spoon. "Oh, I shouldn't have said anything. It's just that I was thinking of quitting teaching this coming year and of doing my senior year straight through at Morningside. Instead of over another three summers."

"How much do you need? Not that it is any of my business."

"I was thinking of about four hundred dollars."

"Well," Karen said, "I've got four hundred dollars for you. You see, when the Hamiltons died last winter"—for a second the shadow of a sad memory touched her eyes—"they left me a small bequest of five hundred. And then too I've saved up some of my own."

Kon said, "I wouldn't think of taking it."

"Well, if you want it you can have it." Karen toyed with her pale pears. "That money isn't going to do me much good. I'm never going to get married anyway."

"Don't be foolish."

Mother again broke in. "Son, take it. She means it. She's like me."

"But, Mother—"

"Take it." Mother quirked shrewd eyes at Karen. "How much interest do you want?"

"Oh, but I don't want to charge him interest. He can just use it until he can pay it back. We teachers've got to stick together, you know."

Pa awoke at his end of the table. "Miss, now you're not using your head. With friends as with strangers you must always be sure and get the old John Henry on the dotted line."

"Oh, but surely not with an old friend, Mr. Harmer."

"Old friends make the best enemies. As I've found out."

There was a silence.

Kon didn't know what to say.

Karen thought of something. "Well, maybe Kon can talk his school board into hiring me in his place. That'd be more than enough interest."

Kon's eyes opened. "You'd teach at Rock Number Four?"

"If they'd accept me."

"You would?"

"It's time for a change anyway where I am. I'm getting so sick and tired of living with the Murrays. They expect too much of me for my room and board. They think they own me body and soul."

Mother hunched her chair closer to the table. First she turned to Kon. "Son, take the money." Then she turned to Karen. "Child, you stay here. Make this your home while you teach at Number Four."

"Oh, but Mrs. Harmer, really. . . ."

Mother's eyes closed for a moment. "Ohh, it'll be such a wonderful thing having a girl in the house at last. To keep me company like a daughter."

Pa slowly shook his head at his end of the table. "The interest will eat you up."

Mother snorted. "The way she eats? Hoh."

So it was done. Kon went to Morningside College for a year. Karen resigned at Rock No. 3 and accepted an offer from Rock No. 4.

Karen moved her things to the Harmers' and was put up in the guest room. Or, as the Harmer boys always spoke of it, the cold room.

The only fly in the honeypot was the way Brant took it. Brant resented Karen's stay at the Harmers'. Brant grumbled to Mother that Kon should have asked him for the money instead of a stranger.

"There's got to be something in back of it," Brant said, "her slickin' her way into our nest like that. Like some stray cat. I don't like it."

PART THREE

❖◇❀◇❀◇❀◇❀◇❀◇❀◇❀◇❀◇❀◇❀◇❀◇❀◇❀◇

Karen

1

The next summer Karen and Kon found themselves in somewhat of a quandary. Kon had got his Bachelor of Arts degree all right, but he still hadn't been able to find a position teaching in high school. Karen decided that since she'd replaced him at Rock No. 4, he should have his old job back and she would go look elsewhere. Kon refused to consider this idea, saying he had made up his mind never to return to Rock No. 4. He was going to teach high school, or nothing. Even hire out as a hired man on a farm if need be.

Then early in June he got a reply to one of the many applications he'd sent out. It came from a high school in Whitebone, just across the line in Minnesota, some twenty-five miles away. There was an opening in the sciences, in biology, and could he come for an interview?

Wasn't that just dandy?

But it also created a further problem. Neither Kon nor Karen knew how to drive a car. Pa had at last bought himself a new Buick touring car, but he was so fussy with it that Kon didn't dare ask him if he would show him how to drive it.

Karen got an idea. Her brother Alfred, who now rented a farm two miles south of the Harmers', had once in passing remarked that he didn't have much use for his fancy trotter Daise anymore. He too had bought a new Buick. Karen wondered if maybe Alf wouldn't let them use Daise. She and Kon could take the horse and buggy to Bonnie and from there catch the Old Omaha train to Whitebone. The Old Omaha left Bonnie at ten in the morning and arrived in Whitebone at one. After it turned around in Whitebone it left at three and arrived in Bonnie again at seven. Kon would have two hours for the interview. Karen in the meantime could do some shopping in Whitebone. They'd take a picnic basket along and eat on the train on the way.

Brother Alf took a rather dim view of the idea. He spoke brusquely over the country telephone. "You drive old Daise? Not hardly."

"What about it if Kon drives her?"

"Is he going with?"

"I just said he was. That's why we're going up there, for goodness sakes."

"That's right. Well-l. . . ."

"Is there anything the matter with Daise?"

"Naw, she's all right. It's just that in her old age she don't like strangers much and with her having a mind of her own anything's liable to happen. She's worse than a dog there almost."

"Alf, after all, Kon's been raised on a farm too. Goodness."

"Well . . . all right. But ain't you forgot the last time you had something to do with a horse?"

"Alf. That was when I was just a girl. Besides, I rode it horseback, not drove it. This'll be in a buggy with Kon driving."

"I mean that time you and the kids went to drive to Bonnie. You know, with Free and Everett. When Daise didn't like the looks of the sky and turned around and came home and you cussed a blue streak because she wouldn't mind you. Because she was the smarter."

"Oh, Alf, but that was because a whirlwind on the road spooked her."

"Trouble with you is, Sis, you're too fine for the animals."
Pause.
"You're sure now Kon knows his horses?"
"Alf."
"All right. I'll bring Daise over tomorrow."

Karen and Kon left at dawn the next Friday morning. The grass was dry. The sky overhead promised fair weather.

They took the Walker road to Bonnie, straight south. With Kon on the ribbons Daise ran fine. Her slim flared nose, her streaming black mane, her sleek roan shoulders, plunged head-long through the opalescent light. Eight little plumes of soft brown powder lifted off the dirt road, four from the flying hoofs and four from the rolling black wheels. Both Karen and Kon tucked their knees under a yellow silk duster to protect themselves against the stiving dust. Karen was wearing her favorite white dress and Kon his light-blue suit. A yellow rose lay pinned on the brim of her wide white hat and a red woodpecker feather stuck up out of the black band of his yellow straw hat.

Soon the sun lifted over the horizon. Warmth came with light. After a while both Karen and Kon began to feel uncomfortable under the yellow duster and they folded it up and put it up behind them. With the buggy top up their head and shoulders rode in shadow.

They rolled by alternate fields of dark-green corn and light-green oats. Alfalfa fields were already purple. Pastures lay blue in the draws.

Old Daise ran like a demon. Her black ears took turns working the road ahead. Her left eye, which with its off-color eyebrow resembled a daisy, checked all unusual objects.

Karen nodded to herself. "I told Alf you could handle her all right."

Kon smiled. "We're not there yet."

"She isn't even smiling her old sly smile today."

"Well, not so far anyway."

"And she hasn't once shown us snaky ears."

"Shh."

"It's when you see that sneaky smile and those clapped-down ears that you got to watch out."

"Shh, or she'll hear you."

"Oh, she can be a little dickens all right."

"Spunky, you mean."

"Alf says I'm too fine for the animals." Karen drew up her nose. "Well, not any more I'm not, after what I went through at Rock Number Three."

"With those stinkers."

"Yes." Karen saw that some dust had settled on her white gloves. Gently she flapped them clean. "The only trouble is, Daise still thinks like Alf. That I'm too fine for her. Alf should keep still around her about me. Animals can catch onto things real quick. Oh, but they can be smart sometimes."

They passed slow-going grain wagons and stately carriages. Daise showed that she was used to the new contraptions on the road, the sputtering gas-engine cars, even the noisy popping Dorts.

They rattled by a farm orchard. Duchess apples were just turning white, showing through the green leaves like the half-exposed paps of a fresh mother, while crab apples were turning pink near the tops of the trees. The pioneer apples were still green, hard to make out amongst the leaves.

A half mile farther on, climbing a hill, Daise plumed her black tail and punctuated the pale tan road with a row of golden apostrophes. It was all daintily done. It would have been even neatly done had it not been for an intervention, the breeching.

A wry expression drew up Karen's lips on one side. "Thank God I'm not a rural mail carrier."

"How's that?"

"With nothing but a horse's sitter to look at all day long."

"Ha. How about riding a sulky at the races? Where the horse practically sits in your lap?"

Karen's lips twitched. "Funny they didn't stop to think of a woman's sensibilities when they invented the buggy. I would have put the cart before the horse. With the passenger riding up in front."

Kon considered the idea for a ways. He held a steady rein on Daise. "How would you drive the horse then?"

"I'd lead-drive her. And fix some kind of a clapper behind her so as to speed her up when needed."

Kon laughed a fine silver laugh. "You ought to get a patent for that idea."

"Maybe I will."

Mushrooming dust showed over the next hill.

"There comes one of those pesky cars again," Karen said.

Kon took a firm grip on the reins.

"So far they haven't been going too fast. But I'm afraid this one is different."

The car exploded over the brow of the hill. It raised four furious tails of dust, all of them coalescing into a rising cloud. The car was a black Velie and its roar was deafening. It came straight down the center of the road, right at them.

Daise refused to give ground. If anything, Daise seemed to brace herself for a collision. Her ears and eyes came up and her sturdy back took on the stiffness of a mud puppy.

"Daise!" Kon cried, and tried to jerk her over by hauling hard on the right line.

At the last moment, as if reluctantly, with a twist and a side lurch, the black Velie veered over onto its own side of the road. A second later the Velie was by, enveloping horse and buggy and passengers with a rush of stifling dust.

Karen coughed. Angrily she brushed off her white clothes. "Road hog!"

Kon let up on the lines. "That was Tom Priester!"

"What? Who?"

"Oh . . . nothing."

"Did you say Tom Priester?"

"Yes. And it's just like I heard. He's become a town sport." A melancholy, even poignant, look came into Kon's eyes.

The dust thinned out as they reached the top of the hill, then slowly wisped away over a green cornfield.

Karen said, "I know how you feel. Tessie Windmiller was uptown the other day with a new baby on her hip. And here she already had four hungry little piglets tagging along behind her. An old woman before her time."

They rolled down toward the Big Rock River. Trees fringed the stream, coming out of the northeast and angling off to the southwest. All the trees were neatly cropped off underneath by farm stock. The effect was like that of a well-kept park.

Beyond lay Bonnie, on a rising slope of land surmounted by a white water tower. In some places gray shingled roofs barely rose above what seemed like a huge grove of trees.

Daise spotted a team of pacers with a carriage ahead. Daise dearly loved a race and she set sail for the pacers and carriage with a sudden lunge of power. The buggy's black wheels hummed and their spokes vanished into blurs. Daise's whirling hoofs beat up a swift drumming roll.

"Daise, now," Kon warned. He pulled hard on the lines. "Whoa now, old girl."

"Can't you hold her?"

"Of course I can hold her." Kon hauled back even harder on the lines. "Whoa, you!"

But Daise had a mouth of tough old leather. Her nose pushed out, and in so doing she lifted Kon from his seat a little.

"Hold her!" Karen cried.

"Can't you see I'm trying?"

"Trying? Oh, dear God, I can already see what's going to happen next. This is going to end up wild."

"Whoa!" Kon cried. "Whoa!"

A duck pond ovaled by on their right.

The black carriage ahead rolled onto the bridge spanning the Big Rock River. Instantly the plank flooring set up an awful clamor. The shod hoofs of the trotters clopped in rhythmic clanging rolls.

Karen cried, "For mercy sakes, man, do something. Or we'll have a runaway."

"That horse is possessed." Kon spoke through set teeth. "I'm doing all I can to hold her and now she's pulling the buggy through me by way of the lines. Instead of through the traces."

"I can see that."

Kon set his feet astraddle the corners of the dashboard and pulled for all he was worth.

Still Daise continued to lick it over the ground and gain on the dark carriage ahead.

Hardly had the carriage finished crossing the bridge when Daise and buggy were on it. Then the bridge planking really clamored, booming like big hills falling down.

Karen let her eyes close.

The clamoring spurred Daise on even more. She sailed. A moment more and they were across the bridge. The clangor instantly fell off. Only the sound of Daise's snare-drumming hoofs flittered on the pale tan road. Another moment more and Daise and buggy were moving into the dust kicked up by the carriage ahead.

Karen coughed. Kon coughed. Hoarsely.

A few seconds more and they were free of the driving dust and were drawing up even with the carriage.

The driver of the carriage looked around to see who might be coming up that fast. The driver of the carriage turned out to be Cletus Pettengill. Cletus lived two miles west of the Harmers. Cletus began to shout at them over the noise of their going. "My wife's having a baby!"

"What?"

"My wife's having a baby!" Cletus gestured with his chin toward the back seat of his carriage.

Karen and Kon looked.

A woman lay bobbling on the back seat with her blue gingham dress worked up over her hips. Her fat white dimpled legs lay spread wide apart and her belly resembled a pan of risen bread dough.

A moment more and Daise surged ahead of the trotters.

"Tell Doctor Tom to get ready for us!" Cletus shouted after them. "We'll be along in a minute."

"But we've got a runaway on our hands," Karen cried over her shoulder.

"Runaway? Christ, I sure wisht I had one then."

"Goodness gracious," Karen gulped.

Daise made sure she had a good lead on the carriage, and then, smiling her old sly smile, eased up, resuming her usual strong-shouldered pace. She let her head be drawn back some so that after a bit it seemed Kon had her under control again.

"Thank God," a white Karen said. "At least the runaway part of it is over. And I don't have to be ashamed when I return Daise to Alf."

Kon threw a glance back at the Pettengill carriage. "Now there is one of the reasons why I never wanted to get married. That was obscene, that was. That woman that way."

Karen pinkened on her side of the buggy. She rose a little. "What's wrong with motherhood, I want to know?"

"Well, like I said, that woman that way."

"You really have got your mind made up never to get married, haven't you?"

"Yessiree! After what I've seen of it anyway."

"What have you seen of it?"

"All you have to do is to go take a good look at Charlie and Inez."

"You can't go by them."

"And then there's Brant. He's not really happily married with Mildred either."

Karen seized on this. "Yes. And that's something I'll never understand. She's a wonderful woman, she is. There must be something the matter with Brant that he isn't happy with her."

Kon threw Karen a hurt look for Brant.

Karen went on. "Brant's a little funny in the head, if you ask me. Because Mildred couldn't be nicer to him."

Kon said shortly, "I'll thank you not to talk about my brother Brant."

Karen went on as if she hadn't heard him. "Well, me—I for one am glad my father and mother got married even though they didn't always get along. And even though I'm not interested in marriage for myself. Because I'm here now."

Kon paid strict attention to his driving.

Daise peered around with her daisy eye to make sure the carriage was still at its proper distance behind her.

Karen let her eyes rest on a field of green alfalfa unrolling past them on their left. "Because just suppose you and I had a chance to get married, but didn't, and suppose the child we could've had, but didn't, suppose it could speak up? It would have said the same thing I just said. That it for one was glad that Konstant Harmer and Karen Alfredson got married. Because it was here now."

Kon all of a sudden couldn't help but burst out laughing. "Karen, you're trumps, you are. But I catch you."

"I don't see anything so funny about that."

"You don't?"

"No."

"A-ha-ha. In any case, I have no desire to become a father. An uncle, yes. But a father, no. And for another, while we've always been good friends, you and I, for years even, I can hardly see us as man and wife. Certainly not with me as the man. No, never." Kon flushed a little as he spoke. "Just like it's hard for me to see my own father and mother as man and wife. Eigh!"

A smile touched the corners of Karen's lips. "But they must have been. Or else you're one of those suppose babies I just talked about."

Again Kon burst out laughing.

Karen glanced back at the carriage following them. "I suppose you're going to stop at Doctor Drury's and tell him the Pettengills are coming?"

Kon pulled out his watch. "Well! Daise went faster than I thought. It's hardly nine o'clock. We'll have plenty of time to stop at Doctor Tom's first."

A shadow touched Karen's face.

A newly opened sandpit lay slack and golden on their right. Then they entered the outskirts of Bonnie. Handsome creamy cottages gleamed behind white fences. Dogs came rushing out from behind honeysuckle hedges and barked at the ringing buggy wheels.

Karen spotted activity over in the Old Omaha yards. A big black steam engine stood just outside a red roundhouse. "I see the steamer's fired and ready to go."

"We've still got plenty of time. It's when they've got her nose headed north that you start to worry."

The steam engine stood like some great old contented boar in a barn lot. Gray smoke drifted out of the old fellow's tall smoke-stack at the same time that white steam hissed from his pet cocks. An engineer, the bill of his blue cap cocked up, touched the old fellow here and there with the long spout of an oil can. Every so often the old black fellow gave off a low deep satisfied grunt, and coughed, once, at the same time that his single eye came on for a second.

Daise threw the old engine a wondering look; brooded to her-self about it a moment with ears flatted back; decided it was all right.

A dozen children played rag baseball in an open lot. A yellow kite sashayed high over the Cannonball depot on the west side of town. A loaded grain wagon crunched heavily down a graveled incline toward a red elevator.

They turned east up main street, going past a smoky blacksmith shop, an aromatic lumberyard, a gritty cement works, a lonely weighing station, the dull orange Old Omaha depot where two green passenger cars stood waiting, and a false-front garage.

Kon slowed Daise down near the Bonnie Hotel, managed to get her stopped directly in front of Dr. Drury's door.

With dark aversion Karen read the black-and-gold lettering on the window in the door:

THOMAS DRURY, M.D.
Physician & Surgeon

Kon handed her the lines. "Hang onto them a minute, will you, and I'll quick go in and tell Doctor Tom the Pettengills are coming."

"I don't like it."

"It'll only take a minute."

Daise wondered around at their talk with her daisy eye.

"See?" Karen said. "I think you ought to tie her to a hitching post."

Kon spoke roughly. "Just you hold these lines a minute, please, will you?"

All too well Karen recalled the time Bets had bucked her off almost on that very spot, to the delight of the loafers sitting on the long veranda of the Bonnie Hotel.

"Woman, will you please take hold of these lines while I go in and quick tell Doctor Tom?"

"Oh, all right." Karen took the lines in her right hand. "But I don't like it."

"Finally." Kon jumped down out of the buggy and disappeared into Dr. Drury's office.

Karen sat with her knees held tight together. She kept a wary eye on Daise's ears.

Daise stood at ease on two legs, the other two sagging.

Occasional souls appeared on the street. A woman emerged from the millinery store carrying a new hatbox. Old man Rexroth came out of his red-rock store and let down a long tan awning. Two loafers sitting on a bench in front of the pool hall watched a dog baptize a line of hitching posts.

A tremor popped up in a muscle over Karen's right shoulder-blade. Like a wave in water it moved down her arm and then down the lines. Why didn't Kon hurry up? Karen shifted the lines to her left hand.

Daise resettled her weight on her other two legs.

A door slammed up the street. Someone had come out of the Corner Café.

The someone instantly caught Karen's eye. What on earth?

It was a man. An odd fish of a man. He came waddling toward them. His short arms flailed the air like paddles, his shirt hung out at the sides like fins, his nose resembled the sloping lip of a coal shuttle, his eyes glowed like balls of marsh gas, and his bald head gleamed as if he'd been born without a hair on his body, slippery with mucus.

Karen stared.

The stump of a fellow came on, slithering more than walking.

Karen rubbed her eyes to make sure she wasn't seeing things. "Dear Lord, I wonder what swamp he crawled out of."

Daise spotted the strange fellow too. Her head came up and her ears shot forward.

One of the loafers in front of the pool hall across the street recognized the fellow. "Hey, if there ain't old Pidge Browne." Then the loafer called out, "Hi, Pidge. Back in town, I see."

Pidge heard the salute and turned to see who it was. Happy that someone had bothered to speak to him, he smiled. And the smile he smiled was suddenly so cavernous it gave him the look of a bullhead. Huge teeth were set wide apart in his jaw. "Hallow," he said.

Daise constricted, her nostrils flared out, and she rose on the tips of her hoofs.

"Now, Daise." Karen tightened her grip on the lines ever so little. "You behave now."

Then Pidge Browne spotted Karen and the horse. His weird phosphorescent eyes looked right through Karen; then, shifting, looked right through Daise. By this time Pidge and the horse and buggy weren't more than twenty feet apart.

Daise's eyes bulged out; also took on a phosphorescent cast.

An even wider smile, full of tender love for animals, opened Pidge's brownish-green snout.

At that moment Kon emerged from Dr. Drury's office, letting the screen door slam shut behind him. "Well, Karen, that's done. Now let's—"

Kon never finished.

Daise snorted; popped her tail; then exploded sideways. She whirled so short around that the iron rims of the narrow buggy wheels screamed on the graveled street. The buggy lurched over so far that Karen banged her head on something. She had to hang on, grimly, to keep from falling out. Snowflakes and stars whirled in her head.

"Karen!"

Daise straightened out in a dead run and the buggy righted itself.

Despite the sudden muzziness in her eyes Karen managed to keep her head. "That horse's got to be stopped right now or our whole expedition is spoiled." She forced herself to look down at her hands. Horrors. One of the lines, the left one, had slipped out of her grasp. It was slowly sliding off the dashboard past the whip holder.

Daise was going lickety-split.

The snowflakes and stars in Karen's head steadied; one by one winked out. She thought: "By ginger, I've just simply got to get hold of that line or for sure all is lost." For a moment the speed of the buggy held her pinned back against the seat. "Even Kon. And I must have him." She leaned forward with all her might against the rush of the buggy. She thought: "Did I really say that?" Then she thought: "I've got to get that line."

"Karen!" Kon cried again.

The two loafers in front of the pool hall came to their feet. "Hey! Runaway!"

"Karen!"

"Runaway!"

Heads, then whole bodies, popped out of the doors along main street, the grocery stores, the cafés, the hardware store, the bank, the post office, the garage, the grain elevators, even out of the lumberyard and the cement works down the street.

"Jerk back on your lines, Karen!"

"Runaway! Runaway!"

Karen thought: "Shoot, you can talk, Kon, safe on the street there."

Dark figures ran out onto the street to block the way, forming a quick impromptu line. The Old Omaha stationmaster ran out waving a pair of big flared blue mittens.

"Whoa!"

"Whoa! Whoa!"

Karen at last caught up with the buggy's momentum. She reached down to pick up the loose line.

Daise decided there were just too many dark figures in front of her for her to bust through, so, flicking her right ear once, she abruptly veered left around the corner, going along the west side of the Bonnie Hotel. As she did so, the end of the loose left line slipped past the whip holder and fell to the ground, trailing in the dust.

"You little dickens, you," Karen said. "Now look at what you've done."

At the next corner Daise again veered left, going around past the old livery stable with its row of buggies and carriages for hire.

Karen's lips thinned. "That's enough of that now, Daise. At the next corner—"

On the dead run Daise dropped a single golden apple.

Karen gave a yank on the one line left her, the right one.

Daise merely shot out her nose against the yank on her mouth, fairly lifting Karen half out of her seat, and turned left again.

"You little devil, you."

Again at the next corner, in front of the very Corner Café from which Pidge Browne had first emerged, Daise held against Karen's yank as she turned left. They'd completely circled the block.

"Runaway! Runaway!"

Ahead, the lower end of main street was by now a solid mass of men out to stop the streaking horse and buggy.

Behind the men the black tender to the Old Omaha backed into view, and then the steam engine itself. It eased across main street, completely blocking it, and made connection with the two green passenger cars standing beside the depot.

Spotting the hissing black engine, Daise once more decided that that was too much to bust through and again veered left around the Bonnie Hotel.

Hoarse male voices roared at her. "Whoa! Whoa!"

"Karen!" Kon called after them.

The Old Omaha let go with two quick fluted toots and then the engineer began to ring the bell.

"Oh, my," Karen agonized, "that's the last call for the passengers to board the train. That I remember from the old days."

As Daise veered around the livery stable once more, Karen tried pulling right with all her slender strength. Daise held against the pull.

"If I don't get this horse stopped, I'm never going to make the train. And then of course Kon won't make the train either because he'll wait for me. And then he'll never get that job in

Whitebone. And then we'll never leave home and get married."

Daise took the next corner left as Karen pulled right on the single line.

"Married?"

The proprietor of the Corner Café and the teller of the First National Bank across the corner and the proprietor of Highmire's Hardware tried to form a line to stop Daise. Daise brushed through their waving white hands as though they were cabbage butterflies.

"Well, it is high time we got married, by ginger."

And yet once again Daise headed down main street toward the mass of men and the grunting train below.

Kon finally ran out onto the street. He yelled, "Woman, stop that horse, for godsakes! The train's about to pull out." He leaped and made a grab for Daise's bridle. And missed. And was almost run down by the near front wheel. "Karen!"

Then Pidge Browne, out of the primordial goodness of his heart, decided it was time he should help. He flippered himself off the sidewalk and onto the street. He took up a position that was in the exact spot where Daise had last dodged left around the Bonnie Hotel. As Daise and buggy bore down on him, Pidge's lizard smile widened wonderfully and his goiter eyes fired up hotly phosphorescent. He waved his short arms. "Hawww!"

Daise, in her abhorrence of the fish man, finally turned the way Karen wanted her to go. Daise threw all four legs left and leaned right. The buggy also turned right, went up on two wheels. A heavy spray of gravel shot into the faces of the men blocking the street.

Karen thought: "At last. Now I've got her going my way."

Daise spotted something. The front double doors to Wickett's Garage were open as well as the double doors to the rear. The garage resembled a covered bridge. With that Daise was familiar. She headed for it.

"Karen! The train is starting up!"

Karen twisted on her seat and leaned out of the buggy and yelled back at Kon. "Well, take the dummed train then! You can see I won't be able to." Karen's green eyes blazed. "I'll see you tonight when you get back." The shadow of the front doors to the garage passed over her. "Put your best foot forward now. We need that job, you know."

The little gray cement garage was suddenly filled with the iron roar of hoofs and wheels. Black mechanics skittered out from under jacked-up cars to see whatever it was that was exploding through their nuts-and-bolts world. Bald Roy Wickett over in the side office just had time to jump up in front of his rolltop desk to catch a glimpse of the backside of a buggy vanishing out of the rear of his garage with a woman leaning out yelling back at somebody.

Karen caught a brief whiff of fresh differential grease along with a rotten armpit somewhere.

Then sunlight burst around her and they were in a green alley. Ahead were houses, and the Bonnie baseball park, and beyond that the open country.

Karen heaved a great sigh. "Oh. Thank God. Safe." She heaved a second big sigh. "At last." And smiling at it all, as well as at herself, she let the other line fall to the ground.

Daise veered one more time, a little, just enough to get onto the King's Trail, and then headed straight for home. Old Daise liked having her own head.

2

An hour later Daise turned into brother Alf's lane, rolled past the cob house, and pulled up in front of the house.

Daise looked mildly around at all the familiar things and then spread her four legs out a little and got set for a rest.

Tall sister-in-law Ada, drying her hands in her blue apron, came stepping down the front walk. Ada's eyes were like big blue flowers. "Karen! I thought you'd be in Whitebone by now with Kon."

"That's what I thought too." Karen had to laugh in spite of herself. "But Daise decided otherwise."

Big Alf came legging it up from the grain stacks north of the barn. His overalls were handsomely patched over the knee and his

straw hat hung down on one side from having been warped a
little in the last rain. He stared and stared, his light-blue carbide
eyes more deep-set than usual. He was so tall his chin came
higher than Daise's ears.

"Where's Kon?" Ada cried.

"Well, by now he should be talking to the principal in his office
in Whitebone." More laughter welled up in Karen. "Poor man,
and he had to go on without his lunch." Karen held up the picnic
basket that she and Kon were going to share.

Alf threw his straw hat down on the ground. "Just as I thought.
Daise ran away with you again." His hair, once a wavy black but
now a flowing white, shone in the sunlight like ripe foxtail. "I
might've known that that lily-fingered boyfriend of yours couldn't
drive a horse either."

"Alf," tall Ada said, "calm now."

Then Alf spotted where the reins were, dragging on the ground.
"Good grutkins! Look at that, would you. Worn to a frazzle. I'll
have to get Daise some new lines now." Alf bent over to retrieve
the lines.

"Alf, now," Ada scolded. "Be thankful she arrived home safe."

"We better thank the horse then," Alf growled. "Because it was
Daise what had the brains."

Karen still couldn't keep from laughing about it all. "Yes, I
guess that's right. Daise drove herself home without any help
from me."

Alf said, "And I suppose that heavy date of yours went and fell
out of the buggy somewhere?"

"No," Karen said, "no." Then, with a roll of her green eyes, she
laughed so hard she wept.

Alf looked at his sister with hard-set lips. "Must be pretty funny
all right."

Karen told about it, laughing and sighing all the while.

"So that's how come," Ada said.

"Well, no wonder Daise headed for home," Alf said. "Daise
was too fine for Pidge."

"You know this Pidge fellow?" Karen asked.

"Saw him uptown last Satiddy. A floater in off the harvest

fields. Good for nothing. Though I guess he means well. His arms are too short for shocking. And his feet . . . well, they're even too short to clear a mouse ball."

"Now, Alf," Ada said.

The Alfredson children emerged from a patch of tall green weeds east of the grove—Free, Everett, and Albert. They'd been playing scouts and Indians. Free wore an old straw hat to one side of his head, pretending he was Buffalo Bill; Everett came holding his nose with thumb and forefinger as though smelling something in his own pants; and Albert came toddling along on fat legs, slowly, holding his little straw hat on with both hands.

"There they are," Karen said. "The little darlings."

"Hey, you kids," Alf said, "who asked for you? You go back to your playing."

"They can see their aunt a minute," tall Ada said.

Karen had an idea. She picked up the lunch basket. "You kiddies still hungry? Yes? Then help yourself to this."

"No, no, that's not necessary," Ada said.

"Oh, let them have it," Karen said. "Children are always hungry. And it'll go to waste otherwise. I know I don't want all that."

"No, Karen, they shouldn't."

"But I really want them to have it, Ada. Really."

"Well—I . . . then I suppose . . ."

"Go ahead, kiddies."

Ada said, "All right then. But what do you kids say?"

All three children chorused, "Thank you, Aunt Karen."

"That's a good boys."

Free, the oldest, took hold of the picnic basket and then he and his two brothers vanished into the weeds.

"You kids bring back that basket when you're through now," Ada called after them. "You hear?"

Silence from the weeds.

Alf stood looking down at the frayed ends of the lines. "Well, I suppose I better get busy and fix this. Women drivers."

Karen stepped down from the buggy. With a demure girlish laugh she fell into tall Ada's arms. "Well, Sis, I guess you and Alf don't have to worry about me being an old maid anymore."

Ada gasped. Her whole face opened in glad surprise. There was also in Ada's manner just a mite of envy. "Did he pop the question?"

"I made up my mind," Karen said.

"You did?"

Karen laughed some more. "It just came to me today what I had to do at last. Set my cap for him."

"Isn't that fine."

"And you won't have to worry anymore either about not having any aunt-sayers. Because all of a sudden I want children of my own."

"Good grutkins," Alf said to Daise, "it was just your rotten luck you had to run into that fish of a Pidge Browne. Well, I don't blame you, Daise. I wouldn't want to be seen on the same street with him either."

Later, Alf brought Karen home to the Harmers.

Karen stayed up for Kon. She sat thinking in the dark, rocking in Mother's rocker on the veranda. Mother and Pa had long ago gone to bed.

It was midnight when Karen finally heard Kon coming down the soft dust out on the road and then across the harder ground on the yard. She got up and waited at the top of the steps.

In a moment Kon appeared at the bottom step, his face as isolate as a pink cameo.

"Hi," Karen said.

"Hi."

"I waited up for you."

"I can see that." He let go a bone-weary sigh. "What a long walk home that was."

"You had to walk all the way from Bonnie?"

"Yes."

"I'm sorry I couldn't make Daise behave."

"That's all right." Kon climbed up to her level. "I understand. I almost bolted myself when I finally got a good look at the Pidge Browne fellow."

They laughed companionably together in the dark.

Karen placed a light hand on his arm. "I hope you bring good news?" She amazed herself at the freeness with which she touched him.

Kon's hand came up and lay over hers. Except for handshakes it was the first time he'd ever touched her. "I do."

"You got the job?"

"Yes."

"You really did?"

"Yes."

"Starting this fall?"

"This fall."

Karen swayed toward him slightly. "Glory be."

The great old cottonwood in the draw casually disseminated cottony seeds on the soft night wind.

"The dear Lord be praised."

"Karen?"

"Yes, Kon?"

Kon's hand pressed down on hers, warmer. "Walking home from town tonight, I had a lot of time to think things over."

Shivering a little, Karen slowly sucked in her lower lip.

"Karen, it came to me . . . Well, so many things happened today. . . . Karen, I'm going to be lonesome in Whitebone without you. . . . You see, we're so much alike. . . . Well, there's only one person on earth I'd be willing to try it with. . . . So I've decided. . . . Karen, will you marry me and help me make a home in Whitebone?"

The sweet words at last.

"Karen?"

"Kon, if I give you my promise now, will you give it back to me in case I should ever want it back before we get married?"

"Karen, you know I would."

Silly giggles began to bubble deep in her. She had an awful time keeping them down. Giggles were for young girls. "Then you will give it back?"

"Of course."

"All right. I just wanted to be sure. Yes."

There was a silence.

Cottonwood fluff touched their faces.

At last, sighing, Kon said, "Maybe we'll still have time for two children."

"I won't have much of a bosom for them."

"Your bosom is just fine. Just right."

"I'm almost like a boy in that respect."

"It'll fill out when you get your first baby."

"How do you know?"

"That's nature's way. God will provide."

"Well, I surely hope so."

Kon's hand trembled on her hand. "And after the second baby it will be even fuller."

"Where did you learn about all that stuff?" They stood close enough for her to sense that his face was flushed and warm.

"Heh . . . from watching the heifers."

"That's where you boys have it over us girls. You're always out in the barn where you can see things. While we're always in the house where there's nothing to see."

Kon began to tremble from head to foot. "Karen?"

"Yes, Kon?"

"Maybe if . . . oh, skip it."

"Tell me."

"No. I can't."

A cow lowed for her calf in the Priester pasture over the rise.

Karen remembered something. "Kon?"

"Yes?"

"Maybe before we go on I ought to tell you something."

"Now, Karen, just a minute. Be careful now."

"Well, if I don't tell you now it'll be on my conscience for the rest of my life."

"Karen, you want to remember we may have all done things some time or other that we're all maybe a little ashamed of."

"Kon, I'm going to tell you anyway. I once lost the first blossom to my maidenhood."

"Oh."

"Dr. Drury took it from me." Pause. "The old reprobate."

"Our Doctor Tom?" Kon almost let go of her hand.

"Yes. You know how it is. An old fool is the worst fool of all. Especially if he's a doctor."

"So that's why you acted so funny this morning when we stopped in front of his office."

"Yes."

Silence. Again the Priester cow lowed for her own.

"You never heard about what he did to me? When he was supposed to be giving me a routine examination for female trouble?"

"No."

"Why, and here I thought everybody knew about it."

"No, I never did."

Karen told him about it, the whole sad story. "And I still say," she finished, "that it was God's will that I should have my roses late and that there was nothing I could do about it. That it was perfectly natural for me. Besides, as an American I have a perfect right to be exactly what I am."

Kon squeezed her hand, fervently. "Oh, Karen. Oh, Karen. You poor dear darling girl, you. All these years . . . What a wonderful girl you are."

"You still want to marry me?"

"Of course. What happened to you isn't wrong at all."

"I suppose we ought not to kiss until after we're married."

"I'm going to kiss you right now."

"Just once, though."

"Karen."

Their lips touched, dry and gentle, as artless as though earlobes had accidentally touched.

PART FOUR

✿✿✿✿✿✿✿✿✿✿✿✿✿✿✿✿✿✿✿

Brant

1

Brant slipped into his blue denim jacket and stepped outdoors.

The sun was halfway up, an orange ball in a chilly green sky. It tinted the evergreens in the cozy windbreak with a sheening blue and darkened the yellow leaves on the ash trees into an old gold and cast streaks of silver over the green honeysuckles.

Brant sniffed the morning air.

Damn. Yes, fall had come all right. It was time to bank the house with warm horse manure again, and put on the storm windows, and hook up the stovepipes to the hard-coal burner.

Brant spat over his left shoulder.

And, goddam it, it was also time to pick corn. This fall that was going to be something. Because his health was not up to snuff. Because in all his life he'd never had such a pain in his belly. It was like some kind of cancer had him in its grip. Low down, on the left side. Steady. Never letting up.

A west wind had risen. It moaned a little as it passed through Brant's cluster of white farm buildings.

Brant decided he might as well catch all that free power drifting across the country. He stepped across the yard and turned on the windmill. The watering tank was full so he switched the water into the supply tank instead. He waited until he heard the strokes go gurling underground, then headed for the barn.

He entered the barn on the cow side. Scowling at life, pushing his blue cap to the back of his head, he opened the stanchions and ushered his black-and-white Frisian cows out into the yard. He watched them shuffle off toward the watering tank, a few of them stopping to stretch a single rear leg, stiffly.

He was about to commence the dirty job of cleaning out the cow gutter, when he heard a car drive onto the yard and then the deep-toned blast of a klaxon. It was brother Charlie in his brown Luverne.

"Wonder what he wants so early in the morning?" Brant set the manure shovel to one side. "Thank God the kids are off to school so they won't have to listen to his rough talk."

Charlie next blatted a greeting on the bulb horn of his old Luverne, two shorts and a long.

"The damned showoff." Brant drew the collar of his jacket up around his neck. "So stuck on himself it's pitiful." Brant kicked a hardened cow pie out of the way. "He ought to have my troubles once." Brant stepped outside, blinking against the morning light.

"There he is," Charlie called out with exaggerated cheer. "Knew I'd catch him on the yard somewhere if I got the lead out."

Brant caught a glimpse of sister-in-law Inez vanishing into the kitchen. So she'd come too, eh? "Well, good," Brant thought, "that'll keep Mildred busy." Brant didn't like the way Charlie had been looking at Mildred lately. It was as if Charlie, having failed to take the old home place away from Pa, was now thinking of taking Mildred away from him, Brant. It was with an effort that Brant tried to match Charlie's cheer. "Your getting up so early in the morning, you're liable to rile up the weather."

Charlie stepped down out of his car. He tipped back his leather cap. His hard yellow eyes went all over Brant. "Well, if riling up the weather will give us a longer Indian summer, I'm all for it." Charlie limped toward Brant. The heel of the shoe of his crippled foot was so worn down, Charlie more rocked on the foot than walked on it. Charlie held out his hand.

For a second Brant stared at the outstretched hand. What? The Harmer brothers shake hands? Something special was up. Brant gave Charlie's hand only a fleeting touch.

Charlie spotted a pair of giant cow pumpkins on the sunny side of the white garage. The pumpkins were of the size of washtubs. "Let's set a spell. There's nothing like sitting on a new chair fresh rolled in from the field, I say."

Both orange pumpkins had their dark-green stems. The stems stuck up like the handles of stove-lid lifters. Brant pointed. "It ain't exactly going to be comfortable sitting on them though."

"That's easy taken care of." Charlie lifted his good foot and with a sideswiping kick knocked off one of the stems. The stem flew across the yard.

"Hey!" Brant cried. "And here I made a point of saving them on. For the girls. They specially asked me to save them stems on."

"What for?"

"To make big jack-o'-lanterns with. For Halloween. You can't have a jack-o'-lantern without a handle."

"Kid stuff."

"Don't you knock off the other one now."

"Suit yourself. Me, I intend to sit on mine without getting reamed."

Brant ground his teeth.

"Too bad the mailman had to run over your dog Bill. Or I'd have sat on him."

Brant's lower jaw worked around and around.

"What's the matter, Brant—the cat all of a sudden got your tongue?"

"You know damned well, Charlie, that there's a sandpaper between us."

"Sit down. I want to talk to you."

Brant groaned and eased himself down on the edge of his big pumpkin. He was careful not to lean back against its dark-green stem.

"Christ, Brant, you sound like you're gonna die."

"You don't know the half of it."

The two brothers sat in silence for several moments. They looked out over the rolling landscape to the east. Both had their lower lips pushed out pink. The one brother brooded to himself as big as a bull, all set to charge; the other brother waited as wary as a watchful dog, ready to snarl.

Presently Charlie allowed himself a short coarse laugh. "Wonder how our Kon is making it these days with that bedful of bones he married." Charlie laughed some more. "I can just imagine them two, going to bed at night. Ha. There they are, all skinny and tired out, he from teaching antsy high school brats, she from scrubbing silk underwear, each on their own side of the bed, not even knowing they're man and wife. Like a monk and a nun together. She says to him, 'Now, Konstant, dearie, please let's not have another one of your nightmares again tonight.' 'Nightmares?' he says. 'Yes,' she says, 'you had an awful one last night.' 'I did?' 'Yes, you did.' 'What did I do?' 'What did you do? Why, you rolled over against me and started doing funny things to me.' 'I did?' 'You attacked me, that's a fact.' 'I did?' 'Yes, you did, Mister Harmer. It was shameful. But I suppose that's all one can expect from one's own husband.' "

Brant felt himself whitening along the edges.

"Yeh, I can just imagine them. Him trying to get his horse between her shafts . . ." Charlie paused. His heavy blond brows knotted together over glittering yellow eyes. "Why, it's unpossible even to imagine it, come to think of it."

"It's none of our goddam business how they go to bed."

Charlie tried again. "Him trying to make her would be like trying to split a slippery tendon with a knitting needle."

"Shut up."

"Or like trying to thread a camel through the eye of a needle."

"Shut up."

"Wonder what he thinks when the lady of the house dons the unmentionables once a month."

"Goddam it, Charlie, shut up about them now, will you?"

"Why, Brantie boy, you sound like you wished you could've married Karen."

"Good God, no, you saphead."

Charlie's hard yellow eyes again went all over Brant. "You ain't by any chance having trouble making a go of it with your wife, are you?"

Brant stared hate at his brother.

"Because if you are, let me know. I'll be glad to take her off your hands. Any day. Man!"

Blue darkness began to gather in the corners of Brant's eyes.

"Brant, you don't know what a lucky dog you are, having Mildred. She's the best, she is."

Brant shivered.

"I'll be more than happy to trade wives with you. Even up."

"You son of a bitch."

"I sure envy you."

"Is that what you came here for?"

"How about it?"

"There's more to it than just sleeping with your wife, you old bull, you."

"Oh, come on now, Brant. You know sleeping with your wife is about the most fun you can have without laughing."

Brant jumped up; paced back and forth in front of Charlie several times; cast Charlie a darting murderous look; then sat down on his pumpkin again.

The faces of the two women in the house appeared above the white curtains in the kitchen. Mildred's face, framed by her dark hair, was paler than usual, while Inez' face, with her high sharp cheekbones, had an eyeless look. Both women were trying to figure out what the men were arguing about.

Charlie allowed himself another short laugh. "Ha. Talking about such things with you and Kon is like talking to a couple of maphrodites, for all the good it does. Both of you are a couple of pikers when it comes to women."

Brant's fists balled up of themselves.

"Neither one of you ever had much sting in your pants." Charlie spat at a late fall dandelion, hit it smack in the middle. The dandelion head bent down under the unwonted load; then, after a moment, when the gob of spittle let go, bobbed up again.

The steady pain in Brant's left side abruptly became a sharp cramp. He had to push in on it with a fist to get relief.

"When it comes to women and hard work, neither one of you has the gumption of a louse."

It had to be cancer. When a pain continued like that and then all of a sudden got sharper it was deathly serious.

"Well, it's like the fellow says, you can't make a pistol out of a pig's tail."

Suppose it was cancer? What a terrible thing that would be. So early in life. Tears filled Brant's eyes. "And then too all the work I've done here on the place. It will all be for nothing. The cement block foundations I put under all the buildings to keep out the rot. The windbreak I planted when we first got married. The cockleburs I picked by hand day after day in the hot sun. The Canady thistles I killed with a handful of salt dropped down into their roots. The neat yard I kept. All for nothing." He wept. "Well, I hope Mildred and the kids'll appreciate it after I've gone."

Charlie picked up a stone and threw it across the yard. It hit the ground and then bounced up against the privy door. "What I've never been able to figure out is how the both of you can be sons of the old man. For a fact, I don't."

Brant thought: "What Charlie forgets is that we can as well be sons of the old lady. Take after her side of the family."

Charlie went on. "Well, forgetting about you for the minute, I suppose it's about time I came to the point."

Brant hunched up a little.

Charlie picked up another stone and hurled it across the yard. This time it bounced with a light crack against the cement block footing of the chicken house. "Brant, for your information I've come over to tell you that I've finally decided to dump my wife."

Brant rose a little on his pumpkin. "Inez?"

"Who else but Inez?"

Brant couldn't help but sneer at the idea. "I suppose you're gonna kill her."

"You dumb bastard, of course not."

"Well, what are you going to do with her then?"

"I'm gonna get me a divorce. For scriptural reasons."

"Scriptural reasons? You?"

"Why not? Nobody can really prove we've slept together. There ain't been any results to show for it anyway. No kids like you got." Charlie pushed his lip out at Brant. "You lucky bastard. Even if it is girls."

"You can't get a divorce on scriptural grounds. Why, you're an out and out infidel."

"The hell I can't."

"Besides, everybody knows you've been a head stud up and down every lover's lane in the county."

Charlie's lower lip hung damp and pink. "She just lays there like an ironing board."

The two women in the kitchen continued to peer out at the men, Mildred with a concerned look, Inez with a constricted look.

Charlie went on. "What I should've done is joined the Mormons. You know? Then I could have been sure that at least one of my women would've had kids."

"What about poor Inez? What's she going to do?"

"I don't know. And I don't give a damn."

"Charlie, what a low dirty dog you are. First you want to get rid of our old man and now you come along and want to get rid of your wife. What next?" Brant got to his feet again and began to pace back and forth. "Why, you're about the worst oldest son I ever did hear of."

Charlie threw another stone across the yard. It hit a neckyoke standing against the granary. "The way we feel about each other, me and Inez, you really can't expect us to fadge it out together for the rest of our lives. Why, like you say, some morning I'm just liable to up and kill her just butting her out of my way." Charlie sneered hugely. "And she for her part is just as liable to poison me."

"Do you hate each other that much?"

"We do."

"Really now?"

Charlie pushed his lip out even further. "Some mornings when I wake up . . . why, it's like I don't know what I'm living for."

Brant thought: "If that don't blow the candles out in church. That's the way I feel."

Charlie rolled his massive shoulders. "A pussy smiled at me a certain way in Sioux Falls the other week and then it come over me what I was missing living with Inez."

Brant thought: "Hey, so it ain't Mildred after all."

"She had close-cropped hair. Like a cougar almost."

"Are you really foolin' around with other women, Charlie?"

" 'Course I know a waitress has to smile at all the men coming in. That's partly what she gets paid for."

"Anybody else know about this, Charlie?"

"Not that I know of."

"Because if they did, they'd give you a Christmas ride on a rail right out of the county."

"You mean that's what you'd like to give me."

"Charlie, if you dump Inez for some waitress somewhere, you'll lose every friend you ever had."

"The hell with 'em." Charlie spat a great spit at the ground. "Screw 'em all but six, I say. And save the six for pallbearers."

A silence fell between the two brothers. Brant paced; Charlie sat huge on his pumpkin.

The cows gradually drifted away from the watering tank, heading for a straw-pile butt near the pasture. The windmill squeaked rhythmically.

Of a sudden Charlie said, "Brant, you hain't told me yet how things are going between you and Millie."

Brant thought: "The son of a bitch. It was Mildred after all."

"Well, Brant?"

"What the hell should I tell you for?"

"I told you how it was between me and Inez."

"And suppose I did tell you?"

Charlie threw Brant a sidelong glance. "Like I said before, maybe we should swap wives."

"Me take Inez?"

"Well, I took her once."

"When I already can't stand Mildred much?"

"Oho! It finally comes out."

Brant's checks burned. "And since when has my wife been Millie to you?"

"It's just a manner of saying."

Brant screamed, he was so outraged. "By God, Charlie, by the great knockers of the Almighty Himself, even if Mildred was the worst woman on earth, I'd never let you have her. Not even if she hated me, I wouldn't." Brant had to suck for air to get his breath. "I'd kill her first. Or kill you."

Again Charlie's blond brows knotted up into bunches over his fierce boar's eyes. He studied over what Brant had just said. "All right. Let's just say you're too good for Inez. Like I am. All right, fine. You are. But now take a good look at me and Millie. Anybody with half an eye can see we deserve each other. We're both good breeding stock. Well built." Charlie nodded in self-appreciation. "Ah, what wonderful pups we'd make together."

"You son of a bitch! I suppose while you're divorcing Inez, I'm supposed to be divorcing Millie at the same time? I mean, Mildred."

"That's the general idea."

"A sort of double divorce? Instead of a double wedding."

"Yeh."

"By God, Charlie, you'd do that, wouldn't you, even if the devil himself stood to the door?"

"Risk little, gain little."

For a second Brant didn't know what he was going to do, he was so mad. His small fists of themselves churned the air like a pair of flywheels. Then his eye happened to fall on the neckyoke Charlie had hit earlier with a stone. "You bastard from hell!" Brant rushed over and grabbed up the neckyoke with both hands and came back holding it high over his head ready to smash Charlie.

At that moment Inez burst out of the kitchen door yelling. "Kill him, Brant! Kill him. Go ahead. Permission I give you!"

Mildred followed her. Mildred clapped a hand on Inez' shoulder. "Here. Here."

Inez kept yelling. "I says too, I says to Mildred, I says, 'That's it, I'm glad Brant killed him!'" Inez began to jump up and down, heavy feet thudding on the cement stoop. "'I'm glad Brant killed him!' I says. 'Killed him!'"

"Inez." Mildred's voice was strong. "Let's not lose our head now."

"I'm glad you killed him while you had the chanct, Brant!"

"Inez!"

"I says to her too, I says, 'For once I'm glad Brant wasn't a chicken and killed him!'"

Mildred next looked at Brant. "And you, Brant." Mildred spoke firmly. "Let's cool off now."

Brant stood transfixed, neckyoke still high over his head. Mildred's alto voice, when it really filled out, had a way of cutting the heart right out of a man.

"Brant!"

Mildred's deep voice and Inez' shrilling together were like enemy cross fire.

"Brant."

Suddenly Brant threw the neckyoke down. A man couldn't go around killing his own brother. "Charlie, by God, killing you is too good for you. But at the same time, by God, Charlie, don't you or Inez push me any further. Or, by God, Charlie, I'll take my double-barreled shotgun to you." Brant walked up and shook a balled fist in Charlie's face. "Now take your goddam mixed-up wife and get the hell off my yard. Get. I give you just thirty seconds."

Charlie got.

The last thing Brant heard as they drove off the yard was Inez' miserable wailing. "Oh, my God! Charlie's took me home again."

2

It was the week before Christmas. There was an inch of snow on the ground.

Brant was carrying a ten-gallon can of milk across the white yard to the house. He had his elbow locked into his right hip. It was the only way he could carry anything, his left side hurt him so. During the past weeks the sharp pain had at last become a great round hot throbbing thing.

He cleaned the packed snow out from under his red rubber boots on the shoe scraper, mounted the steps, then entered the side porch. Knowing that once he set the full can down he'd have an awful time getting it up again, he instead gave the can a rising boost up from his hip and somehow got the can high enough to hook the lip of it onto the edge of the separator tank. "God! How that left side burns." He hung on and began pouring the milk into the tank.

The kitchen door opened and Mildred looked in. A morning smile deepened the gravity of her dark eyes. The smell of frying ham and percolating coffee wafted past her. "Breakfast is ready if you want to eat first."

Brant finished the pouring, then let the can down with a clang. "Should really separate the milk while it's still warm."

"Whatever you want. Thought maybe you'd like to eat with the children. It's almost time for them to leave for school."

Brant shoved his fist into his side. "Oh, all right. 'Tain't too cold this morning so I guess it won't hurt the milk any to wait." He kicked off his red boots. "God."

Mildred slipped her hands into the pockets of her green apron. The gesture brought out the full heft of her strong thighs. It also emphasized the couple of inches of height she had on him. "You better go to a doctor."

"I would, but . . ."

"But what?"

"Doctors around here ain't much good."

"Not our Doctor Tom?"

"Naw." Brant gave his left side another punch. "If I have to go, I think I'll go to the Mayo Clinic. There they'll really know."

"You're afraid to go see Doctor Tom."

Brant tried to face up to her; couldn't quite do it. His eyes troubled off to one side, lidding over. "I'm not afraid to go and see him. It's just that I don't want some old duffer of a pill pusher

to guess about what I already know is cancer." He was in the act
of slipping off his red-and-black mackinaw, one arm still half in
its sleeve, when his sore side grabbed him. He groaned out of his
bones. "Ohh, God! how that catches me there sometimes."

"Cancer," Mildred scoffed. "Ha."

"You don't think so, huh?"

"No. Here. I'll help you." She pulled his arm free of the sleeve.
"Ow!"

"Oh, come on now. It can't be that bad." She hung the mackinaw up on a peg behind the door.

"What makes you so sure it ain't cancer when it ain't you
who's got it?"

"People with cancer don't eat like you do. Like a horse."

The sweet fleshy smell of milk rising from the separator almost
made Brant gag. There'd once been a day when he could drink
milk fresh out of the cow.

"Come. The children wait."

Brant dragged after her into the kitchen.

Edna and Pauline looked up from their places on the other
side of the table. Both girls had begun to bud into young woman-
hood. Pink dawn coming through the kitchen window, along with
a soft lemon light from the hanging kerosene lamp over the table,
gave both their faces a glowing rosy look. Their dark eyes
sparkled. "Good morning, Dad."

"Mrng."

Pauline asked, "Will it storm today, Dad?"

Brant began to soap up his hands in the kitchen sink. "What?
Naa. Not with the sun coming up clear."

"Good. Then Teacher will let us go outdoors and play fox
and geese in the new snow. The tracks will be nice and clear."

"Aren't you girls getting to be a little old for those kind of
games?"

"Oh, but Mother, it's still fun."

Brant scrubbed himself briskly, thoroughly, even reached up
and around behind his neck. He was about done when that
damned pain grabbed him again. "God." It held him transfixed.

Mildred set out the ham and eggs, poured Brant and herself

each a cup of coffee, then drew up a chair on the stove side of the table.

After a few moments Brant extricated himself out of the grab of the pain and toweled himself. He picked up the family comb and cut a neat part through his brown hair and combed it back behind both ears. Then, favoring his side, he went around across from Mildred and drew up his armchair.

"Edna? Pauline?" And Mildred closed her eyes.

Edna and Pauline bowed their heads and said in unison: "Our Father who are in heaven, please bless this food to our bodies, please keep us safely in the long day ahead, forgive us all our sins, in Jesus' name, Amen."

Mildred joined them on the last word. "Amen."

Brant stared down at his plate. He wasn't too sure he liked the idea of his girls being taught the Schwartz Protestant faith instead of the Harmer skepticism. Gramp Schwartz had already done too good a job of making a sober Lutheran out of Mildred.

The girls went brightly about helping themselves to ham and eggs and buttered toast, and of pouring themselves a glass of chilled milk.

Brant also helped himself generously to the ham and eggs and toast. He added a spurt of cream and a heaping spoon of sugar to his steaming coffee. He sipped at the coffee. Ah, at least the java was good today. His eyes settled gravely on his plate.

Mildred helped herself to the ham and eggs and toast last.

Brant's overalls began to pinch him on his game side, so he loosened the side buttons.

Edna asked suddenly, "Mother, will Uncle Charlie and Aunt Inez give us a Christmas present this year?"

Mildred paused in her eating. "I hadn't given it any thought, child."

"Maybe he thinks we're getting too old for that."

"Well, maybe you are."

" 'Course Uncle Charlie really won't give us a present because he's still probably mad at us."

"Oh, I don't think Uncle Charlie ever really was mad at us. Besides, I know he likes his nieces."

Brant stuck strictly to the business of eating his ham and eggs.

Then Edna asked, "Why didn't Uncle Charlie and Aunt Inez have any children?"

"I don't know." Mildred got up to put some cobs in the stove. "That's something for the good Lord to know, not us."

"It would have been nice if he could have just one. And a boy. Then we would've had a boy cousin."

"Yes, that would have been nice." Mildred returned to her seat.

Brant said, "Sometimes it feels like I've swallowed me a whole live crab."

"A crab?"

"That's what it feels like I got here in the center of my belly."

Mildred said flatly, "What you've got is probably just a tapeworm, if it's anything at all, the way you eat."

Brant bristled. "Woman, a tapeworm is a cold fishy thing. While what I got is a hot hard thing."

Edna said, "Dad's turning blue around his eyes again."

Pauline spotted something through the window. "There come the Gatelys. C'mon, or we'll be late for school."

"Oh, my," Edna cried, "now we'll really have to hurry. The Gatelys are hardly ever on time."

Both girls hurried to get their coats and shawls on and skipped for the door.

"Got your lunch buckets?" Mildred asked quietly, arms akimbo.

"Oh, we almost forgot. Thanks, Mother."

Feet scurried back across the kitchen; tin pails clinked together; more swift footsteps sounded; then the door slammed shut.

Outside there were happy cries of greeting, and then slowly childish voices faded away.

Silence in the kitchen.

Man and wife ate with little macerating sounds.

The nickel clock over the sink rocked along. The cob fire in the stove collapsed with soft crinkling sounds.

Out of the corner of his eye Brant could see a troubled look gathering on Mildred's face now that the girls were gone. Her eyes resembled little chocolate puddings being stirred.

Brant coughed quietly to himself. He thought he knew what was bothering Mildred. He hadn't laid a hand on her for almost a half year, not since Kon and Karen got married last August.

An old thought shot through Brant: "Why did that crazy Kon have to get married? Why? He was better off dead. That witch Karen."

Mildred went on brooding to herself on her side of the table.

Brant thought: "Well, it's gone and done now. No use in thinking about it anymore. Besides, from now on it's not supposed to be any of my business what Kon does with his life."

At the same time Brant couldn't help but feel a little sorry for Mildred. Poor woman. There she sat now, sad-eyed and silent, when it was her nature to be full of smiles and overflow with warm joking talk.

He watched Mildred sip her coffee.

Well, in a way it was her own fault. He hadn't asked her to throw her life away on a weak-sister Harmer. It was she who'd chased him, not he her. She'd persisted in dropping in on the Harmers, using anything as an excuse just to see him.

The coffee was rich and flavorsome. Brant held out his cup for more, avoiding Mildred's eyes.

Mildred obliged him, filling his cup to the brim.

Brant put in the cream and sugar and stirred it. He sipped. Ah, good, good.

There was the first time they'd done it together. He, like Kon, had never thought much about girls, about what one did when alone with them. But Mildred kept taunting him that he was afraid to spoon with her because he was scared of Pa Schwartz. Taunting always got him. It drove him wild. So the next thing he knew he was under the lilac bushes with her.

It made him burn, and yet smile too, when he remembered what happened under the lilac bushes. Pa Schwartz had a habit of getting up around one in the morning in his long underwear and wandering out on the grass and relieving himself. Pa

Schwartz liked his glass of home-brew beer at bedtime and so
always had to get up sometime in the night. For some reason,
probably because the grass was wet with dew, this night Pa
Schwartz wandered out onto the edge of the back porch instead
of going out on the yard someplace. To the stiffening astonishment of both Mildred and Brant, Pa Schwartz paused directly
over them. First he hawked up a gob of spittle and shot it over
the lilacs. The pellet of spit landed on the grass like the sharp
fall of a cricket. Then, my God, Pa Schwartz hauled away at the
buttons of his long underwear and let fly into the lilacs. By the
time the stream had worked its way down to where they lay
hidden, it had broken up into tiny drops and fell on them like a
fine rain. It was unpossible. Yet there they were, slowly getting
wet, especially Brant on top. Neither one dared to move. They
just lay there petrified. All they could do was to wait until the old
man finished. And it was Mildred's slow tensing up under Brant,
rising, that suddenly set off a burning in Brant's loins. God. It
was the first time he'd ever had such a sweet fit. At last he knew
what it was that men smiled about when the women weren't
around. Finally Pa Schwartz was finished, and the little shower
was over. Buttoning up, Pa Schwartz went back to bed.

Brant and Mildred didn't do it again until they got married.
Brant shook his head in memory. That'd turned out to be a
funny time too. They honeymooned in a cabin on a lake up in
Minnesota. The first day he got the twenty-four-hour stomach
flu and so had an excuse not to hug her. The second night it
hailed so hard there was too much noise to make love. But the
third night his flu was gone and the skies were quiet. All of a
sudden, as they lay side by side in the dark, Mildred began to
sing, mostly to herself, but also a little to him. Mildred had a low
melodious voice. She sang alto in the choir in her Lutheran
church, and sometimes, on special occasions, sang solos. In the
early days of their acquaintance, the only time Brant ever went
to church was on those special occasions. He was bewitched by
her voice and tried to hear it as often as he could. The large heart
of a woman was in it. The sound of it awoke little sheet light-
nings all through his belly. It was like hearing blood pouring

from a cup. So when she began singing to him in bed he found himself slowly stiffening up. Her voice lulled him at the same time that it thickened him. And then she touched him. God! He thought he'd explode sky-high. At the same time a devil awoke in him and the devil took him and made him grab her. She helped him, still singing in a series of sweet pulsations. He went completely wild inside. With all his might he tried to make himself over into her being. Presently a sweet shivering came over her. It lifted her up under him and abruptly her singing fell away into a low cry. Of a sudden, the sweet fit came over him a second time.

Brant blinked.

Across the table from him he saw that an old smile had appeared on Mildred's lips.

"What are you laughing about?"

"Oh," Mildred said, "I was just wondering what Charlie really will do this Christmas about the girls."

So it was Charlie now, was it? Brant let his cup drop into its saucer. He jumped to his feet. "That son of a bitch!" He took a step around the table toward Mildred.

Suddenly it was as though someone had thrown a pail of hot water all through his belly. He fell heavily to the floor.

Mildred turned white. "Brant." Then she quick got to her feet and rushed to his side. "Brant!"

Brant's eyes turned up under his eyelids. "Guess you better take me to Doctor Tom after all," he whispered. "Right away."

3

By the time Mildred and Dr. Drury got Brant up on the examination table the hot water in Brant's belly had become scalding water.

Dr. Drury's huge shoulders loomed over Brant on one side of the table while Mildred with sorrowed eyes leaned over Brant on the other.

"Can you slip down your overalls?" Dr. Drury asked.

Brant spoke through set teeth. "I'll try." Holding his boiling belly all of a piece, Brant unhooked first one suspender, then the other, and then slid the overalls down over his hips.

"A little farther, please?"

Brant was afraid to lift himself any higher. He shook his head.

"Here, I'll help you," Mildred said.

But Dr. Drury beat her to it. His strong hairy hands deftly slid the overalls well past Brant's hips. "Now your underwear."

Teeth still set tight, Brant obliged him.

"Where does it hurt you?"

"Mostly all over in my belly now."

"Where did it hurt you the most at first?"

Brant held his hand over his left side, not quite touching it. "Down here."

"When did you first notice it?"

"Since late last summer. Wasn't it, Mildred?"

Mildred nodded. "About when school started is when he began to complain."

Brant's brows came together. "Oh. I remember now. The exact time. It was right after Kon got married."

Dr. Drury pressed his thumb down on the middle of Brant's stomach. "Does this hurt?"

"Not specially."

Dr. Drury's thumb moved slightly to the right. "Here?"

"Not really."

"Here?"

"You're looking in the wrong place, Doc. It's over there on the left side."

"When did you last have a bowel movement?"

"Yesterday morning. Like usual."

"Not today?"

"Not yet."

Dr. Drury's thumb moved down and pressed low and hard on the right side. "How about this?"

Brant began to notice a strange thing. The more Doctor Tom

touched him, the more the boiling pain seemed to ease off. "No."

Dr. Drury's thumb at last moved to the right place, left and low down. "This hurt?"

To Brant's surprise the pain there wasn't bad at all now. "Well-l . . . a little. Yes."

"What's it feel like?"

"Well . . . it's kinda like . . . heh heh . . . as if a corncob's caught in there. A rough one." Brant threw Mildred a fleeting look of apology. " 'Course I know that ain't possible." Brant allowed himself a pinched smile at his own pleasantry. "Not even a hog eats a corn ear whole."

Mildred didn't smile.

"Kinda like a whole carrot got in there somehow."

Still Mildred didn't smile.

Dr. Drury kept pressing a powerful thumb into Brant's left side. "I want you to tell me when it really begins to hurt now."

Brant suffered the pressing hairy thumb.

"Anything?"

"Just mostly a round numbness in that one spot."

"Sigmoid flexure."

"Tell you, Doc—what it mostly feels like is a pain inside another pain."

"Mmm."

Brant couldn't understand it, couldn't get over it. His belly was actually getting better and better by the minute, now that he was in the doctor's office. About the only thing left where anything hurt him was where his feet hung over the edge of the examination table. "It comes and goes, like, I guess."

"How's your appetite been?"

"Pretty good."

Mildred folded her arms over her chest, giving her full bosom an emphatic lift as she did so. "He eats like a horse."

Dr. Drury ran a hand up over his balding brow. "He does, eh?"

Mildred went on. "I'll never in my life understand how such a scrawny little fellow can eat so much and yet not get fat."

"Hey," Brant said, "I like that."

"Well, you do eat a lot, Brant."

"Well, woman, but I work hard. I burn it up with all the work I do."

"I know you work hard, Brant."

"And all the worrying I have to do."

Dr. Drury's brow came up a little. "Have to?" Dr. Drury's black eyes looked right through Brant.

"Well, yeh. You know. Making a go of things. These days it takes a lot out of a man just to farm a quarter alone."

"Every farmer has that worry."

Brant bristled. "Hey, I didn't come here to get told I was a sissy."

Dr. Drury cocked his head at Mildred. "Does he tend to be a little high strung sometimes?"

"Very."

"Hey!" Brant sat bolt upright. "I like that too."

Dr. Drury shot them both a question. "You folks didn't by any chance have a family argument this morning?"

Brant's lips turned down at the corners. "Well, no, not so much this morning."

Mildred spoke matter-of-factly. "We've been a little cool to each other lately all right."

"By the Lord," Brant cried, "what's this all about? I came here with a sore belly, remember? An awful sore belly."

Dr. Drury had a faint sneer for him. "In your head."

"I'll be a son of a bitch!" Brant cried. Then he leaped off the examination table and snapped his overall suspenders up over his shoulders. "I've had enough of your trying to"—he threw Dr. Drury a scorching look—"lick me with the rough side of your tongue." Fastening his side buttons as he went, he added, "I told you, Mildred, that the docs around here ain't much good."

Dr. Drury watched him go out through the door with glinting eyes.

Mildred said, "I'm sorry, Doctor Tom. But it is true he gets all wound up sometimes. Like a ball of yarn that's been left out in the rain overnight."

Dr. Drury nodded. "Any time."

Going home, a mile from their house, Brant all of a sudden speeded up. His grip on the steering wheel of the old Ford tightened.

"What's the matter now?" Mildred asked.

Brant only drove the harder. Scarves of white snow began to play off to either side of the rushing car.

"Brant?"

Brant slowed some for their lane; turned in on two wheels, almost tipping over.

"Not so wild, Brant!"

By the house gate Brant stepped on the brakes so hard that the back wheels of the old Ford skated across the powdery snow on the ground. He jumped out on his side even before the car had stopped, then made a beeline for the privy.

"Well, I never," Mildred said.

Brant stayed in the outhouse a long while.

4

It rained during the night.

With the fields too wet to work the next morning, and time on his hands, Brant knew what he had to do. High time too.

He rummaged through the toolshed until he came up with an old rusty sickle, and two weather-blackened pitchforks, and some loose strands of yellow twine string. With an electric drill he carefully drilled a hole through either end of the sickle. He selected two long screws to fit. Then, picking up a screwdriver and a sawhorse to stand on, he headed for the house.

The sun had a hard time breaking through the April mist. There was light out but it lay on the land like a thin smoke.

The cracking sound of a screw being wormed into wood brought Mildred to the porch door. She looked up through the screen at Brant. She asked mildly, "What are you doing?"

"Oh, nothing much." Brant held the sickle in place over the

doorhead as he worked. "Just a little thing I should have taken care of long ago."

She pressed her cheeks against the screen for a better look. "What do we need a sickle up there for?"

"Decoration."

"Oh, come now, Brant. Not really."

"And, just to make extra sure."

"Extra sure about what?"

Brant looked down at Mildred over a half-raised arm. "Don't you see? This sickle is going to be our hexafoos."

"That fable stuff again of your mother's."

"Don't you get too snooty about what Mother believes in."

"Just the same."

"No, this sickle will fix it so them goddam hex witches can't sneak into the house at night. The way things have been falling down off the shelves lately, they've got to be sneaking in somewhere. Let alone the way they've been sneaking little pinches of poison into my food."

Mildred tried to push open the screen door; found it blocked by the sawhorse. "Don't talk crazy now, Brant."

"What about the way my shaving mug fell down yesterday and broke in the sink when nobody was around, hey?" Brant threw a wise look to one side. "Heh heh, that was no accident."

"Why, Brant Harmer, that was because you never set your mug proper on the shelf. I'm always pushing it back where it belongs after you're done. It was finally no wonder it fell off, the way the kids slam the door."

At that very moment the girls Edna and Pauline slammed the door on the other side of the house. They were rushing off to school.

Mildred said, "You see what I mean?"

Brant shook his head. "That ain't the way I see it."

"And sneaking little pinches of poison into your food . . . why, Brant Harmer, are you accusing me of trying to poison you?"

"Oh, I ain't saying that you're doin' it."

"But who else could?"

"I ain't saying."

"Brant, are you crazy?"

"Hah." Brant smiled a sidewise knowing smile. "Let 'em think I am a little crazy. Then maybe they'll stay away."

At that Mildred's eyes opened ever so slightly.

Brant made four more quick turns with the screwdriver, and then one more slowly binding turn, and he had one side of the sickle secured. He dug the other screw out of his pocket, and after making sure the curve of the sickle was level so that it couldn't leak water, began to turn the second screw into the doorhead too.

Mildred folded her arms up under her bosom. "Hexafoos. Good gravy, such heathen ideas. And on my house yet."

"Well, I always kinda believed it was true."

Mildred had in mind to say something sharp, but after a moment of thought managed to take another tack. "Well, I guess it won't hurt none to have it up there as a decoration at that. It might even bring us good luck. Like a horseshoe over the door."

"Shh. I want them hex witches to be afraid of it. Not good luck."

Mildred blinked. She brushed down her hips. Then she gave herself a good shake. "By the way, I forgot to tell you that when I was over to Ma's yesterday, Karen was there."

Brant stiffened. "Kon too?"

"No, he didn't come along. Just Karen and a Whitebone drayman in a pickup. They came to get that old oak table Ma had up in the attic there. You know how Karen dotes on antiques and redoes them for her house. Ma said they could have it."

"Funny she didn't drop by here. Hch. Probably too stuck up for us by now."

"She didn't have time. They were paying the drayman by the hour."

"Well, I still say, a bright daughter makes a brittle wife."

Mildred smiled. "Oh, I wouldn't say Karen was brittle exactly."

"Like Charlie, I never had much use for her. She always reminded me of a witch."

"A witch? Oh, no. It's the other way around. It's more that she always acts a little kiddish. Like a little girl who doesn't know anything about what's what."

The sun at last broke over the veil of mist in the east. It lay like a gouged-out eye on a wad of gray cotton.

Mildred's eyes drifted off. "All you have to do is to take a good look at that marriage of theirs."

"How so?"

"If one can believe what she says."

Brant made three more turns with his screwdriver. He was almost finished with the second screw. At the same time he cocked an ear to hear what else Mildred might have to say.

"Both still as innocent as babes."

The sun behind Brant continued to brighten. Its warm rays touched the sore side of his body. "As innocent as what, did you say?"

"As babes."

Brant's hand stilled. His eyes fixed on the curved rusty sickle in front of him. "You mean . . . ?"

"Well, from what she says they ain't true man and wife yet."

The rusty sickle began to waver in front of Brant. "You mean, if they was to break up now, their marriage could be annulled? Even by the church?"

"Yes. Like the Bible says, Kon still has not known his wife. According to her."

The sun brightened even more upon Brant's side. He suddenly, wonderfully, felt very warm and happy inside. Maybe Kon hadn't ruined his life after all. "So. By God."

"It's hard to believe."

Brant all of a sudden stuck his tongue out at life as far as he could, so far he caught sight of the tip of it protruding under his nose like a fat ripe strawberry.

"That a man and a woman can lay in bed together night after night and not touch each other as God intended. . . ." Mildred shook her head.

Brant went back to turning the screw into the doorhead. The rusty sickle began to set firm.

"Not human not to."

A whistle rose from Brant's lips. He shaped it to sound like the morning call of a meadowlark.

"At least you and I behave normal compared to them." She threw Brant a look.

Brant cocked his head sideways, once. Now Mildred was fishing.

"At least we can point to Edna and Pauline." Mildred sighed. "Though I often wished we could point to more." Her eyes hazed over. "One boy at least more."

"We could've had two boys if you'd've let me start the show them two times."

"That didn't make any difference."

"Oh, yes it did. It's the way you think at the time you do it that throws the dice one way or another. And you wasn't thinking like a true woman was supposed t'."

"Oh, good gravy, Brant, what kind of talk is that now?"

"True, though."

"Prove it."

"I don't have to prove it. Because I've got something a whole lot better than proof."

"And what is that?"

"My firm convictions." Brant gave the screw a final turn, so that a rising squeak came out of the wood. Then he stuck the screwdriver into his back pocket and jumped down off the saw-horse. "There, that's done."

"It still ain't too late, you know."

Brant shot a finger at her. "Hold her. And hold her right there. That's where I draw the line. There'll be no more children in this house if I got anything to say about it. Two is more than enough as it is." A look of sly cunning moved across his face. "Unless'n of course you want to take up with my stud brother Charlie."

"You must be cr-azy."

"Maybe I am. But that's the way it is." Brant next picked up the weather-blackened pitchforks and started into the house. As he did so, he happened to brush against Mildred and one of the black tines pricked her a little in the thigh.

"Ow," Mildred said. "Watch out where you're going."

"Sorry."

"And where do you think you're going with them dirty things?"

Brant looked at her in surprise. "Why, I'm going to tie them under our bed. To the springs."

"You're what?"

Brant decided that here was something he should explain carefully to her. "You see, pitchforks is the enemy of broomsticks. Pitchforks always has been and always will be. You see, a pitchfork just likes to stick itself into anything riding a broomstick. When them hex witches see these pitchforks under our bed tonight, black ones, like they's been stained black with blood, maybe even with witch blood, why, they'll know that here at last they've got hold of a man's bed, as well as God's bed, and not a woman's bed, and then, by God, they'll fly away like all get out." Brant coughed to one side. " 'Course, that's supposin' they get past this sickle up here." Brant coughed again. "I'm just making doubly sure, you see."

A look of slowly dawning horror came into Mildred's eyes.

"Just you watch tonight," Brant went on. "Right on the dot at midnight, when them hex witches spot these black pitchforks of the Lord Jesus' under our bed, you'll hear a screech from 'em that'll melt the wax right out of your ears."

Mildred sat down beside the kitchen table. She gradually turned white over the cheekbones.

Whistling, Brant proceeded upstairs to their bedroom. He got down on his back and slid under their brass bed. With the twine string he tied the pitchforks to the bedspring.

Finished, he lay looking up at the undersides of the bedsprings a moment.

Come to think of it, though, them hex witches just might get overmad with both of them hexafooses put up against them. Maybe he ought to give them a kind of a going-away present to soften their wrath a little. A nice little present of some kind. A special favor. A gift of food. Yep, that's what he'd do. Tomorrow he'd move the road fence over a couple of rods into his field so they couldn't use the excuse that they didn't have enough room to get away. And come next harvest time he'd let stand a couple of acres of oats in the corners for them. That ought to soften their hearts a little.

Slowly he slid into his favorite reverie.

Wouldn't it be wonderful if he and Kon could live them good old times over again, and play they were wild horses in the old slough under the champion cottonwood, galloping and neighing and frisking around, free, having a great time? Or play they were famous bird hunters, looking for redwing nests in the deep grass and counting the brown lines on the green eggs, all the while sweet-talking up at the mother bird hanging nervous in the air above them. Or play they themselves were a pair of hungry red-wings chasing yellow butterflies down the slough to see who'd be the first to catch one. Or, if it was raining, play they were sailors on a big boat up in the haymow, going hand over hand down the hay-carrier rail, until at last, laughing, they'd drop bouncing on the whiskery hay below.

Oh what fun oh what joy oh what heaven.

PART FIVE

✿❀✿❀✿❀✿❀✿❀✿❀✿❀✿❀✿❀✿❀✿

Karen

1

Whitebone lay in a valley on the west bank of the Big Rock River. Even in Indian times there'd been trees along the river, and the early settlers had been wise enough to plant more trees as they built the town out, so that Whitebone became known as that little city with all the trees. Except for the new developments on the west side of town, it was difficult to make out, as one approached Whitebone, the roof of a single house. Only the red roof of the county courthouse stuck out over the treetops. Since the red roof was similar in color to the scarlet quarries at the base of the Blue Mounds north of town, it appeared to be more of an outcropping of nature than an edifice erected by man.

For a little while Karen and Kon wondered if it'd been wise to build where they did, at the end of a lane on the north side of town. The nearest house was three blocks away, the city still hadn't dug the sewer line out that far, and the spot was quite high and windy. But they'd got the lot dirt cheap, and Kon liked the idea of pioneering, while Karen didn't mind, and so they'd taken the plunge.

They lived in their new house for perhaps two months when

they noticed an odd thing. Whenever they ran into any of their nearest neighbors it was as if they'd just missed catching them talking about them. Whispering about them. Gossiping.

The whispering puzzled them. What could it be? So far as they knew they were living perfectly decent lives as man and wife. They kept their place neat. He worked hard at his teaching in school. She was a good housewife.

Karen was a little angry. She thought the people in Whitebone were ungrateful. They should have been happy to see that their new teacher had enough faith in the future of the little city to want to build where he did.

Then the very first Saturday night in May they found out why their neighbors were whispering. It was Karen's keen ears that caught it.

They were already in bed, asleep, when something awoke Karen. At first she thought something was the matter with their new Westminster clock downstairs. There seemed to be some kind of squealing in the works. Kon had wondered a little when the local clockmaker said the new clock would never need oiling. Having lived on the farm, Kon was sure that any and all moving parts needed oil from time to time. But no, the clockmaker had said, not this clock. Wind it every eight days, and it would run until doomsday.

Karen was lying on her right side, knees drawn up a little. She could more sense than feel Kon lying on his right side too with his knees drawn up. Every few breaths, when Kon took a deeper one than usual, she could feel where one of his knees almost touched her on the sitter.

There it was again. A squealing noise. Downstairs in the clock all right.

Could it be mice squealing in the clock instead of a squealing in the works? She stiffened at the idea. Mice in the clock? "Well, I should say not," she thought, "not in my house."

The big tall clock downstairs clicked. A moment later its chimes pealed clear and gentle, four gongs, followed by a gathering pause, and then the slow clangs for the hour.

Karen counted them. ". . . ten, eleven, twelve." Midnight.

Well, it couldn't be mice. They'd never live in the clock with all that racket around. Besides, how could they get in?

There it was again. Squealing. Kind of a giggling even.

She opened her eyes, her right eyelash making a wisping sound against the pillow.

Light from a full moon filled the bedroom with gentle illumination. Her dolly Kathryn's little walnut cradle stood clearly limned on the golden hope chest. Sweet dolly Kathryn lay sound asleep in it, of course. Someday a real child Kathryn would take its place and sleep in it. Later on the real little Kathryn child could play with the doll and in turn name it after her mother.

Karen turned her head until she could make out the entire bedroom. The white curtains on the windows shimmered like fragile silver netting. The walnut antique chest of drawers with a lamp standing on top for a fleeting moment resembled her square-shouldered strong-willed father, Alfred Alfredson V. Father sometimes wore his straw hat exactly the way the shade on the lamp was tipped up on one side.

Again the squealing.

With both ears free of the pillow, she now knew for sure it wasn't in the clock, neither mice nor the works. It came from outside the house. The south window in the bedroom was cracked open an inch—Kon was a fresh-air fiend—and it was through that that the sound had come.

"Kon?" she whispered.

"Yes?"

She was always amazed at how lightly he slept. The merest whisper, the slightest motion on her part, and he was wide awake. "Kon, listen once."

"What is it?"

"Shh. Listen. I heard some squealing."

Pause.

"Hear it?"

"No."

"Listen carefully."

They listened. This time there was nothing.

"Where?" he whispered.

"That's funny. I was sure I heard something."

"You probably dreamt it."

"First I thought it was maybe the works in the new clock. Squealing. You know." She didn't mention her notion it might be mice. "But then I heard it outside through that partly open window there."

"Maybe something's hurt. A dog or so. Run over by one of those wild drivers who sometimes nose into here."

"Listen."

There it was again. Quite clear. A giggling more than a squealing. Tender. Somewhat dewy even. Someone was having a high old time.

Both Karen and Kon rose to a sitting position in bed. Hair a little disheveled from sleep, they looked at one another with widening eyes.

A young girl's voice cried out quite clearly. "Rodger, you quit that."

A young man's voice groused in loving admiration. "Aw, c'mon, be a sport, Tatsie."

A series of squeals and giggles followed.

"Rodger, now you behave yourself!"

"Aw, c'mon."

Both Karen and Kon knuckled out of bed, quick, each on their side, and in their long white nightgowns scurried barefoot to the window.

There below along the lane, where it fell away to the west, were parked at least a half-dozen shiny new cars. The cars were all just far enough over the hill to be out of sight of anyone looking from the highway. Each car had its lover couple.

Karen turned to look at Kon at the same time that Kon turned to look at her. They said it together. "This is a lovers' lane. That's why everybody is whispering."

"Rodger!" the young girl cried again.

"Be a sport, Tatsie. It won't hurt."

"Well, forevermore," Karen whispered. "Those little stinkers."

A smile appeared at the roots of Kon's nose. "Little stinkers? I wouldn't say they were so little."

"Big or little, they're stinkers just the same."

"Now, Karen. People have a right to live their own lives."

"Those kids are people?"

"They're old enough to have babies."

"Wonder what their parents would say if they knew."

"You don't suppose those boys stole their own dads' cars?"

"Konstant Harmer, are you defending fornication?"

"Of course not."

"Well, you sound like it. And you know what our good Lord said about that."

"He that is without sin among you, let him be the first to cast a stone."

Karen leveled a pair of blinking green eyes at Kon. "What an odd passage for you to be quoting from the Bible."

"Not at all. I know of some people who think us pretty strange too. What with us still having no children and all."

Karen looked down at where Kon's thin knotted calves showed below his nightshirt. "Well, that's true."

"And yet don't we have the right to live our lives as we see fit?"

"Yes, I guess we do."

"Fair is fair."

"Yes, I guess a person does have the perfect right to be let alone."

The sound of more dewy squealing came from the parked cars below. And again a girl's voice feigned protest in loving notes. "Rodger, you son of a gun, you"

"Aw, c'mon, Tatsie, don't always be such a wet blanket."

Kon looked down at the lovers some more. "Well, I suppose if the youngsters are going to spoon they're going to spoon. But, dear Lord, do they have to do it right under our very noses?"

"No, they don't."

Kon nodded to himself. "Well, I'm going to do something about this. And I know just what I'm going to do too."

"What's that, dear?"

"You'll see tomorrow." Kon shut the window with a slight slam, then toed back to bed.

Karen first had a peek at the walnut cradle to see that all was well with her doll Kathryn. The big doll lay flat on its back. In the muted moonlight its eyes were closed, blank, and its big broad forehead, framed by curls of real brown hair, gleamed a pale alabaster. Karen whispered, " 'Night, honey, and be a good girl now." Then Karen lay herself down beside Kon, quietly.

Karen and Kon lay on their backs awhile, each on their side of the bed, staring up at the ceiling.

After a time, Kon, sighing, slowly rolled over on his right side.

Karen could feel his kneecap where it touched her slender thigh. She liked Kon. They'd become very good friends. They could easily have been born brother and sister, so attentive were they to each other. "While those stinkers out there have rushed ahead of themselves." Presently Karen sighed too, and also slowly turned over on her right side.

Downstairs the Westminster clock struck the quarter hour.

Karen's body sighed yet again. Then, as she always had ever since she was a little girl, she hunched up a little, making a deeper figure S of her body, until her sitter was almost in Kon's lap.

So they slept.

The next afternoon, after school, Kon came home carrying something in addition to his briefcase. The thing was furry and he was holding it in the crook of his arm.

Karen saw him coming from her window in the kitchen. Wondering, she went to the back door and opened it just as he came up the steps. "What in the world have you got there?"

"Wolf," he said.

"A wolf?"

"German police dog." Kon set his briefcase on a chair and came cradling the furry thing toward her. "It's a puppy."

"Why, Kon, it's a darling little dog."

"Feel him. But be careful. He's got sharp teeth. And he really can bite, the little rascal." Kon ruffled the puppy playfully over the neck. "Now the cats around here are going to have to look out, aren't they, huh, Wolf?"

Karen touched the little puppy gingerly, then stroked it a little.

Its liquid bluish-brown eyes gazed up at her. After a moment it waggled its tail a little. "You aren't really going to call him Wolf, are you?"

"Yes."

"What an awful name. Wolf."

"Well, he's got the markings of a wolf. A brindle gray with streaks of black. Besides, it's going to be fun watching what our squealing friends along lovers' lane are going to do when we start calling him home for supper. 'Here, Wolf. Come, Wolf.' "

"Kon. You wouldn't."

"They'll think twice about parking around here with that big wolf police dog running up and down the lane. Panting with his long red tongue out and his big white teeth showing."

Karen drew in her nether lip, thoughtfully. "Just so Wolf doesn't get it in for me. I never yet was able to get along with animals."

"Oh, but you will this one," Kon said. "Because you're going to raise him from baby on. As if he were your own child. With a bottle and a nipple. It'll take you over as its own mother."

"I only hope so. I always so wanted a pet."

Wolf came to love Karen. He waddled after her everywhere she went. It was with difficulty that she got him to sleep downstairs in his own blanket-lined box behind the stove. Karen very carefully had to explain to him in her play-pretend manner that only dollies and babies slept upstairs with their papas and mamas, while good little doggies, if they really were good, always slept behind the stove.

By the time Wolf was a year old all the lovers had vanished from lovers' lane. He grew to be almost three feet tall. When his big head pricked up and his neck ruffed out, not even the town bullies hanging out at Barth's filling station near the high school cared to toot their horns when they drove past. They were afraid he might tackle the car itself.

Sometimes Kon took Wolf out for a walk at night, especially when the moon was shining.

He'd say, "Wanna go for a dog walk, huh?"

Wolf would rear up from behind the stove and pad over to the door.

"So you wanna go for a dog walk, huh?"

"Woof."

"Shall we go scare all those lovers away? Scare 'em right out of their pantses?"

"Woof!"

"Boys and girls both?"

"Woof! Woof!"

"Now, Kon," Karen said.

Kon only smiled. "But supposing they won't want to go away, then what, eh?"

At that Wolf first made a slashing feint with his jaw, sidewise, then shot his head forward in a loud gobbling swallow.

"Attaboy, Wolf. Now we're ready to go. Let's go get 'em."

Out into the night they went like a couple of mischievous boys.

2

May came. Time to enlarge the garden.

Every morning Kon was up before breakfast and every afternoon was home early from school turning over sod with his spade. Slowly new furrow after new furrow edged across what had once been pasture land.

One evening at supper, Karen wondered out loud why he didn't get a farmer to plow up the sod for him. "It would only take a minute and save you a lot of back-breaking work."

Kon's light-blue eyes opened a little. "Now, Karen, please."

"It takes you so long, the way you do it."

"Karen, please don't interfere."

"So primitive."

"Karen, please don't rob me of one of the joys of my life. I enjoy digging into the earth. Doing it my way."

"I'm not scolding you, honey. It's just that I want to make it easier for you. You sweat so."

"Sweating is good for me." He cut his meat into neat little pieces, all of them square, and then, dipping them deftly in a little puddle of gravy in one corner of his plate, began to eat them one by one. "Besides, I do a much better job with my spade than any farmer can do with his plow. By far."

Karen cut her meat into even smaller pieces. She ate sparingly, thoughtfully. Strong sunlight from the west flashed all through the kitchen. The light-green walls in the breakfast nook deepened the green of her eyes. "You're through for the day now though, aren't you?"

"I should say not. I want to turn over that far corner near the little crab apple trees and put in some strawberry transplants before dark. Strawberries like to be put to bed in the evening. With a good watering. Why?"

"Our off-the-kitchen bathroom isn't working very well."

"What's the matter with it?"

"Sometimes it keeps running after you flush it."

"That's funny. It's almost still new."

"That's what I thought. The one upstairs is all right."

Kon gave it a little thought. "Tell you what you do. Pour a little vinegar into where that brass stem slides through that brass collar. You know, that brass stem that's got a rubber bulb at the end? Vinegar acts as a lubricant in water."

Karen held her head to one side. "Where did you learn all that?"

"From Pa."

Karen ate little bit by little bit. "You miss the farm, don't you?"

"Well, yes and no." Kon finished his meat and potatoes and pushed his plate to one side. "I like to live out in the country, yes. But I don't like the farm work itself."

"But you do miss your folks though, don't you?" Karen replaced his empty plate with a dish of quivering raspberry jello.

"I miss my brothers a lot." Kon pitched into the dessert. "Especially Brant."

"We should probably buy a car so we could drive home more often."

"Maybe we should."

Karen mulled to herself some more. "You're sure now that this vinegar will keep it running good?"

"You'll maybe have to keep lubricating it until it wears itself a proper groove."

"It'll keep doing this off and on for a while then?"

"Probably."

She gave it all some more thought, then said, "Maybe we should buy one of those noiseless toilets."

Kon looked up questioningly. He had just spooned up some jello and held it quivering pink to his lips.

"Because besides that running after, it also makes a funny pfhooming noise. So that sometimes it even makes Wolf howl."

Kon continued to look at her wonderingly.

Karen gave a little nervous laugh. "Anyway, what I was going to tell you was that a salesman came around today trying to sell me one of them noiseless toilets."

Kon swallowed the spoon of jello all in one lump. "A salesman actually came to our door trying to sell you such a thing?"

"Yes."

"For godsakes."

"What's wrong with that?"

"Why, just that I think it's sort of indelicate for someone to go around from door to door selling . . . toilets."

"You think so?"

"Yes, I do."

"Well, and I think there's something to be said for it. Especially if they're selling noiseless toilets. Noiseless toilets call less attention to something that is nobody's business in the first place. While noisy toilets are a betrayal of the privacy of one's own toilet doings."

"You're not serious."

"I am."

"You listened to this . . . this fellow?"

"I did."

. . . Karen was ironing curtains when she heard a crisp knock on the back door.

Wolf barked and got up from his spot behind the stove.

"Quiet, Wolf. Let me see who it is first."

She looked out, and was surprised to see it was a salesman. She and Kon were seldom bothered by them, living as they did three blocks away from their nearest neighbor.

Reluctantly she opened the door a crack. "Yes?"

"Madam, I have something here of special importance for the genteel housewife."

"What is it?"

The fellow took off his gray hat, revealing a pink forehead and a receding hairline. He was a good-looking chubby man. He wore a dark-brown business suit. The toes of his shoes shone like a pair of black billiard balls.

"What is it?"

The fellow lifted a large suitcase a little. "It will be difficult to demonstrate my product out here. May I come in? Please?"

"Well . . ." Karen opened the door a crack farther.

The fellow pushed boldly past her into the house. And without asking her, placed his hat on the hall seat. "Ah, you have a lovely home."

"Thank you."

"Could I please have some water?"

"Water? You mean a drink of water?"

"No. Just some water." The fellow fixed her with hard, unblinking, gray-edged eyes. "For what I wish to show you."

"What is this thing you want to show me?"

Again he adroitly stepped past her. "Ah, I see you have a half bath just off the kitchen. May I have a look at it? Please?" He stepped into the little toilet, and to Karen's amazement flicked the handle to the stool, making it flush. The stool let go with a "Pfhoom!" followed by a noise as if it were both choking and clearing its throat. "Ukk-achh!"

Wolf let go with a sad howl from his spot behind Karen.

"Quiet, Wolf!" Karen's brow gathered into a deep frown. "Just what in the world do you think you're—"

"Shh. I just wanted to see if it was functioning properly." He cocked an ear. "Ah. It also keeps running afterward. You poor woman, you."

"Yes, it sometimes does that."

Quickly he set his suitcase on the floor and opened up. There, shining white, and built in the most modern of streamlined styles, was a miniature stool. "Could you let me have a quart measure of some kind?" He took the demonstrator stool out of its case and set it squarely on the open seat of the Harmer stool. "Please?"

Karen, by now caught, got him an empty milk bottle.

"Thank you." He listened to the larger stool to make sure it was still running, then, nodding, and using the quart bottle, filled the small demonstrator stool from the faucet in the sink. "Now," he said. He gently pressed down the handle, then lifted the lid to the little seat so she could watch the flushing action.

The flushing action was beautiful. The water swirled around and around, easily and gently, almost silently, and then, with only the softest of coughs, flushed down and up around through the trap, and dropped into the Harmer stool.

"You see?" he smiled. "Hardly any sound at all. Super-quiet flushing. Decent. Considerate of my lady's feelings. Whereas the old-style toilet, such as the one you have here"—again he tripped the Harmer toilet and again it flushed with a strong pfhoom! with Wolf letting go with one short doleful howl—"the old-style noisy toilet is a betrayal of the privacy of one's own toilet doings. An outrage to my lady's sensibilities."

Karen was dumbfounded. The new model did run wonderfully silent compared to the old model. Why, it could hardly be heard above the old model's running over afterward. What wouldn't they think of next?

As a clincher, he once again filled his little demonstrator model with two quarts of water and, gesturing, asked her to flush it.

Karen tripped the handle.

Once more the new model made hardly any noise at all as it emptied itself into the stool below. Yes, it was a wonder all right.

Karen couldn't resist asking, "How does it manage to flush silent like that?"

"It's all in scientific designing, Mam. You see, one of our laboratory men noticed one day that certain waterfalls made an awful roaring noise while certain others did not. He investigated the matter and discovered that the water going over the noisy waterfall fell into a round flat-bottomed hole below, while the water going over the relatively less noisy waterfall fell onto a sloping wall below."

"Oh. I see."

"It also has another feature that should interest you. It . . . heh heh . . ." He laughed disarmingly. "I can hardly demonstrate that other feature for you, of course. But the point is, in voiding urine, there will also be little or no sound. This too is based on the scientific fact that when you dash water against this same sloping wall, at a thin angle, it makes little or no noise. Whereas when you dash water against a wall that is at right angles to it . . . well, there will be a considerable splash."

Karen drew back a step, thinking. All this was very good. It would be nice to have such a noiseless toilet next to the kitchen all right. A person couldn't be heard using it from either the kitchen or the living room. And then too it was always distasteful to hear the old toilet pfhooming and going ukk-achh when one was eating in the dining room, especially when visitors used it.

"Notice the contour of the seat itself, Mam, as compared to your old-style seat. It has a special splash guard molded to fit the human form."

"The sitter, you mean."

"Umm. Yes, that."

"I see."

"And here, note this, if you will." As he leaned over to point it out to her, his pink cheeks flushed a little. "This extra-large trapway assures you of a powerful flushing action. It positively will not overflow."

"Well, we only do number one"—Karen to her own astonishment found herself about to giggle, and that in front of a stranger—"in this toilet."

"Oh. Well, I was hoping I could persuade you to buy two of these, one for this half bath here and one for your full bath."

"Well, I don't know now."

"Is your husband at home?"

"No. He's at school. Teaching."

"Could I make an appointment to meet the two of you at home some evening?"

Karen was angry at herself for almost having giggled. Also, she'd been a little taken aback by his mention of urine. He was overbold, he was.

"Perhaps tonight?"

"No, I don't think so."

"We'll take the two old ones in trade and it won't cost but a trifle more?"

"No, I think we'll just make do with what we have now. Both our toilets have served us well. They're still not really old yet. This is a new house."

"I know, but—"

Karen finally got up enough nerve to speak emphatically. "No." And abruptly she went to the door and opened it. "Please."

The salesman turned a deeper pink. He swallowed, once, then decided he had pushed in far enough. Quietly he put his super-noiseless demonstrator toilet back in its case. As he picked up his hat from the hall seat, he said, "At least may I leave my card? You just might change your mind. After you think about it some more."

Karen did take the card.

"Think of me the next time your toilets go pfhoom." . . .

Kon said, "Did he really talk that fresh in front of you?"

"I guess he did."

"The nerve of him."

"Well, he did have a good point though. I do get awfully tired of hearing our toilets go pfhoom every time we use them. And then hearing Wolf howl."

Kon finished his jello.

"I wish I'd asked him the price," Karen mused. "And asked him what he'd give us for the old ones in trade."

"Say, it sounds like you really want these noiseless toilets in our house."

"Well, it would be nice, Kon."

"Would you really like to have them?"

"Oh, they'll probably be too expensive."

"Listen, if you want them, go ahead—call him and order them. You have his card."

"Well, it would be more decent. Civilized."

Kon got up. "Get 'em, then." And, all business, he went back to his garden.

Karen watched Kon from her kitchen window as she washed dishes. What a dear husband he really was. Filling the day with good work done. And work meticulously done. Yes. Even when working in black soil he rarely ever got his tan work pants dirty. He always wore cotton gloves to keep the palms of his hands from blistering and thus always had the pliant hands of a gentleman. And now he was willing that she should have toilets that were less noisy. She smiled indulgently as she saw him attack the green earth almost with a run and a jump.

Kon had bought himself a spade with a special long flat blade and a tough long ash handle. By jamming the blade down into the earth to the hilt he could come up with a chunk of sod and dirt some eight inches square and more than a foot deep. First he cut off the sod portion of the chunk and chucked that upside down into the bottom of the deep furrow ahead, then broke up the dirt part of the chunk on top of the piece of sod. As he'd once explained it to Karen, that way he made sure the sod would more rapidly decay down under and he could also immediately begin growing things in the dirt on top of it.

Wolf sat on the grass near Kon, watching for birds. Kon had trained him to chase them away—sparrows looking for choice bits, crows looking for freshly turned up white grubs, robins for angleworms.

Karen put away the dishes, emptied the dishpan, cleaned up the sink, hung up the dishcloth and the dish towel, and finally put away her apron. She did number one in the toilet off the kitchen and was pleased to note that this time, though it still went pfhoom, it didn't continue running after she'd flushed it. She decided to lubricate the brass stem with vinegar anyway, just to make sure for the next time. It would be at least a week before they could get the new noiseless wonders installed. She took off the crock lid and, getting a tablespoon of vinegar, poured it through the brass collar Kon had mentioned. She thought it strange that tarty vinegar should act as a lubricant in water.

She washed her hands with a bar of fatty soap. She sometimes had trouble with dishpan hands, the backs of her slim fingers turning red and scaly. She finished up by anointing her hands with a fingerdip of cream lotion.

Stepping outside, she found that Kon had added another furrow since she'd last looked. She strolled smiling toward the spading man and the seated dog. The man didn't look up but the dog did. She settled on a seat in the grape arbor entrance to the garden.

The new concord transplants at her feet had just begun to stick out tiny baby fists for buds, bronzy and sticky. The little apple trees and the little plums bordering the garden were also well-budded and about to burst into blossom. The young hackberries along the north side of their lot were already frilled out with small light-green leaves. And the sugar maple saplings appeared to be dappled all over with drops of congealed dark syrup.

"Are you about done, honey?"

Kon demolished a clump of dirt with the back of his spade. "This row and then one more."

Karen studied the long shadows everywhere reaching east. "It'll be dark in another hour."

"I'll finish the strawberries by flashlight then."

A fat robin wheeled in from above. It was a wary mother and it landed on a lump of fresh upturned sod as far away from the dog as possible. Lady redbreast cocked her head, once, and instantly spotted a squirming angleworm. She hopped over and pulled at the worm. The worm at first resisted. But robin pulled hard and the worm was stretched out until it resembled a thin rubber band. Finally the worm had to let go and it came free with a feeble snap.

Wolf came awake to his responsibilities with a roar and a jump. He'd been caught napping, and to make up for it put on a fierce show of dog outrage. That a mere bird had dared to invade his bailiwick! "Woof! Woof!" Wolf made two huge springs, one to get past Kon and the other to pounce on the bird. But he was just too late. Lady redbreast managed to squirt out of his reach and, soaring up and away, carried off the long dangling angleworm. Just as lady redbreast passed over the farther plum tree, she released a farewell flag of white birdsplash.

Wolf chased the rising bird with great springing jumps as if he meant to sail up after it by sheer dog will power. "Woof! Woof!" Wolf roared in frustrated rage.

Kon had to laugh. "Attaboy, Wolf. That's telling 'em off."

Karen smiled and shook her head both. "Poor mother robin. Half scared out of her wits. What a story of a close escape she'll be able to tell her little ones when she gets home."

"Oh, come now," Kon said. "Poor mother robin nothing. All birds are rascals."

"Not robins."

"Robins are the worst strawberry robbers around."

"Oh, Kon, giving the birds a tithe from our garden won't hurt us any."

"Besides, she steals worms. And I need all the angleworms I can get into this soil, being as it's mostly clay. It needs a lot of openings, or veins, to breathe, and that's what the worms give it. As well as manure it up from the subsoil."

Just then another mother robin landed in the freshly upturned soil.

This time the hair on Kon's neck ruffed out. "Look at that, would you! Wolf, go get 'em. Get 'em now."

Wolf charged straight through Kon's spread legs, almost upsetting him.

But this robin was also too quick for Wolf and spurted up and away. "Wik-wik-wik!" it cried in anger.

"That's a good dog, Wolf. At least that one didn't get one of our worms."

Karen laughed, and shook her head again. "Oh, Kon, the fuss

you make over one little ordinary worm. And making a bird hater
out of our Wolf."

Kon put a hand to his back and stiffened himself up straight.
"I'll tell you why I'm making a bird hater out of him. I want him
to learn the limits of. . . ." Kon paused. He'd just spotted Wolf
running across an already seeded portion of the garden. "Hey!
Hey! Get out of the garden there, Wolf. Bad dog, you. Bad dog.
You stay on the grass part there. And stay off the loose dirt."

Wolf quickly slunk over onto the grass part and sat down, hanging his head.

"Oh, Kon. Look at him now. So sad."

"Karen, just you leave the outdoor training part of that dog
to me. You can take care of the indoor part."

Karen sighed. She crossed her legs under her long green dress.
Sometimes even the most perfect of husbands could have his
touchy side. Sister-in-law Mildred said she sometimes didn't
know what to make of her Brant either, he could be so awful
touchy. Well, the truth was the two brothers Kon and Brant were
much alike. While that awful Charlie, Lord, he was in a class
by himself. Pure brute. It was as if the good Lord knew He had
to come up with both a Kon and a Brant to make up for the
mistake He'd made in Charlie.

Karen had to admire the way Kon kept his yard. Kon was every
bit as neat outdoors as she was indoors. The lawn was always
close mowed. Each tree had its perfect little well dug around it,
with coarse gravel to catch extra water. The flower plots were
weedless. The hedge out front was clipped as level as a human
eye could make it. The more slender of the dark maples were
securely tied to stick supports with strips of rubber inner tubes.
And the garden . . . well, it was his pride and joy. Already the
lettuce and radish lay in trim straight rows across the far side
of the garden, the one a yellow-green and the other a blue-green,
while the two rows of onion sets stood out like long green eyelashes. Several of the beans in the bean rows had just popped
through, having tossed aside the clod of earth that blocked their
opening to the sky.

Her eyes lifted to the east, to the fringe of trees bordering the doubling and redoubling Big Rock River. The leaves on the ashes were thick and tender green.

Involuntarily, as she often did, she looked north, toward where the red escarpment of the Blue Mounds ridge reared up out of the earth like a petrified redwood log just emerging from a wallow of humus. Harsh rocks lay strewn down its sides, some in attitudes suggesting they were still tumbling. The crags along the top were sized over with gray-green lichen, which in contrast to the green grass below them appeared bluish in color. The blue was especially pronounced in the sidewise-striking sunset. A huge shadow loomed off the east point of the escarpment. The shadow already had in it a little piece of night.

Karen said, "Really, aren't you about done?"

"This is my last furrow."

"Working so hard like that, the first thing you know your gloves'll have calluses. Honey."

Kon hardly had a grunt for her.

"And your right leg, the way you jump with it on your spade like that, it's pretty soon going to walk different from the other one."

At that a smile appeared on Kon's face.

"Really, honey."

"Why don't you get the strawberry transplants ready? That'll hurry it along."

"Where are they?"

"I put them in that peach box on the back porch there. Under some wet paper."

"All right."

"And while you're at it, why don't you also fill the green sprinkling can with water and have it ready to hand."

"Why don't you use the garden hose?"

"Strawberries prefer to be put to bed gently. With a loving rain."

Karen obliged him.

The sun changed to a ball of boiling copper, too hot and too heavy for the fragile silvery horizon beneath to support it, and it sank from sight immediately. Within moments the knoll on which their house stood was suffused with a rusty incandescence.

"There," Kon said, breaking up a last spadeful, "we did it." Carefully he cleaned off the shining blade. "And now for the frosting." He leveled the new spading with a rake and then with a gardener's trowel put in the strawberry transplants. "Karen, would you water them behind me?"

"Is that an order, honey?"

"It's a loving request."

"In that case I'll do it."

They finished at about the same time.

As they each picked up a garden tool, Karen felt the first dew of evening mist down on her cheeks.

"Whew!" Kon breathed in relief. "All done at last."

"You're tired."

"Tired but triumphant." He slipped his free arm through hers. "Now to sleep the sleep of the just."

As they strolled across the lawn, Karen said, "Kon, we ought to adopt a baby sometime."

"Does gardening make you think of babies?"

"I'd hate to see all that wonderful training you've had in being a good man around the house go to waste. Die with you. You should pass that on."

Kon chilled noticeably. "We'll think about it."

Karen drew his arm dear to her. "You aren't mad at me now, are you, honey?"

"No."

"Because I couldn't stand that. You're all I have in the world." Again she pressed his arm tenderly against her side. "But a baby would be nice sometime."

They mounted the back stoop together and set the garden tools to one side on the back porch. Then he held the kitchen door open for her and Wolf and all three passed inside.

"It's hard to imagine oneself a mother with just a doll," Karen added. "Or a dog."

Sitting down on the hall bench, he began to take off his work shoes. "Well, I have been thinking it would be nice to have a little one around at that. Sometime when we can afford it."

"You have?"

"A boy. Of around ten or so."

"Ten years old to start with?"

"Thereabouts."

"Why, Konstant Harmer, if we are going to adopt a little one, I don't want one that is already half grown. I want one that's a tiny baby. Like I'd just had it myself. I don't want to miss out on all those little infant secrets. It's bad enough not to—"

"I know, I know," he cut in hastily. "For you it would be better if we got a little one." He shoved his shoes under the bench. He wriggled his toes inside his brown socks. He sat a moment lost in thought. Then, with a blink and a shake of his head, he gave her a smile. "I want you happy, dear. And I guess if we adopt a child we'll have to get you what you want."

Of a sudden Karen wanted to do something nice for Kon. "Why don't we have a nice cup of hot chocolate, after all that hard work?"

"That would go just right."

3

"Kon!"

"What, dear?"

"Did you just do number two in the kitchen toilet while I was down in the basement looking for a jar of canned beef?"

Kon looked up from his hoeing in the garden. "How would you know?"

"Never mind. Did you?"

"How could that new wonder toilet have betrayed me? I thought it was supposed to be noiseless."

"For your information, Mr. Konstant Harmer, I can tell for another reason than just the noise part."

Kon smiled. "Well, I cannot tell a lie. Yes, I guess I did use the kitchen toilet."

Karen pushed through the screen door. "Why, Konstant Harmer, shame on you. You know we agreed we'd never use that toilet for number two. Because of you-know-why. You know I would never otherwise have agreed to having it there. Except in emergencies."

"But that's just what I had. An emergency."

"Oh," she said, "that's different." Her voice was quickly one of concern. "What's the matter, honey, you got a stomachache?"

"Oh, not that exactly. A little, maybe."

"Well, have you or haven't you?"

"Not so loud."

"The neighbors can't hear us way out here."

"I'm thinking of the time when we'll have them close next door. Practice for it."

"Konstant Harmer, have you or haven't you?"

"Must you always be so blunt, Karen?"

"I'm not being blunt. I'm just speaking my mind. The truth always smarts."

"Karen, do you expect me to take off my shoes in the middle of hoeing the corn just so I can go to the bathroom upstairs?"

"Kon, that off-the-kitchen toilet is not to be used for number two. That's final."

"Now, Karen, let's be sensible about this."

"Kon, a promise is a promise. You said it was never going to be used for number two. And I'm going to hold you to that promise. You can always go out there in the fresh air of the garden afterward, but me, I've got to walk back and forth through it in the kitchen while I make your supper. And that's not very nice."

The dog Wolf was sitting on his haunches in the grass near Kon. Wolf followed the squabble back and forth between Karen and Kon for a few moments; then, abruptly, howled once and ran forward a few steps and barked at Karen, sharp.

Kon laughed. "Attaboy, Wolf, that's telling her. Your opinion in the matter is much appreciated."

"It isn't any laughing matter, Mr. Harmer. Not to me, it isn't." Karen let the screen door slam shut and, nose up in the air, went back to making supper.

Later, Kon tried to make up for it by carefully removing his shoes while still out on the back stoop and by flaffing the dust out of his socks on the cement steps. He even changed his clothes out on the enclosed porch. When he sat down to supper he was as well groomed as their Reverend John Marrow at the Methodist Church.

But Karen remained prickly all through the meal. And she wouldn't eat any of the canned beef.

Kon ate his meal with modest relish. He gave her several compliments on her cooking.

Karen's nose stayed up.

It was an hour later. The lights were on in the living room, one lamp glowing where Karen sat tatting near the Westminster clock and another blazing where Kon sat working at his desk in the alcove near the fireplace. The dog Wolf lay curled up on the blue rug at Karen's feet.

"Karen!"

"What?"

"Did you dust my desk today?"

Karen looked up from her tatting. "I guess I did. Why, what's the matter?"

"Karen Harmer, what must I do with you? Here I've told you again and again never, never to touch my desk." Kon glared pale-blue eyes at her. "You know I never even used to let Mother touch my study corner at home. I always cleaned it myself. Like I do here." He gave his desk a slap with the flat of his hand. "Or maybe I don't keep it clean enough to suit you?"

"How could you tell I dusted it? I thought I left it just as I found it."

"How could I tell?" He jumped to his feet. "In the first place, you lost my place in the bird book. So that now I can't find it."

"I thought you didn't like birds."

"I love birds. It's just that I don't want them in my garden. And that's my right too. But I don't mind them out in nature, out there. Besides, I teach about birds in school."

"The way you sic that dog after the robins, I didn't think you'd care what I did with your bird book."

"And then the one book you did mind where I had my place, that fat flower book, you put an eraser in it as a bookmark." He fixed her with cold male eyes. "Karen, woman, helpmate, if there's one thing that breaks the backs of books it's when you use fat things like erasers or pencils or shoes for bookmarks in them."

Karen let her tatting fall into her lap. "Oh, honey, I was just trying to be helpful. You work so hard out in the yard."

"Suppose you'd have thrown my lesson plans away for to-morrow, eh?"

"Honey, I saw some dust on your lamp shade and so when I dusted that I just sort of without thinking dusted the rest of your desk too."

"Karen, there's one thing a man wants. And that's one little corner that nobody touches. In his castle."

"I'm sorry, dear."

"I don't touch your doll in your little cradle upstairs."

"I know you don't."

"Well, then, don't ever touch my spot again. Not until I'm dead at least."

Karen couldn't help but get in one last little lick. "The trouble with you Harmers is, you're all too touchy. Like your brother Brant."

The pale blue in Kon's eyes again turned a cold male gray. "Don't you say anything against my brother Brant."

"Well, you Harmers are too touchy. Though, thank God, you're not as bad as Brant is."

"Not as bad?"

"No. But then that's probably because he's sometimes off his rocker a little."

Kon slowly balled up a fist. "Off his rocker, is he?"

"Or notional. I saw that in him the very first time I met him. And the way Mildred writes about him in her last letters proves it. About that imaginary pain in his side. And then those odd things he does around the place. Putting a sickle up over the doorway to keep out the hex witches. And such. Mighty odd."

Kon took a sudden threatening step toward her. "Karen, there's one thing you mustn't ever do. And that is—don't ever talk bad about us Harmers. Even if you're married to one. Even if you're dead right."

"Why, Kon, you don't have to get so mad. It's just what I simply think."

"What you think I don't give a fig for." Kon's ears slowly began to stick out, he was so furious. "Brant is . . . is . . . !"

"Why, honey, you're. . . . Why, Konstant, I've never seen you like this before. Not even for my sake."

The words came stuttering out of Kon one by one. "I—want—you—to—shut—up—about—my—brother—Brant. He's . . . He's . . . I don't ever want you to say anything about my brother Brant! He's—my—dear. . . ." Kon took yet another threatening step toward Karen.

This time Wolf resented the way Kon was getting after Karen. He jumped to his feet and started toward Kon, ears down. And he barked once, deep, showing long flashing teeth.

That stopped Kon. It made him stare down at the dog, away from Karen. And after a moment he managed to get hold of himself. He inhaled a huge slow breath and went back to his desk.

Karen also fell silent, and went back to her tatting.

Karen thought: "Of the three of us, the dog had the better sense."

When Karen and Kon went to bed, each on their side, they first lay facing away from each other, each thinking their thoughts.

Karen felt bad. While it was a good thing that both she and Kon had fallen silent on Wolf's reprimanding bark, it was still a bad thing that they hadn't made up afterwards. They'd worked for another hour or so, and then both had gone silently about their bedtime chores: take Wolf out for a last walk, lock up the house, wind the kitchen clock, turn out the lights, take a shower. It hurt her even more that neither had knelt on their own side of the bed and offered up a prayer of thanksgiving to the Lord for the good day He'd given them. Of course, in one sense, not kneeling to pray meant that they at least weren't hypocrites. But it was still bad that they hadn't made up. In all the months they'd been married they'd never once gone to bed mad at each other. Always it had been lovingly, as a loving brother and sister should, with nothing held against each other. Both believed it a wrong to let the sun set on a trouble. Now this was going to be the first time if one of them didn't make the first move. Karen wept a little, silently. What she really should do was to count the many blessings she'd received living with Kon. Yes. Just think. He never ever bullied her, really. He never bothered her like some racy men she knew would've. He worked hard. He shared all he had with her. He never swore. He was usually in a good humor. He was mean about those robins, yes, a little, but that was understandable when one thought of all the hard work he put into the garden. He sometimes called her lady friends "the cats," but that was also understandable because he was a man and not a woman. He was neat. He was always a gentleman in his habits—except for that one slip in the off-the-kitchen toilet. Yes, he was a wonderful man, and what she should do now would be to turn around and take his cheeks in her hands and kiss him on the lips and let him know she was sorry she'd spoken so sharply and then turn over and sweetly go to sleep. She gave it all one more thought; and then, a smile opening her lips, she did turn around and she did reach for his face with both hands.

To her surprise, she discovered that Kon had also just then turned around and that his hands were reaching for her face too.

They held each other's faces a moment in the silver moonlight, then gave each other a sweet dry kiss.

"I'm sorry for what I did, Konstant."

"And I'm sorry for what I did, Karen."

"Our first real spat."

"Let's say it was only our first tiff instead."

"Yes."

"Yes."

They looked at each other, warming toward each other, smiling, and then both at the same time as with one thought slipped out of bed on their own side and knelt down and prayed a silent prayer.

Finished, they climbed back into bed. She curled up on her right side facing her dolly Kathryn. He curled up on his right side facing Karen's back. Still smiling, they fell sweetly asleep.

An hour later, something awoke Karen.

She lay blinking on her side, waiting for whatever it was to make the sound again, wondering if it was lovers squealing again, knowing it really couldn't be that because it sounded more like a dog whining.

She let her eyes rove around in the bedroom. It was bright with light like the other time. A big moon had already ovaled halfway up the sky east of the house.

"Dear Lord, if it's those spooners. . . ."

There it was again. Through the open window. An urgent whining. She listened intently. Why, it was dogs. Not people.

Where was Wolf? Strange that he wasn't barking by now. Wolf always heard everything.

She sat up.

"What's the matter?" Kon whispered from his pillow. "Is there something we forgot?"

"Listen. Outdoors there. Through the window. Hear it?"

He listened.

It came again. A pleading sort of whining.

Kon sat bolt upright. "That's our Wolf."

"It is?"

Kon hopped out of bed and footed it over to the window. "That's just who it is. Our Wolf. With some bitch from town."

"Kon!"

"First time I ever heard of a bitch looking up a male dog. I always thought it was the other way around."

Karen had to see for herself. She got out of bed and joined Kon at the window. Peering down, she saw Wolf standing at right angles to a smaller brownish dog, a mongrel. Wolf was nosing and slicking the mongrel and wagging his tail like a fool.

"Darn," Kon said, "I must've left the back door open a crack when I went to bed."

"Maybe Wolf opened it himself. You taught him how to open the basement door, you know."

"That's right, I did."

"That's what you get for teaching him all those clever tricks."

"I better go down and get him inside."

Before Kon could make a move, the brown mongrel bitch presented herself to Wolf. Overjoyed, Wolf promptly mounted her, and after a few uncertain probes, made connection.

"Why, the hussy!" Karen cried. "She deliberately set her cap for him."

"The fool," Kon said.

Both Karen and Kon stood transfixed. In the bright moonlight they saw it happening as plain as day.

Both Karen and Kon breathed through slightly parted lips, Karen's lips softening and Kon's nether Harmer lip hanging a little. The bottoms of their nightshirts hung level with each other. Twice Kon made a hitching motion, more inward than outward, to do something about stopping the dogs, but didn't. Karen blinked. They watched the whole performance.

When at last Wolf slid off, luckily without much trouble, both Karen and Kon broke out of their rapt freeze.

"I'm going down and get that darn dog inside," Kon muttered.

And Karen went to bed.

Karen lay flat on her back, looking up at the ceiling. She saw the whole thing again, vividly. Presently she heard Kon come in with Wolf, heard him scolding Wolf for being such a bad, bad dog.

Some ten minutes later Kon came stamping upstairs again and reentered the bedroom.

Out of the corner of her eye Karen watched Kon go sit on his side of the bed, and then get into bed.

He too lay flat on his back looking up at the ceiling.

They lay awhile looking up at the ceiling together, breathing almost in unison, a little faster than usual.

Finally Karen said, "So that's the way the animals are."

"Of course."

"Nothing sneaky. All out in the open there. Innocent of sin."

"Of course." Kon twitched on his side of the bed. "Didn't you know that?"

"No."

"You didn't?"

"No."

"But you knew this about human beings?"

Silence.

"You saw that Adolph Horsberg and Tessie Windmiller that time."

"That was different. They were children who were supposed to know better. And they were being sneaky about it. And on the school grounds yet."

"Do you really mean to tell me you've never seen animals do it before?"

"No." Karen shook her head, her hair rustling against the pillow.

"That's hard to believe."

"You want to remember, Kon, we women are always in the house where we can never see any of the important things."

"Well, that's true."

Karen moved past maiden shame. "Kon, if that dog hussy— what is it you called her? bitch?—if that bitch has little ones out of this, I want one of those puppies."

"I should say not."

"Why not?"

"One dog in the house is enough."

Silence.

"I mean that now, Karen."

"All right, Kon."

"He's enough of a fuss as it is."

Karen couldn't help but marvel at it all. "So our dog Wolf will soon be a father. Have offspring. While. . . ." Her thoughts scattered.

Kon spoke aloud in the moonlit room. "Tomorrow I'm going downtown and get Wolf a leash. Because he's got to be tied up nights, now that he knows how to open doors so good."

Karen thought to herself: "Perhaps it has been my fault all along."

Kon turned on his side, facing Karen, nuzzling the side of his face into the pillow, getting ready to go to sleep again.

A sideways smile came over Karen's face. As the smile grew her lips filled out.

She let the new mood gather strength, and then, at last brimming over, slowly turned on her left side, facing Kon. She drew her nightgown well up over her hips. Instead of taking his face in her hands to kiss him, she first drew up his nightgown also well up over his hips, gently. Then she took hold of his shoulders and drew their bodies close together. It was the first time their bellies had ever touched. Warm. Naked.

The Westminster clock downstairs chimed the half hour.

Then the sting of desire at last came to Kon, and Kon took Karen, and in the manner of a man turning over virgin sod went in unto her, and she became his wife, and the Lord gave her conception.

PART SIX

❀❖❀❖❀❖❀❖❀❖❀❖❀❖❀❖❀❖❀❖❀❖

Brant

1

Once more it was late September. Shortly there would be frost and then all of Siouxland would turn golden for a few weeks.

Brant finished his morning chores, walked out to the back pasture to see if the heifer Gypsy had calved during the night, then was ready for his ten o'clock cup of coffee.

As he headed for the house, he saw the mail carrier, Warts Berry, coming down the road. Even at a distance it was easy to spot the mailman coming because he always sat in the middle of the front seat of his car, driving with his left hand so that he could reach the mail into the mailbox with his right hand.

"Might as well go pick up the mail while I'm at it." There just might be news of Kon in a letter. Karen and Mildred corresponded quite regularly.

Brant looked out to the mailbox to see if the two hex hooks were still in place. They were. That meant that if there was a letter from Karen it would be a good one. Ever since he'd hung a pair of whiffletree hooks under the mailbox he'd had nothing but good news. They'd worked like a charm. As long as he could hear them jingling in the wind he knew all was going well with Kon.

Brant reached the mailbox at about the same time that Warts Berry pulled up in his mud-spattered Ford.

Warts reached the mail out to Brant. Warts was a cigarette fiend and because of it had the breath of a turkey buzzard. His fat face was speckled over with bumps and freckles. "Well, Brant, and how do you like this for weather so late in the year?"

In accepting the mail Brant spotted Karen's familiar low angular handwriting on a letter tucked inside *The Review*. Good. The hex hooks were working today. Already he felt better. "Well, we could use a frost."

"Frost? Hell. Me, the longer winter stays away, the better."

"Do the corn a lot of good. It needs drying."

"You farmers are never satisfied."

"That's because we take all the risks."

"How're Kon and Karen getting along these days?"

"Fine." Brant shied off from looking Warts in the eye. Why should news about Kon be skin off Warts's nose? It made a man wonder if Warts didn't sometimes steam open the letters at home to know what to gossip about. If Warts kept this nosiness up, a man might have to get out an extra set of hex hooks to take care of him.

"Gettin' any lately?" Warts asked with a confidential leer.

"I think there's one today." Brant gestured with the mail in his hand.

Warts's face quickly became bland. "Oh. That's right. So I noticed."

It took a moment for Brant to catch on that Warts had meant something dirty. "Oh. That. No. Yes." A chill moved up Brant's spine. Another one of those damned jealous studs lusting after Mildred. Ha. If they only knew. Only knew.

Warts goosed his motor. "Well, I guess I better be pushing on. I'm already a little behind schedule. See you."

"I wouldn't run over any more dogs if I was you." Brant had never forgiven Warts for killing his dog Bill.

Warts drove off as if he hadn't heard.

"The son of a bitch," Brant muttered. Then, taking another

peek into the mail to make sure he'd really seen the letter with Karen's handwriting on it, Brant headed for the house. Heart beating a little higher than usual in his chest, he had the odd feeling that there was too much blood in his system. He felt drunkish. And every now and then his heart doubled up on itself, sent out an extra beat.

Brant was careful to enter the house through the kitchen door. By going in under the sickle he was sure of clearing the air of any possible hex a witch might have set for him.

Mildred had some good rich coffee ready for him when he stepped inside. Good.

"Got the mail," he called out. He placed the mail on Mildred's side of the table. He couldn't stand to read Karen's handwriting himself. Mildred usually read the letters aloud to him. "Mildred?"

"Coming." Mildred was in the basement.

He slipped out of his blue denim jacket and hung it on the back of his armchair. He pushed his blue cap to the back of his head. The hairline over his forehead had been receding of late and with the rest of his dark hair drawn back tight by his cap, he gave the appearance of having a very high forehead. He sat down.

The clinking of glassware against a crock came out of the basement.

"What're you doing down there, Mildred?" Brant gave the yellow tablecloth a light whack. "Here it's past ten already and you ain't even got the cups and saucers set out yet."

"I'm getting some fresh cream for the coffee." Mildred started up the cellar steps. "I'll have everything set out in a second."

"Well, I'm kind 'f in a hurry."

Mildred appeared, swarthy face pink from the climb. She carried a small white pitcher of cream and placed it in the center of the table next to a matching sugar bowl. She glanced at the mail. "Ah. So that's the reason for your hurry."

"Well. Yeh. But I do have a lot of work to do today. Getting ready for corn picking and all."

Mildred poured the coffee. Soon both cups were steaming like wide chimneys. She also set out a plate of sugar-coated dough-nuts. She sank into her chair with a sigh.

Brant helped himself liberally to the cream, a good thick spurt of it. He next checked the surface of the sugar to see if there were any hex prints in it or any strange markings. There weren't any. Good. The power of the sickle over the door was still holding up. Helping himself to two heaping spoons of sugar, he stirred his coffee briskly.

Mildred put cream and sugar in her coffee. She stirred it slowly.

Brant tried to hurry Mildred along by willing her along, silently, directing all the will power he had in him straight into the core of her. "Woman! Read that letter. Pronto."

Mildred resettled herself comfortably in her chair. She pondered the problem awhile as to whether she should have a doughnut or not, finally did take one. She took but a small bite, hardly breaking through the frosting into the yellow insides.

Brant sipped his coffee. That woman sure knew how to rile a man up into a blue fume with that slow steady way of hers. He too took a doughnut and bit into it, lustily.

Mildred chewed solemnly; took a slow sip of coffee.

Brant took another big sip of coffee, then set his cup down with a light clap. "Well, hell's bells, woman, if you're going to take all day about it, I might as well read what new dirt *The Review*'s come up with instead." He reached across the table for the paper, gave it a light jerk so as to make the letter stay on her side while he got the paper. He opened the paper with a crack-ling flourish.

Mildred smiled. She took yet another bite of her doughnut and a sip of coffee, and then at last picked up Karen's letter. She opened the letter with a prying finger and removed three sheets of linen paper filled on both sides with Karen's low angular pen-manship.

Jesus. That damned Mildred.

Slowly Mildred began to read. Mildred always liked to scan most of Karen's letter first before she read it aloud to Brant.

Brant gave his newspaper another flourish, a light one, and dared a peek past the edge of it at Mildred. He breathed audibly through his open mouth, nether lip moist.

As Mildred read, her wise brown eyes slowly opened in astonishment and her dark brows ascended halfway up her forehead. She became lost in the letter. Her swarthy face pinkened some. She began to read faster.

Brant in turn became absorbed in Mildred's reaction. What in the world was up with Kon? Slowly he let his newspaper drop into his lap. He leaned forward a little as though to read in Mildred's eyes what she might be reading in the letter.

Mildred turned over the first sheet; read the back side of it; began the second sheet. "I don't believe it," she whispered.

Brant became alarmed. What? What?

As she read the back of the second sheet, Mildred's face gradually softened into a warm sisterly smile. "Isn't that wonderful," she breathed. "I'm so glad for them."

Brant's brows shot up in turn. And his mouth clapped shut. He instantly guessed what the news was. Oh, God. Oh, God. It wasn't true then that Kon never touched Karen. Kon and Karen were going to have a baby.

"After all these years, isn't that simply wonderful." Mildred counted on her fingers. "Let's see now. From the middle of next February back . . . that'd be last May sometime. Isn't that wonderful."

Brant brushed the newspaper from his lap; got to his feet; slipped into his blue jacket again; started for the door. He could feel himself turning white all along the edges.

Mildred broke off reading. "Hey, where are you going?"

"Out."

"But I haven't read you the wonderful news yet."

Brant pulled down the bill of his cap with a jerk and hurried outside.

Mildred jumped up and followed him to the door. "Brant?"

Brant scooted around the side of the garage and out of sight.

"Brant!"

With an awful shudder Brant fell flat on his face.

A half hour later he came to, slowly, face in the dirt. He still felt white all along the edges. He breathed roughly through open dry lips.

He lay awhile longer; then, stiffly, got to his feet.

He looked around bewildered. Where was everything?

His eye fell on a winter apple tree in their orchard.

The next thing he knew he was going over and picking one of the yellow apples. He didn't know why. He sat down on a small stump. His hand automatically searched through his pockets until it came up with his jackknife. With his thumbnail he pried open the longer blade. Slowly he began to cut the yellow apple into neat precise slices. He ate the slices with dry lips and a heavy chopping motion of his lower jaw. He didn't know why.

But he did know Kon was gone. Kon was gone.

All those wonderful times they'd had together as boys, they'd been for nothing.

. . . The most wonderful times were in the summers.

Once after supper Pa had sent the two younger boys out to the cornfield north of the grove to go weed out some cockleburs.

Brant and Kon found the cockleburs without much trouble. The cockleburs were a foot high to the corn's three feet and their leaves were a light green to the corn's dark green. Also they already had seed with stiff hooked spines while the corn still hadn't put out either tassel or silk.

As Brant and Kon pulled out the weeds by the roots one by one, they gradually drifted apart a dozen rows or so. The sun was setting. Where the sun's light hit on the top surfaces of the green corn, the blade leaves shone as if varnished while underneath in the shadows the stalks took on a horehound-green hue. The boys stood in the rippling greens up to their chests.

The freshly cultivated earth, a rich chocolate brown, was full of wonderful clods. It was Brant who first thought of it. After pulling up a cocklebur, he also stealthily picked up a clod the size of an egg and when Kon wasn't looking threw it high over Kon's head so that it dropped on the other side of him.

"Hey," Kon said, looking up. The setting sun lay like a flash of lightning over his blond hair. His eyes opened, surprised, full of light-blue wonder.

Brant feigned innocence. "What's the matter?"

"Something almost hit me out of the sky." Kon stared up at the yellow stripes of light arching across the heavens.

"What makes you think that?"

"Something just fell over there."

"Maybe it was a meteor or something."

"You think so?"

"Did it make a kind of sizzling noise?"

"No."

"Maybe it's a hex witch then."

"You mean it's one of them bad hex teasers?" Kon's boy eyes opened very wide and filled to the brim with sunset. "Like Mother used to talk about?"

"Could be." Brant had to work hard to keep a straight face. "You remember them Oorts living by Starum there? In Outlaw Country?"

"No."

"Well, I guess you was too young then to remember. Well, every time you went by the Oort cornfields by Blood Run Creek there, where them old Indians used to have their mounds, clods would suddenly fly out of the corn and hit you."

"They would?"

"They once even had the sheriff out there. And then the sheriff called up a college professor and asked him to dig up one of them mounds. Called him long distance too yet."

"Did they find anything?"

"A couple of skulls and a whole lot of bones."

"Then it was maybe them Indian ghosts what was throwing them clods."

"That's what they think."

"G-o-s-h."

"Maybe we got one of them mounds in the field here, a little low one that's been all plowed flat, and them Indian wizard ghosts are trying to chase us out of here. Maybe even trying to hex us. Because this land really belongs to them."

The sun set. The rim of the earth was scissored free of the sky for a moment.

Brant was touched by the grave look on Kon's boy face and couldn't go on with it. He said instead, "Well, I guess we better get to work or Pa'll be after us."

"Maybe we better tell Pa about them wizards throwin' things at us."

"Aw, maybe it was only a meteor after all. A little one."

"I'm kind of scairt, Brant."

"Oh, don't be scared. C'mon, or we'll have Pa on our tail." Brant began picking cockleburs again.

Still puzzled, somewhat stiffly, Kon also went back to pulling up cockleburs.

They worked awhile in silence. Sometimes the cockleburs had deep roots and it took all their boy strength to yank them out. The boys had to grunt on occasion.

The dark east came on. Overhead the sky turned a green purple. A glowing brilliant rust lay all along the western horizon. Each cornstalk, and both their boy bodies, took on a separate atmosphere of amber light. It was so clear out, so pure, that to breathe was to drink air.

Ten minutes later Brant found another handy-sized clod. He couldn't resist it. Choosing a moment when Kon wasn't looking, Brant hurled it high over Kon's head so that it landed well beyond him. This time Brant accompanied the clod's falling with a low sizzing sound. Then Brant quickly stooped over and began to tug at another cocklebur.

Kon jerked erect. "There it was again."

Brant looked up, nether lip hanging a little, moist. "Say. I heard that too."

The expression on Kon's face slowly changed. His keen ears had caught an odd nuance in Brant's voice. "Brant."

"What?"

"It was you."

"Me?"

"You did that."

"What?"

"It was you making that sizzing noise. I heard you."

"You couldn't've. It wasn't me."

"Why, you. . . ." Then with a laugh, and pretended ferocious anger, Kon leaped across the rows and jumped on Brant.

They fell to the ground, wrestling, laughing. They rolled over and over, first the one on top, then the other. They flattened several cornstalks. Ground and dust worked into the sides of their overalls and in at the necks of their shirts. They laughed until their bellies hurt, until they had terrible stomachaches. And it got worse and worse. When one would start to get over it, the other would start it up again. One look and they'd fall into a fit of it again. They laughed until they almost couldn't get their breaths anymore. Their throats hurt deep in back. Even their sitters hurt. They completely emptied themselves out, they laughed so long and hard.

Oh what fun oh what joy oh what heaven.

But all for nothing.

And then there was the time when once after breakfast Mother wondered if the two younger boys shouldn't go plumming in the Wasteland. The Wasteland lay along the Big Rock River north of Bonnie. It was the last Saturday of summer vacation, before school was to start, and the wild plums there just might be ripe.

"Oh, boy," Brant cried, "can we really?"

"To the Wasteland," Kon cried, "really?"

"Well, why not?" Mother said. "I'm sure Pa will let you have a horse. Anse?"

Pa smiled at their cries of joy, his lip hanging a little, moist.

"Oh, boy."

Pa helped them hitch up Whitetail to the stripped-down running gear of the old family carriage, and Mother gave them a couple of pails and the old washtub to pick the wild plums in, plus some sandwiches, and off they went.

They arrived at the black iron bridge around eleven. Brant

opened the gate to the Faber pasture on the near side of the
river and Kon drove the horse and running gear through. A quarter of a mile farther on, they tied old Whitetail to an ash tree.
Then, each with a pail, and the tub and the bag of sandwiches
between them, they pushed into the Wasteland.

They followed an old buffalo trail. White man's cattle had
kept it up, well marked. They stepped across rotting trunks of
fallen trees. They ducked beneath broken branches. They skip-
roped through hanging loops of grapevines. Fifty yards in, the
foliage high overhead became so dense it was as if the sun had
gone into an eclipse. Occasional plum trees appeared in the green
dusk but they had only sparse leaves and tiny pale-green plums.
Green moss coated the trunk of every standing tree on the south
side as well as the north side, so that in the prevailing gloom
directions were impossible to make out.

There was a riot of bird cries overhead: scolding crows, mourning turtledoves, chipping song sparrows. Once a flicker rapped
on a hollow tree, trying to chase out the beetles, so loudly that
both Brant and Kon jumped.

Raccoons with the manners of monkeys peered down at the
passing boys.

Kon finally stopped. "I don't see any ripe plums here."

Brant stopped with him. "Oh, they're here all right. Otherwise Mother wouldn't remember it."

"Well, I don't see any."

"They'll be mostly yellow when you finally spot them. With a
little red on them. Like a Chinaman with a touch of rouge on
his cheeks."

"This place is scary."

"It's not either. It's just that we're not used to it. C'mon, somewhere in here we'll find them plums."

They pushed on. Vaguely off on their left they could hear the
river rippling over a sandy shallows. The path into the dense un-
derbrush almost vanished. They had to work their way through.
Their pails banged; their big tub boomed.

A dozen tough steps more, and they exploded into sunlight.
Before them opened a glade. The river ran rippling through the

middle of it. And there, on both banks of the river, stood a scattering of little prickly trees laced with pendent rows of yellow drops.

"Plums!" Kon cried. "Look at all the plums."

"I told you."

"Millions of 'em."

"Trillions."

They looked into each other's eyes full of delight. They'd found the plums together.

They dropped their pails and tub. They rushed up to the first little prickly tree and reached up and picked themselves each a plum. Each took a tasting bite.

"Ripe," Kon said. "Mmm. And sweet."

"Mmm," Brant said. "That first little clear drop is the best. Like pure syrup."

"Like nectar."

Brant threw his arms around Kon and kissed him on his silver-blond hair. "Boy, this is fun."

Kon smiled shyly.

"Boy," Brant cried in joy, "am I glad Mother sent us."

Kon looked at the myriad plums again. "Now Mother can make a lot of plum preserve and jelly."

Brant sampled plum after plum. "Nicest wild plums I ever saw. Not a worm in the bunch."

They drifted from tree to tree like bees.

The outer plums tasted warm. The sun was in them.

Presently Kon went back and got his pail. "I guess we better start picking."

Brant got his pail too. "Boy, will these taste good on warm fresh bread. Buttered."

"Don't eat too many now," Kon warned. "Or you'll get a bad stomachache."

"Not when they're so ripe like this you won't."

"Well, maybe you won't."

Brant held up a handful of plums. "See, I told you they'd be yellow with a little red on their cheeks."

"Mmm, they're good," Kon said. "Just like nectar all right."

They felt safe inside the clearing. There wasn't a breath of wind. The sun shone warm on their bare heads, the one a fine bleaching blond and the other a somber walnut brown. Being alone together was like being tickled all over.

There were so many plums within easy reach, their pails filled rapidly.

Brant was first to empty his pail, gently, into the tub. "It's like it ain't true."

Kon emptied his pail too.

"What're you thinkin', Kon?"

"Nothing."

Brant wished he could jump like a grasshopper, straight up into the air. "If only we had us a big mirror."

Kon's eyes opened in blue wonder. "What for?"

"Well, then I'd hold mine up to you so that when you looked at me you'd see you in me. And I'd see me in you."

Kon didn't catch on.

"Sometimes I get the funny feeling you and me wasn't supposed to be two people. That we've really got one me together but that somehow we got split up. Like I'm only half there without you."

Kon still looked puzzled.

"I once even dreamt that."

"You didn't."

"Kon, I just bet you that if you was to take our blood, yours and mine, you couldn't tell the difference between us."

"Our hair and eyes are different."

"Sometimes I don't even feel I'm me. But that I'm you, Kon."

"Maybe that's what it means to be brothers."

"Yeh."

"But then there's Charlie."

A shiver ran down Brant's spine. "Now why did you have to mention him? That spoils it all."

Kon studied to himself a moment. "Let's pick plums."

"That's right. Mother's expecting us with lots of plums."

They moved from tree to tree, picking the outside plums, the best and easiest to reach.

When the tub was half full, they stopped to rest awhile. They got out their bag of sandwiches and, finding a soft grassy spot, sat down and had lunch. They chewed solemnly together. After the plums, the dried beef sandwiches tasted salty sweet. The thick butter made the bread easy to eat.

Finished, Brant rolled up the empty bag into a ball and threw it into the shining water in front of them. Both watched the ball bob down the river.

A yellow-green apple dropped into the water, landing with a light splash immediately behind the floating ball of paper.

Kon looked up and spotted the tree from which the apple had fallen. Part of the apple tree hung over the water. "Say, there's a real wild apple tree."

Brant's dark eyes lighted up too. "Just the thing for dessert."

They jumped to their feet and went over for a closer look. The tree was a good fifteen feet high, slender, with stiff spiny branches. It had been neatly trimmed underneath by cropping cattle. It wasn't nearly as thick with fruit as the wild plums were.

Kon said, "The thing about a wild apple is, it's a prairie crab apple really."

"Where'd you learn that?"

"Read it in my nature book. The one Teacher gave me."

"Wisht I could read fast like you."

Kon jumped for one of the little yellow-green apples; missed. Then Brant jumped for one; and got two. He gave one to Kon. They each took a good bite. They chewed, gravely savoring.

Kon nodded. "Tarty but sweet."

"Real sweet."

Kon took a deep sniff of the open bite in his little apple. "If you smell it slow like, you can catch a whiff of perfume in it."

"Yeh. Like mothers put on for church."

Kon finished his apple, threw the core of it into the river at their feet. He studied the apple tree some more. He spotted bigger apples near the top. "I'll bet those up there ain't so tarty. They've had the most sun."

"They look riper."

"I'll go get us some." Kon began to climb the little tree.

Brant looked down at the river. It had the dark-green look of depth. "Don't fall into the river now."

"I won't."

"But those big apples hang over the edge of the bank."

"Brant, sometimes you act like an old woman."

Kon climbed swiftly. Soon he was at the very top of the little apple tree, riding on a willowy branch. He snatched at one of the top apples; got it. He threw the apple down to Brant. Then Kon made a grab for another big apple; missed it. The other big apple was just out of reach. Kon placed his foot in a slightly higher crotch, set himself to make another grab for it.

"I wouldn't do that if I was you," Brant warned.

"Are you being afraid for me?"

"But you can't swim if you fall in."

"I don't aim to fall in."

"That water is awful deep." There was a shivery catch in Brant's voice.

Kon tested the higher crotch. He decided it would hold him. He gave himself a heave and up he went. He got the apple. But when he came down, the crotch parted under his foot, and the lower half broke off, and Kon lost his hold, and Kon came tumbling down through the tree on the river side. One of the bottom limbs, a sturdy one, caught him for a moment. It first gave a little under his weight; then, springing up again, boosted him outward. Kon somersaulted once in the air and then fell like a broken frog into the deep green water. Under he went. First water splashed out; then water fell in. Rippling rings widened out from the spot.

"Kon."

More rings widened out.

Brant stood stunned. "Kon!"

The yellow-green apple Kon had just picked bobbed to the surface. After a moment it began to drift downstream with the current.

"*Kon!*"

The knuckles of a white hand appeared on the surface. The knuckles vanished.

Brant stared great dark eyes at the water. For a deep moment. Then, throwing his apple away, he scrambled down the bank. Black earth broke off ahead of him. He slid to a stop just at the water's edge where gravel showed.

There was some boiling action in the water directly in front of him. After a second Kon's head popped to the surface, eyes pinched shut, mouth drawn back as if trying to shout. Then down again Kon went.

"Kon!"

Brant spotted a thin polelike branch sticking out over the edge of the brown bank above him. He ran to get it.

A dozen feet downstream there was more boiling motion under the surface of the water.

Brant followed it along the edge of the water. He held his long pole out toward the spot, hoping that when Kon's hand came to the surface again he would grab hold when he felt it.

The back of Kon's head washed to view. His blond hair lay parted like the mane of a horse in a wind.

Brant reached as far as he could with his pole. Too short by far. Kon was drifting toward the center of the current.

"Kon!" Brant threw the pole away.

Kon slowly sank from sight.

"One more time and he's a goner. God."

Too bad the both of them hadn't learned to swim.

"Got to save him before the third time. Somehow."

No sign of Kon.

"We both might as well be dead if one of us is to be dead."

Then Brant took a deep breath and sprang into the river. He hit with a big whacking splash. He went under; came to the surface; went under. He remembered to flail his arms; came to the surface again.

He gasped for breath; flailed his arms, gasped and choked and gasped.

It came over him that his flailing and struggling were keeping him afloat. He was swimming. God, he was actually swimming. For the first time in his life.

He opened his eyes. Sure enough. His head was out of the

water and above him hung the brown riverbank and ahead stood all the trees of the farther wall of the Wasteland. God.

He kept flailing and pounding and kicking. Of a sudden, directly ahead of him, Kon's fine white hair washed to the surface once more. Brant grabbed for the white hair with his left hand. And got hold of it. Then with a second effort he got hold of a bigger handful of Kon's hair. Then, brain and eyes crackling with terror, he began pounding for the shore with his right hand. His breath came in erratic gasps. Shivers of wildest terror shot up and down his spine.

Slowly he gained on the shore. He was keeping both afloat. God.

Kon felt dead under that hair, dragging so heavy in the water. Maybe he was dead already.

Brant's elbow hit solid earth. He scrabbled out of the water on all fours. He tugged Kon with him. A dozen feet ahead there was a crack in the riverbank. It was a place where cattle came down to drink. Brant crawled toward it, still dragging Kon with him. When he got to where he could get some leverage, he heaved Kon up on dry ground. Then he carried him up the cattle path to a flat place above.

He rolled Kon over on his belly. He slapped him on the side of his head. "Kon!" He whacked Kon on his back. He lifted Kon up and let him drop. Whoosh.

He couldn't get Kon to come out of it.

He rolled Kon over the other way. He opened one of Kon's eyes with a fingertip and yelled down into it, crying, "Kon!" He shook Kon.

Kon lay as limp as a dead herring.

"God in heaven, now what?" Anguish came out of Brant with a hinnied sound. "What am I going to do? Pa! Mother!"

Kon lay on the hoof-pocked ground like a broken sack of oats.

"Mother's got a dead son now."

A trickle of water ran out of Kon's left nostril.

Brant shook Kon one more time. Hard. Wild. Desperate. He slapped Kon's cheeks with loud cracking sounds. He called his name with a great loud call. "Kon!"

Kon's mouth sagged open and a gush of water spilled out.

Brant stared. "Kon?" Quickly he put an ear to Kon's chest. Something faint.

"Kon?"

A mourning dove called, "Ooah—koooo-kooo-koo."

Brant pressed his ear closer.

Heartbeat. Kon was still alive.

Brant picked Kon up again and shook him ferociously. Then he deliberately dropped him hard on his belly on the rough cattle path.

Kon's neck cracked. There was a sigh. "Huhh-ahhh."

"Kon! You're alive. Oh, thank God." Brant bawled. "Thank God, thank God."

Another sigh.

Brant kneeled beside Kon and rolled him over, face up. "Kon? Kon? Can you hear me?"

The wonderful blue eyes opened.

"Kon?"

Kon broke into a wet choked cough. Deep. He coughed and coughed. The coughing grabbed hold of him so deeply it brought him up to a sitting position.

"Kon, oh, God, I thought sure you were a goner. Dead."

Kon finally got on top of his coughing. When he could talk again, he asked, voice hoarse, "Where's my apple?"

"Your apple?"

"Yes. I wanted it. I gave you one."

Brant stared in disbelief. "You crazy nut, you blame near drowned and yet you're still worried about them apples?"

Kon looked down at his soppy overalls, at his dripping shoes, then at Brant's wet clothes and shoes. "What happened?"

"You fell in the river. And I fished you out."

"You did?"

"I sure did. I swum and hauled you in."

"You can't swim."

"Well, I sure as the devil learnt how getting you out."

Kon's blue eyes softened. "Then you saved my life."

"Well, somebody had to."

"You saved my life."

"How do you feel now?"

"Fine."

Brant got to his feet. "C'mon, we better take off our wet clothes." He reached down a hand to help Kon up. "Before we catch something."

They sludged to their tub and pails. They undressed back to back and spread out their wet clothes over a fallen log. They poured the water out of their shoes and opened the sides wide so that the sun could get into them.

The sun shone warm on them. Dry air made their white backs itch.

Brant looked at the half-filled tub. "Suppose we might as well keep on picking while our clothes dry."

"Might as well."

They avoided looking at each other. They moved apart from tree to tree. The grass gave underfoot. The plums still came easy and fast. Soon the tub was full.

Kon spotted a strange green tube of grass. "Look." He kneeled and parted the grass around the green tube, the better to see.

Brant came over. He recognized it. "Snake grass."

"Ma calls it scouring grass. She used to use it to clean pans with in the old days."

Brant kneeled beside Kon. "You can take and pull them apart real easy. Like toy stick sets." Brant pulled the green tube apart. The several sections let go with easy releasing sounds.

"Don't do that!"

"Why not?"

"They're precious."

"It won't die. You can stick 'em back together again." Brant gently pushed the sections back into place. "See?"

"I bet it'll die though now."

"No, it won't. I've done it many times."

"Are you sure?"

"Of course."

They mused on the striped tube of grass. It had the sinister look of something one might see in a nightmare. Even in the Wasteland it seemed out of place.

Brant wondered aloud to himself. "Wouldn't it be something if we could grow trees like that? If you wanted a log for the stove, all you'd need to do would be just to take out what section you wanted, the right thickness, the right length, then stick together what was left again and let it grow some more. You wouldn't even have to plant new trees and yet you'd have all the firewood you wanted."

Kon smiled. "Or take out the size you wanted for fence posts. You'd never need to buy them."

"Say, wouldn't that be something? Maybe someday the world will grow trees like that."

"That'd take millions of years."

They smiled together. Under the warmth of the sun, they felt a glow coming from each other's naked bodies. The clear air in the middle of the Wasteland was sweet with the scent of the ripe plums and wild apples.

"I'm glad we came plumming," Brant said.

"The Wasteland is fun," Kon said. He continued to look down at the sinister tube of scouring grass.

"Kon, sometimes I get funny ideas."

"We all get funny ideas sometimes."

Brant looked away as he spoke. "Like I wish we could try standing back to back close together once and at the same time I could throw my arms around you."

Kon had a shy smile. "That'd be a funny sight."

"Maybe someday in a dream we can do that, huh, Kon?"

Kon got to his feet. "Let's see if our clothes are dry. We can't stay here all day."

"Yeh. I guess we better mosey on home at that."

The clothes weren't quite dry.

Brant said, "Maybe we ought to fill the pails too in the meantime. Keep busy."

Kon nodded. "By that time the shirts should for sure be dry."

They went back to picking.

When they finished filling the pails, Brant found a long stick and went over to the wild apple tree and poked down a half dozen of the top yellow apples. He gave Kon half of them. He went over to his wet overalls and got out his jackknife and cut one of the apples into thin slices and popped the slices one by one into his mouth.

Kon got out his jackknife too. "I should've thought of poking 'em down in the first place."

"They fall and bruise easy that way though."

Kon was first to finish eating his three apples. He went over to test his shirt. "Let's head for home. They're dry enough now."

Back to back again, they got into their clothes and shoes.

Brant was sorry it all was over.

They returned home heroes. Mother just couldn't get over it that they'd picked so many plums.

Pa thought they'd done pretty well too. "Maybe we should give them a medal. They didn't wreck a single solitary thing. And they even look cleaner somehow."

"Well, if not a medal," Mother said, "surely all the plum jam they want all winter long."

Neither Brant nor Kon ever told about the near drowning. All they ever talked about was the best most wonderful time they had. . . .

2

Brant could hear Mildred's hand sliding toward him under the quilt. He knew what she wanted. She'd complained lately that he'd been fidgety in bed. She said that one minute he'd lay stiff like a post, then the next minute like a curled-up crab.

Mildred's hand came warmly up on his hip. She shook him gently.

Brant burned. The humiliation of it. Who was she that she should touch him gently, out of consideration? God.

Again she shook him. Gently.

Suddenly Brant gave her a hard elbow in the side.

Mildred grunted. "Ow."

"That's what you get for it. And it serves you right."

"Why, Brant, you're hot."

"Of course."

"Worse than a red-hot stove almost."

"Keep your hands to home."

"Well, you don't have to get that mad."

"Just leave me alone."

"I can't help it that you're so jumpy."

"Just leave me alone, I said."

"Oh, Brant, please, I'd like to get some sleep too, you know."

Brant got a good hold of his corner of the quilt and turned hard on his side, and in so doing took a good share of the quilt with him. He snuggled under cozy and tight. "Kon never complained."

"That was when you was boys."

"Just don't touch me." Brant spoke with his mouth half buried in the pillow.

Mildred slowly rolled over on her side too, away from him. The quilt became taut between them.

Soon Brant could feel cold air flowing in under the quilt. It touched all the way down to his seat. "Damn women."

Mildred gave her solid hips a flounce, the better to settle in. The motion stirred up the black pitchforks under the bed. They jangled softly. Mildred mumbled, "You and your crazy pitchforks."

Brant bit back a bitter reply. She didn't know any better. If it hadn't been for the sickle over the door and the pitchforks under the bed, the hex witches would long ago have got them.

Mildred murmured into her pillow. "I ought to have my head examined, living with you like this."

"I suppose you think I'm crazy."

"Well, sometimes, Brant, I tell you, the way you act, I might as well go to bed with a corkscrew as to try and straighten you out."

Oh.

"But then, we all have our bad side. So who am I to point the finger? Just lay quiet now and go to sleep. I've got a hard day of work ahead tomorrow."

The need to make water awoke in him. Goddam. Now he'd probably have to get up. And that just when he'd got himself nice and cozy.

Silence.

The alarm clock ticked on the bed table. The oil stove downstairs cracked. The last crickets of the year sawed sad cheer outdoors.

Mildred stirred on her side of the bed.

"God," Brant thought, "if she'd only lay still herself. One more move like that and I'm done. I'll have to get out of bed for sure."

More silence.

Brant willed hard.

Mildred stirred again. Then she rolled over on her side toward him. She whispered, "I'm sorry for what I said, Brant. It was mean of me to talk that way to you. Please forgive me." Once more she placed a warm hand on his hip. "I love you, husband."

That tipped it. Now he couldn't stop it. Balefully he cried, loud, "Goddam you, woman, keep your goddam hands off me." He threw back the quilt on his side and swung out of bed. He quick got down on his knees and reached under the bed for the chamberpot. It wasn't there. "Oh, Jesus Christ to hell, I suppose you got that goddam thing on your side of the bed tonight." Hanging on, almost stumbling over his own puddle of clothes, he ran around the foot of the bed to her side and again knelt and reached under. He found the handle of the chamberpot, jerked it toward him, and stood up holding the pot so as not to miss it in the dark. "Goddam it!"

"Brant. Please. You don't have to swear like that, do you? Get hold of yourself."

"Get hold of myself? Christ, woman, I have got hold of myself. And that's just the trouble with me, goddam it. I've got too much hold of myself. While what I ought to do is to let go more. Be my true self. Do what comes naturally." Cold air moved up under his nightshirt and touched him over the belly. "And by God, that's just what I am going to do. Let go. Do what comes naturally." And Brant, instead of making water in the chamber-pot, suddenly switched over and made water all over his wife, up and down the length of her form where it lay under the bed-clothes. "By God, if your goddam pa could pee all over me under them goddam lilac bushes of his, I sure as hell have a right to pee all over you in my bed."

With a wild cry Mildred heaved herself over onto his side of the bed, out of range. "Brant! Are you out of your mind?"

"What was good enough for him is good enough for me."

"Brant, in the name of God, what's the matter with you?"

"It's one of the best ways to put out a fire I know of."

"Well! This is the last straw." Outraged, Mildred bounded out of bed on his side and stamped off to the girls' room.

"Good riddance!" Brant cried after her.

"Och!" came from the girls' room.

At last, finished, he hopped back into bed on his side, the dry side.

The black pitchforks underneath jangled pleasantly.

3

Brant made up his mind.

He slipped into his mackinaw and boots and put on his mittens and got to work.

First he got the screwdriver and sawhorse and took down the rusty sickle over the kitchen door. Then he went upstairs to their bedroom and crawled under the bed and untied the weather-blackened pitchforks.

He was just leaving the house when Mildred came up from the basement, where she was washing clothes.

Mildred immediately spotted the sickle and pitchforks he was carrying. "Good." Mildred spoke plain and flat. "I see you've at last come to your senses."

"I have."

"It was about time."

"Yes, it's about time."

Mildred closed the door after him.

Brant carried the sickle and the pitchforks across the yard and threw them onto the junk pile behind the garage. In the cold air, metal hit metal with a high-pitched jangling sound.

Next Brant went out to the mailbox and removed the whiffle-tree hooks hanging under it. He threw them onto the junk pile behind the garage too.

Brant also looked at his fence lines along the road. "Too bad the ground is frozen or I'd move them back where they belong today too. Well, it can't be helped. She can hire somebody else to do it, come next April. And good luck to him, whoever it'll be."

Brant opened the garage doors, hooked them back. He set the spark and the gas on the old Ford, went around front to crank it. He was careful to hold the crank handle with his thumb held back. He didn't intend to have the old tin lizzie kick back on him and give him a broken arm. Not today anyway. He spun her hard three times, and on the fourth time around she fired. Good. At last everything was going just right.

He hopped in, backed out in a sharp turn.

Mildred saw him through the kitchen window. She came running out. "Where are you going?"

He tried to ignore her.

"Wait!" she cried.

He saw she had him and pulled up on the brake and lowered the window on his side. He said nothing: just stared down at her. That damn woman didn't miss a trick.

"Are you going to town?"

"I was thinking of it."

"You didn't tell me."

"There's lots of things I don't tell you."

"Well, can you pick me up some groceries?"

"What do you need?"

Mildred puffed. "Well, as I didn't know you was going today, I didn't have a list made out. Can you wait a minute?"

"No. I'm in a hurry."

"Well, could you take along at least a couple of things I need?"

"Shoot."

"I need a sack of sugar. Salt I got, so I don't need that."

Brant goosed the motor. "Get on with it. I'm in a hurry."

"And I need some bluing." Without her sweater Mildred shivered in the cold. "And, oh, yes, we're almost out of oatmeal."

"That all?"

"I—guess—so. I can't think of anything more. I know there's more, but . . ." Mildred's look sharpened. "Say, what are you going to town for?"

"Business."

"Can't you tell me?"

"Not today I can't."

"What darn fool thing are you going to buy now?"

"You'll see soon enough."

"I hope nothing foolish. Something we can't afford."

"We can afford this all right."

"You can't tell me?"

"Nope."

"When will you be back?"

"In about an hour or so."

Mildred nibbled on her lips to keep her curiosity in check. "Good."

Good?

Mildred went on. "I thought maybe we'd go over to your mother's this afternoon. So I'll need the car."

"Oh?" Brant lighted up inside. That might be just the ticket.

"Yes. There's some kind of teachers' meeting in Rock Falls this afternoon, so there's no school for the children. And I thought maybe we'd all go quilting at Mother's."

"I'm not going."

"Brant, what makes you so edgy? Of course I didn't mean for

you to go quilting. Though I thought maybe you could visit with
Pa a little."

"I visit him often enough."

"Well, suit yourself. But I do think me and the girls should
go."

"Good." Brant goosed the motor. Things were really beginning
to work out perfect.

"You'll be home in an hour then?"

"Yep."

"I'll call Mother up and tell her we're coming."

"Do that."

Brant let go of the brake and the old Ford ground off the
yard.

Brant aimed the black car accurately down the right side of
the road. There was going to be no accident on this trip if he
could help it. Thank God it'd been an open winter so far so that
the road wasn't slippery.

"So Karen is due the middle of February, is she? Well, we'll
see about that."

He entered Bonnie in low gear. Main street was dead. No cars.
No buggies. Nobody around. The morning Omaha had already
left on its run north.

He rolled past Doctor Tom's office. That bastard. That blacksmith. Doctor Thomas would never never get his hands on Brant
Harmer again.

He pulled up in front of Fraser's Drugstore, easing the right
front wheel into the curb. He got out and walked briskly into
the drugstore. He took off his gloves and stuck them into his
back pocket. He chafed his hands to stir up the circulation.
They'd got cold holding the steering wheel.

Dick Fraser appeared from behind a partition. He had a stiff
brush of blond hair, an open friendly face, and crinkles in the
corners of his blue eyes. He wore a tan smock. Fraser said, "Well,
if it isn't old Brant Harmer, the champion hen hopper of Rock
township."

Brant cautioned himself not to get mad. It was only Fraser's
way. Fraser meant well. Actually Fraser had a kind heart most

times. "Hi." Brant let his eyes rove over the counters and shelves. There were glistening brown bottles of pills, gleaming white boxes of lozenges, soft blue packages of womens' napkins, cardboard posters of fountain pens, racks of black combs, displays of hot water bottles.

Fraser was quick to catch Brant's mood and next waited for Brant to speak his mind.

Brant first showed Fraser the cracked skin over the knuckles of his hands. "I could use me a little arnica."

"Got just the thing for you. Special preparation just in from Sioux Falls." Fraser reached for a slim brown bottle from a shelf behind him. He read from the label. "Ingredients: glycerin, rose water, tincture of arnica."

"How much?"

"Fifty cents a bottle."

"You guarantee it?"

"I do."

"Then I'll take one."

Fraser set the bottle of hand lotion on the counter near a wide roll of brown wrapping paper. "Anything else?"

"Yeh. I could also use me a little strychnine."

"What do you need that for?"

Brant looked Fraser in the eye. "What's it to you?"

"Nothing. Just that state law requires that I ask."

"For rats then."

"Rats? On your place, Brant?"

Brant's ears clicked. "What's wrong with my place that it can't have a few rats?"

"Nothing. I was just joking."

"Most places have a few rats, don't they?"

"It's hard to imagine rats on a place with cement flooring everywhere. And kept so clean."

"You'll find rats anywhere there's corn."

The crinkles in the corners of Fraser's blue eyes sharpened. "How much do you need, Brant?"

"Enough to kill off a couple of dozen. In case they come back later on."

Fraser held his bristle blond head slightly to one side. "You'll sign a receipt for it?"

Brant seethed inside. Questions. Questions. He swallowed to control his face. "Why that?"

"State law."

"Oh, all right."

Fraser got out a receipt book, entered a notation, then turned it about for Brant to sign.

Brant wrote his name in an uncertain boyish script.

"You know how to use this stuff?"

"Uhh . . . no, I don't."

"Best way is to put a pinch of it in some hamburger or meat scraps."

"Okay."

"Not much now. If you can see it, it'll be enough to kill them."

"Okay."

"It's awful bitter, you know, and rats've got a pretty leery tongue."

"All right."

Fraser went to one side and began filling a brown vial with what looked like powdered sugar. The sharpened crinkles in the corners of Fraser's eyes lingered. "Better not take any of this stuff yourself, Brant. Ha."

"Why not?"

"A whole lot will kill you and this your wife wouldn't like. And a little bit will make you hornier than a wild goat and this she might not like either."

"Ha. My wife'll probably recommend I take a whole lot."

"Ha. In that case, try a little bit first and maybe she'll change her mind about the other."

"Ha."

"And a little bit of that hand lotion each day will help too."

"How so?"

"It'll make your hands soft. Not quite so horny."

"Ha."

Fraser capped the vial, wrote something on a label, and stuck the label on the vial. He set the vial alongside the bottle of hand lotion. "Will that be all?"

"That's all."

Fraser carefully wrapped up the vial and bottle together in several layers of brown paper. "That'll be one dollar even."

Brant extracted a partly torn dollar bill from his pocketbook and paid up.

"Let me know how you make out with those rats, Brant."

"You'll hear about it." Brant took the brown package and started to leave. Everything had gone just right.

"Say, Brant?"

Now what. Brant paused by the door. It wouldn't do to make a run for it.

Fraser came out from behind the counter. "How's your side been lately?"

"My side?"

"Yes. You know, down here?" Fraser stroked his left side low down. "Where you always said it felt like a whole carrot had got in there somehow?"

"Oh, that. It went away."

"Good for you."

"Yeh, it just quit of itself."

"I'm glad to hear that. Everything's going just fine for you then, is it?"

"Couldn't be better."

"Good."

Brant nodded. And left.

Brant got Mildred her sugar and bluing and oatmeal, and went home.

4

At one o'clock Mildred and the girls still hadn't left for Mother's. Mildred was dawdling over her coffee and the girls were still on their apple pie. The girls were thick with food and winter underwear.

Brant himself had long ago finished eating. He'd only taken a bite of this and a sip of that. A near empty stomach was best.

Mildred smiled at her girls. "It looks like I'm in luck today."

Brant threw Mildred a high look. "How so?"

"Well, I've got me two dishwashers this noon. Other days I have to do it alone."

"Skip the dishes."

"Why?"

"It's getting on to where you should've already been busy quilting at Mother's, ain't it? If you want to get something done yet today?"

"I'm not so sure we're going now."

Brant held himself tight. Here he was ready and now this. "Why not?"

"Well, the thing of it is, I had to call Mother back after I talked to you this morning and she wondered if maybe we shouldn't come tomorrow."

"What's the matter at Mother's?"

"Her rheumatism is bothering her pretty bad today."

"Go anyway. Stirring her up will do her good."

Slanting February sun had slowly begun to veer in through the west kitchen window. It gave the whole room—the black nickel stove, the brown cabinet, the blue wallpaper, the yellow linoleum floor, the oak table and chairs—a look as though all had been stained with dandelion wine.

Edna finally finished her pie. In the last year or so her face had slowly become longer than Pauline's. "I know what we can do. I can do Gramma's share."

Mildred smiled. "You know what your gramma will say to that."

Pauline also finally finished her pie. Over the last months she had begun to show signs that she would be another patient Mildred. "And I'll give Gramma a rubdown with some of Grampa's liniment."

Mildred laughed. "Gramma will surely appreciate that." Mildred finished her coffee. "No, first we do the dishes. Then we'll call up Gramma to see if she feels any better."

Brant sat stiffly erect. "Listen, I'll do the dishes for once. If it's for Mother, I'll be glad to do 'em."

"Hey, hey, listen to the man," Mildred said.

The girls lighted up. They hated doing the dishes.

Brant said, "You don't need to call Mother up. You know she's always glad to see the girls. Especially now that they're growing up so. The next thing you know, after you're there awhile, she'll have forgot all about her rheumatism."

"Well, that's true."

"So I say, just go." Brant got to his feet and began stacking the dishes.

"Your coffee," Mildred said. "You didn't finish it."

Brant looked down. "Oh. Yeh." He picked up his cup and drank what was left all in one gulp. Then he went back to stacking the dishes again.

"Are you trying to get rid of us?"

"Maybe I am."

"Well, it sure looks like it, the way you're hurrying us."

"Take your time. But if I'm to wash dishes, I'm getting at it right away."

Mildred studied him. She sensed that he was up to something all right.

Brant busied himself with the dishes. With a yellow bar of soap he worked up a good head of suds.

After a few moments, Mildred decided to humor him one more time. Maybe it was all in her own head. With a sigh she got up from the table and made ready to go, getting out her black fur coat and her blue hat.

The young girls flew through the house as they too got ready to go, back and forth, chirping happily, putting on their blue coats and blue stocking caps and blue mittens. Going to Gramma's was always a treat. There would be ice cream and honey, and a trunk full of old pictures up in the attic to look at, and Grampa even had a radio where you could hear people talking all the way from Denver.

Brant dropped the silverware in with a clatter.

Mildred gave him yet another wondering look as she passed through the door. But she said nothing. The young girls in their excitement forgot to say good-bye.

Through the kitchen window Brant watched Mildred set the spark and the gas on the old Ford and crank it properly with the thumb held back. Soon a puff of smoke shot out the back and it began to shake rhythmically. He watched all three of his womenfolk get in. Then the old tin lizzie rolled off the yard with a steady purr of power.

"Now," he said, "quick."

He found his hands still immersed in the suds. He looked down at them a second.

"Hell, I don't need to finish the dishes now. Nothing matters now. I won't know about it afterwards anyway."

He jerked his hands out of the dishwater and dried them on the dish towel.

"The main thing is to get the top job done and get it done before they come back."

He'd left the vial of strychnine up on a ledge in the garage when he'd earlier brought in Mildred's groceries. He went out to get the vial.

The skull and crossbones on the label caught his eye. "WARN-ING: Poison!!! Antidote: Charcoal and egg white administered promptly. The patient should be kept as quiet as possible. Artificial respiration may be necessary."

He pulled out the stopper and had a look inside the brown vial. He sniffed. The dope not only looked like powdered sugar; it smelled like it.

The druggist had said something about its being awful bitter. Maybe it would be better at that to mix it in with something to cut the bitterness.

He reentered the kitchen. Mildred had set the coffee on the back of the stove. Good. That might be just the ticket. Some coffee with bitter powdered sugar.

He decided he'd use all of it in one blast. The quicker he got it over with, the better.

He got out an old-fashioned coffee mug, a big one that Mildred had once picked up at an antique sale, and shook all the powdered strychnine into it.

To make sure that no one would find the vial in time to give him the antidote, he went outside again and smashed the empty vial into the junk pile where the sickle and the black pitchforks and the whiffletree hooks also lay. Splinters of brown glass shot like flying crickets everywhere.

Back in the house, he poured in the black coffee, stirring as he did so.

The strychnine didn't dissolve well. It rode in the coffee like sour cream. Stirred fast it seemed to mix all right, but stirred slow the separate curds showed again. He mashed the larger lumps of powder against the sides of the mug.

"So Karen is due the middle of February, is she? Well, we'll see about that."

He looked out over the yard for the last time. The sun shone lemon pale across the faded cornfields and the frost-seared pastures. The trees were the only things that had much color. They stood like sticks of chocolate. February was always the worst month of the year to live through.

"Well, after today not for me anymore."

His eyes closed of themselves. Instantly he saw again the time when he and Kon had gone plumming: white naked bodies moving sweetly across the deep green grass, a warm big-eyed sun shining on little rows and rows of hanging yellow fruit, a lone wild apple tree leaning over the riverbank.

"We should've both died then. It would've saved everybody a lot of trouble."

A cow bawled for her calf out in the barnyard. In his mind's eye Brant could see her standing in front of the closed calf-pen door, waiting, listening for some sound of her precious one inside, tail risen a little, ears pricked up, dumb mind all of a small burning pain at the separation.

"Even dumb animals can miss each other an awful lot."

The oil burner cracked behind him.

"Kon, Kon, what you did to me, what you did to me!"

Brant looked at the kitchen clock. It was one-forty-five. By two-fifteen it would be all over. Let's see, wasn't he born shortly after one in the afternoon? Yes. That's what Mother said anyway.

"Our dearly beloved son and brother and father, our neighbor Brant Harmer, who lived upon this earth forty years, forty days, and forty-some minutes, has gone to his final resting place. Amen."

Nice round figures. Out of self-mocking curiosity Brant checked the marble clock on the piano in the living room to make sure. Yes. One-forty-six.

"Well, we shall see what we shall see, Mrs. Konstant Harmer."

Best place to do it would be upstairs. Drink the dope and then lay down in bed, the bed on which both Edna and Pauline had been conceived. And where the beginning began of his losing Kon.

"Kon, maybe you're thinking of naming that baby after me. To make it up to me. If it's a boy. Well, Kon, by God, I for one am never going to know about it."

He climbed the stairs, mug in hand, stirring with a spoon as he went.

"I'd sure like to see Mrs. Konstant Harmer's face when the telephone rings tonight."

He entered their bedroom. He made it a point to close the door behind him. Sunlight coming in through the parted white curtains gave the walnut dresser and the walnut chest of drawers a chocolate-gold tint. The shiny brass bed was neatly made. The chamberpot was in its proper place under his side. You couldn't beat kicking off in a neat room.

"She might even throw her kid. I've heard of women having miscarriages on littler things than that."

He set the mug on the stand beside the bed. Then, before he lay down, of a sudden, unhooking a suspender, he lowered his overalls and had a quick look at himself. Then, equally sudden, he lifted his overalls up again.

"Two clots and a hollow tube of flesh. Almost lost on a fellow if you didn't know where to look for 'em."

He picked up the mug. He gave the mug a good swirling shake so as to thoroughly mix in the curds again.

"Come to think of it, why not go out in style? If I am going to save them the fuss of carrying me upstairs to bed, I might as well do it up right."

Setting the mug down again, he took off his work shoes and socks, his overalls and shirt. He dug out a white shirt and blue bowtie, his black dress shoes and blue socks, his black suit. He watched himself dress in the mirror over the dresser.

"Serves them both right."

He checked the clock. Two bells even. He'd be gone by two-thirty then. Mildred and the girls wouldn't be back until at least four.

"But if the Harmer luck holds out they'll have a girl. That's what I had anyway."

He observed himself in the mirror. A little peaked over the cheeks. Black eyes shiny. But yet for his age not a half-bad looking gaffer. One of the pillars of Rock township.

"A crucifix with the crossbar low down."

He picked up the mug once more. He stirred up the contents until it looked as smooth as a cup of coffee with fresh cream.

"I have a right to take my own life. It's mine, ain't it? To do with as I please? Yes, I have a right to long for my heavenly home."

He laid the spoon aside. He hoisted up the drink to toast the fellow in the mirror. The fellow in the mirror toasted him back.

"Well, old man, bottoms up, and then Charlie will be free to make a pig out of your wife."

He drank. The first couple of swallows went down smooth as silk.

"This cup, which my brother hath given me, shall I not drink it?"

He drank again. But from then on the drink began to bite something fierce. He caught at his throat with his free hand. He coughed.

"By God, it is pretty spicy at that."

Yet he kept drinking and swallowing until it was all down. He set the mug down and wiped his lips with the back of his hand. Ul-lck. He'd made the dope too thick.

"Now I lay me down to sleep. I pray Thee, Lord, my soul to keep."

He stretched out on his side of the bed. He composed himself as he thought one should look after being laid out in a coffin, legs straight out and slightly parted, hands crossed over one's private crucifixion, head lightly sunk into the pillow, eyes shut like a pair of white four o'clocks closed for the last time, Adam's apple high, lips curved in a faint smile.

"God, it's bitter. I can feel it working in my stomach down there like it's liniment boiling."

He opened his eyes for a last look around in the bedroom. The shaft of sunlight coming through the south window touched the foot of his bed. The room seemed to be flooded with cider.

"What I should've done was to 've cut it off and pickled it in a jar as a memento for Mildred."

He licked the bitterness off his lips.

"Well, too late now."

The cider air in the bedroom tasted surprisingly sweet. Even to let the eyes dream around in it was like smelling heady wine. It was like being sucked down deep into one's blood.

Ah, dying was wonderful. Dying was like waking up on a frosty morning and knowing the corn was all out. Dying was like being born a boy again. The perfume of wild plums was all around one.

The phone rang downstairs. Two shorts. It was their ring.

"Holy hell."

The phone rang four times and then stopped. That meant that someone was now waiting for him to answer it.

"God."

Then the phone rang again. Two shorts. Then a pause. Then two more shorts. It rang and rang.

He counted them. It rang two shorts eighteen times before it finally quit.

Ringing silence followed.

"Of all the goddam luck."

It was as though his stomach had tongue and could taste the thick dope.

"That has to be Mildred."

He bounced upright in bed.

"It has to be."

He saw himself in the mirror across the foot of his bed. That fellow was Brant Harmer? Never in his life had he seen such a crazy wild-eyed nut.

"God, what if she's decided something's gone wrong here? She did give me a wise eye when she left."

He fell back into his pillow.

"Well, it'll take her ten minutes to get here. By then the dope should have the job done."

The instructions for the giving of the antidote were safely in the junk pile. Even if she did arrive on the yard before he was gone she'd never think of looking for it there.

The back of his neck began to feel odd. And his bowels began to burn.

"Good. That means it's beginning to take hold at last."

The bitterness in his throat spread down into his gullet. Slowly his breath came faster and faster.

"Leave it to her though to think of something to make me vomit if she gets back here in time."

His back was stiffening. He rolled his shoulders a little as if to welcome it.

"Dear God, let it hurry."

The stiffness in his neck and back deepened. It was as if a big white crab had lighted just below the back of his skull and were digging into his spine with its pincers and feet both. Deeper. Deeper.

"It had better hurry. Because if it don't, I'm gonna have to go down and lock all the doors. To keep her out until it's over with. Because as sure as hell that was Mildred ringing. She knows."

He waited. Throat, gullet, belly burned. He coughed.

"But suppose she busts in here anyway? I can't have her watch me die. Or the little girlies."

He lay stiff in bed. The white crab dug in deeper.

"Well, if she busts in here, I'll just have to take the double-barrel shotgun to myself."

His neckbone cracked.

"Thank God, the shotgun's got a short barrel."

A single tremor coursed through his body.

"Let's see now. I know where the double-barrel shotgun is, but where the hell did I put them shells?"

After threatening Charlie that he'd take the double-barrel shotgun to him if he didn't leave the yard in just thirty seconds, Brant had discovered that he didn't have any shells on hand. So he'd bought a boxful. But for the life of him he couldn't remember where he'd put the shells. Up on a ledge in the garage? He couldn't remember seeing them there when he'd gone out to get the strychnine a little bit ago. Up behind the clock where he sometimes put things—matches, gloves, jackknife? No, not there either. Goddam, where were they?

"I know I haven't used any. So them shells must be where I put 'em when I came home from town that time."

He tried to recall that trip home from town, minute for minute. He got himself back on the yard in memory all right, but from there on his mind ran blank.

"Maybe Mildred found the shells and hid them. Be just like her."

Muscles all over his body began to twitch. His legs and arms behaved as if they had minds of their own. They jerked and let go and jerked like they might be clowns gone crazy.

"Where the devil did I put them shells?"

A spasm shot up his gullet and closed his throat. He had to fight to get his breath. It was an awful feeling. It was like he was going to choke to death. He clawed at his throat. He tried to stick his finger down it. Couldn't. He gagged. It was awful the way it was working out.

"Great balls of fire."

Convulsions seized him. First they doubled him up into a tight ball; then they bent him backward until his belly arched up out of bed like a barrel hoop.

"All doubled up like a poisoned pup."

Was that their old Ford already purring onto their yard? He listened wild-eyed. Listened. No. It couldn't be. It had to be the poison buzzing in his ears.

The convulsions let go of him. His body relaxed. He poured out to his further extremities again. Exhausted, he lay slack on the bed.

"What a way to go."

To his amazement he discovered he was aroused. The one place the convulsive seizure hadn't let go of him was there. Druggist Fraser had hinted something about that. For once Mildred would have been proud of him.

"Get it over with. God."

It boiled all through him.

"Just so I took enough now. Then I won't have to find them damned shells."

The clock on the piano downstairs struck the half hour.

"If she piled into the car right after she hung up she could almost be here by now."

All of a sudden he recalled where he'd put the shells. They were in with his underwear, in the chest of drawers. He'd put them there after Mildred had suggested he shouldn't keep the shells and the gun in the same place. With the gun hanging over the table in the kitchen, and the shells upstairs, he'd have a couple more seconds to think it over before he did anything rash. She was thinking of Charlie, of course.

"Good. Now I'm ready for her. If I'm not dead by the time she drives on the yard, I'm gonna run downstairs and lock all the doors, then grab the gun and run up here and ram two shells in and let 'er go. Both barrels."

He lay waiting, listening, boiling.

"Kon, look at all I'm doing because of you."

PART SEVEN

Mildred

1

The girls made a happy racket in the front seat beside Mildred. Gramma sometimes had an extra surprise for them when they came over, and they were wondering what it would be this time.

Edna said, "Some new red mittens. I need 'em for school."

Pauline said, "Homemade candy. I surely love homemade candy."

Edna said, "I just know it'll be a barrette."

Pauline said, "Cookies. With maple frosting on top."

"Or a young girl's brassiere."

"Some special homemade ice cream. With homemade honey on top. And on top of that some homemade walnuts."

"Pauline Harmer, nobody makes ice cream this time of the year. In the middle of the winter."

"They do too."

"They do not."

"Well, it's the middle of February already. And next month it'll be the middle of March. And that's when spring begins."

"Stretcher."

Mildred gave the steering wheel a shake. "Will you girls stop it? All that ruckus. Mother's thinking."

Both girls, taken aback, turned to look at Mildred.

"It's about time you girls started acting a little grown up." Mildred gave the wheel another good shake. "And I mean that."

The two young girls became very quiet. Mother didn't often talk that way.

Gramma's lane came into view. Mildred slowed for it; turned in. "Something funny is going on," she said to herself. And without thinking, she pulled up sharply in front of the house gate, so hard that the rear wheels chattered on the frozen rutted yard.

"What's the matter, Mother?"

Mildred stared out over the yard. Her hand reached for the ignition key; then paused.

"Mother?"

Mildred let the motor run. "I think maybe we ought to turn around and go right back home."

"But we only just got here, Mother."

Gramma appeared on the veranda. She hadn't bothered to put on a coat and the moment the cold struck her she began to hug herself. She resembled a nubbin of corn with only a few husks left on.

Pauline said, "Gramma won't like it if we don't stay for at least one minute."

"I don't like it," Mildred murmured. "He's up to something."

"Who, Mother?"

"He was too anxious to get us off the place."

Gramma couldn't understand why they didn't right away pile out of the car. She gestured sharply for them to come on and hurry up.

Still Mildred let the motor run. The back of her head opened up as though it were a river clam, and like a straining muscle her whole soul reached out of it toward Brant.

Gramma came down the stoop and then the sidewalk. She walked as if she had to break and rebreak her knees on every step.

Edna, on the outside, lowered the window. "Hi, Gram."

Gramma stopped by the gate. She stared at them. "I suppose

now that Grampa and Gramma are old and dying, we stink too much for you young ladies, hah?"

Mildred blinked.

"Ha?"

After a moment a smile of a sort stirred on Mildred's lips. "We forgot something, Gramma, and I was wondering if we shouldn't go back and get it. That's all. So don't get mad."

Gramma's head jerked back like a gobbler's. "Turn around and go home and get it then. This house won't float away."

"Oh," Mildred said, giving in, "I suppose it can wait. What we forgot." She shut off the motor. She also tried to shut off that part of her that was reaching out for Brant.

"Yippee!" Edna cried. Opening the door, she jumped down out of the car and ran over and gave Gramma a tight hug and a big kiss.

Pauline followed. She too loved up her gramma.

Gramma accepted it all with stiff knees. She was much shorter than the two girls. Two yellow tears wriggled down her wrinkled stiff cheeks. "So your old gramma don't stink too much after all, hah?"

"Oh, Gramma, such an awful thing to say."

"So you still like Gramma's homemade candy with homemade walnuts, hah?"

Pauline gave Edna a look of triumph. "See? I told you."

Edna said nothing.

Mildred got herself out of the car and stepped to the frozen ground. She brushed down her black fur coat, then reached back into the car for her purse. "Anyway, we weren't sure you wanted us over today, Ma."

"Ptuey! I needed a little stirring up."

"That's what Brant said." Mildred leaned down and kissed Gramma. Her lips touched one of the yellow tears on Gramma's cheeks. The taste of it was like that of pickling brine.

Gramma pretended she didn't want Mildred to kiss her. "Och!" But two more tears appeared in the corners of her eyes. To hide them she in turn began to love up the girls. "Come. First a treat. The quilting can wait."

The girls and Gramma traipsed up the walk to the house.

Mildred dragged behind. She found herself looking off toward the northeast, where Brant was home alone. "What I don't like is that lately he's somehow turned sneaky quiet on me." She nodded to herself. "We were better off when he was busy with all them fool notions of his about how to outfox them hex witches. At least then there was something going on I could pick at."

Gramma held the door open for Mildred and the two girls. "Come, move along, we can't afford to heat up the whole county."

The moment warm air touched her on the face Mildred knew what she had to do. She didn't even bother to take off her coat or her mittens. She walked straight to the wall telephone and, grabbing the little nickel crank, began to ring it. Two shorts. Four times. Then she put the black receiver to her ear.

"That's our ring, Mother," Edna said.

"What's the matter, Mother?" Pauline asked.

"Shh. I want to ask your daddy something." Mildred listened, listened. "Don't take off your coats just yet."

Gramma snapped, "Did you and Brant have a fight?"

Mildred shook her head.

Gramma watched her.

The girls waited.

The only sound in the receiver was a low moaning on the wire as of far-off angels singing endlessly in monotone.

"That's funny."

Mildred rang again. Two shorts. Two shorts. She whirled the crank on the brown wall telephone until her whole body shook with the motion of it. Two shorts. Two shorts. Surely one set of the two shorts would be heard.

Gramma said, "The way you ring it's enough to wake the dead."

Mildred heard clicks all up and down the country line. They were so loud they hurt the ear. "Yes, as well as wake up all the rubberneckers in the county."

Edna said, "Maybe Dad went out to the barn or something."

"No," Mildred said, "no. He hears me ringing all right. But he's made up his mind he's not going to answer."

Pauline said, "Sometimes Dad can be stubborn all right. Worse than a doll even."

Mildred could smell Brant. Right there in his mother's kitchen. A man's sweet male smell. Yeasty. What he smelled like when he was young and full of beans. When he was eighteen. It was almost enough to turn her into soft warm butter again. "I still love that funny little runt."

Pauline looked around to see where Gramma might have set out the walnut candy to harden.

Edna viewed Pauline with huge disgust. "You don't like your dad, that's why you can say such a mean thing about him."

Pauline puffed herself up. "I love him just as much as you do."

Mildred snapped her hand at the girls. "Shh, you kids!"

Gramma's eyes flared open for a second as if she had just then come upon an awful thought.

Edna said, "Dolls don't feel."

Pauline stuck out her chin. "Mine used to."

Gramma's eyes hooded over. She drew both girls down to her old husk of a bosom and enfolded them in her arms.

Mildred found herself staring at Gramma. Was the old mother thinking what she was thinking?

Edna said, "That was because you was always feeling for her. By herself she couldn't've."

Pauline said, "Anyway, that's a lot better than going around playing pinching and such."

Edna said, "Who plays pinching anymore? That was when I was a little girl and didn't know any better."

Gramma gave the girls a sudden convulsive hug. "Eiii!" she cried out as if she couldn't hold it back.

It caught Mildred in the heart. The hair over her temple prickled out and she could feel herself blanch all the way down to her throat. "Brant!"

The girls broke free of Gramma.

Mildred slammed the black receiver into its nickel hook. "Get into the car, you kids!" She surged for the door herself. "Hurry."

Scared, the girls rushed outside ahead of her.

Gramma's head fell forward.

Mildred pulled the door shut behind them so hard it made the house boom like a huge bass drum.

The girls ran through the house gate, then trembling stood waiting in their blue clothes beside the black-and-copper Ford.

Mildred jerked the car door open, threw her purse inside, reached in to set the spark and gas. She cautioned herself to think straight. "Don't flood the car now." She hurried around to the front of the car and grabbed the crank. She took a deep breath. "Please, God." Then she quick spun the old Ford's tail.

The old car caught on the second turn; immediately began to purr smoothly.

"Thank God." Mildred dodged around the fender and bounced into the car. "All right, girls, get in. Quick, now."

The girls obeyed her like they might be part of her.

Mildred put the old car in gear and, cramping the steering wheel over, whirled off the frozen yard. "Please, God, don't let it be too late."

The girls sat as still as stunned raccoons.

The sun was halfway down. It shone slanting through the frazzled cornstalks. There were no shadows. The muted yellow hue lay reflected over the road. A line of gold shone in a long crack across the windshield.

With her forefinger Mildred pushed the gas lever all the way down. The old car gradually got itself up to its top speed.

"For once I wish we could go sixty."

Two pheasants, a brilliantly colored male and a muted tan hen, exploded out of the ditch on the right. The pheasants angled up in a blur of popping wings, then, leveling off, streamed across the road. Gradually their flight flattened out, until, sinking, they vanished into a field of dark plowing.

The section corner came up. Mildred stepped on the brake a little, turned right almost on two wheels. The girls couldn't help but lean against her a little. The car backfired once. Then, leaning ahead over the steering wheel, Mildred gave the old car the gas again.

Black eyebrows creased into paired arrows. Mildred probed the grove ahead for some sign of Brant, for any kind of movement at all. All she saw were some black-and-white cows dreaming out by the straw pile in the barnyard and two black horses nosing through the butt of an old haystack along the pasture fence.

Gradually the old car got itself up to its top speed again.

A rough rutted stretch loomed up ahead in the road. It was where a spring was always working through. Mildred took a good hold of the steering wheel. Twice the car bounced high enough to leave the surface of the road entirely; came down square again.

"Mother—"

"Shht!"

The old motor began to buzz with heat. Alcohol fumes from the radiator drifted back into the car.

The Harmer mailbox appeared ahead.

Mildred moaned to herself. "Dear God, let him still be alive when we get there."

"Mother—"

"Shht!"

Mildred reset herself square to the car's hard leather seat.

The eyes of the girls opened wider.

How she loved that tough funny little runt. The two children she'd luckily had by him were wonderful. They couldn't have been better by any other man. Compared to that horse of a brother Charlie, Brant was a gentleman. And compared to that overfine Kon, Brant had real sand to him. "Brant. Brant. Don't do it. Everything's still gonna turn out all right."

The lettering on their mailbox came up clearly.

Edna broke out, "Mother, you're going too fast to turn in."

Pauline cried out too. "Mother, look out!"

Mildred blinked, and came to. Lord. She flipped up the gas lever; stepped on the brakes; hauled back on the steering wheel.

Both the slowing motor and the brakes took hold. The car shuddered; slowly began to skate sideways.

"Mother, we're going to tip!"

Mildred waited until the very last second; then, leaning left as hard as she could, turned left. The girls leaned with her. The old Ford lurched up on two wheels; ruggled a little on the rutted entrance; held; then made it, just barely.

All three heard it. Bangbang.

"What was that?" Mildred cried.

"The car, Mother."

"Didn't sound like it to me."

"It backfired, Mother. It did that back there by the corner too."

"You think so? Oh, God, let it only be that."

Mildred shut off the motor in front of the house gate. "Out, girls. Quick."

The girls scrambled out.

Mildred grabbed her purse and surged heavy-kneed up the sidewalk. Her eyes went all over the house, especially the windows. She hurried up the back steps to the kitchen. Looking up, her eyes caught sight of the two raw screw holes where Brant had once had his crazy sickle stuck over the door. She grabbed hold of the handle to the storm door and gave it a pull.

Locked. From the inside. Lord. And she never carried a key because they never locked the house.

"You girls wait here."

"But—"

"Wait here." Mildred ran around the other side of the house to try the front door. She hurried onto the porch. The wood flooring cracked underfoot. She grabbed the handle of the storm door. It opened with a sigh of escaping air. Good. Next she grabbed the knob of the inside door, turning the knob as she gave it a push.

Locked. Mercy sakes alive.

She stood a moment thinking. Again she could smell him. A man's sweet male smell. Yeasty. "Brant."

She took off her mittens and looked in her purse to see if she might not happen to have a key anyway. Her fingers paged through the contents of her purse: last letter from Karen, two pink combs, compact, several store bills, little black leather pocketbook lumpy with coins, extra car key, bulletin from the last church service. But no house key.

"That's right. I remember now. Both keys are up in the clock on the piano."

Brant.

She ran back to the kitchen door.

The girls still stood waiting to one side, eyes black dots in white faces.

Mildred made up her mind what to do. She put her mittens back on and took her purse by the handle and smashed in the lower glass pane. Triangles of glass fell inward, tinkling.

"Now."

Reaching in, she unlocked the storm door, opened it. She grabbed hold of the doorknob of the inside door and gave it a firm twist and push.

Also locked.

"Brant!"

The children reached for each other's hands.

The wide overhang of the roof slanted darkly down over the three of them. A pallid tan sun struck warped across the yard. Only the white barn and the white granary had bulk enough to raise shadows.

"Better get a crowbar and break into the house." She snapped a look down at the girls. "Wait here."

Mildred ran to the toolshed. She hunted around in the dusky insides. No crowbar.

"Wonder where in the world he keeps it?"

As she stepped outside, the junk pile behind the garage caught her eye. Ah. Should be something there she could use to prize open the door. She hurried over. Her black eyes looked everywhere almost at once. Lots of broken glass. Tin cans. There was that dratted rusty sickle and those black pitchforks. Some broken cultivator shovels. A long iron rod still tied to a wheel. Discarded bull wheel from a binder. Bent wagon box rods. Rusted gas can. Crushed milk pails.

Bits of freshly broken glass caught her eye. A piece of paper was still stuck to one of the slivers. There was some writing on the piece of paper. She picked it up. It was part of a label from Fraser's Drugstore.

"WARNING: Poison!!! Antidote: Charc—" The rest was torn off.

She sniffed the broken piece of glass. No smell really. With her tongue she tip-tasted it. Bitterish, whatever it was. She looked at the date on the label.

"Why, it's dated today."

She stared down at it.

"Today?"

Vomit trembled in her belly. Calm now. Calm.

"Wonder where the rest of this label went?"

She looked. Looked. Couldn't seem to spot it in the tangle of all the junk.

Her eye next caught something rusty lying at the very edge of the junk pile. She leaned down for a better look. An old house key.

She picked it up. She rubbed it. Rust came off on her mittens like a smear of old dried blood.

Well. It might just work. House keys all looked pretty much alike. That'd save having to break open the inside door.

Gathering up her skirts and her black fur coat, she surged back to the kitchen door. The girls still stood waiting, in their blue clothes, holding hands. She held open the storm door and stuck the key into the inside door. It slipped in. Trembling, she tried it. It turned over.

Too easy. The key hadn't caught.

"Have to break in somehow after all."

Yet she tried the rusty key again just to make sure. This time she turned the key in a cramping manner high up against the top of the keyhole.

The key turned a bit heavier. She could feel it. Slowly, gently, but forcibly, she wedged the key around. Halfway around, the tumblers clicked inside. The key turned easy the rest of the way. She tried the doorknob. Open. Ah.

"Now."

She shot into the house, the girls following her, the mother in black, the other two in blue.

Nothing in the kitchen. Quickly she ran to look in the living room. Nothing. The parlor. Nothing.

Next she ran to the cellar door and, jerking it open, hollered down. "Brant?"

Nothing.

"Brant, are you down there?"

Nothing.

She took a couple of steps down the stairs and, kneeling, looked around in the gloom. Nothing.

Wild rags of terror raced across her line of vision.

Calm now. First things first.

She stepped back up and closed the cellar door.

That bangbang they heard as they drove onto the yard—maybe the girls were wrong after all that that was the car backfiring.

Warped sunlight wavered on her hips as she stood in the kitchen.

Edna spoke up. "He's upstairs, Mother."

"What!"

Edna pointed up at the ceiling. An old look had come over her face. It was the same hooded look that had come over Gramma's face a dozen minutes earlier.

"That's right. We haven't looked upstairs yet. Why didn't I think of it before?"

Mildred pounced for the knob of the stair door. She flung the door open so hard it hit the wall with a bang. She bounded up the dark steps.

The girls followed.

The door to the master bedroom was closed.

That wasn't right. None of them ever closed their bedroom door. They'd made it a habit to be within easy call of each other at night.

Mildred hesitated. Her hand hovered just above the doorknob.

"Dear God, please, please make everything be all right on the other side of this door. In the name of our marriage made holy in Thy name. Because I love him so."

Her hand continued to hover above the doorknob.

The girls bumped into her from behind.

"Shht."

Pauline said, "Don't you want to go in and see Dad, Mother?"

Mildred closed her eyes.

"Mother?"

"Yes, Pauline." Mildred turned the knob and pushed in.

On their shiny brass bed lay what was left of a body dressed in Sunday black. The upper part of the body lay toward them. It resembled the stalk of a red cabbage with the head chopped out. Even the blasted bits of something lying about the room resembled scraps of shredded red cabbage.

Brant.

Brant's double-barreled shotgun lay across his hips. The thumb and forefinger of his right hand were still caught in the trigger guard. There was a sharp smell of burnt powder in the bedroom along with a sickening smell of what seemed to be sweet cream.

A mug with a spoon in it stood on the stand beside the rumpled scarlet bed.

Mildred understood what had happened in a glance.

He'd taken the poison. He'd lain down, waiting for it to take hold. Then for some reason, maybe because he'd heard them coming down the frozen road and didn't want them to see him die, he'd hopped out of bed and had quick got his double-barreled shotgun and had loaded it, and then had stuck the barrel end into his mouth and had pushed down on both triggers. Because it looked like there'd been two heads of red cabbage where the two blasts had come out.

Blood and what looked like ground-up mushrooms still oozed out of the decapitated stalk. Gone forever was that darling hanging lip.

Mildred heard breathing beside her. The girls. She should never have let them come upstairs with her. Now they were ruined for life.

She turned and put her arms around her girls. "Come."

They resisted her. Their eyes gleamed like dark glass marbles. "Come, girls."

The girls continued to hold against her and stare at the scarlet bed.

Mildred gave them a push, firmly. "Come now. This is not for us anymore."

The girls gave way slowly, dragging their feet until she got them out in the hallway.

Mildred closed the door behind them. "Go on."

The girls began to stumble stiff-kneed down the stairs.

Mildred followed. Her knees also behaved as if they'd been broken.

Down in the living room all three stood staring at each other. The two daughters in blue moved a little ways apart from the woman in black.

Pauline couldn't help but talk out loud. "Mother, did you see that ceiling?"

"Pauline! Please."

"How will we ever get it off?"

"Shht, child. Please."

"Blood doesn't wash off easy."

"Pauline!"

"There'll always be a stain there."

Edna spoke up. "Will you shut up, Pauline? Can't you see that Mother is a wreck already?"

Mildred dropped into a rocking chair. She covered her face with her hands.

No.

No.

2

"Operator, I want to talk to Konstant Harmer in Whitebone. He's a teacher up there. In high school. Mr. Konstant Harmer."

"Do you have his number?"

"No, I don't. We've never called there before. Long distance."

"You want me to try him at the high school first then?"

"Oh, he should be home by now. It's going on five."

"Do you have his home number?"

"No. Like I say, we've never had to call there before. We always just wrote letters. When we wasn't visiting back and forth."

"Just a moment."

Rapid clicks followed. Distance had the sound of a warped blank record slowly revolving on an old heavy turntable.

"Whitebone."

"Would you ring the Konstant Harmer residence, please? For a party here in Bonnie."

"One moment, operator."

More rapid clicks followed.

The sound of a hollow humping continued to come out of a deep cave.

Someone lifted a receiver far away and the line was open. "Hello?" It was a woman's voice. A little tired. Karen Harmer.

"Go ahead."

"Karen?"

"Yes?"

"This is Mildred. In Bonnie."

"Oh. What are you doing on the wire all the way from there? It's so expensive."

"Is Kon there?"

"Yes, he is."

"May I talk to him?"

"What's the matter, Mildred? Is there something wrong?"

"You better let me talk to Kon."

"Mildred, what's the matter down there?"

"Let me talk to Kon."

"Oh, Mildred, I do hope there's nothing the matter!"

"Just let me talk to Kon."

"All right. I'll go get him. He just got home from school. Hold the wire. He'll be here right away. I'll hurry him along. The wire costs so much."

"There's no need to hurry now. Just get him."

The receiver on Karen's end was placed down on something hard.

Distance had the sound of a barrel organ turning tunelessly around and around.

"Hello?" It was Kon.

Mildred took two great breaths, one right after the other, to get on top of her heart. Her two eyes stared at the two nickel bells on the top part of the wall telephone.

"Hello? Mildred?"

"Kon, you better come down here and clean up the mess your brother Brant just made."

"What!"

"You better come down here right away."

"What happened, Mildred!"

"I can't talk about it over the phone. The line's already full of rubberneckers hanging on. So you better just come down here."

"What did Brant do!"

Mildred's eyes drifted off. Outside the bay window the sun had just set. "I guess there wasn't enough for him to do around here anymore. This winter anyway. To keep his nerves quiet."

"What'd he do! What'd he do!"

Mildred's eyes slowly closed. "I probably should've had him committed long ago."

"Mildred!"

"God knows I thought of it a couple of times. But then just when I thought I'd had about enough, he'd straighten out a little, and then I'd forgive him his funny stunts all over again."

"For godsakes, Mildred, what did Brant do!"

"You get used to the funny things people do if the funny things come at you only one at a time. With a little time passing between them."

"Mildred!"

"I don't know which is the worst: not all there and in the crazy house, or just plain dead and in the grave."

Kon began to gasp over the wire.

"You two were always so close, so maybe when you get here you can tell me why Brant killed himself today."

PART EIGHT

❁◈❁❀◈❀◈❁◈❁◈❁◈❀◈❁◈❀◈❁◈

Karen

1

The tall dark Westminster clock struck the hour of five in the other room.

Karen was sitting beside the kitchen table. As she listened to Kon shouting at Mildred on the wall telephone, Karen held the sweet burden of her belly close in her hands. Thank God, the baby at least felt warm and safe under her heart. A canary, newly bought to humor her, chipped lightly in its white cage near the window. The dog Wolf, one glistening eye sometimes on her and sometimes on Kon, lay at her feet.

Kon began to gasp as he listened to what Mildred was saying. What Karen could hear of Mildred's voice sounded exactly like the chipping of the canary.

Suddenly Kon turned white. The sharp overhead light in the kitchen made it seem deathly white. "He couldn't've!" Kon cried. "Not my brother Brant."

Karen could feel herself turn pale. She whispered to herself. "Oh, my God, I wonder what's happened down there."

Kon cried, "Somebody else must've done it. Somebody who had it in for him. Because Brant wouldn't do a thing like that."

"For godsakes, Kon," Karen cried, "did Brant kill somebody?"

Kon listened with wild blue eyes a moment longer; then wilted. "All right, Mildred." Pause. "All right, Mildred."

Karen's face felt as though it were freezing over. "Kon! What did he do?" She crossed her arms over her belly in protection. "Kon?"

Kon hung onto the mouthpiece with one hand. "I'll come right away, Mildred. Tonight yet."

It was Karen's turn to gasp. "Why! Wait a minute. You're not leaving me here alone tonight. Not in the condition I'm in. You can't leave me just like that, Kon."

Kon said, "Just lock up the house until I get down there, Mildred. Then we'll call the sheriff and the rest. Not before."

"Wait a minute," Karen cried, "wait a minute. I'm not going to let you run off just like that."

Kon waved his hand at Karen for her to keep quiet. Into the mouthpiece he said, "Just go over to Mother's and wait for me there. And don't you touch anything, hear?"

Karen struggled to her feet. The dog Wolf stood up with her. She wavered. She grabbed hold of the edge of the table for support. She was like a slender river willow bent down by a sudden swarm of bees. "Kon, you're not going to leave me here alone. This baby is too important for that." She gave the table a rap with her knuckle. "You hear? Nothing is as important as this baby. Nothing."

Kon went on talking into the phone. "If there's no train or bus connection, I'll borrow a car. Even buy one if I have to. It's about time we had one anyway."

Karen almost fell over. "You'll buy a car? When we're so poor and need all the money we can scrape together to even have this baby? What's happened down there that you can forget about this baby?"

"All right, Mildred. I'll take care of everything. Bye." In hanging up Kon missed the receiver hook and had to make a second try at it. Kon looked like he was about to keel over with a heart attack.

One hand on the table for support, Karen blocked Kon's way. Her bones felt like they were turning to icicles. "I'm not going to let you go, Kon. You hear? It's your duty as a husband to stay right here by the side of your wife when she's about to have her baby. Her first baby." Karen slowly stroked her belly. "This is your child too, you know."

Kon stabbed her belly with a green-edged look.

The dog Wolf caught the look and instantly bristled a warning at Kon.

Kon said, "Now, Wolf, you lay down, you."

Wolf held his ground.

Kon went on. "Karen, I'm going home. Brant needs me."

"But I say you're not going home."

Kon stuck his face into Karen's face. "Get out of my way. Please."

Karen backed a step. "What's Brant done that he needs you more than I do?"

"Please, Karen, don't stand in my way."

"In my condition? With the baby due in about a week?"

"Karen, please, please don't make me do something we'll both be sorry for later on."

"Well, but . . . Kon. . . ." The child in her belly suddenly thrust out its legs. "Ow. Aren't you at least going to ask me if you can go?"

"Brant's dead and that's all that matters to me right now."

"Kon!"

"After I've got him safely in the grave, then I can start thinking about you."

"Kon, why, what arc we doing here? We never fight. Why, we've never had but one little spat in our whole life. Kon!"

Kon turned abruptly and, snapping on the hall light, ran upstairs.

Karen gasped. Holding her belly, she followed him, Wolf padding after her. Lately her heart had stumbled some when she had to climb the stairs. "Kon?"

Kon was already in the bedroom upstairs. The drawers to his

bureau were squeaking and cracking as he jerked them open one by one.

Halfway up the stairs she had to stop and catch her breath. The dog stopped beside her. "Dead, Kon?"

"That's what I said." His voice came choked out of the clothes closet.

"So that's it."

"He killed himself." Kon sobbed as the words ripped out of him. "He took his own life."

"Oh, dear God, anything but that. No!" she cried. And the child in her belly jumped.

"Another one of those who should never have been married."

What? She couldn't quite believe what she'd just heard. Another one of those . . . what? She gasped and caught at her throat with her free hand. "Kon."

"But it's true though."

"What an awful thing to say."

"Take it or leave it, it's still true."

"What about his two girls? Isn't it a good thing they're in the world?"

"Sometimes I wonder."

Karen had to sit down on the stairs. What? What? And here Kon had always been so loving and sweet to his nieces Edna and Pauline? The world was coming to an end.

Kon made several stomping staggering noises in the bedroom as he stepped into his trousers. "Damn."

Wolf barked once, very loud.

The child in her belly dodged toward her spine.

Between moans, Kon said, "If they'd've been boys it might've been different."

The clock struck the quarter hour.

"Dead. Dead." He cried it out. "Ohh. Ohh. Brant dead. I can't believe it. Can't."

Karen panted. She forced herself to think of the other person, of Mildred and what must be her awful grief. She stroked Wolf's big bold head. "Yes, poor Mildred."

"Poor Mildred, nothing. She's still got her life. She's still alive." Kon broke. "While my poor Brant is dead, dead." Out of sight, Kon wept uncontrollably.

A chill struck the child in her belly. "What about me? Is it wrong for me to be alive too?"

Through sobs Kon said, "No, not you."

"You're still going to go?"

He appeared suddenly at the head of the stairs, all dressed up in dark blue. The hall light shone brightly on him. He carried a suitcase and a coat over an arm. He was struggling with all his will power to get control of himself. "Of course I'm going to go."

"Can't someone else do this whatever it is you're supposed to do?"

"No." The muscles over his cheeks worked, worked. "It's my duty. Mine. I don't want anybody else to touch him."

"Doctor Michaels won't like this, what you're doing."

"That's right. You've got Doctor Michaels here in Whitebone to take care of you."

"But why can't someone else touch your Brant? What did he do in taking his own life?"

He said it brutally, viciously, as if at last he really meant to crush her with it. "He blew his brains out with a double-barreled shotgun. And left an awful mess in their bedroom upstairs."

She stared great-eyed at Kon. "Why, he must have been out of his mind."

"Huu, you don't know the half of it."

She shied away from imagining what that grim sight might be like. What an awful thing to have happen to them all. "I don't want you to go, Kon."

"I've got to go."

"I'm now thinking of you and what it'll do to you as the father of our child."

"I've got to go."

"What about your teaching job? You'll be gone at least a week."

"Oh, my goodness. That's right. I forgot. Well, you can tell

them up at the school for me. Can't you? About what's happened?"

"What shall I tell them?"

"Well, just say that there's been a death in the family. That's
usually excuse enough."

Tears ran down her white cheeks. "Oh, Konstant, I can't let
you go. Suppose our child decides to be born while you're gone?
I can't go through that alone. I need you beside me. I'm getting
on to be having my first baby. My husband."

He started down the steps toward her. He gestured with his
suitcase for her to get out of the way. He was biting the inside
of his lips to keep them from trembling.

Wolf, bristling, moved up past Karen and blocked his path.

Kon snapped, "Wolf, you lay down, you."

Wolf leaned up instead, ready to charge.

Karen placed her hand on the dog's back. "Now, Wolf. Down,
down."

Wolf looked over his shoulder at her. In the hall light his eyes
burned small blue coals.

Kon said, "Get that dog out of the way."

Karen said, "Wolf, you lay down now."

Wolf, slowly, reluctantly, sank down.

Kon quickly stepped past both woman and dog. He hurried
down to the front door.

"Kon! aren't you even going to kiss me good-bye?"

Kon stopped. He half turned toward her. His face was as
though carved out of old snow. "Oh, God, Karen, I hardly can."

With a hand on the banister, and still sitting, Karen slid down
the stairs a few steps. She held out her arms to him. "Kon?"

"Oh, Karen, let me get over this first."

"Kon?"

"Oh, God. Oh, God." He shuddered. "That this should have
happened to us." He made a slight move toward her out of conscience; then, with yet another shudder, suddenly whirled and
was out of the door with a slam. The house boomed.

The dog lifted a paw to cover his ears against the sound.

Karen cried out, "He didn't kiss me."

Wolf lifted his black nose and howled piercingly.

For a moment echoes filled the new house with old primordial sounds. The mirrors and the windows rang with them.

The tall dark clock struck the half hour.

Karen staggered to her feet and stumbled to the easy chair near the Westminster clock. One hand on her belly and child, the other on the arm of the chair, she let herself down easy.

The clock talked to itself.

Karen sat bowed.

After a bit Wolf began to pad restlessly around in the half dark of the living room. His toenails rattled on the bare patches of varnished floor between the carpets. His eyes glowed at each window.

The furnace clicked downstairs. Soon warm air breathed over Karen, coming out of the hot air register beside the clock.

The baby within had fallen still. It was hardly a wonder. It had never been around such wrangling before. Karen stroked her belly over and around with her cupped hands, thumbs up.

"Sleep, baby, sleep. Save your strength for the big day."

Wolf heard her whispering. He came over and placed his dark muzzle on her knee. He looked up at her soulfully. The half light from the hall made his eyes gleam a sacred smoke blue.

It struck her then how wonderfully peculiar it was that at last she'd found a friend animal. There was a lesson in that. She'd been especially loving to Wolf ever since the night she'd conceived. Wolf had returned the love.

She patted Wolf's noble head. She stroked his fur back over his powerful shoulders. "Wolf. Wolf. Maybe you'll turn out to be the best friend I ever had."

Wolf loved the stroking. The bluish gleam in his eyes deepened. He whined a little.

Warm air continued to pass over her. Yet the chilling shock of what Brant had done was still settling in her, sinking deeper and deeper with each passing moment.

"I'd better stir around a little before it touches the child."

She got up, one hand on the arm of the easy chair, the other on her knee.

She checked the temperature. It was seventy-two degrees. She turned the heat up to eighty degrees.

The tall dark clock struck the quarter hour.

She looked down at Wolf. "Isn't it about time for your supper? Come,. I'll give you a bite." She willed herself to the kitchen.

The dog padded on the kitchen floor behind her, toenails ticking lightly.

She poured some milk into the dog's dish as well as put out a piece of meat left over from yesterday. The sight of the shrunken cold fried meat almost made her gag.

She turned to go to bed.

Wolf looked up as though to follow her.

"Finish your meal first, Wolf. Then you can come up."

She mounted the stairs sideways, right foot first, then the left, labored, and made it to the bedroom.

Kon had left the light on. It shone brilliantly in the white and walnut room.

The first thing to catch her eye was the closed eyes of the doll in its cradle. She stopped. She stared at the closed eyes.

She spoke aloud. "It's time I put away childish things." She stroked her high belly with the inside of her thumbs. "There's a real doll coming and I don't need you anymore." She took the doll from its cradle, tenderly, and placed it far back on the upper shelf of her closet, out of sight. She folded a blue blanket over it so it wouldn't get cold. "I hope we have a girl."

She got out an extra comforter and spread it on her side of the bed: She undressed; got into her nightgown; and, shivering in the warm room, got into bed.

After a while Wolf came padding up. The German shepherd placed his big muzzle on the edge of the bed almost beside her face.

Karen stroked him a few times; then said, "Wolf, you go lay down now. On the carpet there."

Wolf whined.

"Go on."

Wolf whined again; at last lay down.

The baby swung heavy against her lungs.

Presently the tall dark clock struck the hour: six solid lingering bongs.

2

Sunday she walked almost a mile in a loving sun to attend services at the Methodist Church. Karen liked and respected their minister, the Reverend John Marrow. Reverend Marrow was both a warm man and a blunt man. And he was an open man. He could still make simple horse sense out of what others thought complicated.

Kon hadn't either called or written. Karen missed him. She prayed that God might comfort him in his ordeal. She tried not to think of the awful things he had to do for Mildred.

Karen slipped into a back seat on the right side, lifting the baby within her belly past the knob of the bench ahead.

The church was only a third full. Most of the congregation were farmers. The modest women wore hats and dresses several years behind the times, bought at closing-out sales in the local style shops. Their hair was put up simply, a tight roll in back, a braid above the ears. The humble men wore suits with the crease from the hanger showing. Their hair stuck out in back somewhere, a rooster tail that wouldn't stay down, a bristly neck needing a trim. Only the wives of the few well-to-do men in town were handsomely dressed. While the lawyer and the banker came with a well-groomed dome, full head of hair or bald.

Except for an occasional footfall, a creaking bench, it was quiet in the church. The sun coming through the colored tall windows cast a rainbow light over the varnished benches. Motes fell gleaming onto the folded American flag to the right of the pulpit. Two big candles twinkled in the chancel. Their pale light gave the scarlet velvet runner on the altar a varying phosphorescent cast as though every now and then someone were breathing over it.

Organ music dreamed through the church.

Karen found herself looking, as she often did, at a special pane of glass framed in a band of black in the near window. Inside the black band were the words done in gold: "Sacred to the memory of Emily Ellsworth. First white child born in Siouxland. Killed by the Indians on August 19, 1862. This window was presented to the church by her sorrowing father and mother."

Slowly Karen's mind filled with fleeting little daydreams tinted over with colors from the tall windows.

Full of baby as she was, Karen felt only half there without Kon.

Presently Reverend Marrow, dressed in a black robe, emerged from a side door and seated himself in an imperial chair behind the pulpit.

Karen looked at the good reverend with hope. Perhaps today he would have a special word for her, one that she could take home with her and hold close to her heart and her baby.

Reverend Marrow prayed to himself, head bowed. His long black hair slid forward a little like a horse's mane might upon grazing.

Karen dreamed upon him with her green eyes half closed. It was good to see a God's man who was all man.

Reverend Marrow looked up. He ran a hand over his ruddy cheeks. His black glittering eyes roved freely over the congregation.

Karen hoped his eyes would fall upon her. She waited.

Soon Reverend Marrow's probing eyes swung to her sector. Just as he was about to leave off his survey, he spotted her. His eyes rested on her a moment. His big hand came up and cupped his square jaw. Even from that distance the black eyes under the flowing black hair seemed to look right through her.

Karen was thrilled by the look. It uplifted her.

Reverend Marrow stood up and approached the pulpit. Thick arms akimbo, he leaned over the big Bible and offered the invocation. "Bless this assembly, O Lord, and may we all find that comfort this morning for which our soul longs. Amen."

Karen wondered why the baby had fallen so silent under her heart.

Reverend Marrow led the singing with a powerful bass voice. He sang with the fervor of a little boy in a Christmas program. His broad voice rode well over the organ and was stronger than all the other voices limping along in unison.

Karen dream-moaned through the singing.

Reverend Marrow paused to give the announcements. He spoke in a conversational tone of voice. "We have received a complaint from the city hall that the sidewalk in front of the church, and along the east side there, was not cleared of snow soon enough after the last snowfall. Your pastor was out of town that day, otherwise it would never have happened. What we need are a couple of volunteers from the younger people who can step in when your pastor is away. Write your name on a slip of paper and hand it in when the collection is taken." He smiled magnetically. "I expect at least a dozen volunteers. From whom I will choose two."

A rustling noise, not quite a chuckle, passed over the congregation.

Reverend Marrow's voice turned sober. "Our hearts go out to Mr. and Mrs. Konstant Harmer in their bereavement. May the Lord open His hand and give them of His healing love all that they may need in a difficult time."

With the mention of their name aloud in church, Karen's whole body for a second stiffened upon her baby.

Reverend Marrow prayed all through the long prayer as if he were engaged in a passionate argument with a dear close friend. "Yes, O Lord, we often question Thy wisdom. For example. Why didst Thou create the mosquito? What good is it? So far as we can see it has no value whatsoever. All it does is bite and raise bumps, and in some instances infect people with malaria, and in certain corners of the earth even kill people with yellow fever. From no man, not even from the learned at our universities, have we ever yet heard even one single thing to be said in the mosquito's favor. Why, then? Why?" Pause. "Yet we believe in Thy infinite wisdom. So there must be a reason. So we shall continue to search for it, even as we smite in vexation to the right and the left of us at the troublesome pest. O Lord, we love Thee, so send us wisdom and insight. Amen."

Karen had herself often wondered why the mosquito had been created. But the mosquito wasn't the only thing wrong with this world.

Reverend Marrow again led the singing in the next hymn:

> Life is good, for God contrives it,
> Deep on deep its wonder lies;
> Death is good, for man survives it,
> Lives again in better guise.
> This they knew the night they nailed Him,
> When He came through that which veiled Him,
> Alleluia, alleluia,
> Smiling, wonderful, and wise."

Sometimes when Karen moved a little in her seat it seemed to her that the baby felt more like a big rutabaga than a living soul.

Reverend Marrow rested both elbows on the pulpit, one on each side of the great gold-trimmed Bible. "Beloved tillers of the soil. Neighbors in the Lord. Today we shall attempt once again, as we do every Sunday, to leave the profane world behind us and to go seek that sacred source from which all truth and beauty flow."

The congregation settled in their benches as though about to embark on a long voyage. Most heads tilted back to hear the better. A few heads tipped forward to catch a little catnap between points.

Reverend Marrow spoke of sacrifice. There was no way of setting a value upon life unless and until one had made a sacrifice of some sort. "It is not until you have lost a crop of corn to the drouth, or to the grasshoppers, that you learn to appreciate what it means to have a bumper crop. It is not until you have lost a friend that you come to appreciate what it means to have a warm dear friend. It is not until your house burns down that you come to appreciate, fully, what it means to have shelter in the middle of the winter when it is thirty below with a raging blizzard outside. Those who have lost something or someone in their life have a far richer life than those who have always had everything they wanted. It is good for the tongue to sometimes taste a bitter radish."

Karen nodded. Yes. That's why a cook always served up potatoes with a touch of salt first before she served up strawberries with a sprinkling of sugar.

Reverend Marrow's black mane began to flow back and forth as he got deeper into his sermon. "It is not that you must seek sacrifice. Because that would be a sickness. But rather that when sacrifice seeks you out, when it is thrust upon you, that you accept it, and that you go on from there and live the next day a wiser man, more fully appreciative of such blessings as do come your way. You farm families who survived the terrible drouths of recent years, in some instances at great personal cost, know how to live with fat crops. You are not swamped by success. Your ship comes in with all hands hale and hearty."

Karen thought: "Wouldn't it be something if the baby all of a sudden decided to be born here? Right here in this back bench? It's been quiet enough for that. The quiet before the storm."

Reverend Marrow stood a little apart from the pulpit. "If you would appreciate good times, have some bad times first. That is, if the Lord will be so kind as to give you some bad times. Yes, if you would appreciate the sweet evening air of Whitebone here, hie yourself down into the valley along the Big Sioux River some late afternoon, into the swales and swamps of Outlaw Country, and let yourself be bitten by mosquitoes. The mosquito there has the bite of a mad wasp. The mosquito there will teach you to appreciate the bug-free higher ground of Whitebone."

There was a pause. The whole church seemed to creak. Once.

Reverend Marrow's eyes closed; after a moment opened again with a sheepish look. Then, turning a little pink, Reverend Marrow said slowly, with a half laugh at himself, "Ah, now I catch on as to why the good Lord sent us the mosquito. He created the mosquito so that we might by contrast enjoy our evenings here in Whitebone, sitting out on the lawn, going for a walk in the pasture, picnicking out at Blue Mounds Park."

Another pause.

Reverend Marrow next closed his eyes toward the high dark rafters above. "Forgive this Thy servant, O Lord, for daring to presume to criticize Thy handiwork. It was born of the impatience of a shortsighted man."

Again a rustling noise, not quite a chuckle, and this time indulgent, passed over the congregation. They loved their pastor.

Reverend Marrow went back to standing behind the pulpit. "The difference between a man and a pig, between a human being and a human pig, lies in the fact of sacrifice. I speak now not of a mother's sacrifice for her child, of the ruffed grouse, say, who pretends to have a broken wing to save her chicks. No, I speak of the larger sacrifice, where one dies for a cause not for personal reasons but for impersonal reasons, dies because it is simply the good and the right thing to do."

Karen thought: "My baby is strangely quiet. When it should be happy and kicking here in church."

Reverend Marrow placed both big hands on the sides of the pulpit and leaned on them until his arms bent inward at the elbows. "One has to die that some may live. One has to suffer that some may prosper. Yes. It is an old story, and a wonderfully human story, both in fact and in legend. It is the story of the hero in battle, of the scout on the frontier, of the original philosopher searching ahead in the darkness, of the seer-prophet foretelling of disaster, of the martyr on the cross. Of a Horatio at the bridge. Of a Frisian boy with his finger in the hole in the dike. Of a doughty Wellington at the battle of Waterloo. Of a valiant Leonidas at the pass of Thermopylae. Of an idealist Ikhnaton in the sunny valley of the Nile. Of a comely lad and lass immolated on a Maya pyramid temple. Of a Socrates in old Athens. Of a Jesus Christ on a cross." There was a concluding pause. Until again the whole church creaked as if it were an old boat. Once. Then, with a significant closing of the eyes, Reverend Marrow intoned, "Amen."

After the benediction Karen lingered in her seat.

The rest of the parishioners thronged toward the main door. Reverend Marrow gave them each a firm handshake and a cheery word as they passed outside.

When the last "God bless" had faded away, and the big outer doors had been closed against the world, Karen got up and slowly moved up the aisle toward the front of the church.

The baby hung heavy under her heart.

Karen stopped in front of the chancel. She looked around at the pulpit, at the choir loft, at the cross in back, finally at the two winking candles.

It was so silent she thought she could hear the tiny flames pulsing on the two candles.

"Kon should have been here with me to hear that sermon."

She kneeled at the kneeling rail, bowing over her baby. The scarlet cushion was mercifully soft.

She waited.

The gold cross emblazoned on the scarlet runner on the altar shone like a flame.

Her baby lay quiet on her thighs.

The colored windows shed greens and reds on her gray coat.

Her lips moved. "Pray God that my husband and I may once again draw close to one another. Pray God that this difference between us may pass. Pray God that this child I am about to bear may be born healthy and well, for, oh, God, it is so heavy."

Faint scents wavered in the air, of mothballs, of cologne, of peppermints.

"Please, Lord, have my husband hurry home to us. My baby and I, we need him. We need him almost as much as they do in Bonnie."

A bench cracked in the back of the church.

"Oh, God, save me from jealousy. Oh, God, save me from a bitter tongue. Poor Brant was my husband's brother, and through my husband and because of my husband, I shall try to cherish his memory. By Thy grace."

The tiny flames on the two candles made little mouthing sounds.

"This burden that I bear, it is as though it has divided into twins, it is so heavy."

A bench cracked closer by.

"Help me to accept what my brother-in-law has done. Even though I still do not understand how his act can be part of Thy divine purpose."

A rafter shifted high above.

"It is so hard for me to understand."

A voice spoke above her. "Mrs. Harmer?"

Karen turned startled on her knees and looked up.

It was Reverend Marrow. He stood directly behind her, black robe hanging to his knees, arms folded over his broad chest, red face quizzical with concern. "Mrs. Harmer?"

"Yes, Reverend Marrow?"

"Did I hear right that you're questioning God's purpose in this matter of your brother-in-law's death?"

"I'm not really questioning God, Reverend."

"What then?"

"Well. . . ."

"Come, come, speak up. God does not like equivocators."

"All right then." Karen got to her feet, heavily, and faced her minister. "All right then. If God prefers that I be blunt, I'll be blunt." She took a deep breath. "It's that I've got some pretty awful thoughts about my brother-in-law."

"What are these awful thoughts about your brother-in-law that the Devil has been putting into your mind?"

Karen ran the tip of her tongue across a tiny crack in her nether lip. "That Brant killed himself on purpose."

Reverend Marrow's black eyes looked down into the very center of her. "And why should he do that?"

"To take my husband away from me just when I needed him most. Because Brant was always jealous of me. Sometimes even like you might expect a woman to be."

"Go on."

"Brant hated it that we were going to have a baby. And he wanted to hurt that baby."

"Hrm!" Reverend Marrow's black eyes fixed on her with magnetic power. "So that's what the Devil has been telling you."

"Yes."

"All right," Reverend Marrow said, "all right. This is what we'll do. We'll catch the Devil by his crooked tail and look him straight in the eye. Let's just say that your brother-in-law did take his own life on purpose to place a stone between you and your husband. So what? Must you sink to your brother-in-law's level and like him harbor thoughts that are also evil? Sufficient unto each Christian is the evil within him."

Karen ran her hand over her belly, thumb up. Her mind caught at one of the Reverend's words. "A stone. Yes. Huu." An involuntary sob escaped her. "Maybe that's what I am carrying here in my belly. A stone. For, oh, Reverend, it is so heavy."

Reverend Marrow's black mesmeric eyes held her up. "And also sufficient unto the day is the evil thereof."

"Like it might be dead."

"Oh, come now, woman, buck up, buck up."

"If you only knew how it feels here. If you only knew. It is so strange."

"All mothers, even mothers out in the pasture, have black thoughts just before their babies are born."

"But I am not a mother out in the pasture, Reverend." It upset her that their minister sometimes talked like her brother Alf. "Begging your pardon, Reverend, but I hope that I have a soul. As compared to a mare."

Reverend Marrow's face opened red and boyish. "I only meant that in a manner of speaking, Mrs. Harmer. You of all people, never."

"I was going to say."

"What I meant was for you to take comfort in the fact that you were not alone. That even far down in the animal kingdom you might find friends who could sympathize with you."

"Oh, I see."

"Animals have feelings too, you know."

"Well, that's true." She thought to herself a moment. "Wolf has, I know."

"Comfort ye."

"Thank you, Reverend Marrow."

"It will be given you."

Karen opened her hand further. "But, Reverend, what if I have other dark thoughts?"

"Such as?"

"Well, for one thing, it's that I'm afraid I won't have enough milk for my baby." Karen touched her slim bosom on the side. "And I so want to nurse my baby like all good mothers do."

"That also will be given you."

"Do you really think so, Reverend?"

"My dear Mrs. Harmer, God is not asking you to do the impossible. You are a woman and such things are given to a woman." Reverend Marrow continued to smile upon her, boyish, pink. "Now if you were a man and God asked you to give birth to a child as well as have the milk for it . . . well, then, yes, perhaps then we might dare to question His purpose a little. But you're not a man. You're a woman. And you were meant to bear children, not stones. So take comfort in exactly what you are. It's fine. It's right. It's what God intended."

"Yes, I suppose I do have a perfect right to be exactly what I am."

"Having a baby is about the greatest thing that can happen to a human being here on earth."

"Yes. Men can't have babies."

"No greater gift could God give to a human being. So take heart."

"That's right."

"Now, is there anything else that seems to be troubling you?"

"Well, I'm also worrying that Kon won't be home in time. I want him to be here when I have our baby."

"Again, that too will be given you. God will so arrange it that whatever happens will be the best for the both of you."

Karen wept in relief. "Thank you, Reverend. It's always a comfort to talk to you. You remind me so much of my father. He was a rough man too. Yet we kids always knew he spoke his mind flat out because he loved us."

"Flat out. That's right."

"At the same time he taught us to love the flowers. He even taught my brother Alf to play the harmonica a little."

"Remarkable."

"So thank you, Reverend Marrow. Because even though this" —she placed both her hands on her belly—"even though this still doesn't feel right, I feel a lot better for having talked to you. And of course for having prayed to God."

"Can I give you a ride home?"

"No, thank you. Doctor Michaels says it's good for me to walk as much as possible. At least until the baby comes."

"You're sure now?"

"Yes."

"All right. As you wish. God bless."

3

She walked about a half a block, and then the first big pain came. It cracked all through her pelvis. And she didn't recognize it right away. She thought it a bad gas pain.

For about a minute she stood in the middle of the sidewalk as if impaled on something. With both hands she pressed down on her belly. Then, thanks be to God, the big pain passed on.

It hit her again when she got to the next corner. This time it was even worse. Her innards seemed to want to drop out all in a push. And again she stood a minute transfixed, absolutely still, hands hard on her burden.

It came to her what it was. "It's my baby coming," she whispered. "This is what the doctor said it would feel like. Now I know. Glory be."

Pain subsiding, she immediately turned east and headed for the hospital three blocks away.

She managed to get to the next corner before the third pain grabbed her. This time it felt like a great fist closing on her stomach. She stood still and suffered it, all the while that her eyes watched a boy chinning himself on a horizontal ladder on the public school grounds across the street.

"Patience, sweet lamb, and in a little while I'll be holding you in my arms."

The big fist relaxed its hold on her belly, and she started walking again. Her footsteps echoed off the wall of a dark-red stone church. The low sun was on the other side of the church and its light passing through the tall windows just barely illuminated the colored panes on her side, yellow becoming orange, crimson becoming plum violet, blue becoming purple.

The fourth pain caught her as she turned the last corner north. This time she forced herself to walk through it. She swung along as though astride a long stick, as a boy might playing horse.

Again the pain passed on. She noted how dead the grass was around the noble red courthouse and the square red jail. The two quartzite buildings resembled molds of raspberry jello. Too bad the high ash trees on the courthouse grounds had neither leaves nor birds.

Halfway down the block she jaywalked across the street and headed directly for the front steps of the Whitebone Hospital. There were pigeons under the eaves of the Grecian gables of the brick hospital, cooing, fluttering, prinking. Below, streaks of bird-squit ran all the way down the sides.

A nurse spotted Karen coming. She opened the door for Karen just as Karen made the top step. The nurse was a short slight thing. She had concerned dark eyes.

"Just in time, I see," the short nurse said.

"Yes." Karen stepped inside, puffing. "I think I'm . . . I was just on my way home from church when. . . ."

"Right this way. The delivery room is on the first floor. In back."

Karen followed her. "Are you the nurse in charge?"

"I'm Miss Chambers. Yes."

Karen drew back a little. "But you're such a tiny thing to be a charge nurse."

Miss Chambers laughed. "In here, Mrs. Harmer."

The fifth pain hit Karen before she could reach the long white metallic bed in the far corner. She felt as if she were about to be upended.

Little Miss Chambers caught her before she fell. Miss Chambers had surprising strength. She helped her onto the bed.

Karen suffered it. She lay straight out on her back.

"Are you all right?"

Slowly the pain subsided. "Yes."

Miss Chambers helped her remove her coat and shoes.

Karen puffed. "You remind me a lot of my mother-in-law. Reka Harmer. She was a little woman too but she sure could surprise you sometimes with her strength."

Miss Chambers smiled. "I was raised on a farm. An only child. So I had to help Dad with the horses and chores and such."

"Sometimes I wish I'd been born on a farm. I'm so ignorant when it comes to the important things of life."

"Well, that's a switch." Miss Chambers smiled a wide hearty smile. "And here I've been wishing I'd been born in town."

It was with an effort that Karen spoke over her belly. "Well, I guess we've all got a perfect right to be exactly what the good Lord intended us to be."

Miss Chambers continued to smile.

Karen panted. "Nurse, it's so terrible heavy."

"They all are the last couple of hours, Mrs. Harmer. It means that at last they are ready to enter the world."

"But this one feels funny heavy."

"It'll be all right."

"I know that when it's going to be your first one everything is going to be a little strange for you. But this one feels a little too much that way."

"Does Doctor Michaels know you're here?"

"No. It's like I said, I was on my way home from church when it started."

"I'll call him. Meanwhile, can you undress yourself?" Miss Chambers handed her a white hospital gown. "And put this on?"

"I'll try."

Dr. Michaels came quietly into the room, stethoscope dangling from a white jacket pocket. Miss Chambers followed him, carrying a tray with a white basin and a nickel forceps.

Dr. John Michaels of Whitebone was the other side of the coin to Dr. Thomas Drury of Bonnie. Dr. Michaels was a slender gentle man with fair skin and light-blue eyes. Women instinctively trusted him; men spoke well of him. Karen and Kon had liked him the very first day they went to see him.

Dr. Michaels spoke in a warm baritone voice. "Well, well, I see the baby couldn't wait until your husband got back. The little rascal."

A smile found its way to Karen's lips. Immediately she felt better. "It can't be helped, I guess."

"Of course not." Dr. Michaels felt of her pulse. "Perhaps it's just as well." He placed a warm good hand over her brow. "We don't need the husband around for this really. He just gets in the way. As in nature."

"Kon meant to be here though."

"Of course he did." Dr. Michaels took hold of the sheet lying over her. "Well, now, let's see what we have here. Would you please place your feet in the stirrups here?"

Karen did as she was told.

Dr. Michaels went in.

For the first time in her life Karen found herself liking the touch of a man's hand under her clothes. She wondered how it must be there for the baby in its warm nest.

"Well, young lady! Things are moving along much faster than I expected. Nurse, the medicated tray. Pronto."

Miss Chambers hurried to the cupboard to get the tray.

"Is it bad, doctor?" Karen asked.

"It's good, Mrs. Harmer. V-e-r-y good. In fact, I find it hard to believe that this is your first baby. And at your age yet. Better than many a veteran mother, believe me."

"I'm glad."

"Well, now, you should sound more enthusiastic than that."

"Oh, doctor, I'm worried I won't have enough milk for it."

"You'll have more than enough."

"Somehow it still doesn't feel quite right though."

"How so?"

"It's so funny heavy."

Dr. Michaels put his stethoscope to his ears and began moving the black endpiece over the high mound of her belly. He listened intently for a while, then put the stethoscope back into the pocket of his white jacket.

"Is the baby all right, doctor?"

Dr. Michaels went over to a washbasin. He soaped his hands and thoroughly scrubbed them, then rinsed them with hot water and shook them dry. He came back to her bed. His mild blue eyes had become strong blue eyes. With both hands he took a full hold of both her wrists.

"Doctor?"

Dr. Michaels gave her a man's smile. "Karen, each to his last. You do the pushing, I'll do the worrying."

"Doctor?"

"Please, Karen."

"All right, doctor."

Miss Chambers, standing to one side, gave Karen a smile exactly like the doctor's.

Another pain spread through Karen's hips. "Oh, doctor, it's all so strange. I feel like I'm a building that's coming apart."

"Good, Karen. That's just what we want."

"I hope Kon's all right wherever he is."

"Let's not worry about him now."

"All right, doctor."

"Now, Karen, I must examine you further. It may hurt a little this time. But just relax and remember it's for the baby."

"All right, doctor."

Dr. Michaels went in again.

"Doctor?"

"Shh, now. Nurse?"

"Yes?"

"I think perhaps we could use a hypo at this time. Our Karen here is out to break the record."

"Is it really going very well, doctor?" Karen lifted her head off the pillow to see him the better. It hurt her high in the chest to do so.

"Girl, so far as you are concerned, it couldn't be better."

After the hypo, Karen dreamed off.

An hour later, Dr. Michaels again took full hold of both her wrists. "Karen?"

Karen opened her eyes. "Yes?" She saw Dr. Michaels as a wavering silhouette.

"Are you all right?"

"Where's my baby?"

"Karen, are you all right?"

"Doctor?"

"Karen, listen to me. Do you feel all right?"

"I feel fine. I feel as if I'm floating. But where is my baby?"

"Karen, can you hear me clearly?"

"I hope I have enough milk for it." Karen tried to cup her breasts. But her hands moved as if they were hardly connected to her, fumblingly.

There was some rustling beside her bed. Then Dr. Michaels said to Miss Chambers, "I think we should wait a bit."

"Yes."

Karen rose up out of her pillows. Her eyes opened very wide and green. She saw that she was now in a different room. She also saw that Miss Chambers knew some bad news. "Doctor, is my baby dead?"

Dr. John Michaels gave her the grave eyes of a veteran general. "Yes, Karen. It was stillborn. A boy."

Karen's eyes slowly narrowed. "It never was alive?"

"It was alive two weeks ago."

"Two weeks ago! What happened to it after then?"

"I don't know. It was a perfect baby boy in all respects at birth. It was all there but the breath."

"You can't tell me what happened to it after two weeks ago?"

"No, Karen."

"Did you ever have another mother who lost her baby like this?"

"Yes."

"And you couldn't tell her either what happened?"

"Not really."

"Was it because she did something wrong? Or her husband?"

"No, not really." Dr. Michaels continued to keep a full grip on both her wrists. "Karen, I'm sorry."

Karen sank back into her pillows.

Tears appeared in Dr. Michaels' eyes. His cheeks quivered. "If ever a woman deserved to have a baby, you did, Karen. You did."

4

It was late afternoon. Karen was home in bed. The dog Wolf lay on a braided rug nearby.

Karen heard a car stop out front. She thought: "That must be Doctor Michaels. Good man."

Then she heard a key in the lock in the back door downstairs. That was odd. She'd left the front door open for Dr. Michaels to use.

The back door opened softly.

Wolf slowly came up on all fours.

Ah. Kon was home.

Karen's first impulse was to be a little mean to Kon because of what he'd done. It wasn't right that he'd run out on her just as she was about to have his baby. Such a husband deserved to be punished a little. She nodded to herself. Yes. What she'd do would be to lie back in her pillows and first see what he had to say. She grimaced darkly to herself. It had better be pretty good too.

There was a silence downstairs.

Wolf lowered his nose and his ears shot forward as he listened intently.

Karen could just imagine Kon. He was probably standing stockstill just inside the door, grieving, feeling guilty.

The Westminster clock struck five times, slowly, clearly, with long lingering echoes.

Of a sudden Karen felt sorry for Kon. Tears rimmed her green eyes. And she forgave him. It really hadn't been his fault that Brant had gone off his rocker and killed himself. Kon, Kon, poor man. And, oh, what an awful thing it was that now she also had to tell him that he'd lost a son.

"Kon?"

The silence downstairs deepened.

"That's you, isn't it, Kon?"

The white lace curtains hung very still in the bedroom.

She sat up. What was this? "Kon?"

Wolf threw her a glowing look over his gray shoulder; then, toenails ticking on the golden oak floor, he padded softly to the open door of the bedroom and looked downstairs.

"Kon!"

"Coming, Karen."

"Oh, thank God."

She heard him moving around downstairs. The door to the back closet squeaked. That meant he was hanging up his coat. There were other noises.

Wolf continued to listen intently too, head cocked to one side.

"I'm up here in bed, Kon."

"I'm taking off my overshoes."

Thoughtful man. She could just see him doing it one foot at a time standing on the rubber mat.

Presently he started up the stairs, his steps coming slower as he neared the top. "Hi there, Wolf. You been a good dog, huh?"

The feelers on Wolf's muzzle prickled out.

Karen said, "Now, Wolf."

Kon's hand appeared in the doorway and reached for Wolf's head. "So you've been a good dog, huh?"

Wolf drew away and looked back at Karen.

"Wolf," Karen said.

Wolf then tolerated him.

Kon stepped through the door and came toward her.

"Kon!" Karen cried. "Oh, my dear husband, but you've aged so. Hhh."

His face was ravaged by darkest grief. And his light-blond hair appeared to have turned completely silver-white. Even his light-blue eyes seemed to have turned gray.

"Oh, Kon, how awful it must have been for you."

His glance first fell on her stomach. Slowly his gray-blue eyes opened in shock. "Karen!"

"Yes, Kon."

"Oh, Karen, it did come then while I was away."

"Yes, Kon."

His eyes swept the room; finally settled on the doll's cradle. "Then where is it?"

"Right after you left, I put the doll right up on a shelf. But as you can see, it's back in its cradle again."

"What happened?"

"You didn't hear about it?" She was tormenting him a little, she knew, and that after she had decided not to. But she couldn't help it.

"Karen!"

"It was born dead, Kon."

He stood staring down at her. "It was?"

"Stillborn, the doctor said."

Kon turned chalky over the cheeks. "I did that too then?"

"Oh, Kon. No, Kon."

"It's dead then?"

"Oh, Kon, let's just say it couldn't be helped." She held up her arms to him.

A vast groan broke out of him.

Karen thought: "If anybody did wrong, it was Brant."

Kon dropped to his knees beside the bed. His head landed near her hip. He began to cry silently.

Karen thought: "Maybe Brant took the baby away from us. Yes. But I still have Kon. And I have him all to myself now."

Kon's arms slowly encircled her and without looking at her he clutched her to himself.

Karen looked down at his strange silver-white head. Then she stroked his hair, back. "It's all right, my husband. Nothing could be helped." She mused upon him. "We all have a perfect right to be just what we are and to have happen to us what happens to us. It's something we can't help."

Pretty soon Wolf came toenail-ticking over and licked Kon's cheek where it showed above his arm.

The next morning Kon brought up their breakfast on a couple of trays. Karen had her breakfast in bed and he had his across the room from her sitting by the white curtains.

Sunlight streamed in brilliantly, both down from the sky and up off the snow, so that there was as much light under their chins as over their hair. The golden light glossed over their silvering hair and heightened the winter pink in their cheeks.

Karen was sipping her coffee, slowly, looking off to one side with a thoughtful air, when all of a sudden it hit her that Kon had driven up in a car the afternoon before and that that car was still standing out front.

"Kon, whose car is that out there?"

Kon brightened for the first time. "Ours."

Karen set her blue cup down carefully in its blue saucer. "Did you say . . . ours?"

"Yes."

"Where'd you get it?"

"I bought it."

"Well . . . but then . . . but where did you get the money?"

"From our savings."

"Oh, Kon, you didn't throw away all our savings, did you? You know we were saving that for our old age."

"There'll be more where that came from."

"Spender!"

"It had to be done, Karen. I had to get home to Bonnie quick and there was no other way but to buy a car." A smile edged into the corners of his thin lips. "Besides, it was time we owned a car. Now on Sundays we can take little sightseeing trips out in the country."

"What kind did you get?"

"A Buick."

"For goodness sakes."

Kon added with a laugh, "Buick means big belly or paunch in Dutch. And our car looks a little like it's got a big paunch too."

Karen didn't know whether she liked that or not.

Kon sipped at his steaming coffee and continued to smile to himself.

Presently another question popped into Karen's mind. "Who'd you get to drive for you?"

"I drove it myself."

"You didn't. You couldn't've."

"But I did."

"But when did you learn?"

"Right after I bought it. Mr. Jacobson showed me how to start it and how to stop it." Kon allowed himself another short laugh.

Karen stared at him.

"Well, there was more to it than that, of course. Mr. Jacobson also showed me how to shift the gears. And then I got in and drove off. I had to. I was desperate."

"You really did this?"

"You can do all kinds of things if you have to."

Karen took another sip of coffee. "I suppose that'll mean we'll have to build a garage for the car now. To preserve the finish."

"Yes, I suppose so."

"And a driveway."

"Yes."

Karen sipped some more, "Well, there's at least one good thing to be said for it. You can keep your garden tools out in the garage now. Instead of having to cart them onto the back porch every time."

"Say, that's right." Kon's light-blue eyes opened some. "And I can also build me a woodworking bench in the garage. I've always so wanted one."

Karen mused upon the snow-white world outside. "Kon, when I get up and around again, I'm going to learn to drive that old Buick. Just you watch."

September 16, 1967
Blue Mound
Luverne, Minnesota

About the Author

Frederick Feikema Manfred was born January 6, 1912, on a Siouxland farm north of Doon, Iowa, in Rock township, just a few miles from the Minnesota and South Dakota borders. Mr. Manfred is the oldest of six brothers. His mother died in 1929; his father now lives in California.

He was educated in northwest Iowa until he attended Calvin College, Grand Rapids, Michigan, from which he graduated in 1934. For the next three years he wandered back and forth across America, from New York to Los Angeles, stopping off now and then to take on odd jobs to pay his way—busboy, filling station attendant, driver, harvest hand, warehouse roustabout, factory hand, weekly newspaper reporter. In May, 1937, he became a reporter for the *Minneapolis Journal*. In 1939 he did social work and opinion polls. In 1942 he married Maryanna Shorba; they have three children, Freya, Marya, and Frederick.

In 1943, after working as an abstract writer for *Modern Medicine* for several months, Mr. Manfred decided it was now or never and began to devote his full time and energy to writing. Since then he has published nineteen books, including the novels *Lord Grizzly*, *Riders of Judgment*, *Conquering Horse*, *Scarlet Plume*, *Morning Red*, *King of Spades*, and the trilogy *Wanderlust*. He has received several grants and writing fellowships from such sponsors as the American Academy of Arts and Letters and the Huntington Hartford Foundation. He is currently a writer in residence at the University of South Dakota, Vermillion, South Dakota. Until 1951 he wrote under the pen name of Feike Feikema, an old Frisian family name, of which Frederick Manfred is a translation. In Frisian genealogy his full name is Feike Feikes Feikema VII. (The Frisian people were once tribal cousins of the Angles and Saxons and still speak an old "Anglo-Saxon" language today.)

Mr. Manfred has lived in the Upper Midlands, mostly in Siouxland, all his life. He likes gardening, fixing fence, and chopping wood; and enjoys taking long rambling walks alone through the countryside.